"[The] imagery is striking, almost lyrical . . . Cook's prose sets it a notch above many like novels. . . . It could make out like a bandit."
—*Publishers Weekly*

"Lively, darkly comic, enormously entertaining."   —*Houston Chronicle*

"If Elmore Leonard lived in Texas, his name would be Christopher Cook."   —Kinky Friedman,
author of *The Mile High Club*

"An impressive first effort."   —*Kirkus Reviews*

"This is familiar plot territory, but Cook covers it with fearless originality, in a lyric voice that sings itself raw."
—*The New York Times Book Review*

"I can't wait for the next one."   —James Crumley,
author of *The Last Good Kiss*

"From Elmore Leonard's laconic flair with the dumb and dangerous to James Lee Burke's lyric feel for dark hearts in a New South—*Robbers* ranges wild and wide, deep through the heart of Texas. Cook has a talent big enough to take his natural-born killers in richly traveled territory he makes memorably his own."   —Michael Malone,
author of *Time's Witness*

"[A] fine debut novel . . . an exciting and welcome addition to the modern noir fiction scene."   —*The Austin Chronicle*

ROBBERS

a novel

Christopher Cook

BERKLEY BOOKS, NEW YORK

A Berkley Book
Published by The Berkley Publishing Group
A division of Penguin Putnam Inc.
375 Hudson Street
New York, New York 10014

The publisher gratefully acknowledges the following for permission
to reprint from previously published material:
Richard Wilbur, for excerpt from "The Pardon" in *Ceremony and Other Poems*, 1950
Clarity Music Company, for excerpt from "Black Cat Bone" by Harding Wilson

This is a work of fiction. Names, characters, places, and incidents either
are the product of the author's imagination or are used fictitiously,
and any resemblance to actual persons, living or dead, business
establishments, events, or locales is entirely coincidental.

Published simultaneously in Canada.

PRINTING HISTORY
Carroll & Graf Publishers hardcover edition published 2000
Berkley trade paperback edition / April 2002

Visit our website at
www.penguinputnam.com

Library of Congress Cataloging-in-Publication Data

Cook, Christopher, 1959–
Robbers / Christopher Cook—Berkley trade paperback ed.
p.   cm.
ISBN 0-425-18346-7
1. Fugitives from justice—Fiction. 2. Automobile travel—Fiction.
3. Male friendship—Fiction. 4. Blues musician—Fiction. 5. Texas
Rangers—Fiction. 6. Guitarists—Fiction. 7. Murderers—Fiction.
8. Texas—Fiction. I. Title.

PS3553.O55316 R6 2002
813'.6—dc21   2001043204

PRINTED IN THE UNITED STATES OF AMERICA

10   9   8   7   6   5   4   3   2   1

For Corinne, Jan,
and all the other brave folk

I dreamt the past was never past
    redeeming:
But whether this was false or honest
    dreaming
I beg death's pardon now. And mourn
    the dead.

—Richard Wilbur, "The Pardon"

Part 1

1

Eddie didn't intend to shoot the guy. Didn't mean to rob him either. What happened was—

They were sliding south down Lamar after rib sandwiches and beer at T-Bones Bar-B-Q House. Going no place particular on a lazy day in May. Laid back under a babyblue sky, the sun floating in it like a warm dab of butter. Cruising the street past used car lots flying plastic banners, the whole foods market, record stores, saloons. Moving through bright southern light and summer heat, vehicle exhaust rising acrid off asphalt, the hypnotic afternoon postpotative haze.

Eddie and Ray Bob, jazzing in low gear. Radio on soft, Lyle Lovett.

They rolled on southward through the commercial verge, crossed the Colorado bridge above a shimmering turquoise river. Upstream high greentreed banks flanking the course and a solitary racing shell sculling the windskipped surface, a waterborne centipede. Downstream, bridges over First Street and Congress and the snaggletoothed profile of the glassy city center.

Austin, state capital, university town. Former counterculture magnet and slacker haven now balling the jack on a fulltilt bender. Sucking wind under the onslaught of money, a stripmall gangbang straddling the Balcones Fault. The mellow chilled-out days mere mythic history. Silicon Gulch now, hightech hysteria and the California influx, a city overrun by cyberokies on the rebound two generations after the dustbowled western plunge, returning flush, pockets stuffed with plundered gelt.

Come back to take Austin mainstream. And succeeding. Beyond a few longhaired relics holed up in canyoned university enclaves, the only surviving outlaw instincts career through a juicy music scene in the rambunctious downtown club district. Rebellious tattooed youth there possessed of mutinous ideas and unencumbered time. Elsewhere, jackleg politicians seeking cool capitol cuties and dot.com commandos stroking bearphobic bull lust. Free market lechery for profit, unleashed.

To this scene come Eddie and Ray Bob, outsiders from the rural frontier, from the unseen and forgotten bumfuck outskirts of the urban media landscape. Rubbernecking the city, seeing what it's about, not much impressed. Just more folks humping the dollar. Two men alien among distant kindred, young and unemployed and broke, trawling boredom after a late greasy lunch. Scoping the street past fastfood joints and pawnshops in a boosted Eldorado convertible.

When Ray Bob says, Gimmee a smoke, hoss.

Eddie fished the packet from his T-shirt pocket, crushed it, tossed it over the side. Said, I'm out, pull into this 7-Eleven.

Ray Bob wheeled the Caddy ragtop into the empty lot, parked nose up to double glass doors plastered with signs advertising RC Colas by the twelvepack. He shoved the gearshift into park, let the motor idle.

Listen, he said, don't buy those fuckin straights. Get some filters.

Eddie on the sidewalk put a boot on the bumper, rolled a Zippo lighter across the back of one hand. Man, you know I smoke straights. You want filters gimmee some money.

I'm broke.

Eddie shrugged. All I got's four dollars, I'm buying straights.

Fuck you.

Yeah? Well up yours sideways, asshole.

In your momma's mouth.

Already tried it.

I ain't surprised, Ray Bob said. How was it? His face serious.

Yours was better, said Eddie. No teeth.

Try her pussy next time.

Them talking that way because they were running buddies.

Copper cowbells jangled on the door when Eddie went inside. Kaleidoscopic view: consumer *soixante-neuf*. Anything you wanted in there, racked up tight to please the eye and move fast. He paused, shaking his head. Then stood at the counter between the lotto ticket stand and a display of Lone Star keychains saying, Gimmee a packa Camel straights.

The clerk, a plump young man with burnished bronze skin and a black mustache, either Indian or Pakistani, laid the pack on the counter and rang it up. Four dollars and one cent, he said.

Eddie glanced at the register readout. I got four dollars here, pardner. Where's the spare penny bucket?

The man pointed to an empty plastic ash tray. All out.

Hey, no problem, I'll catcha next time.

The clerk put a hand on the pack of Camels, pulled it back to his side. Saying, It's four dollars and one cent.

Eddie looked at him. You gonna hold up this deal over a penny?

The young man adjusted the collar of his red 7-Eleven shirt, gazing somewhere over Eddie's left shoulder, as though preoccupied. As if he didn't care. Saying, That is what it costs.

Eddie frowned, not believing it. Flipping the top of the Zippo open and shut in one hand. Snap, snap. Man, you jerkin my chain.

I am jerking nothing.

Hell you ain't. What kind of fuckin country you come from?

A good country. The clerk meeting his eyes then for a moment before turning to put the pack back on the shelf. He faced the counter again, splayed both dark brown hands flat on the surface. Fingernails ivory as bone. Hair black as creosote, features resolutely braced. Maybe defiant. Very fine country, he said. Where we pay for what we get.

Hot flash. A spasm sideslipped over Eddie's shoulders, crawled up his neck, hit his jaw. He eyeballed the guy. You giving me the redass, pardner. Listen to me. This is America. Gimmee them cigarettes.

Four dollars and one cent.

I ain't believing this.

Only the guy didn't budge. Not one word, just standing there like a chocolate Deputy Doright. A corner of his mouth lifting slightly, either a smirk or a twitch.

Eddie said, Goddammit to hell.

That's when he hoisted a leg and reached into his boot. Pulled out a .22 revolver, an old Colt Police Positive with a four-inch barrel, looked like a toy. Pointed it at the guy. Arm straight out, finger on the trigger. Saying, Gimmee them fuckin cigarettes.

Robbery, the man squawked. He stared at the gun, dark eyes blinking, teethed his upper lip, jaw thrust forward. I call the police. Get your license plate.

So Eddie pulled the trigger. A sharp crack, the barrel kicking up. The bullet caught the clerk square in the forehead. His head snapped back, a small black hole in the bronze curvature. He stood there with his hands on the counter a moment, eyes crossed, then slid down onto the floor out of sight.

Eddie leaned over the counter and looked down. The guy lay on his side on the thick rubber floormat, head across one arm as if taking a nap. You dumbshit, said Eddie, look what you did. He reached over the open space and took a pack of Camels off the shelf, left the four dollars on the counter. Slipped the gun down his boot and went outside, cowbells clanging behind. He got into the Caddy.

The fuck you do? said Ray Bob. Shoot somebody?

Cocksucker wouldn't give me the cigarettes.

No shit?

Cause I didn't have a penny.

Ray Bob grunted. Don't fuck with a man and his smokes.

Man oh man, Eddie said, I thought they trained them camel jockeys. You fuckin believe it?

I believe it. Where's the money?

Left it on the counter.

Not that money, asshole. Ray Bob drumming the steering wheel with the heels of both hands. The register money.

It's in the register, where you think? Eddie tamped the pack of Camels on the back of one wrist, tore open the cellophane with his teeth. His hands were shaking. Went in for cigarettes, he said, I got cigarettes.

Goddamn straights, too. Ray Bob wagged his head. Man, I told you filters. Shit, gotta do everything myself. He opened his door with the Caddy still idling in park and legged it inside griping. He returned a minute later carrying a plastic sack bulging with dollar bills and rolls of coins and loose change, a carton of Marlboros tucked into an armpit. He sat behind the steering wheel counting the money.

Eddie exhaled a thin stream of smoke, snapped the Zippo open and shut. Don't you reckon we oughta be headin out?

Just a second.

Count that shit later, man, it ain't goin nowhere.

Neither is that A-rab in there. He dead.

Reckon he is. I plugged him in the head.

Ray Bob snorted. That'll sure do it. He tucked the plastic bag under the seat, put the car in reverse and hit the brake. He peered through the windshield at the storefront. Saying, Dammit to hell, shoulda got some beer.

I ain't thirsty, Eddie said. Let's git.

They rolled on down South Lamar in the slow lane with the sky spread softly overhead, transparent and cloudless, a pale blue altitude without end and the sun suspended in it. The radio on low with Dwight Yoakam singing about love come and gone. They didn't listen and they didn't talk. They were moving and that was enough. Going anywhere and everywhere, going nowhere in particular. The motor of the Caddy purring beneath the hood.

Down near the Brodie Oaks shopping center Eddie said, Man, ain't this some weather?

Ray Bob nodded. It is that, hoss. Gimmee a smoke. Open up that carton.

Eddie tore out the end of the cardboard carton and handed Ray Bob a hardpack of Marlboros. His hands were still trembling. How much in the sack? he asked.

Ray Bob shrugged. Didn't finish counting, you was in such a rush. Not much. Musta just made a deposit. He pulled the cellophane off the cigarettes and leaned sideways for the wind to whip it back past his shoulder. Forty fifty bucks, maybe less.

Shit, said Eddie. For that you make me an accessory to robbery?

Wasn't robbery. You can't rob a dead man.

Hell you can't.

You can't.

Bullshit, said Eddie. They got a law for everything.

2

He parked the Dodge Ram pickup on the 7-Eleven lot and climbed out, straightened the cattlemans crease in his Stetson. Tall lean man wearing black eelskin boots and western khakis, longsleeved white cotton shirt with a black bolo tie. Silver star pinned to his shirtfront. A double leather belt rig with a government model Colt .45 strapped to one side, belt buckle big as a fist. Tanned face, windweathered, crow's feet framing dark brown eyes.

The law.

He squinted into sunlight. The lone noble pose, Marlboro perfect but for a long narrow face and pointed chin.

Out beyond the concrete apron a slopeshouldered wreck holding a plastic bag foraged in the D npster. The man's gaze hovered there, then scanned up the rise behind the store. Houses nestled on the hill among the trees, half hidden in the mottled shade. South Austin, old working-class homes crowded onto small lots, revamped and spruced up for the highdollar white collar trade. Hot tubs and xeriscaped yards, wraparound decks, glassed-in porches. Still cramped though, houses packed hip to thigh. While a few feet away a homeless tramp scavenged trash.

Why he lived out of the city.

The tall man strode over the cement lot toward the front door and the single police officer on guard, young milkfed guy with the hint of a mustache, peachfuzzed yearling trying to look alert. He nodded to the officer and passed inside, saw no one there, heard a noise behind the counter. Setting an elbow on the Formica top, he leaned forward, lowered his gaze to the body laid out prone on the rubber mat. A heavyset man in a suit crouched near it.

So who we got?

Abraham Krishna.

Damn, where'd he get a name like that?

Same place everybody gets a name, said Bernie Rose, APD homicide. Somebody give it to him.

Rule Hooks touched the brim of his Stetson and said he reckoned so. Said that was the usual case, it surely was. Nobody got to choose their name no more'n they chose to be born. Said it was probably why the fella on the floor left home all the same. Leave a whole damn country, name like that.

Well, I wouldn't know, Rose replied, not being psychic. The overweight detective sighed, pulled up his suitpants legs and kneeled on the floor. He put his face down close studying the hole in the man's forehead. A small round indentation filled by a purpleblack gob of blood pudding. He grunted. Small bore, probably twentytwo or twentyfive.

The detective bent his head even lower to the mat, broad cheeks turning dark red. Rule shifted the gun on his hip and watched, said, Don't have a stroke, Bernie. Any idea who did it?

Well, from the evidence, I'd say a skinny fella about five foot ten or eleven wearing a pocket T-shirt and bluejeans and a fair-sized ring in his left ear, with straight dark hair pulled back in a ponytail.

No shit, Sherlock. What's his name?

Rose glanced up. Said I ain't no psychic ferchrissakes.

No, said Rule, but you got that faraway look. Just close your eyes and hum, Bernie, say the first thing that pops into your head.

The detective smiled. I dunno, but he looks like one of them guys in a rock band, Mick Jagger with all those lips maybe, or that guy in Aerosmith that wiggles his ass.

Rule stared at the detective as if he was speaking in tongues. Rose winced, said, I see'um because my daughter's over, she's always got MTV on. He balanced awkwardly on one arm and pointed upward and backward over his shoulder. Rule followed the finger to a video surveillance camera mounted high on the wall in the corner.

Rule pulled at his lower lip. Got it all, huh?

Rose leaned his head down again and poked at the skin around the bullet hole. Saying, Either he didn't know or he didn't care. He wasn't hiding. Neither was his partner. Shooter splits, the partner shows up a minute later and lifts a carton of Marlboros and rifles the register. All on the tape.

How you know they're partners?

The detective shrugged and stood up, wiping his pants legs. Saying, Goddamn look at that. He pointed to a wad of chewing gum stuck to one knee. That's a new suit, too. He gimped past Rule holding out his pants leg to the soda dispenser and pushed the ice button, caught a big chunk from the noisy cascade and pressed it against the gum, hints from Heloise at work. He held it there.

Don't know it, he said, could be they aren't. I don't think robbery was the motive anyway. All we got's black and white video, no audio. But it appears like some kind of argument with the shooter. Over a pack of cigarettes maybe. Or maybe it's something else entirely. That's what the deputy chief thinks.

When he start thinking?

The stocky man inspected his trousers leg, frowning. Well, it comes in fits. You know how that goes. But he's got a point. Know how many Indian convenience store clerks we had shot in Austin the last month?

Rule said he didn't know, hadn't been counting. He went over to the coolers, took out a plastic half-liter bottle of Dr Pepper. Snagging a bag of salted peanuts off a rack, he bit open the end, drank off some of the soda pop, then made a funnel with his hand and poured the peanuts into the bottle. He put his thumb in the neck and shook it. The countrified cocktail fizzed and boiled.

Well I sure have, Rose said. Too many, that's how many, too many for coincidence.

Smoke and mirrors, said Rule. Statistical hankypanky all that is. Matter of interpreting numbers. Majority of car wrecks occur in moving vehicles, like that. Ever notice most folks choke to death on knockwurst is Germans? With death by crawfish heads it's coonasses. Mexicans it's knives, black kids it's AK-47s. At 7-Elevens you get your gunshot Indians.

The detective stared at him.

Rule shook the Dr Pepper some more, watched it fizz. Saying, Convenience store clerking's a career with a high mortality rate any way you look at it. Why it pays so well. He winked, raised the soda and swallowed down half the bottle, wiped his mouth with the back of one hand. Plus if you're one a them Hindus you get to come back anyhow. Get you another chance on the merry-go-round, many as you want. Not so bad that way. Rule grinned. Kinda convenient, you might say, probably why they end up working 7-Elevens.

The detective screwed up his face. Yeah, well, tell that to the deputy chief. He's hardshell Baptist and thinks this ride is the big banana. Plus he's catching heat downtown. Word is it might impede his promotion to chief. Rose frowned and tugged at the wad of gum still clinging to his pants leg. For cripes sake, he moaned, this ice ain't doing it.

Rule waved his hand holding the soda bottle toward the gum. I'll tell you something else that works, Rosie. Brake fluid.

Yeah? Brake fluid? No kidding, Beth says ice. The detective went down the aisle to the automotive section and opened a can of brake fluid, poured a smidgen on the gum. Anyhow, he said, the civil liberties crowd is in an uproar. Writing letters, calling the mayor, phoning radio talk shows. They making noise, claiming it's some kind of hate thing. A conspiracy. Organized rednecks plugging foreigners. The Klan, Neo-Nazis, skinheads, whatever. Like that, racial.

Might be, you never know. That why I'm here?

Rose lifted one shoulder absentmindedly, his eyes still glued to the gum. I suppose so. The chief said he might ask the mayor to call the governor, get the Rangers involved. You guys being such elite, highly trained investigators. Scotland Yard with boots and a Texas twang. Not to mention it'll look good on TV.

Reckon the mayor picked up his phone then, Rule said. Governor calls the colonel, he calls the captain, captain calls lieutenant.

He calls me. Regular circle jerk. Anyhow, here I be. One riot, one Ranger.

Detective Rose looked up, cocked his head. Hesitating, then remembering. Saying, Surprised it's you though, Rule. Heard you was suspended.

The Ranger swirled his cocktail. Over that Mexican in Red Rock? Don't believe everything you hear, Rosie. Took a temporary leave is all, pending investigation. And it's finished.

Short investigation.

He had a gun.

Heard that, too, Rose said. A thirtyeight revolver. Only you tapped him with a rifle from a hundred yards out.

Guy raped and killed three women. Rule lifting his chin like that explained it. Don't take no chances with a hairball like that. Besides, you know I'm conscientious about procedure, everything by the book.

Uh-huh. Rose rolling his eyes. We all know your rep.

Then good on you. Rule grinned. Well, let me get my kit.

He pushed the Stetson back on his head and went out the front door past the officer on guard. The rookie clicking his heels, snapping to attention. Ranger romance. Rule half amused, thinking, Jesus Christ. Thinking too much TV. Chuck Norris juju.

In the parking lot he opened the passenger side of the pickup, lifted the evidence kit from the floorboard, shut the door. Squinting again, watchful. The tramp still foraging the store Dumpster, two bags now. Overhead a blank blue sky. The day turning more than warm. City a heat sink, all that pavement.

He stood observing the traffic on South Lamar for a moment. Recollecting something he'd read. Millions of years ago all this a great inland sea. Tectonic upheaval, sea sent packing, limestone bed exposed, then hills and unpeopled plains. Few Indians maybe. Now all concrete and noise, the afternoon sun keening off car windows and chrome. Surprising no one had seen anything. The street here a well traveled commercial thoroughfare. But not a clue on what the shooter was driving. Other guy either. If the two were together. And if they were driving. Might've been walking. Or riding bicycles. Or rollerskating in drag. No telling in Austin.

He locked the truck door and went back inside. Getting an eager rookie salute this time. Rogue idea: sell the boy a Ranger autograph, give the money to the Dumpster diver. A T-bird contribution. Forget it. Rein in.

Focus.

Rule set the kit on the floor near Abraham Krishna. He unfastened his gun belt with the holster and laid it aside, kneeled to unsnap the kit latch. Saying, Alrighty, pardner, let's see if you left us any clues. Let's see if there's anything left to this crime scene after all the commotion.

An hour later he stripped off the latex gloves and put the kit back together and fastened the latch. In the bathroom he washed his hands, then wet a paper towel and wiped the polymer print powder off his eelskin boots. He straightened the bolo tie, leveled his hat, gazed at himself in the mirror. No kidding, he did look a little like Porter Wagoner without the pompadour hairdo. Woman the other night in the Broken Spoke told him that, walked right up to his table holding a whiskey sour and said you look just like Porter Wagoner, you play guitar and sing? No ma'am, he'd replied, but I wish I had the man's money. Porter being a successful Nashville entertainer, old-timey cowboy singer, had his own TV show for a while. Ever since then Rule'd noticed the resemblance. Only not quite so tall as Porter, who could've played basketball. Not quite as long in the jaw, either, but that was all right, that was plain good luck. Plus Porter wore those crazy outfits, enough sequins and rhinestones to make Liberace salivate. He took a final glance in the mirror and walked out.

Rose was standing in front of the counter near the lotto ticket rack holding out the knee of his trousers staring at it. Consternation on his face, genuine. A large dark splotch had spread over the gray fabric.

I'll be goddamned, Rule, would you look at that shit? That brake fluid done stained my pants.

The Ranger took a look. I'll be, it sure nuff did.

That's a brand-new suit, too. Cost an arm and a leg, Beth bought it for me herself. Damn brake fluid. Where'd you hear about that?

I don't rightly recollect, Rosie. Rule put on his gun belt and buckled it. Reckon it works, though. Got the gum off.

Shit, Beth's gonna kill me.

Well then, least we'll have a case with evidence and motive. Cause I'll tell you what, pardner, on this situation here we ain't got jack.

Nuthin? The detective seemed disappointed.

Naw, not nuthin. What we got is too much. Only found about a hunnerd latent prints and smudges. How many people you expect leans on that counter in a day?

How about the register?

Well, we'll take a closer look at the lab, see what we got. Maybe use the laser. But I'll be surprised we find more'n our buddy Abe there and a coupla other clerks.

There's the video. The detective sounding hopeful.

Yep, you're right, there's that much. It's a start, Rule agreed, we'll take a run at it and put the pics through the system. He picked up the evidence kit and headed for the door. I'll be in touch, Rosie. Say hello to Beth.

He was driving away in the red Dodge pickup when Rose went out front and stood on the asphalt lot. Late afternoon heat, radiant waves waffling off the tarmac. He mopped his wide forehead with a handkerchief. Back up in the balconied west a bloodred sun hung low over the treetops. He heard the officer standing solitary sentinel behind him scraping his shoes on the pavement.

Must be important to call out the Texas Rangers, the patrolman said. I heard they was better trained than the FBI, only a lot less of 'em. You see his badge? They bang that star out of a silver Mexican coin, 1948. Heard they got an eagle on the back.

The detective gave the rookie a brief contemplative glance. Guy young enough to be his son, almost a kid. Practically swooning.

So what did he find out, sir? We got anything?

Not very much, Rose muttered.

Sir?

I said not very much. Not much at all.

The detective took a gander at his suit leg, regarded the taillights of the Dodge truck disappearing up South Lamar. Said, I can tell you one thing worth knowing, though. You ever get gum stuck on your pants, don't use fuckin brake fluid to get it off.

Aw, hell no, the boy agreed. He wagged his head. It'll sure lay in a stain, sir, and that's a fact. You ever try it?

3

An accounting—

A quarter against two dimes . . . dime against two nickels and a dollar bill . . . that's all the rolls. Mine, yours. Here's the loose change, you keep it.

Ray Bob playing cashier.

Eddie glanced at the separate piles, said, We gotta go to a bank, man. I ain't hauling around no rolls of nickels in my pocket. Look stupid all them bulges.

Then carry the dimes, they smaller.

Hell with that, I'll take it to a bank you don't. What's the big deal?

I don't like banks, Ray Bob said. Got popped robbing a bank.

Eddie looked at him. Thought you said you never skanked a joint before.

I lied.

What for?

I need a reason? You don't like it, call the cops.

Ain't illegal to lie, said Eddie.

That's right. Ray Bob smirked. But I do it anyways.

Whatever. I still ain't hauling these rolls in my pocket. Could use 'em to buy supper, though, I'm getting hungry.

Them arguing because Ray Bob liked to, because Eddie was feeling antsy.

They perched on a smooth limestone shelf in Zilker Park down the creek from Barton Springs, legs overhanging the edge. The stone ledge jutted outright from the embankment beneath a towering pecan. Nearing twilight, and balmy. Purple martins cut gliding arcs over the water poaching insects on a breeze. Upstream the shallow current murmured among the waterworn rocks, rippled there in the race. Then the creek deepened between the steep-flanked banks coming down and the rocks went under the surface and the deeper water was still.

Eddie tugged at his earring, watched two swans drift along the shore. Big white mounds of feathers with slender curving necks. All right, he said, what else you lie about?

Ray Bob grinned. Get real, hoss. I pulled more heists you can shake a stick at. Case you didn't notice, I ain't no Boy Scout.

I was, Eddie said, only they booted me out.

What you do, shoot the scoutmaster?

Naw, his old lady did. Caught him in bed with her sister, shot 'em both. Used a twelvegauge with buckshot. Fat jackoff died in the saddle. A real asshole, too, always yelling about our uniforms, how we looked. Shoulda give her a merit badge for civic duty.

Or marksmanship. Ray Bob sniggered. He stacked the paper money, straightened the corners.

Why I never got past Tenderfoot rank, though, Eddie said. Didn't like all those rules, all that yelling. Hat's on crooked, a wrinkle in your pants, and this guy's screaming in your face.

Ray Bob lit a cigarette, let it dangle from a corner of his mouth as he began dividing bills, mostly singles. He closed one eye against the smoke. Said, Maybe more dinero here than I thought. Back in the old days, your old lady mess around you could shoot her, no questions asked. Crime of passion.

Twelve years old and you're in the fuckin marines, said Eddie, watching the swans disappear downstream. Who can take that? So they bounced me, bad attitude.

She got off, right?

Eddie shrugged. Don't remember. Bummed me out though. I wanted to be good at sumthin.

Being good for nuthin is being good at sumthin.

That don't make no sense.

Why it's true.

You got some funny logic. Hey, lookit that. Eddie pointing toward the creek.

Two girls in an aluminum canoe floated past and they stopped talking to watch. One girl was blonde and chubby with short hair and the other was a thin brunette with long straight hair. They both wore shorts and halter tops, held the paddles across their laps.

Which one do you want? asked Ray Bob. He scratched an armpit.

I like blondes, Eddie said. Don't bother me if they husky.

Shit, that gal ain't husky. She's fat.

I like a little meat on the bones.

That's some high-cholesterol beef, said Ray Bob. I'm a lean-meat man.

Then you take the skinny one.

All right.

Ray Bob stuffed the bills and rolls of coins into the plastic bag and took off his T-shirt and wrapped the bag in it. A thick mat of red hair curled over his pale chest and belly. Why they called him Red in the pen. He was short and wideshouldered with a narrow waist and thick muscles. He wore his hair closecropped and a gold nugget earring in each ear.

C'mon, said Eddie, they getting away.

They ain't goin nowheres, Ray Bob said. Just let me do the talking.

The two of them hoofed it along the dirt path following the creek bank beneath the trees. The early summer air lay mild and dry and cicadas sang in the green trees overhead. When they drew even with the girls Ray Bob yelled, Hey there you purty thangs! Wanna beer?

The girls looked to one another and the brunette in back rolled her eyes. Then they put the paddles in the water and began to stroke. They moved awkwardly, paddle blades slapping the water, handles scraping the gunwales of the canoe. They pulled away toward the farther shore.

We got beer! hollered Eddie.

What the fuck'd I say, growled Ray Bob, let me do the talkin.

Oh yeah, uh-huh. I done seen your sweet talk. They can't hardly wait, look at 'em go.

I told you they ain't goin nowheres. C'mon.

They went hustling on down the narrow path lipping the creek, hopping tree roots, ducking a fallen cottonwood trunk, staying even with the girls in the canoe. Ray Bob calling out to them: Looks mighty hot out there! Wanna cold beer? We just wanna talk to you gals. C'mon now, slow down!

Where the Barton Springs Road spanned the creek they slid down the slope grabbing scrubwillow branches beneath the concrete bridge arches. A mallard drake and hen drifting the near shore bobbing for dinner spread their wings, scuttled away in a panic. The girls hugged the far bank stroking in uneven tandem, the paddles beating against the canoe, striking the surface stiffly to send up roostertails of spray. The blonde one in front started to giggle and the other one told her to paddle faster. She sounded scared.

Ain't no need to get worried! hollered Ray Bob. We just a couple a fellers wanting to talk!

The dirt path along the bank deadended at the earthen bulwark of a walking bridge carrying the creek and they climbed the steep pitch, taking short quick steps digging boot toes into the hard surface, sliding back one step for two. They finally reached the top and stood on the narrow bridge panting. The canoe was already downstream, headed for the creek mouth where it broadened beneath overhanging trees and dumped into the river.

Shit, I told you, Eddie said. They done got away.

Naw they ain't.

Let 'em go. They don't wanna talk to us nohow.

Sure they do, Ray Bob said. Coupla fuckdogs. C'mon.

He ran across the bridge, the hard heels of his boots pounding on the wood planks. Eddie followed. At the far end of the truss they dropped over the rail onto the dirt path and started running along the bank. The path was wide and smooth among the trees and soon they drew even with the canoe. When the girls heard their footsteps the thin brunette screamed and they began to paddle harder. The blonde in front had stopped giggling. Her breath now came in short ragged spurts. She shifted suddenly to one side to stroke deeper and the canoe tilted and careened. She quickly slid back toward the middle and the canoe leaned far the other way, its gunwale dipping to the surface. Both girls scrambled for balance, the upper rail lurching downward to the surface dipping once, twice, three times. The canoe began to ship water. Then it tipped for good. They pitched over the side and began flailing water.

Ray Bob slid down the low grassy bank and went in after the brunette. You get that other'n, he called to Eddie.

He hesitated a moment, then waded in. She almost drowned him. She threw her arms around his neck and his feet slipped out from under him against the mud bottom and they both went down, her holding so tight Eddie couldn't get his head up. He swallowed water, choking. He finally got his feet down and shoved toward the bank and the girl came with him. She was heavy, body limp, a dead sagging weight but for the vise of her arms. He pulled his legs up and tucked and dug in one more time and pushed and they sprawled over the verge of the bank, her still gripping his neck so tight he popped her upside the head to get her off. She let go, rolled sobbing to her side.

Hey now, hey now, Eddie said. He got over her on all fours, water dripping. You all right, you was just scared's all. Here, let me help you with this.

He began to push the wet halter top up over her breasts and she threw her arms across her chest to stop him but he pushed them back. Saying, Easy now, easy easy, no need to get upset. Then her body went slack and she began to cry again, moaning, Don't hurt me, don't hurt me, please don't hurt me.

Shoot, I ain't gonna hurt you, he said. He pulled the halter top up around her neck. Her breasts were heavy and soft and plunged to either side of their own weight. The nipples were large pinkbrown nuggets of taut flesh and the surrounding coronas even larger circles of lighter pink and he took her right nipple between his lips and began to suck. She laid still, whimpering softly. He unzipped his pants but his pecker was flaccid and stayed that way. He stroked it for a while but it wouldn't get hard and finally he gave up and lay down beside the girl. Thinking he couldn't get a hard-on cause it didn't feel right. Knowing it wasn't.

I'm really sorry, he said, reckon I ain't that relaxed.

That's all right, she said, still on her back, eyes skyward. It happens more than you think. Her voice subdued now, a low flat monotone without feeling. Lying there in her shorts without moving, hands folded over her belly. If her eyes hadn't been open he'd have thought she was a corpse. Scared him to look at her. She started to speak again but her voice broke and she was silent. After a bit, she reached up and pulled the halter top down over her breasts.

Eddie said, Didn't mean to scare you. Speaking quietly. Without reply. Guess I wasn't thinking, he said.

A few minutes later he got up and found Ray Bob down the grassy bank on the other side of a weeping willow tilted out over the water. He was lying on his back with his feet crossed holding his gun in one hand, fondling himself with the other. Nearby lay the skinny brunette, her legs spread open on the grass. She was naked and unconscious, blood smeared over her inner thighs near the dark thatch of hair. Eddie stood watching, tried to see if she was breathing. He couldn't tell. Her mouth was twisted to one side, her bottom lip badly swollen.

Shit, man, you didn't kill'er did you?

Naw, Ray Bob said. He zipped his pants and stood up, slapped his hips, looked around for the T-shirt bundled with the money. She just passed out's all. Right when I was cummin her eyes rolled back. Happens all the time. He grinned. How was yours?

Eddie tugged at his earring. Well, she didn't move much.

Them fat ones is sluggish.

Eddie thought about it. Reason I think is, she was scared.

Goddamn right she was scared. C'mon, hoss, I'm hungry. Let's go eat.

They went up the trail, passing the blonde girl curled up in the grass on her side, forehead against knees. Mute, heavy shoulders trembling. After they passed Eddie told Ray Bob to hang on a second and went back to the girl. He stooped and leaned over her, hands on kneecaps. Hey, I'm sure sorry, he said, cause you a real pretty girl.

She became still.

Eddie hesitated, bent lower, cleared his throat. He tugged at his earring and spoke low, almost a whisper. Listen, I know it was wrong and I'm really sorry. I mean that. Don't know what got into me. You got a right to be scared. You ain't the only one feeling it either, and that's a fact. But you gonna be all right, just watch.

What you doing, asshole? called out Ray Bob. Apologizing? C'mon.

Eddie stood up, uncertain. Wasn't sure she'd listened or heard. She still wasn't looking at him so he turned and went up the trail. They walked along the path toward the bridge in the dusk. Their clothes were wet and water sloshed in their boots. They stopped and sat beside the trail under a sycamore to empty their boots. Cicadas were murmuring in the trees and crickets in the grass. In the east a slim crescent moon floated over the skyline. The air warm yet from the long day.

Man, I sure like this weather, said Ray Bob.

It's okay, Eddie said. Sounding indifferent, distracted.

Where you wanna eat?

Anywhere'll do.

I wanna chicken-fried steak.

Eddie didn't say anything.

With cream gravy. Fries. And buttered rolls.

Eddie looked up, closed his eyes. Shit that sounds good.

Let's go to that place down the road, said Ray Bob. Threadgill's they call it.

They got music?

Sometimes.

What kind?

Hell, I dunno, said Ray Bob. Music music. Guitars and shit.

Eddie nodded, said it sounded good. Said he used to play guitar hisself. In a rock band.

Yeah?

Man, we was good too. He took a deep breath, chewed his lower lip, remembering. Southern boogie, R and B, rockin blues, like the Allman Brothers. Gigs all over. Wish I'd stuck with it.

Go ahead, said Ray Bob, wish all you want. I wished a lot of things. Wish and a nickel don't buy squat.

They got up and walked on. The woods were quiet save for insects courting and a breeze whispering high in the limbs. They crossed the truss bridge in the dusk and slipped down the steep supporting bulwark to the trail. They followed it along the bank, Ray Bob in front carrying the T-shirt bundle of money. His short thick form strode through the shadows.

Well, I ain't gonna stop wishin, Eddie said from behind. Being a musician's all right. Feels good up there. Like you're doing sumthin what matters. Folks like it, women friendly. Get laid a lot without trying. Free beer, too. Better'n robbing places.

Ray Bob stopped abruptly and turned. He scratched his bare chest with the knuckles of both hands like he was working a washboard. Speaking of which, dickhead, you told me you never killed nobody.

I ain't, Eddie said.

Well, now you have.

Didn't want to. Eddie shook his head, frowning. Didn't mean to either. No way. I ain't been planning nuthin, I just wanted them cigarettes.

Ray Bob grunted. Done killed a sand nigger.

That wasn't it. Was the way that guy acted, looking down his nose at me, like I was some lowlife cheat . . . I dunno, it was reflex. Eddie still frowning, shaking his head. Like I slipped a gear, man. Ain't like me, and that's a fact. Never even shot at no one before. Never. Only reason I got this gun is you give it to me.

Then why was you in jail?

I told you. Auto theft.

Shit, that's right. Ray Bob snorted. Got caught stealing cars.

Wasn't caught, another guy was. Eddie paused. Only he talked.

Uhn-uhn-uhn, said Ray Bob. Some motherfucker squeals on me— He drew one finger across his throat.

They walked on in the twilight and passed the limestone ledge where they'd counted money and climbed up the pecan-groved hill to the Caddy parked in the picnic lot. Ray Bob opened the trunk and they changed into spare dry jeans. Eddie found another T-shirt, stripped off the wet one. Ray Bob stared at his thin hairless torso, the smooth white skin. There was a dark blue jailhouse tattoo above his left nipple. Five short horizontal lines with some musical notes.

So, you get that motherfucker back?

Who.

Cat what snitched.

Naw, said Eddie. Never could find him.

What's his name.

Ledoux. DeReese Ledoux.

What's that, a nigger name?

Coonass from Lafayette.

Well, let's go find that fuck, said Ray Bob. Cut him a new asshole.

Eddie pulled the dry T-shirt over his head and put his arms through the holes. Saying, He ain't there no more. Done went to Houston.

Hot damn. Ray Bob grinned. Look out Houston, here we come.

What you care anyhow? asked Eddie. He tucked the shirttail in his jeans. Ain't your concern.

Bullshit. Ray Bob looked at him like he was stupid. We runnin buddies or what?

Eddie shrugged. Thinking that after about two weeks now maybe it wasn't such a great idea, lookit what happened, shit, shooting people, almost raping women. Thinking he might oughta reassess the situation.

But saying, Yeah.

All right then. Ray Bob grinned again, cocked his hand and pointed a thick finger at him. What else you got to do?

Eddie thought about that, too. Not much.

4

Bernie Rose called his wife, Beth, from the downtown station, homicide division, suggested they meet for dinner at the Jalisco. When she asked what's the occasion he said nothing special, just an urge for Tex-Mex. Felt like putting on the ritz, a swank beaner whimsy. Drop a double sawski on tacos with his favorite lovely lady, he said, just call it romance. Call it caprice.

Bernie chatting her up, enjoying it. Bernie thinking with the kids grown and flown they should eat out more, had more money to do it with. Thinking it was usually his idea. Beth always asking what's the occasion, having a hard time turning the corner. Empty nest syndrome. Schoolteacher tired. Age transition, a crisis barely mentioned. Thinking this too shall pass.

You got other plans, hon? he asked.

Well, I've been hoping to see a certain man, she said quietly. I was looking forward to it.

What he look like?

A handsome brute.

Suave? Like me?

A real charmer.

You trying to make me jealous?

Is it working?

Better believe it. Now I suppose he done asked you to dinner.

That's right, Beth said.

Damn. You say he's a looker? Let me guess. His name's Bernie.

How'd you know?

Bernie Rose grinned. Your eyesight's going, sugar, but you still know how to talk.

Not all I know how to do.

Bernie thinking, Whoa now, Beth on the make, a good sign.

Goosing him, stirring that old *goood* thang. Three alarm schnitzel alert. He whooped, the other guys in the bureau glanced his way. He turned his back, talking low, told Beth they'd get around to that later, start with dinner, work up to it. Just now he was thinking some south of the border ambience. Thinking chips with hot salsa and a cold Modelo dark. Thinking juicy charbroiled fajitas, fat or no fat. Plus they got the mariachi tonight, he added. Chachacha. Like he might ask her to dance. To which she'd reply no thanks. And he'd feel grateful. Thirty pounds past nimble.

Okay, Beth said, the Jalisco. What time?

Meet you there in thirty minutes.

Love you.

Mi tambien.

He hung up the desk telephone, looked down at the stain on his suit pants. Jesus, he was gonna catch it. Good thing Beth was in an upbeat mood. Talking wicked sweet. Revving his motor. *Zoooom.* Schnitzel action not dead. *Very* good sign. Not spring chickens anymore, either. Another peek at his trousers. At least the Jalisco was sort of dark inside, she might not notice until later. If he was lucky.

He finished the paperwork and kibitzed with Blaine, dropped by Garcia's desk to practice his Spanish a bit, then signed out. He took the department car up the Sixth Street ramp onto I-35 and headed south over the Colorado, the river here called Town Lake because it was so wide, backed up by the Longhorn Dam. The narrow greenbelt along the downtown shore passed below in twilight and then the broad water lay black and smooth between shadowed banks. A scimitar moon hung above the river downstream to the east, a pale sliver of platinum floating among early stars.

On the far bank he turned off onto Riverside and headed west through deeply shaded curves. It was his favorite time of day, work done, the evening ahead, a time for silence and contemplation. That time in his life, too. Might just up and retire, see what that was about. Beth would agree, tired of surly students, public schools a war zone. He drove slowly, car windows down, listening to the low familiar hum of hoppers in the grass, cicadas in the trees. A sweet sound, elemental. The sound, he believed, of the Maker kicked back in a La-Z-Boy with a frosty glass of beer.

He cruised along, contemplating that latter image. When the car phone rang. It was Rule Hooks calling from the state lab.

Mi amigo, Bernie said. *Que pasa?*

That's some accent, said Rule.

Yeah, well, I'm working on it. Maybe I'll call it quits and buy a place down in Cancun, Playa del Carmen, see what this siesta thing's all about. I got this tape, ten easy lessons. *Como esta? Quiero uno cerveza frio*. Like that.

You're too old, Rosie. The ear goes first.

Says who.

Says Katie. She's taking Spanish at the university, tells me she's too old and she's only nineteen.

How's she doing?

All right, I reckon. Don't see her much. No time for the old man.

Well, that's how it is with kids. They go through stages. She'll come around.

Maybe, only I ain't sure it's age. Could be she's a lone wolf like me.

Even loners get lonesome.

I reckon.

And God gave Adam Eve, Bernie said. You ever consider remarrying?

Rule paused, cleared his throat, said, We way off the subject, Rosie. Listen up, Moline here in the lab says one a them boys on tape looks familiar. Thought I'd let you know.

The detective moved the phone to his other ear. No kidding, he know the name?

Not yet. But he's thinking on it. Moline's got one of those photogenic memories. Only it works slow.

Bernie nodded and shifted his buttocks on the seat. Thinking he really needed to lose some weight. Time for diet action. Drop by a bookstore, check out the latest nonpainful fad. Buy the book, feel better already. Mental thing. After the fajitas. *Mañana*. Saying, I guess you scanned the pics from the video?

Done sent 'em through the system, pardner. But I'll put my money on Moline. Rule snorted. The bad boys ever learn how lousy these damn computers are we all be in trouble.

How about the prints?

Like I said, we got some. Oh, I reckon we got a hunnerd unique latents and smears. Want to work the list?

Damn, said Bernie.

That's how it is, Rule said. You boys do any better?

No.

Imagine that. We'll be in touch. He hung up.

Bernie returned the receiver to its dock and shot through a yellow light at South Congress. He neared the intersection with Barton Springs Road and saw the Jalisco, large white stucco building with red trim, a gringo builder's idea of Mexican architecture. Looked like the Alamo with a lowbid face job. To the left, the blinking lights of Threadgill's. Place belonging to a local restaurateur specializing in downhome cooking at midtown prices. Jim Hightower, populist agitator, political gadfly, broadcast his syndicated *Chat & Chew* radio program live from it. Bernie's second-best favorite place to eat. As he was passing two fellas in the lamplit parking lot climbed out of an old Eldorado convertible. He slowed to scope out the Caddy, a classic, and pulled a doubletake on the men crossing the lot. Both wearing jeans and T-shirts, one slender with a ponytail, the other short and stocky. Too dark to tell much, though. Half the dudes in Austin wore ponytails.

Working on impulse Bernie swung the Ford left across the street into the Threadgill's drive. He stopped near the side entrance, foot on the brake. The two guys approached from the lot and veered to pass behind the Ford. Bernie leaned out the window.

Hey fellas!

They stopped and looked.

This place good to eat? Bernie asked.

The stocky one walked alongside the car and stood at the driver's window looking in, thumbs hooked in his jeans pockets. You oughta know, he said, you a cop ain't you?

Bernie smiled. From outa town.

The skinny one drew up then and said, We ain't from here neither. He wore a gold ring in his left ear.

That right? Where you boys from?

The ponytail glanced away, then back. El Paso.

Now I suppose you wanna see some ID, said the other one. He had short red hair and two gold nugget earposts and freckles.

Bernie smiled again. Casual, friendly like. That might not be a bad idea.

Redhead shrugged and said, All right then, my wallet's in my boot. He lifted his leg and reached into his boot before Bernie could say hold on. He pulled out a pistol and stuck it through the window against Bernie's face, pushing the barrel hard into his cheek alongside his nose.

He still had both hands on the steering wheel, hardly had time to recognize the make of the gun, a 9mm Walther, when Redhead pulled the trigger. The sharp report was muffled by the barrel end pressed against flesh. Sounded like a cap gun going off. Bernie jerked and slumped in the seat. His foot slid off the brake and the car began to roll forward. Redhead walked alongside and thrust the gun inside against the detective's temple and squeezed off another shot. Then he put the pistol back in his boot and watched the car roll slowly down the drive toward the rear of the lot.

Motherfuck, said Eddie. You done it now.

Don't I know it. Ray Bob scammed the ejected shells off the pavement, stood gazing at the outside corrugated metal and brick wall of the restaurant. I done fucked up dinner.

Jesus, said Eddie. That ain't what I mean.

What I meant, Ray Bob said. He reached under the T-shirt and scratched his belly, staring at the building. Shit, I can almost taste that chicken-fried steak. They make it good.

Well, it's gonna have to wait. Eddie dancing on his feet, jerking his head around, checking who was where. Jesus Christ.

Goddamn cop, muttered Ray Bob.

Man, we better get the git outa *gone*. Eddie already on his way, backpedaling. Ray Bob still scratching his belly, not even moving.

A middle-aged man came out the side entrance of the restaurant then and stood on the sidewalk beneath the awning lighting a cigarette. Wearing a dark western cut suit and cowboy boots. Ray Bob eased away among the parked cars then and they faded back into the lot, moving hunched over down the aisles toward the Caddy. Eddie saying, So why you think he stopped us?

Asked us about the food.

Hell with that, that ain't why he stopped us.

If you know then don't ask.

When they reached the Caddy they heard a dull metallic thud and crunch from the back of the lot. Then a car horn that didn't stop. The man smoking out front swung around to look. After a moment he began to amble down the sidewalk in that direction. Ray Bob waited until the man was down near the Ford, then he cranked the motor and pulled onto Riverside Drive toward the freeway. He drove with his elbows while he lit a cigarette.

Well how about that, he said. Now we even.

We ain't even, said Eddie. He was fooling with his earring, pulling it down and letting it spring back up, over and again. He glanced back over his shoulder, blinking. That was a fuckin cop, man. You way ahead.

Ray Bob grinned, said he agreed. Said, You don't even know how much I'm ahead, hoss. Adding, I didn't know you was from El Paso either.

I ain't.

Lied like a dawg.

Eddie shrugged. I suppose you wanted me to say Dallas. Eddie thinking Dallas because that's where the two of them had crossed trails in a southside bar, hooked up on the spot. Ray Bob just off a prison jolt, restless, eager to get it on. Ready to hit the road, get *moving*. Eddie on the drift, aimless, braced by the other's bounce. They'd buddied up just that fast, that easy, hardly even talked about it, what drifters do.

Fuckin Dallas, said Ray Bob. Rotary Club nazis in pinstripes, whole city. That where you from?

Naw, Louisiana. Down in them swamps and bayous. How about you?

I ain't from nowhere.

Well, I been there too, said Eddie. You can bank on it. Everywhere and nowhere.

Ray Bob drummed the steering wheel. All right then. You know.

They went through the dark closed-in curves on Riverside and then the trees fell back from the pavement and the road turned uphill toward the intersection with the interstate. Ray Bob shot up onto the freeway and merged into traffic going south away from town.

Tell you what I know, said Eddie. He slumped in the seat, leaned his head to one side and cracked his neck. I ain't believing it, but I'm still hungry. That's what I know.

Cause you got a taste for this stuff, Ray Bob said. Nuthin makes a fella hungry like a good day's work. Look, there's a Denny's up there, next exit.

I ain't eatin at no Denny's. Not that goddamn hungry.

Must do sumthin right, said Ray Bob. They everywhere.

Like a virus. Where we going?

Where you wanna go?

I dunno. But it better be outa Dodge. Plus if you see a McDonald's stop. Grab me a burger. Eddie hunched forward to jam the wind sheering over the windshield and lit a Camel. You really think they had music back there?

Probably. What I heard.

Damn.

He turned on the dash radio and rotated the dial, paused on a preacher bawling in cadence, warning against the new millennium. The devil done busy, time's gonna get worse. Here it comes now, look out. A prostitute riding a sevenheaded beast, naked as a jaybird. Listen to her screeching, listen to her laughing. Beast foaming at the mouth. Land filled with plagues and awful suffering. People falling like flies. Blood over Babylon.

You hear that? Eddie said. That's some bad news rising.

He turned the dial some more, wishing the FM worked, observed it was next to impossible to find rhythm and blues on

AM radio, everything straight talk or country western. He settled on a country station, lowered the bass and boosted the volume. George Strait singing about Texas, how all his exes lived there. Didn't sound that sad about it though, kind of happy, like it was more or less convenient.

They shot down the highway in the Caddy, roof folded back beneath the early evening starlight. Darkened office buildings sped past above the sloped embankment of I-35. Motel signs advertising low rates. An eighteen-wheeler stopped on the shoulder with flares. A city patrol car running radar from an overpass. The silver splintered moon coming up high.

After a minute Eddie said, Talking about end times, I heard more'n two hundred million people been killed the last century in wars and concentration camps and such as that.

No shit? said Ray Bob. That include women and children?

Beats me. Just a number I heard. Eddie reached back and smoothed his ponytail. Tell you sumthin else I heard. A lotta clocks stopped working on the year 2000. Right when it hit. At midnight.

Ray Bob nodded. Like he'd heard it too. Then he said, What the fuck for?

I dunno. Sumthin to do with zeros. Screwed up a shitload of computers too.

That right?

What I heard. Shut 'em right down. Everything inside disappeared, lost forever.

Police computers too?

Eddie nodded. What I heard, they got some chaos.

Shit, I hope so, said Ray Bob. Lose my sheet.

Man, I ain't even thought of that. Eddie fiddled with his earring. Saying, Thinka that, dude, a clean record. Whoa. Get me a guitar and get back to music. What you gonna do?

What I'm gonna do? Ray Bob grinned. Gonna hit a 7-Eleven and start all over. Same as you, hoss.

He punched Eddie on the shoulder.

Same as you.

5

Rule Hooks stood by the open car door in the dark and studied the body of Bernie Rose lying sideways on the seat. Keeping it clinical. Face and temple, close-in work. Not a lot of blood, considering the mess. He shined the highbeam flashlight on the floorboards and over the dash.

Anybody moved him?

Guy who found him.

Who's that?

Shitkicker from Dripping Springs dressed up on a date. Said he was leaning on the horn. Moved him back, he fell over.

Lieutenant Blaine shrugged, stood against the rear left fender of the Ford rubbing the bridge of his nose between a thumb and forefinger.

Rule bent forward and flipped the flashlight beam into the backseat, then outside along the pavement near the sedan. Anybody see anything?

The lieutenant shook his head, lit a cigarette. Bony guy with a gaunt pockmarked face beneath a head of straight black hair smoothed back with gel. A country boy pushing sixty, supervisor in Austin homicide. His white seersucker suit hung loosely, a couple of sizes too big.

Beth come over and seen him after, though, Blaine said. She was across the street at the Jalisco waiting for him, saw the hubbub. Says she don't know why Bernie was over here.

Rule wagged his head, clicked his teeth, pointed the flashlight beam beneath the sedan. You see her?

I saw her, you bet. Blaine palmed his forehead, rubbed an eye with the heel of one hand. She passed out, some waitress from inside brought her around with ice. When I got here she was in shock, stumbling around like a zombie. He tossed the cigarette, half smoked.

Where's she now?

Squad car took her up to the daughter's place in Round Rock.

Blaine stood away from the car and bent his head back, looked at the sky. Pale floating stars, a slivered moon, aurora borealis of the nightlit city. No breeze stirring, it'd laid at sunset. Night way too quiet, an eerie fallen hush. He waved one thin hand helplessly.

You know, I talked to Bernie earlier at the station, Blaine said. Seemed fine. Talking that pigeon Spanish, complaining he'd fucked up a new suit. Said something about brake fluid. Don't use brake fluid, he told me, two three times. Otherwise in a good mood. You know Bernie. He said you was working that 7-Eleven case.

Rule flicked off the flashlight and pushed his hat back. He hooked both thumbs in his gun belt, looked at the detective. Reckon there's a connection?

How the fuck I know? Blaine's country twang twisted with outrage, with apprehension. He folded his arms and took a deep breath. Saying softly, All right, now, all right. Telling himself to get a grip. Then saying, Me and Bernie we go back twentyfive thirty years. He sighed. This is some shit.

Rule looked past the detective at the people milling in the crowded lot beyond the yellow crime scene tape. TV lights, reporters on the make. Customers finished eating or on their way into Threadgill's stood in loose clumps near the entrance lights discussing the show, asking what happened. Something to watch, an unexpected spectacle, gaga delicious, witnessing a real-life crime-film shoot. Several uniformed patrolmen positioned just inside the line of tape stood ramrod stoic, arms crossed, or turned in tight circles, ignoring questions. Agitated, frightened, brother cop down, stonecold dead. Rule gazed at the two TV trucks parked on the lot and saw the deputy chief talking into cameras.

What's he got to say?

Blaine frowned, glanced backward over his shoulder. Who?

The chief? The usual, I reckon. He'll mumbojumbo through it. That's his job.

Just keep him clear of me.

That ain't my job.

Rule tapped the flashlight against his thigh, not looking at Blaine. Everybody uptight, angry. Bad mojo working. He watched the deputy chief motioning stiffly into one of the cameras. Too far away to hear, but you could mark down what he was saying: We have an officer down, but that's all I can say at this time, the investigation is in process. As soon as I have more information I will make a statement. No, I cannot identify the officer now. Give us a few minutes until the family is notified. We will release the appropriate information once that is done.

Etcetera.

Rule spat to one side and turned to Blaine. Saying, All right, but keep back the reporters anyhow.

You reckon I gotta be told.

Just following procedure. I'll get my kit.

Rule went off in a sideways direction and ducked the yellow tape away from the crowd—a murmuring buzz there, someone giggling, stupid nervous—crossed over an aisle to his truck. Inside the cab he dialed the headquarter's lab on his cellular phone. Moline had left. He dialed another number and Moline picked up. Where are you, pardner? asked Rule.

Almost home. Round Rock's the next exit. What we got?

You remembered that ol' boy yet? The ponytail?

Not yet.

Well, don't quit on me.

I'm working on it.

So was Bernie Rose.

Moline didn't say anything for a moment. Then said, I've heard the name. Homicide detective at city.

Was.

Jesus. Line of duty?

Could be.

And you're thinking the ponytail.

Maybe. Gunshot, up close and in.

Damn. Moline paused. Guy I'm thinking of wasn't a shooter though. He paused again. Auto theft's what I'm thinking.

Rule looked through the windshield across the parking lot. Another TV van pulled into the drive, jammed the lot honking, pushing the crowd for space. A reporter got out and began fixing her hair in the side mirror while the cameraman set up. The deputy chief went over and shook her hand, smiling.

Well, keep at it, Moline. Maybe this ol' ponytail boy done got promoted.

I'll call when it comes.

Rule put down the phone and carried his crime kit back to the Ford. He worked the scene for almost an hour but came up with zilch. The examiner would have to pull the slugs, see what they said. Thirty-eight or 9 mm, looked like. He was kneeling on the pavement packing up when Lieutenant Blaine drew up close saying, Here he comes. Rule glanced over to see the deputy chief approaching. Short careful strides, asshole tight, long arms swinging. He snapped the latch shut, picked up the kit and started away at an angle toward his truck.

Ranger Hooks.

Rule kept walking.

Sergeant Hooks, just a moment there, sir.

Rule stopped and turned, waiting. The deputy chief was tall, broadshouldered and balding. Rimless glasses and a dark pin-striped suit, pressed white shirt and maroon tie humped over a well-fed belly. He carried himself like a deacon and wore a worried look. He stopped three feet away.

You find anything?

Nope.

The deputy chief grunted, touched his glasses.

Detective Rose was working these 7-Eleven murders, he said. Now Rose is dead, a good man, irreplaceable loss. There may be a connection. I understand you were called in on that investigation personally. We're depending on you to give it your best, sir.

His voice was deceptively high for a big man, the tone senten-tious. Tenor in the First Baptist choir, Rule figured. Office player, budgets and policy, hadn't scuffed the streets in twenty years.

Hobnobbing city council, cozy lunches with bureaucrats, Kiwanis club speeches. Lawman politician. Handshakes and photo ops, scrumming for an edge. Play hardball politics all week, rise above it on Sunday. Chickenshit his way through this world, sneak into the next.

Another reason Rule worked alone.

He eyed the deputy chief, a knot working in his jaw. Then said, Save it for the press, pardner. I don't need no pep talk.

The other man either ignored the remark or didn't hear it. He turned the Mason's ring on his right hand, red stone glinting in dull light, and continued. Said, As you may know, these recent convenience store homicides have the public disturbed. They indicate a certain ill will towards Indians, Asians, what have you. We have placed them on the front burner, Sergeant Hooks. That's why you are involved. Rangers have statewide jurisdiction, special resources. You can cast the net wide. I'm also told Detective Rose discovered an important lead today.

The man ran a beefy hand down the lapel of his suitcoat. Now, we don't want to let that slip away on us, do we?

Rule felt his chest constrict as if the other man had reached in through his breastbone and torqued a screw too tight. For a moment it paralyzed him. Then he grinned with his teeth, turned and spat to one side, turned his back and walked. He was lifting the crime scene tape and ducking under when he heard the deputy chief behind him speaking to Blaine, his loud voice labored with dismay. Saying, What in God's name is wrong with that man?

He didn't hear Blaine's response.

When he opened the truck cab the cellular phone was ringing. He put down the kit and answered. It was Moline.

You ought to carry that phone, Rule. What it's for.

He put the truck key into the ignition and cranked the motor, rolled down the window. Warm night air, honeysuckle on it. Said, You calling for a reason, Moline?

I got a name for you.

Shoot.

DeReese Ledoux. A Louisiana boy. From Lafayette. But they heard of him in Oklahoma and Arkansas, maybe Mississippi. He gets around. I'll give Jackson a call tomorrow. I already phoned Crime Records at headquarters, they're running him through. We'll put it on the NCIC, check the Triple-I. Auto theft's what I recall but we'll see.

How you spell it?

Moline spelled the name. It's Cajun.

Coonass, Rule murmured. Appreciate it, Moline. Good work. Have a whiskey on me.

Doing just that.

Rule heard a glass clink in the background.

Johnny Walker, Moline said, Black Label. C'mon over. Gotta extra glass and a big old lonely house. Dana's gone out again.

Better pass, pardner. I'm gonna head back to the shop and see what records has on Ledoux. Rule waited a second. Then, Go easy on the whiskey.

I'm missing Dana.

No reason to wallow in it, Moline. She's a bitch.

I know it. But she's my bitch and I miss her.

It's good riddance.

She wants a divorce.

Give it to her.

Rule punched the button and the telephone went dead. He put the truck in drive and pulled off the lot into evening traffic. Moline getting drunk. The guy was all right. Crime analyst, liaison between Ranger investigators and the state crime lab. Had a brain like nobody. Worked hard, knew his business. Only problem was Dana. Rule waited for the stoplight at Congress to turn.

Not that he couldn't understand. She was a slinky little thing, cute as a bug. He'd fucked her a coupla times himself. A real screamer.

6

They got off the interstate in South Austin and headed east on State Highway 71, following the outer lip of the river valley through the low nightstreaked hills. In Bastrop they filled up on gas at a Diamond Shamrock and stopped at a Sonic Drive-In. Ray Bob ordered two number one burgers with jalapenos, Eddie wanted a foot-long Coney with chili and onions.

Ray Bob punched the speaker button. Said, And bring two orders of onion rings and fries with that. Plus ketchup. He punched it again. And two chocolate malts.

They paid the carhop with three rolls of dimes when she brought the tray. She stared at the rolls like she might have to break them open and count. A high school student, sixteen maybe, foxy, wearing skintight red corduroys and a striped Sonic shirt. Ray Bob winked at her, said keep the change and called her darlin. She smiled and sashayed away, tight little butt wiggling in the pants.

They sat in the Caddy and spread out the feed and ate.

What time you reckon she gets off, asked Ray Bob. He stuffed a wad of fries in his mouth and chewed.

Eddie said they were open late, probably midnight.

Well, I ain't waiting that long.

What?

Ray Bob swallowed the fries and sucked some malt through the straw, drawing hard. We shorta money, hoss. Maybe we oughta go back to that Diamond Shamrock.

No way, said Eddie. Right in the middle of town.

You got a better idea?

Mmm-hmmm. He leaned forward between his knees to bite off a chunk of hotdog, trying to keep his ponytail from flopping in the chili. There's another one just like it down by Columbus, just this side of Interstate Ten.

Man, don't talk with your mouth full. Ray Bob folded an onion ring and dipped it in ketchup, bit off half. Saying, All right, we'll hit it and then the freeway. He stared at Eddie, making a face. You and that fuckin chili. Don't get it on my goddamn car.

Where?

Shit, you got it everywhere.

Eddie wiped his chin with a napkin, checked his pants. A glob of chili there on his left knee. He fingered it off and licked. Only don't shoot this one, he said.

Ray Bob said, I ain't gonna shoot nobody. Don't have to. He pushed the speaker button and ordered more ketchup. He jerked a thumb toward Eddie. It's your turn.

No way, Eddie said. I don't like shooting people. We can lock the clerk in the restroom.

Still gonna see us.

Eddie thought about it, snapped his fingers. Put my shirt over my head.

I can see that now, dickhead, said Ray Bob. Where's my ketchup?

But that's what he did. An hour down the road they waited back on the shoulder of the highway in the dark until a white Chevy pickup pulled away from the pumps. Then Ray Bob put it in gear and slowly rolled into the Diamond Shamrock. He parked to one side where the clerk couldn't see. Eddie pulled his T-shirt over his head and went in looking through an armhole with the .22 revolver in his hand.

Inside he waved the gun and said, This is a robbery.

The clerk was an old man, stooped over like a hunchback with blue bumps bulging off his hands and thin gray hair plastered to his skull with rose oil. Wearing khakis and a longsleeved flannel shirt when it wasn't even cold. Eddie told him to empty the register. Speaking through the armhole of the shirt, voice jumping, his bellybutton showing. The man nodded once and fumbled with the register keys. He moved slow and deliberate but his hands shook like he had the DTs. He bent closer to the register and squinted, eyes boomeranging between it and Eddie.

Just don't squeeze that peashooter, he said, I'm near enough dead already.

Eddie watched the old geezer fussing with the register buttons. He reminded him of his mother's brother Uncle Wade. The blue swollen hands, a grizzled face full of bones, the voice, the smell of rose oil. Even the khakis and longsleeved flannel shirt, which his uncle wore year round because of arthritis in one shoulder, poor circulation all over.

Your name ain't Wade, is it? Eddie asked. He adjusted the armhole of the shirt so he could see better. Wade Hebert?

The old man stopped, stared at him. His gray washed-out eyes watering. Naw, it ain't.

Well, gimmee that money. Put it in a sack.

The man said all right. Said he would. Said that's what he was doing. He put the bills in a plastic bag and set it on the counter.

You ain't got no rolls?

The old man studied the T-shirt over Eddie's head, looked up the armhole, then turned his wet gaze to the side toward a stainless steel warming oven for pastries. Sorry, son. We all out.

Said it just like Uncle Wade. It caught Eddie off guard. He hesitated, followed the old man's eyes toward the oven. It was empty. He quickly swung back waving the gun. Jesus Christ, I mean rolls of coins.

No need for that kinda talk, the man said. I ain't deaf. Them rolls is in the safe and I ain't got the combination.

Eddie thought about that. What safe?

The man slowly looked down the cement floor between his feet, then back up at Eddie. You new at this, ain't you, son?

Like Uncle Wade again. Just like him. Jesus Christ. Eddie couldn't believe it.

Course, you could just turn around and walk out. The old man rubbed his stubbled jaw, the gnarled hand still shaking. That'd be my advice, son. Just change your mind, walk on out, save everybody the trouble.

Eddie stared at him.

I won't even call the law.

The prospect sounded so reasonable Eddie thought about it. He kept the gun on the man, peering out the armhole while he pondered. He was still thinking about it when he heard the door open behind and the old man looked past him and slowly raised both arms. Then there was a loud explosion and the man jerked back with a hole in his shirtfront. His chest buckled, he stood there wavering, then dropped like a body bag buried at sea. Eddie heard his skull pop when it hit the floor.

What the fuck you doin, discussin the weather? Ray Bob standing just inside the front door holding his gun.

Eddie didn't move.

Goddamn, do everything myself. Just point and pull, that ain't hard. Ray Bob grumping now. But no, you gotta make everybody feel good about it, don't want no hurt feelings. He tucked the Walther automatic down the front of his britches. You can drop your shirt now, dickhead. Where's the money?

Eddie motioned at the plastic bag on the counter. Ray Bob came over and looked inside it, grunted, then scooped out the loose change from the register compartments. He went behind the counter and stepped over the old man and put a carton of Marlboros and a carton of Camel straights in the bag. Said, Grab that empty cartridge off the floor. What else?

Eddie shook his head.

C'mon then.

Outside the front door Ray Bob stopped. Beer, he said, forgot the goddamn beer again. He went back inside to the coolers and took out a twelvepack of Bud. He snagged a big bag of Fritos off the rack in passing and half a dozen bags of M&Ms.

In the car a few minutes later, after the state highway ran out and they'd merged onto Interstate 10 going toward Houston, Ray Bob opened a can of beer and took a big swallow. Good golly miss molly, he said, that's some good stuff. Cold too. They keeping their freezers right. He looked over at Eddie. What the fuck's with you, hoss?

Eddie bent forward, cupped a cigarette and tried to light it. His hands were shaking. Man oh man, I think you just shot Uncle Wade.

What?

That old man. Eddie wagged his head in wonderment, finally got the cigarette lit. I swear to god that was my mother's brother Uncle Wade.

Well, why the hell didn't you ask?

I did.

And?

Said he wasn't. Eddie took a long drag on the Camel. But I swear to god.

Shit, you all fucked up, said Ray Bob. He frowned and reached into the backseat and came back with another Bud. Here, drink one of these.

Eddie took the beer but didn't open it. Man oh man, that was some weird shit back there.

Your uncle, huh? Ray Bob gunned the accelerator and the Caddy picked up speed, the wind gushing back over the windshield. Uncle Wade. He grinned. Was you close?

Eddie pulled up his T-shirt tail and wiped off the top of the can. He took a deep breath. Naw, man. Shit naw. Always telling me what to do. Couldn't stand him.

Then why didn't you just shoot the motherfucker?

Uncle Wade? He opened the beer and took a sip. Same reason I didn't like him, I reckon. Same reason he pissed me off.

Yeah? What's that?

Cause he was always right, that's why.

They rode in silence then. The Caddy skimmed over the smooth pavement through the night. There were a million stars set into the sky and the sky stretched high and forever over a darkened earth, the end of which could not be seen. Way down south sheet lightning played at the fringe.

After a while, Ray Bob said, I tell you what, my ol' momma was like that. He knuckled a nostril and wiped it on his pants. Flat drove me crazy.

Always thought she was right?

You bet. Never was wrong.

Well, said Eddie, why didn't you just shoot her?

Ray Bob leaned his head back against the seat headrest with his lower lip poked out like he was studying the question. Then he lit a Marlboro and shrugged. Staring out through the windshield past the long palewhite hood into the pale light of the onrushing road. Saying:

Who the fuck says I didn't?

7

Down in Houston at a Holiday Inn on the west side Della Street sipped her screwdriver and pushed away the man's hand. It was creeping up her skirt. They sat side by side on high upholstered stools at the atrium bar, and the screwdriver was the third drink he'd bought her. But he'd been outdrinking her two to one and now he was stewed.

What you say you do? the man asked.

I'm a model, Della said.

Lies lies lies. She hated it but no man wearing a business suit in a nice Holiday Inn was gonna take a beautician from Sugar Land seriously.

A model, huh? Like on stage? The man smiled. Leered, actually. A stripper?

He put his hand on her knee again. She pushed it off and remembered to sit up straighter on the stool, square and relax her shoulders. She sipped the screwdriver, ignored his remark.

Finally he said, All right, allrightarooty, okay, what kinda model? His words slurring.

She flipped a strand of hair back over her shoulder. Said: Fashion. Like in catalogs. Montgomery Wards, JC Penney, like that.

She looked at her reflection in the mirror behind the bar. Long blonde hair falling in waves over her shoulders, her best feature.

Her face maybe too long for her nose and her eyes set too close, but the hair distracted from all that. Especially the bangs. Big fluffy bangs. Learned that back in beauty school. Still, she never said like a model for Sakowitz or Neiman Marcus. Or for fashion magazines, *Cosmo* and such. No use overdoing it.

I seen you in one, the man said. Okay, I remember now.

Yeah? Which one?

Wards, he said. He nodded. That's right, the bra section. You got nice tits . . . boobs . . . you know, breasts.

Della scraped the corner of her mouth with a little fingernail. Thinking about that. It was true in her own opinion, lord knew she used that Suzanne Somers exercise thingy enough. Before work every morning, while watching Letterman before bed. First she'd worked on the size, now it was lift. But she sniffed and said, No you didn't. I don't do bras. I do panty hose. And shoes.

The man looked down where her feet perched on the stool rail. He wagged his head. I don't believe it, uh-uh. Your ankles too big.

She crossed her legs self-consciously, pointing her top foot away. Thinking that was true, what he said, but what could you do? Nature had its limits. Bone structure not being like waist or boobs. Or hair. She glanced into the mirror and fluffed her bangs.

You gotta have skinny ones, the guy said. Real dinkers. He weaved on his stool and leaned on the bar with one elbow and made a tiny circle with a thumb and finger. He closed one eye and leaned toward the circle, peering through it. Like that.

Della's shoulders slumped, she blew her breath out slowly. Jesus, the guy was a jerk. A whole evening wasted. Scrimp all week to get a new outfit off layaway at Dillard's and go out to a nice place, you end up with a drunk. A real stinker. And he'd started out so nice. A salesman for Tyler Pipe. Good haircut, smelled clean. Gray suit with a silk polka dot tie, color coordinated. Even wore a hanky in the breast pocket. Sat down next to her and smiled. Sell pipeline by the mile, he'd said, install it by the yard. Big fat commissions. You want a drink?

She'd replied yes and thank you. Listened to him talk about pipe. Acted interested. Nodded a lot and smiled, hands folded demurely in her lap, just like that quiz in *Redbook* said. And now this shit.

My wife got ankles like that, the man said. He frowned and his head nodded forward then jerked back. My ex-wife. Did I say wife? I mean ex-wife.

Della put her hand on her purse to excuse herself to the rest-room. Spend a little while in there, touch up her face, brush her hair. Maybe the guy'd get tired and leave. Or pass out. Maybe there'd still be time to meet someone else. Although it was getting late. She glanced around. Most of the tables were empty. The atrium bar was clearing out.

When without any warning he reached over and squeezed her right breast through her brand-new rayon blouse. Hand right on the boob. Fingers spread for a good grip. Squeezing hard. Saying, Yeah, it was the bras, I remember.

She flung up her right arm and smacked him in the nose. He fell sideways off the high upholstered stool and landed on the parquet floor. Whap, thump, thud. Not a soft landing. Sprawled there, looking dazed. But only for a moment. He was up fast, very quickly for a drunk, she thought, and unhurt. No surprise there. Boozers never get hurt. Drunk in a Ford Escort smashes into a Greyhound and half the people on the bus die, the pisspot bumps his eye. But the speed surprised her. He came up in a snap, snarling. Saying, Dammit, you just like that stuckup bitch, you just like her. Then he balled up his hand and took a swing.

No time to move. That fast.

So Della just closed her eyes and waited, flinching, knowing how it'd feel. Except the punch never landed. Waited another second, you never know. Then she opened her eyes and saw a man standing behind the pipe salesman twisting his arm backward. He was tall and slim with black hair, a curled lock falling down his forehead, like it was put there by some *True Romance* illustrator, and blue eyes. Square jaw, fair complexion. Wearing the nicest suit she'd ever seen, as if it had been made just for him and no other. Looking just like the movie actor who played James Bond, no kidding, the Remington Steele one. Then he opened his mouth—even bobbed his head once, a courtesy bob, like tipping a hat—and said, his voice calm, deferential: Is this man bothering you, miss?

She almost fell off the stool.

Bitch led me on, the salesman protested loudly. He wriggled in the other's grasp, tried to turn out of it. She's a user, what she is.

Mister Dreamboat lifted up the man's arm twisted behind and the salesman made an ugly face and grunted. Mister Dreamboat saying, That's no way to talk to a lady. Then he marched the guy away through the low tables with smoky glass tops and across the atrium past the green potted plants and the piano player in the tuxedo playing soft moonlight music and right past the salmon nainsook love sofas and chairs with rattan frames in the lounge area near the elevators and on out past the check-in desk toward the front door. Della couldn't see after that.

She sat on the stool and waited. She crossed her legs, folded her hands in her lap. She crossed her legs the other way, ankle hanging down there low, inconspicuous. Uncomfortable, though. She uncrossed her legs and perched her feet on the crossbar out of sight. Much better. She looked at herself in the mirror behind the bar. Smiled, reached up to relax her hair, fluff the bangs. Hand back in lap, she discretely tugged at the elastic top of her panty hose through the skirt. Not to presume anything. But she didn't want those unsightly red marks. Just in case.

The bartender came over and asked if she wanted another drink. A young guy, college student with a Jan Michael-Vincent swagger and a slight smirk. When Della shook her head, he said, Sure? It's on the house. Well in that case, she told him, she wouldn't mind a little something, but not a screwdriver, something different. Something more exotic maybe. No problem, he said, and brought it to her.

She sipped the Tom Collins and waited. Glanced at the clock. He sure was taking his time. Front door of the hotel wasn't that far away. Then it occurred to her he might not return. That thought was negative and depressed her, so she stopped thinking it. Power of positive thinking, she knew all about that. At least theoretically. Articles in every magazine, lots of good advice, but hard to follow. You had to remind yourself, usually when you were already occupied, that being the catch. She closed her eyes and imagined Mister Dreamboat coming back, sitting on the stool next to her. Very nice. Positive.

She opened her eyes, glanced at the clock. Damn. She debated lighting a cigarette, Benson & Hedges menthol. She usually smoked generics what with being a single mother on a budget, if you called minimum wage a budget. But not in a Holiday Inn where you might meet someone. She picked up the pack from the bartop, hesitated, put it down. Maybe she should wait and let him light it. Nice thought. Positive. She smiled into the mirror. Only what if he couldn't stand smoker's breath? She fished in her purse for a Certs.

The Certs was sucked down to a tiny little ring Della was trying not to crunch, which wasn't easy, especially with nerves, when he appeared beside the stool and asked if he could join her. Yes, she said. She rearranged her hands in her lap. It's so nice of you to ask.

I assure you it is my pleasure.

She closed her eyes and sighed.

He sat down and straightened his suitpants and cuffs, then put his elbows on the bar and clasped his hands in front. Nice hands, with long tapered fingers and perfect nails. He leaned his chin against them thoughtfully. Eyes focused somewhere out there. No, not out there. Inward, right in there, composing himself. Della patiently waiting for him to say his name, ask hers. Then start talking about his job, or football teams, which one would win which division, all depending, or the state of the economy, which was hard to predict. Something like that.

She was all prepared to listen, reminding herself to nod and smile at every opportunity, to agree with whatever, no matter what, when Mister Dreamboat turned his head to face her, his crystalline blue eyes gazing precisely into hers, and said, I'm an executive with a Fortune Five Hundred company and I stay so busy I hardly take time to eat, much less have a social life. I'm also very direct because it's the shortest way to the heart of any matter. Right now I have a dozen things to do—the demands are exhausting, all of them pressing—but I'm tired and lonely. You are the most beautiful woman I have seen in a long time. Would you care to join me in my room for a drink?

Della put her hand out on the bar to steady herself.

If I seem too forward, forgive me, he said. One beat pause, tip of the head. But I sensed our interest is mutual.

Yes, Della said. She felt a little dizzy and forgot to smile but remembered to nod. Yes, oh yes, and thank you.

8

Rule Hooks sat in an undershirt at his kitchen table. To the side lay a dogeared James Lee Burke paperback, *Burning Angel*. He sat still, a bigknuckled hand wrapped over a bottle of cold Dos Equis. Behind him, the back screen door propped open to the night, his hound Lefty lying across the threshold sleeping, wide tan and white head between his paws. Crickets chirred in the backyard. A soft breeze floated through the open doorway, the scent of honeysuckle lightly on it. A whippoorwill called out of near darkness.

The midnight hour.

He raised the bottle and swallowed, set it down on the oilcloth. Looked at the oilcloth, old and worn. Small hairline cracks weaving through it beneath the somber kitchen light. A spidery topography of years mapping out time's relentless passage. In the beginning, nonexistent, or at least unnoticed. Then perceived, but barely. Then the steady increase, an advancing pressure felt with intensifying concern, and the quickening that follows. Finally urgent, with moments of panic. Which one resisted. Which one resisted. He took another sip, listening.

I hope you don't mind me dropping in on you like this, Rule, at this hour of the night and all.

Her voice coming from across the table.

But you been on my mind. She reached to pick up her bottle of beer and gingerly sampled it. She tapped a fingernail against the bottle. This is pretty good. You sure it's Mexican?

Rule looked at her and waited. She wore a gabardine western swing shirt with a light green bodice and a dark green zigzag yoke. Smile pockets and pearl snaps. Piped with white cotton cording, sequins on collar and cuffs. A woman's Bob Wills shirt. Plus fancy pants to fit and a handtooled leather belt with white buckstitching. Tiny pinto boots with silver conchos under the table. An outfit Porter Wagoner might wear, if Porter went drag. Only thing missing was a hat.

She patted her hair, cut in a thick shag, tinted gold like Farrah Fawcett's. I left my hat in the car, she said, cause it wrinkles my hair.

Rule grunted, stroked one thigh through his khakis. She was cute as a button but he didn't like the way she crawled into your head. It didn't seem healthy.

She said, I was thinking about that time you met me out at Pedernales Park. Last fall. Remember? We hiked up the river and laid in the sun and made love on a boulder. Seemed so natural. She smiled. That was nice.

I heard you asked for a divorce.

Well that's right. She narrowed her graygreen cat eyes and looked at him. Where you hear that?

On the street.

What street?

Street with no name, Rule said.

Ain't no street with no name. She tossed her head. You been talking to Moline?

Most every day, said Rule. I work with him.

Well, I *know* that.

Where you been all dressed up?

She sipped her beer. The Broken Spoke.

You get stood up?

Don't be mean, Rule. She slid the bottle over the oilcloth to the middle of the table and left it there. I just didn't like him, that's all.

Rule listened to the crickets chirring outside, heard the whippoorwill call again. Soft and musical, like an echo. Saying, I suppose you don't like Moline neither.

He's all right. She frowned. No he ain't. He drinks too much.

You give him a reason.

Moline don't need no reason. When he tell you?

Tonight.

She picked a piece of lint off her pants with her nails, flicked it away. Well, it must be important, him working at night.

Gotta make that overtime, Rule said. He leaned an elbow on the table and shot a long finger from his fist toward her shirtfront. Gotta pay for that snazzy outfit you wearing. How much that cost?

None of your business.

She got up and walked around the table to stand behind him in the doorway looking outside into the darkness. The kitchen light fell in a skewed rectangle over the wood steps and near ground with her shadow cast in it. Lefty stirred on the threshold. He opened an eye, shut it back. You need to cut your grass, she said. What kind of dog is this?

That's Lefty, said Rule. He didn't turn his head and spoke straight ahead as though she still sat across the table. Lefty, meet Dana. He's a Walker. A coon hound, when he ain't sleeping. Lefty likes to sleep.

She turned back and took two steps and stood close behind Rule's chair with her hands on his shoulders. Just sitting there, light as butterflies, on either side of his undershirt straps. Then she began to knead. Her hands were small but her fingers were strong and she dug in deep. After a minute she bent over and laid her face against his neck. I'm kinda sleepy myself, she said. Wanna go to bed?

Rule told her he wasn't tired. With her head still laid against him, she said that wasn't what she meant. Rule said he knew it. She told him she knew he knew it. Then we all clear, Rule said.

She cuffed him on the far ear. Rule, why you being so damn mean?

Comes natural.

It sure seems to. I oughta slap you upside the head.

Rule picked up his beer and took a long swallow, emptied it. He set the bottle down hard. You do and I'll tan your hide.

I'm gonna bite your neck.

You don't know what trouble is, he said.

That's just big talk's all.

She bit the back of his neck. Her teeth were small and sharp. He didn't stir. She moved back around the side and took a fold of neckskin under his ear between her teeth and bit harder. He still didn't move. So she bit down until she drew blood. She raised her head and looked at the teeth marks. Said, Now look at what you made me do. She leaned back to the spot and licked it, mouthed it, then sucked it. Sucked hard, leaving a mark.

You finished? said Rule.

Darlin, I ain't even started.

Maybe you ain't, he replied, but I'm damn sure gonna finish it.

Rule pushed back his chair and stood up in one smooth motion. He shoved the chair aside with his leg and grabbed her around the waist, swung her up sideways and over his hip. Holding her horizontal over the tabletop like a man hauling a stepladder, only lighter. She yelled and reached back and dug her nails into his far side below the ribs, clawing his skin through the thin cotton undershirt. He ignored the mauling nails and lifted her higher, carried her through the kitchen into the living room to the hall and down the hallway to the bedroom, her kicking and squealing the whole way. He pushed open the door with one foot and tossed her on the bed.

He was in his socks and she was pulling at her boots but she was naked before he was. Her clothes flung over the floor. Laid up in the sheets. When he finally got stripped down and spread her legs and topped her she commenced to screaming and didn't stop until he lay panting in slaked suspension above her, his back layered with sweat and strung with the long red welts. He rolled off and lay back with an arm under his head while she nibbled at his chest.

Christ, she was a screamer all right, and that was a fact. A scratcher too. He'd forgot about that part. Truth was, he couldn't figure how Moline had ever held her.

9

The night was dark and moist and the highway ran out under the stars like an unstrung arrow flying toward some destination straight and true. The twin tunnels of light the Caddy bored forward into darkness never faltered but seemed to gain no ground different from any other. The FM still didn't work, and they changed from one AM station to another as they ran out from beneath the reach of each into broken waves of static. That's how they knew they were moving. Otherwise they might not have known in that broad charcoal sweep beneath wheeling constellations.

By Sealy they were out of beer and soon after they needed to piss so badly they pulled off the interstate beneath the Brazos River bridge. They stood on the high broken bank with the stars blinking up from the surface of a wide rippling current the arcs of their piddle could not reach. The night was warm. They had drunk much beer and their bladders were swollen and they both groaned and sighed.

Damn, said Eddie, that feels good. Only thing better'n a good fuck's a good piss.

Ray Bob stroked his cock, allowed he'd take a good fuck first any day.

Well, I was just talking, Eddie said. It's a saying.

Worst fuck I ever had was good, said Ray Bob. He stood holding his cock long after he was finished listening to the lap of the river against the bank in the darkness below. I never had a bad fuck.

You ever fucked a cow? asked Eddie.

Shit no. I don't fuck cows.

Well, Eddie said, that's why.

Man, I don't want to hear about it.

After a minute, though, Ray Bob admitted he'd fucked a watermelon. Out on the prison farm at Huntsville. Fuck anything that don't move in prison, he said. That's why you keep moving.

I ain't never been cornholed myself, Eddie said. It's a record I aim to keep.

Ray Bob zipped up his pants. Ever let someone suck you off?

Naw, Eddie said. They gonna want it back.

Not always. Ray Bob lit a cigarette. It ain't bad. I had me a swish in Huntsville. Black guy from Beaumont. He could blow some tunes.

No shit?

Yeah. Begged me twice a day. Liked to eat jam too, but I didn't go for that.

Uh-uh-uh, I reckon not. Eddie grimaced.

You don't even know what I'm talking about.

Eddie shrugged. Said, Don't think I wanna know.

Living in ignorance, said Ray Bob.

Well, sometimes it's better that way.

They stood silently on the high scabrous bank eroded by runoff and flood. The Brazos running below, tenebrous, its felt presence a wide unseen crevasse of power and movement. Their eyes came round to the darkness and they soon made out eddies and pinwheels in the swift current and the darker shadows of logs and dead trees floating midstream down the drift. It was quiet save for the river's purl and the occasional whine of tires on the bridge above and the rapid *whapwhapwhap* of the tires over bridge joints. After a while they heard the motor of the Caddy ping and creak as it cooled beneath the hood.

You really shoot your momma? asked Eddie. He spoke low but his voice seemed loud in the quiet, almost a shout.

Ray Bob didn't answer. He lit another cigarette off the butt of the first and scratched his belly. He kicked a clod of dirt off the bank. They heard it tumble down the steep slope and splash.

You don't want to answer, Eddie said, I understand.

Ray Bob cleared his throat and spat. Said, What if I did?

If you did, you did.

Well, I did.

Eddie fingered his earring and nodded. Well, I figgered you did. Then, after a silence, She must've been one mean old woman.

Ray Bob reached into his boot and pulled out his pistol. See this?

Eddie looked at the gun, looked at Ray Bob, then back at the gun. The short steel barrel glinted wool-blue in starlight and moonlight. Yeah, I see it.

Well, take a good looksee.

Ray Bob stepped close and pointed it at Eddie's chest, raised it higher and leveled so that the barrel stopped and steadied, aimed just above the bridge of Eddie's nose. At that narrow point between the eyebrows. He reached with his thumb and released the slide, his finger tight on the trigger. Eddie stared down the black hole.

Look good, said Ray Bob, cause that's the last thing my momma ever saw. And that's the last thing you ever gonna see you ever talk bad about my momma again. Ray Bob slowly lowered the automatic. Runnin buddy or not. He stuck the gun back into his boot. And that's all I got to say about it.

Eddie tilted his head to the side and pulled up one sleeve of his T-shirt to wipe the sweat off his forehead. Well, I understand, he said. I surely do.

All right, said Ray Bob. C'mon now, let's git. We almost to Houston.

He turned and walked back to the Caddy, his stocky figure striding over the thin grass into the bridge shadows like a man going off to war. Eddie stayed behind and unzipped his pants. I'll be right there, he called out. I got to piss again.

He stood holding his pecker listening to an owl summon the night from somewhere along the bank downstream. It called once, hesitated, called again. The low sweet sounds rose softly down the way like dapples in the air to dissipate over the water. He listened some more but it did not call the third time.

Well, I shoulda knowed better, he told himself, asking someone sumthin like that. He shook the last drop off his pecker, then shook it again. Saying, Yessir, sumthin like that's bound to be personal.

10

Rule Hooks lay in bed with the sleeping form of the woman curled against his flank. One silky smooth leg thrown over his, an arm across his chest holding to his side. Felt like he was wearing a straitjacket. He couldn't move without waking her and he didn't want her awake. Didn't even want her in the bed, that was the damn truth. He never could stand to sleep close to nobody.

He lay looking up at the ceiling in the dark thinking about the woman for a while, then he took to thinking about Moline. That was a pitiful subject in the altogether so he left off that and started thinking about Bernie Rose. Poor ol' Bernie. A sad situation. Good cop, a veteran. Probably could've retired. Bastard couldn't have been thinking, letting anybody get that close.

A real fuckup.

Paid for it too. But it happened all the time, you couldn't tell no one, they all knew better. Like that highway patrolman up in Fort Worth just last week. Pulls a car over and approaches the driver, leans down to scratch his ankle, catches a fortyfive slug in the head. Sixteen-year-old kid with his daddy's gun. How it went. A fuckup. And then Abe Krishna who'd been stupid enough to argue with a gun. Fuckups all around. No wonder so many people getting killed.

He dozed off for a moment but the woman moved in her sleep and he awakened thinking about DeReese Ledoux. He'd seen the guy's paperwork, all the way back to juvenile. Possession of narcotics, marijuana. Petty thievery. Creeping houses. Boosting cars, the last thing on the sheet. No muscle in that. Now *boom*, homicide. A giant leap forward. Not your usual career move. Never could tell with a coonass though.

He replayed the video from memory. Something to do with the cigarettes. Ledoux walks in. Pack on the counter, then off. Words exchanged. Abe saying something, excited. Ponytail leaning down, leg up. Gun from the boot, a revolver. Little ol' thing, but deadly. Weren't they all, weren't they all. Gun back in the boot. Ledoux gets the cigarettes, leaves. Leaves the money on the counter. Didn't make no sense.

Then there was the other fella. Comes in, grabs the money. Cigarettes too, by the carton. In and out fast. Knew what he was doing. Shorthaired guy, stocky. Maybe freckled, maybe sandy-haired, hard to tell. But muscle. Ledoux the shooter, the second guy hoisting the money. Put 'em side by side and he'd've guessed Mister No Name for the badass. So much for guessing. Maybe they were partners, maybe not.

He took the woman's arm, which had moved up around his neck, choking him, and pushed it back down. He wondered how long she planned to sleep, wished she'd wake up and leave.

For all he knew they didn't even know each other.

11

Della Street sat naked in the lamplight on the edge of the chair cushion. A beige muslin cushion with flowered print, pastel greens and understated orange. The chair in one corner facing the bed. Room 1114 of the Holiday Inn.

She sat hunched forward over her knees. Her breasts pressing bare thighs, arms hanging limply to either side. Skinprickled all over. The room was cold. She looked at the bed.

Mister Dreamboat lay sprawled faceup across the twisted sheets, the pearl plastic handle of a knife protruding from his chest. A smooth hairless chest with dark brown nipples. A nice chest. But bloody. The sheets bloody, too. Della looked down at her bloodred hands.

Boy oh boy.

She tried to think what to do. Nothing in *Redbook* about this. *True Confession* maybe. "What to Do When Love Goes Bad." Or,

"Those *Really* Bad Hair Days." Or "How I Killed Mister Dream-boat." Or . . . boy oh boy. Damn damn damn damn damn.

Tears welling up, she wanted to cry. She almost cradled her head in her hands but remembered the blood just in time. Hard to miss, all that red goop. Sticky fingers. She wiggled them apart. Yuck. Too scared to cry anyway. Too pissed.

She stood up and passed around the end of the bed toward the bathroom. Turned on the tap, hands beneath. The water swirled rubyred down the drain, then faded to primrose pink. Cold water rush, her bare feet against the cold ceramic tiles. She shivered and pushed the tap handle to the side with one wrist. Much better. She held her hands under the warm flow, stared into the mirror. Jesus Louise. Her hair was a godawful mess, kinked up in back, bangs all aflutter. And her left eye swollen and bruised. She looked a little crazy.

How about, "Love in My Heart and a Knife in His"?

She giggled, then a sob ratcheted up her throat and she caught herself. Maybe more than a little crazy. Better watch it. Things to do, things to do, no time to come unglued. Wig out later.

With dripping hands she poked her head out the bathroom door to see. Still lying there. Without a doubt. Same as before. Mister Dreamboat going nowhere. Gonna miss his next appointment.

She closed her eyes. Damn damn damn. And she'd been so sure. So absolutely certain. Escorting her across the atrium to the elevator, his hand on her elbow. Up to the eleventh, down the hall to the room, touching her all the time. Guiding her gently. Not saying much, his demeanor saying it all. A gentleman. A man in charge. Mister Fortune Five Hundred, whatever that meant.

Then cozy lamplight and the clock radio low on some easy listening station, Barry Manilow and such, crooners and violins, smooching music, a scene right out of *The Young & the Restless*. Him pouring scotch in two glasses, clink clink, bottoms up, eyeball to eyeball, falling falling gone. So easy. Kiss kiss, hug hug, another drink, more kisses, some fondling, clothes off. That had been nice actually. On the couch, on the bed. Tender. Good with his tongue. Very sweet. Little lick here, little lick there, she was moaning and groaning. Legs wide open, c'mon in.

When he excused himself to the bathroom.

Came back holding a wide leather belt and handcuffs.

Her coming off the bed in a flash and him chasing her down in a corner.

Busted him in the balls.

Him whacking her in the eye with the belt buckle. A jolt of sharp heat, then starbursts. Damn that hurt.

Only no time to bother. Another shot to the balls. Easy target. Him being well hung on both counts, dickory and dock, she'd already noticed that much. Who coulda missed it? And him doubling over, gasping, dropping to his knees, cratering, pitching sideways.

Damn damn damn.

Della ducked back into the bathroom and finished washing her hands. Using one of those little hotel soap bars. Dinky, even in a Holiday Inn. Like soap was a highpriced item. Washing, washing. Thinking back, trying to remember. A blur after that, so fast. After the nutshot, the second one, him still doubled up on the floor . . . okay . . .

Right. That's when she got to her purse on the far nightstand and pulled out the pearlhandled switchblade. The one Ruby brought back from Nuevo Laredo. Gave one to every girl in the shop. For self-defense. Cause you know men. Giggling when she said it, like it was a gag gift. Like it was something cute.

Only there she is, by the nightstand holding it. Mister Dreamboat starting to stir. Push the little button on the side. *Ping.* Blade springs out. Standing there buck naked staring at it. Blade shiny and new, slick as chrome. Long and narrow. Not very sharp, but pointed.

Him getting up off the floor then, crouching, one hand between his legs, other side of the bed, not saying a word but murder in those ice blue eyes. Just staring, slowly swinging the leather belt in a circle while it rolled up around his fist, buckle hanging loose. Pausing then, a wicked smile. The sonofabitch actually grinning. Then suddenly leaping onto the bed and diving at her.

Oh Jesus. Here he comes.

Her practically paralyzed throwing one arm over her eyes not

to see and sticking the other arm straight out elbow locked holding the knife pointed forward. And his weight hitting it, knocking
her back. Back against the wall, off balance. Falling on her ass on
the prickly carpet still holding the knife. Handle gooey warm with
blood.

Him not dead though. Writhing on the bed like a snake, as if
demon possessed, grunting, holding his chest. Getting to his knees
grunting low, growling, and her getting onto her knees too, moving ahead on the carpet and them meeting at the edge of the bed
with him lurching forward onto the knife blade again and her not
being thrown backward this time but thrusting the blade on up
into his chest. Between the ribs, must've been, went in so easy, like
stabbing a mushmelon.

And down he went.

Like that.

Della holding a white huckaback towel stuck her head out the
bathroom door again as if she couldn't be sure. Yep, there he was.
Mister Dreamboat. Dead as a dodo.

Damn damn damn damn damn. Guy like that, all that poise,
the manners. Who would've believed it? Not her, no way. Not that
jerk the pipe salesman either. Or the bartender. Or others she
hadn't even noticed. Witnesses all over the place.

Della went back into the room and sat on the edge of the
muslin-covered chair in the corner. She stared at the body
sprawled on the bed, blood oozing all over.

Shit, who *was* gonna believe it?

12

They rode down on Brookshire just after midnight. The top was
still back off the Caddy and the stars wheeled round in the deep
blueblack void. They'd hit the flatlands that ran off the inland
country down to the coast, and to the southeast the horizon lay

dark and starless, a blank slate of formless clouds drifting in off the gulf.

The town spread out over the plain from the interstate north-ward though there wasn't much to it. Eddie wanted to stop at an all night Exxon for some coffee. Ray Bob took the exit and coasted along the narrow access road until they reached an inter-section marked by fastfood joints and service stations. He rolled into the Exxon lot and stopped in back by the restrooms.

They climbed out and stretched. A yellow forty-watt bulb threw a pale spray of light over the pavement. Beyond its perime-ter the squat outline of a storage shed stood against a broad shad-owed swale of farmland and pasture. From it came the low hum and whir of insects singing in the damp. They stood for a minute and listened.

Then Ray Bob went toward the restroom saying, I'll tell you one thing, hoss, the only thing better'n a good fuck's a good shit.

Whatever, said Eddie. I ain't gettin into that again.

He walked around to the front entrance shaking his head. Inside he nodded to the clerk and stood at the coffee machine try-ing to decide what size cup to buy. He was pouring from the Pyrex pot when he heard Ray Bob come in and ask for the restroom key. Here I am about to bust a gut, he griped, and the damn door's locked.

The clerk was a bony redhead about forty years old snapping gum and smoking a cigarette and she didn't seem too interested. She was listening to the radio. She handed Ray Bob the key with-out looking at him.

I asked you a question, honey.

Eddie put two sugars in the Styrofoam cup. He heard the woman say, First of all, you didn't ask no question. And second of all, my name ain't honey. She had a smoker's voice that crackled around the edges. Eddie looked over his shoulder. The woman had turned to fiddle with the radio dial, conversation finished. Ray Bob spun in a small impatient circle then stood there holding the restroom key, a single bronze-colored key wired to a round slab of plywood as big as a Frisbee.

I asked why you lock the bathroom, he said.

The woman wasn't looking at him. She said, No you didn't.

Eddie couldn't see Ray Bob's face but the back of his neck was red and his shoulders were shaking. Man oh man, muttered Eddie, here we go again.

Like hell, said Ray Bob. Like hell I didn't.

The woman looked at him then and she didn't look very interested and she didn't seem afraid. She said, If you in such bad shape why you standing here talking? She snapped her gum and went back to the radio. Anyways I just work here. Them's the rules.

Say Ray Bob, Eddie said, you want some coffee? He took a sip from the cup and it scorched his mouth. It ain't that old, man.

Naw, I don't.

After a minute Ray Bob turned and went out the door lugging the slab of wood with the key and disappeared down the sidewalk.

Eddie surveyed the candy rack and settled on a Butterfinger and a bag of M&Ms. The clerk rang up the total. Dollar seventy four, she said. Eddie patted his pockets and told her he'd be right back. He went out, returned with a roll of nickels. The woman took the gray roll of coins without comment.

Kinda slow around here, said Eddie.

She took the cigarette from between her lips and held it in the vee of two fingers straight out and upward at an angle. Her fingernails were short, painted metallic brown. She squinted at him. You boys up to any good?

The question surprised Eddie. He studied the Butterfinger bar while he peeled off the wrapper. What you got in mind? he asked.

I ain't got anything in mind. Her eyes were dark green, almost jade. I was just wondering if you're trouble.

Eddie thought about whether to suck the chocolate off the bar down to the hard caramel center or just bite right in. He decided not to drag it out and bit off a chunk. We just passing through, he said.

Well, that's good. Cause my old man's an auxiliary with the sheriff and I can tell you right now you don't want no trouble in this county. She spoke with a country drawl, her voice crackling like embers in a lowburning campfire.

He carry a gun? Eddie asked.

Damn right he does. He'd do that if he wasn't auxiliary. Same as everybody else around here.

Eddie pondered that. You carry a gun?

That's right, hon. Lifetime member of the NRA. Guns what built this country, guns what'll keep it safe.

Eddie said he wouldn't know about that. He shrugged and bit off another candy bar chunk and chewed. I never noticed guns making anybody safe, he allowed.

The woman looked at him. What I'm sayin is if your friend out there's carrying and has any notions you might better go on out and have a little talk. Before he comes back in. She put the cigarette between her lips and drew long, then blew out a silver cloud of smoke. Cause we don't want him making no mistake.

No, I reckon not, Eddie agreed. He picked up the Styrofoam cup and bag of M&Ms and went out the door. Around back Ray Bob was standing by the restroom under the yellow light zipping his pants. The chunk of wood with the key was hanging from the lock.

Ray Bob bent his knees and cupped his crotch with one hand, rearranging his balls. Only got one question, he said. His gray-green eyes stared out toward the dark expanse of land leading coastward. You wanna fuck'er before or after?

Neither one, said Eddie. We can't mess with her. Her old man's a cop.

Ray Bob grinned. All the better.

Eddie said that was bullshit. Only thing worse'n killing a cop's killing a cop's wife.

Where you hear that shit? said Ray Bob. You been reading a book?

Naw I ain't. Saw it on TV. One a them real-life cop shows.

You dumb fuck. That ain't real. They make that shit up.

Say it's real.

Course they do, asshole. Get people to watch it.

Looks real to me.

TV make anything look real, said Ray Bob. What it's for.

It works.

Goddamn right. You watch it, don'tcha?

Don't you?

Yeah. But I ain't confused. I know what's what.

Anyway, she carries a gun, said Eddie. She figgered you gonna try sumthin. She probably already called the law.

You dumb motherfucker, said Ray Bob. Why didn't you say so? Us standing here talkin. Start the car.

He tossed Eddie the keys and pulled the Walther from his boot, disappeared around the side. A moment later Eddie heard a dull pop and then Ray Bob came back walking fast holding the gun and a sixpack of beer. He grabbed the slab of plywood hanging on the restroom door and jerked the key out. He tossed it in the front seat. Slide over, hoss, I'm driving.

Eddie slid into the passenger seat. Ray Bob threw the Caddy in gear and squealed rubber going around the corner and out the lot. On the access road he slowed down until they went through the intersection light. Then he laid on the pedal and hit the interstate going sixty and soon the Caddy was purring balls to the wall down the highway at eighty with the wind whistling over the windshield.

How far we from Houston, he asked.

Twenty thirty minutes, said Eddie, pulling at his earring. That's the outskirts. Only we hit a place called Katy pretty soon and you better slow down. Speed traps. You shoot'er?

What you think?

Man oh man.

They rode without talking a short while and then Ray Bob picked up the piece of wood with the key and slung it out over Eddie's head spinning into darkness over the high grass verging the shoulder. You touch anything back there? he asked.

Nuthin with a print. He thought about the coffee pot. Least I hope not.

That fuckin bitch was on the phone all right.

Oh Jesus, said Eddie.

So I picked up the phone and told whoever was on it to call the cops.

Hell you did. Eddie dropped his head. Jesus Christ.

Ray Bob grinned. Only I told 'em the shooter was a nigger headed west on the interstate drivin a Thunderbird.

Eddie blew out his breath. Man oh man, you was thinking.

Goddamn right. Ray Bob hooted and lit a cigarette. Gimmee a beer. Yeah, they gonna be all over some jigaboo somewhere.

Eddie frowned. Only they gonna wonder where you are, fella what told 'em.

We in Houston by the time they wonder that. Gimmee a beer, I said.

Still better get off this freeway, said Eddie. He pulled a beer from the plastic ring and handed it over. When we get up to Highway Six head south.

Ray Bob didn't say anything. He put the radio on a hard-rock station and they shot over the cement ribbon through the damp night listening to Pink Floyd and ZZ Top and Led Zeppelin climb the stairway to heaven. Ray Bob drumming the steering wheel with both hands, a beer can nestled between his thighs. When Lynyrd Skynyrd came on Eddie said the whole band got killed in a plane wreck.

Why I don't fly, said Ray Bob. Half them pilots is stoned.

I get the motion sickness, Eddie said, why I don't. Flew from Baton Rouge to Shreveport one time, lost my lunch. Ralphed in a sack.

Motherfuck! Ray Bob pounded the steering wheel with his fist. Motherfuck!

What.

I didn't get the fuckin money. Left it on the counter when I went after beer. Walked right out. Motherfuck!

Eddie shrugged. We can always get money. They got money everywhere.

But Ray Bob wouldn't have it. He cussed and beat on the wheel until Eddie got tired of it and said, Well you didn't fuck'er neither.

I know it. Ray Bob settled down. Said, You damn right about that. Said, I sure do like that redhaired pussy too. It's not every day you get some redtufted boojum.

Pussy's like money, Eddie observed. It's everywhere and you can always get it.

If you know what you're doing.

If I knew what I was doing I wouldn't be here.

Whatever.

Cause the only reason I'm here is I'm not all there, Eddie said, that's what I'm starting to believe.

But Ray Bob wasn't listening. He was thinking back. Least it wasn't a complete loss, he finally said. Sounding philosophical. I did get me a big ol' shit.

Well then, said Eddie. You oughta be satisfied.

13

Sometimes she walked on the shoulder and sometimes she walked on the grass. But the shoulder was strewn with pebbles that hurt her feet and no telling what lay in the grass. Broken glass, stickers, snakes. So mostly Della walked on the road.

She went barefoot along the smooth concrete pavement carrying her high-heeled shoes in one hand dangling by the ankle straps. For a while she'd worn them. Like ten minutes maybe. They were shoes to look at. Shoes to walk in from the house to the car, from the car to some other place. A nice place. Like the Holiday Inn atrium bar. Where you could sit. Which she'd quickly realized. The shoes pinched her toes like pliers and rubbed a blister on each heel in no time flat.

So she hoisted the skirt to her waist not to dirty it and sat on the grass beside the road and took the shoes off. She got up and wiggled, unsheathed the panty hose to her knees, sat back down and pulled them off too. No use tearing them up, just that one little hole in the crotch, they cost good money. Then she started walking again. The shoes dangling in one hand. The Gideon Bible in the other.

She wasn't wearing any underwear, which felt good, and as she went along she swung the shoes back and forth like a purse and swung her hips to either side as if somebody might be watching. Which they weren't. She hoped. For once, she prayed, don't let them look. For godsake don't let them see. She reached up from time to time to feel her bruised left eye. It hurt, touching it.

The stars spun in their cradles against a wide black sky, a crescent moon slid down the curve. She felt very small beneath them and alone in the darkness spreading out into fields beyond the road. Animal sounds in the unseen fields, startled bird cries shrieking then dropping just as abruptly and strange sounds she didn't recognize. In all that darkness. It gave her the creeps. She'd always feared creatures crying in the night.

The Highway 6 loop was deserted. A couple of times she heard cars approaching from behind and she drew aside into the grass to stand still with her back turned as if by achieving immobility she would escape notice. As if they might presume she was but an odd misplaced statue of a woman holding a pair of shoes and a Bible, or an apparition, or might not see her at all. The whine of the engine neared and the headlights swept over the pavement and when very close the whine suddenly fell an octave, then picked up again as the car sped on.

All that time holding her breath.

Then she returned to the pavement and walked on south. Watching the wide bank of clouds obscuring the horizon in that direction. Feet hurting. Swinging the shoes. Swinging the Gideon. Wishing she hadn't brought it now but that had been a last minute impulse, before she knew she'd be walking. That part definitely unplanned: the walking. She stepped on a pebble and cursed, stopped cursing the pebble to curse the Hyundai. Cheap piece of shit sitting back there in the Holiday Inn lot. Wouldn't start again. Ralph said he fixed it, charged her thirty fucking five dollars. Ralph working out of his yard, saying it kept down overhead. Saying it kept down prices. Ralph didn't know squat.

She cursed Ralph a while, then the Hyundai some more. Quit at least once a week. First one thing and then another. Falling apart. Hunk of Japanese junk. Korean, whatever. Still owed notes on the damn thing. Two months behind, too. And the salesman at the used car lot had said it was dependable. Guaranteed it. Only not in writing. Take my word for it, he'd said, she's a honey, been driving it myself.

Lying sonofabitch.

Everybody out to take advantage of a single mother on a budget.

She cursed the salesman and she cursed Ralph and then she went back to cursing the car. Everybody but Mister Dreamboat. She didn't even want to think about him. No way. Him laid up on the bed back there in room eleven fourteen. With a knife stuck in his chest. Mister Busy Executive.

Made her a little wet, though, thinking about it. The before part.

Damn damn damn.

A sharp cry rose from the field to the side and she peered into the forever darkness shuddering and walked faster. She wished she'd remembered to bring the knife. Damn thing worked, that was for sure. Plus it probably had her fingerprints all over it. Not that it mattered. Plenty of witnesses. They saw her in the bar, saw her go up the elevator. Probably even heard her say yes. Yes, Mister Dreamboat. And thank you. Thank you! Like some idiot child. Shit.

She walked on. Walked on through the night thinking it was just like that old movie she'd seen on TV. On the superstation stuck here and there between the commercials. About Mister Candy Bar. No. Something bar. Bad bar, maybe. Came to no good end at any rate. Gruesome. Well, they made movies like that for a reason, they surely did. Like a parable. She'd known it too. But had she listened? Course not. Did she pay attention? No.

Her feet hurt badly and she stopped for a minute. She didn't know if she could make it all the way to Sugar Land. Ten miles at least. Plus those dark clouds ahead were getting bigger coming off the coast. Lightning playing along the edges. A thunderstorm, naturally. What else but that. Trouble behind and trouble ahead. Story of my life.

After a few minutes the wind picked up and she smelled the salt in it and it carried the sharp tang of lightning and rain and she knew she would soon get wet. There wasn't anyplace to go so she kept moving, her feet sore and raw along the soles, limping now.

She heard another car coming then and she knew that if she was going to make it she needed help. The car drew up fast and she stood on the shoulder watching. The headlights came bursting out of the darkness with the motor sound low and deep. She tucked the Bible in an armpit and put out her thumb. She felt stupid, as if she was holding the thumb all wrong, so she tilted her hand first one way and then another, then gave up and waved.

The car came on fast then slowed abruptly. The twin lights blinded her and she closed her eyes against them. She heard tires squealing on the pavement, then come to a stop just past her. She looked over and saw an old white Cadillac convertible fishtailed almost sideways in the road. Long as a hearse. Two guys in front. It was too dark to see more than the rider had a ponytail and the other didn't. The one with the ponytail got up on his knees in the seat and hollered, Goddamn we was going eighty when we saw you!

She stood and stared at them, then took a few steps forward and stopped, watching. Thinking about that movie.

Well c'mon, the driver said, you cummin or not.

The rider opened his door then and leaned forward holding the seat up for her and said, C'mon now, we all right.

She climbed in. She sat in the back holding her shoes in her lap and the Bible to her chest. The rider shut his door, the driver hit the accelerator, tires peeled rubber. The engine rumbled and the car fishtailed again, shot forward. After a minute they were speeding into the darkness ahead and the wind was blowing her hair everywhere so she opened her purse to get an elastic hairband. She bent forward to put it on.

Where you going?

She looked up to see the guy with the dark brown ponytail sitting sideways observing her. Sugar Land, she said.

The driver who had short hair, either sandy blond or light orange, and wide thick shoulders looked at her in the rearview mirror but didn't say anything.

The other guy said, Lucky you. We going that way. Why you walking?

My car broke down.

That's a long walk.

She nodded. My feets tore up.

Why didn't you call nobody?

They weren't home.

He wagged his head as though he understood. Still sitting sideways in his seat, watching her. Oughta be careful though. Dangerous out here at night, all kinds of boogers.

She nodded again. He seemed nice, a thin face and friendly eyes. Don't I know it, she said, I was getting worried.

Well, I reckon you was. What happened to your eye?

She reached up and touched it. She'd forgotten. It was still swollen and hurt beneath her her fingertips. I fell down, she said. In the dark.

Well, you sure got it good.

I know it. And now there's a storm coming up. She pointed ahead.

Yeah, we seen that, the guy said. We gonna put the top up pretty quick. He looked at the driver. If it works, I mean. We ain't had it up yet. You religious?

She frowned, puzzled by the question.

Cause you got that Bible, why I ask. He pointed.

She looked down, saw the Bible clasped to her chest. Well, I didn't figure it would hurt, she said. You never know when you might need some protection.

I heard that, the guy said. Wanna cigarette?

Okay. She gave the inside of the Cadillac a quick once-over. Nice car.

Filter or straight?

You got a joint? she asked.

He glanced at the Bible, lifted his eyebrows. Naw, we all out. Got cigarettes though.

She saw the driver looking at her in the rearview again. His eyes seemed to go right through her. That's okay, she said, I gotta pack. She opened her purse and took out the Benson & Hedges and leaned forward behind the seat to block the wind while she lit one. The ponytailed guy waited until she raised up.

What's your name? I'm Eddie.

Della. She turned her head and exhaled to one side. Where you going?

We on the run, Eddie said.

The driver quickly glanced his way but didn't say anything.

What from?

We're robbers. He pulled at the gold earring in his left ear. How about you?

I'm a model. She hesitated. In catalogs and stuff.

Is that right? He sounded impressed. Like Sears Roebuck?

She nodded. I woulda been in magazines but my face is too long and my eyes set too close.

They look fine to me, Eddie said. They ain't so close. You got nice hair too.

Why, thank you. Della folded her hands in her lap demurely and then picked them up pronto and set them on the seat to either side. You really robbers?

Well, it's just a sideline. Eddie waved one hand. Really we're welders. Only we outa work. We work the pipelines.

I heard all about pipelines, Della said.

Well then, you know, said Eddie. That's why we stay on the move. That and other things. Where's your car?

Back there. She pointed back over her shoulder. It broke.

Maybe we could fix it.

I doubt it, Della said. She turned down her mouth and shook her head. It's a mess.

Foreign job?

She nodded.

Well that's why. He abruptly turned around in his seat and leaned down to light a cigarette, then swung back blowing out smoke. But we could try. Tomorrow I mean.

Della thought about it. It's awful nice of you to offer, she said, but I think I'm just gonna let the finance company take it back. Payments're high anyway.

The redheaded guy was staring at her in the mirror again. Like he saw something no one else could see. She slid along the seat to the right out of his line of vision.

Eddie was shaking his head, his face twisted in a sympathetic grimace. Saying, Finance companies, man oh man, ain't that just like a finance company? All that interest. Take advantage cause you ain't got credit. Nuthin but loan sharks. You live in Sugar Land?

Della opened her mouth to answer, then shut it. She studied the question, studied the answer. It occurred to her that it was only a matter of time before the police showed up. First they'd find Mister Dreamboat. Then ask around, learn about her. Maybe notice the car sitting there on the lot. Trace it down. Wouldn't take long, they'd be knocking at her door. Howdy, ma'am, this knife here belong to you? She had twelve hours maybe.

Well, Sugar Land's where I been staying, she said. Only I'm in the process of relocating. Where you going?

Eddie shrugged. Everywhere and nowhere. Whichever way the wind blows. They any cheap motels where you stay?

Della was quiet.

That ain't what I meant, Eddie said after a moment. Motel for us, I mean. Me and my bud here.

Well, she said, I knew that.

She hesitated. Thinking again. She could name half a dozen motels within walking distance of her apartment. Hollering distance practically. Cheap ones, too, her apartment complex not being situated in the best part of town. Which is what made her decide. I need a ride in the morning, she said. If you could give it to me, y'all can stay at my place tonight. I got an extra room. That last part added quickly.

Eddie looked at the driver. He didn't say anything. So Eddie said, Sounds good to me. Save us some money. Where you need a ride to tomorrow?

She folded her hands in her lap. Still thinking. It was complicated. Mister Dreamboat, the police, her kids, her job, that shitty old Hyundai, and not having any money to speak of, all that crowding in and hard to untangle, make any sense of. She needed some time. Didn't want to get it in a jail cell either. So she said, Whichever way you're going might be fine, I ain't sure yet.

Eddie nodded. Like it made sense. Saying, All right.

They rode in silence then and the storm coming up from the coast passed to the southwest over Fort Bend County so they didn't have to stop or put the top up. The nighttime air was cool and damp and salty. The wind in their faces smelled like the refineries and petrochemical plants along the Houston Ship Channel. When they neared the intersection with alternate Highway 90 Della said they needed to get off the loop and go left.

How about some music? Eddie turned on the radio and moved the dial, stopped on a drawnout moaning vocal and couldn't believe it. Said, Goddamn, would you listen to that? On AM, too. That's Lightnin' Hopkins. Hear that single picked line? Damn, that's Texas blues. You hear them strummed percussive chords, maybe some bottleneck slide, you got Delta blues.

He turned to Ray Bob, smiling, saying, Man, this is the shit I always liked but the band members wouldn't go for it. Said it was nigger music. R and B? Soul? That was fine, electrify and boost it, speed it up, get your Allman Brothers or Lynyrd Skynyrd, basic southern rock 'n' roll. It ain't blues no more but people groove on it. All right, listen to this change coming now, tonic to subdominant—

When Della in the backseat said, Don't you like country music?

Mostly what you get, Eddie said, head bobbing and weaving, why I can't believe they got an AM station plays this in Houston, man oh man. Listen up now, here comes Charley Patton, Mississippi man—

We got good country stations, Della said. Lots.

Eddie stopped moving, turned around and looked. After a moment he grinned and shrugged, said, Well, you're the guest, Della. Name your station.

She did and he adjusted the dial and Dwight Yoakam came up singing, heartbroke again. How his woman done gone cold. Done locked him out the house, gonna get her a divorce, her family's idea. Gonna have to hire him a lawyer and all.

That's ol' Dwight, Eddie said, Dwight Yoakam. Real name, too. I heard he spent sixty thousand dollars on cowboy hats in Austin.

He's cute, Della said. He was going with Sharon. Ain't that weird? Except they broke up. I think that's who he's singing about, Sharon Stone.

Eddie nodded. Could be, he agreed. Sure could, he said, I wouldn't doubt it a bit. He lit a cigarette, still nodding in agreement. Wondering who Sharon Stone was.

The song ended and Mark Chesnutt started singing about his woman leaving him, too, and Eddie observed it sounded like an epidemic but Della said that celebrities were plagued by marital difficulties more than the rest of us. Because of their special situation, she said. Like what happened to Julia Roberts and Lyle Lovett. It was the same for models. Most men love you for your appearance and not your true self, she said, and that always leads to disappointment and grief. Also divorce. Then she directed them off Highway 90 and down several dimly lit streets lined with cars to the parking lot in front of her apartment complex. It ain't much, she said, but it's home. Cause I'm still early in my professional career, she added.

When he put the Caddy in park and turned off the engine, the driver turned around in the seat and looked right at her. His eyes big and strange. Making an ugly face like he'd put up with something for too long, something he couldn't stand. Like he was fed up. Saying, Let's get one thing straight, gal. I ain't no welder and you ain't no model. His voice angry.

Della held the Bible to her belly and looked right back. I had a long day, she said, and I don't feel like having no fight.

Good. Ray Bob opened the door and got out. Cause you wouldn't win it.

Eddie said, Jesus Christ, man, take it easy. We just got here.

And one other thing. Ray Bob balled his fist and pointed a thick finger at Della. Just so you don't get the wrong idea, I ain't feeling too good. Otherwise, if they ain't fat, I get the blondes.

Della didn't even blink. Sat there and told him, Well, I don't see how.

14

Rule woke up with the phone ringing in the kitchen. He was lying on his back in the dark like a cadaver with the woman wrapped all over him. He moved her off and went down the hall through the livingroom, the worn oakwood floorboards cool against his feet. He walked stiffly. His lower back ached and he noodled the possibility he was getting too old for predawn phone calls. In the kitchen he picked up the receiver in the middle of a ring, stood naked by the refrigerator stretching his back side to side.

Yeah?

It was Moline calling from the office.

Rule leaned over and opened the back door so Lefty could go out. A cloud of damp air slipped through the opening. The sky lay heavy in the west, a curved platinum sheet. The line of low hills of mesquite and juniper beyond his property line were shadowed in deep gray, a few skimpy clouds hung high above the horizon sporting dark red underbellies embered in orange.

Hell, it ain't hardly morning, Rule said. What time is it?

Time for you to get up, said Moline. Our boys are on the move.

All right. Tell me about it. He held the receiver between his chin and shoulder and started making coffee. He put a pot of water on the stove and filled the metal drip filter with French Market chicory.

Looks like they're moving south, Moline said.

They leaving a trail.

A bad one. I come in early, been following the reports on the computer.

They a team then.

Looks that way, the two of 'em together. Last night someone hit a Diamond Shamrock outside Columbus on Seventy-one and did the clerk. Hour or so later an Exxon Food Mart in Brookshire got hit. Clipped another clerk. Got pictures on that one. I ain't seen them but I got a description. Our boys all right. I'm waiting for the pics now. They gonna drive 'em up.

The water in the pot hadn't quite started to boil but Rule poured it into the drip pot anyway. The heavy aroma of coffee grounds bursting the grain wafted off the top. They still doing Indians?

Naw, Moline said, they done moved up to white people. Ain't particular about age either. Or gender. They equal opportunity boys.

Rule tugged at his prick and scratched his nuts. He lifted them in one hand, gauging their heft absentmindedly. They sagged more'n they used to, weren't as full. Bad back and a sagging sack. You read about the first everywhere and never heard about the other. One of them private concerns. We need the ballistics, he said.

Moline agreed, added, Can't say about Columbus, but the shooter down in Brookshire wasn't DeReese. It was the other'n.

Do say.

And they said he walked off and left the money on the counter. Fucked up.

They all do, Rule said. Eventually. He poured coffee into a thick ceramic mug, took a small sip, then another. The bitter chicory edge went down with a shudder. He said, Ballistics on those might match up with Bernie.

They might. And tell you something else. This second guy's a coppernob. I saw sumthin in the paper this morning and called city. Coupla young gals got assaulted down in Zilker yesterday evening. Coeds from UT out canoeing. One's in a coma but the other's talking fine. Sexual assault. What she says fits our boys. Second one's a redhead alright.

Christ, muttered Rule. Homicide, armed robbery, add on rape. DeReese was working his way up fast. We know what they're driving?

Witness in Brookshire said a Thunderbird, Moline replied. Guy who called it in. Only he said it was a nigger too. And then he didn't wait around to talk.

Sounds like bullshit.

Yep. Could've been our boys pulling a prank for all I know. They both full of piss and vinegar. But what they're driving's your guess good as mine. DeReese ain't got no car registered. And no current address. He's off the books, like he don't even exist.

Well, he's out there.

That's a fact, boy. They both are.

Rule told Moline to get a line on the second guy. Maybe they were driving a boost, probably were. But maybe the redhead owned a car. We get a name and car make, he said, and we're halfway there. Anything'll help.

That's a good idea, Moline said, that's exactly what we're doing, same as always. Besides twiddlin our thumbs.

Rule grunted. He took a big swallow of coffee and refilled the cup. Well, I sent out pictures of both boys last night. Check if anything's back on the index.

Moline said he had. Nothing but goose eggs. I'll keep trying but don't expect much, not the way this is going.

Well stay on it. I gotta run.

You coming in?

Nope.

He stood in the back door watching the clouds afloat above the hills glowing deep red and orange with sunrise. The sky was dappled in light gray with white streaks glinting off the gray and a mourning dove was calling from the oaks near the back fence. Lefty came in wagging his tail, laid down under the kitchen table, put his head in his paws.

Gonna head down to Columbus and Brookshire, Rule said. Gonna track those suckers down. Keep me posted on the cellular.

All right.

He was about to hang up when Moline said his name. With a question mark.

Yeah.

You know, Rule, I never did get to sleep last night. Reason I'm here early. Dana didn't come home.

Give her the divorce, Moline. She's no good.

Man, I miss her.

I can't fix it. Neither can you. Let it go.

It's hard. Real hard. Moline's voice cracked. You go through this?

Both times, Moline. Both times.

Don't see how you got over it.

Who says I did?

He hung up the phone and stood in the open doorway drinking his coffee, lifting each nut and dropping it by turn. Two squirrels scampered through the limbs of the oaks, then swirled down a twisting trunk into the yard. He drained his cup and rinsed it, filled a plastic bowl full of dry cereal from a fifty pound sack and set it on the floor in front of Lefty.

He thought about calling Katie then, reached for the phone, decided against it. Hadn't heard from her in a month, had already left three messages on her answering machine. What could he tell her? Your old man's thinking about you? I miss you? He'd already told the machine that, hadn't made a difference. The silent stiff. Confusing. Too early to call her anyhow. So he went into the bathroom and showered, returned to the bedroom drying off.

Who's no good? She curled on one side under the sheet and bunched a pillow under her head.

You ain't.

That was Moline?

That's right. He opened a bureau drawer and took out a pair of shorts.

She drew the top sheet back and stretched out on the mattress. Her breasts were small but her nipples jutted out like two long pink antennae seeking some direction or affirmation by touch. The dark blonde pubic hair climbed up her belly in a thin vertical patch. He figured she shaved it that way. She had good legs, small like the rest of her but shaped well. Size wise, she could've been a pubescent girl. Even with her arms extended upward and her toes pointed down her feet didn't reach the end of the bed.

C'mon back to bed, sweetie pie. She held out one arm and drooped the hand at the wrist, wiggling it. C'mon, we didn't finish.

Yes we did. Leastwise I did.

Not me. Sounding pouty.

She dropped the arm to the bed, then ran her hand along the sheet and up an inner thigh and tugged softly at the narrow patch of hair. She watched him, stroking herself. Rule, don't be mean.

He pulled on his shorts and looked at her out of one eye. She smiled crookedly. It ain't like you to start sumthin and not finish, Rule.

The hell it ain't, he said. You don't know me.

Do so. Lot more'n you think.

He opened the closet and took out a pair of brown denim pants. Saying, You don't know me from Adam.

15

He awakened while it was still dark. Wondering where he was. Turned over, almost rolled off the bed. Narrow, a child's bed. He hung an arm over the edge and touched the floor, touched his clothes.

Remembering.

The room where she'd put them to sleep. During the night. Where he was now. Two small child's beds with Smurf sheets smelling faintly of piss, the walls hung with fastfood giveaway posters of dinosaurs, Space Rangers, Disney stuff. The floor sprinkled with broken toys.

The kids' room.

Her apartment.

In Sugar Land.

The kids spending the night with her mother. On the floor, next to his clothes, his boots. He could smell them in the darkness, a familiar odor of aged leather and sweat. He put one hand down the well of a boot and left it there.

He wondered what had stirred him from sleep. Wasn't sure. Then saw the black silhouette of Ray Bob float through the bedroom door, sit down on the edge of the other bed. Saw the shape put its head in its hands and not move for a bit. Then it laid down and pulled up the sheet.

He waited until he heard the other breathing evenly and got up and went out the door in his jockeys and across the short hallway to the other bedroom. He paused in the open doorway. It was too dark to see. He inched his way forward, toes feeling their way over the worn shag carpet, toward where he figured the bed to be. His shins bumped into the sideboard.

She hissed. I told you to go away.

You all right? he whispered.

Is that you?

It's me, Eddie.

Okay.

Yeah, well, you all right?

He come in here. Tried to get in my bed.

Eddie didn't say anything.

I told him to leave.

He blew out his breath. And he did?

Yeah.

Eddie still couldn't see her. He stood by the bed in the dark running his hand over his head, down his ponytail. He'd forgotten to take out the elastic band. Then reached down and adjusted the waistband of his shorts, pulling them up. Saying, I'm surprised he left. Except he knows I was talking with you.

I thought he come back.

Naw. It's just me.

They didn't speak then. He stood by the bed and she lay in it. Not seeing one another. They each listened to the other breathing in the close cloyed darkness thicker than night. He could sense the smallness of the room. He took the elastic band off his ponytail and shook his head, looping the band around two fingers.

You want to get in? Her still whispering.

I guess so.

He heard her draw back the sheet. He put a leg up on the mattress and hesitated. Which end are you?

This one.

He put down his leg and turned and pulled the other up and laid down beside her. She moved to her side. He could feel the heat coming off her body and she smelled fresh like shampoo and some kind of scented flowers soaked in water. She put her hand out then and touched him. Laid it on his chest. Where his tattoo was. Her hand was warm and soft.

I feel better you being here, she said. I don't like the way he looks at me. What's his name.

Ray Bob.

He looks mad all the time. Kinda crazy.

Well, said Eddie, I reckon he is. Mad, I mean.

How come?

Eddie thought about it. Maybe someone close to him got killed, he said. I dunno, I ain't no psychologist.

You're nicer.

Well, I got my own hands full. I ain't no Boy Scout.

I know that.

Sometimes I ain't so nice.

I figgered that too.

Well, I try to be, but it ain't always easy.

Ain't that the truth?

I bet you're always nice.

She was silent for a moment. Then, Well, I try to think positive, you know. Cause you act what you think. Like you are what you eat.

Think so?

Yeah, that's why it's effective.

He lay there working that one out, unraveling it.

Just try it, she said, you'll see.

All right.

They didn't talk then and she leaned over and kissed him on the mouth. Knew right where it was in the dark. He kissed her back and her hand went down and touched him. He was soft. She wrapped her fingers around him and squeezed, pulled up and down a little. Nothing happened.

I might not be able to do anything, he said. I'm kinda uptight.

She let him go and turned on her back but left her hand laying there, on top of him, resting in his hair. You don't seem that way, she said, not to look at you. Tense, I mean. You talked right away.

Well, I can talk. He reached up and rubbed his face in the dark. I'm pretty good at talking. It's just sumthin on my mind.

Just try thinking positive about it.

He took a long breath. Saying, I don't think that would work. Cause it already happened. Sumthin pretty bad.

That don't surprise me, she said, not really. Being a robber and all.

It ain't so easy, doing it right. Things go wrong. Things you don't expect.

Well, believe you me, I know all about that.

Then before you know it you done sumthin stupid. Sumthin real bad you can't take back, even if you want to.

That's cause sometimes we don't have time to think, she said. It's all happening so fast, it catches you off guard. You just do what you can. She lifted her hand and scratched his tangle of hair with her fingernails a minute, then laid it back down on his belly. Saying, Whatever it was, at least God forgives you.

He reached over under her arm and put his hand on her thigh, felt its warmth. I guess so, only I ain't asked him yet, not officially anyhow. I forgot you was religious.

I'm not. Well, I am but I don't show it much. I got other things to think about.

Like what?

Just stuff. She paused. I got them kids, you know. Ages three and four. It ain't easy. Plus money's usually tight.

Half the world living on minimum wage, he said, other half don't even notice, don't care.

I notice.

Reckon you do. Reckon it's hard being a single parent.

You don't even know.

I seen my sister. Five kids from three different men, always scratching to get by. She's looking old, and not even thirty yet.

She said, Tell me about it. Then she ran her hand down his

belly to his hair and put her fingers around him again. You're getting hard.

I know it.

Talking's always helpful, I've found.

Maybe God done forgive me, he said. Sounding hopeful.

Well, somebody sure did.

She turned on her side again, her breasts against him, and put her finger and thumb in a tight circle around him and moved it up and down. The smooth skin moved along. She scooted down after a minute and eased her mouth over him and left it there, not moving, her tongue licking the underside. Then she began to suck.

He put his hand on her head, entwined his fingers in the thick hair. She moved on the bed so he could run his hand down her back to the small of it, and then on down to the curve of her ass. He cupped one round cheek and then the other while she moved up and down over him, and then he lowered his hand between her cheeks to her crack. She was wet. He slid his middle finger inside and she rolled her buttocks. He moved his finger in and out while she sucked.

After a while he said, I'm gonna come if you keep that up.

She swung around then and put one leg over him and held his prick upright and put it inside while she lowered herself. She tried to go down slow. But she was very wet and slippery and he was stiff as a railroad spike and he went in fast and she sunk right on down to the hilt. She groaned.

He put both hands on her hips and held her. She didn't move. After a while he reached up and spread his hands over her breasts and began to knead them. They were larger than he expected. He lifted them from underneath with his thumb and forefinger twiddling her nipples. She made a throaty sound again and then she began to pump him fast and he came right quickly. His pelvis arched when he spurted and she bore down hard and rubbed herself against him so she could come too. Then she laid over him prone, him still inside her, saying, I needed that.

Me too.

Only I usually take more time.

Well, it's been a while, he said, sounding apologetic. Usually I go longer.

Before doing it, that's what I meant.

Oh. Guess I'm just lucky then.

They didn't talk for a while. She nuzzled his neck and bit it gently and he lazily played with her ass. When she finally slid off to the side and lay with her head on his chest and a leg across his thighs, she asked him if he thought her ankles were too big.

They just right, he said. How about mine?

She giggled. You can't see in the dark.

I saw 'em all right, I was looking. He paused, thinking. And if you ain't a model—and I ain't sayin you ain't—but if you wasn't, you could be.

She snuggled down. Well, you don't have to worry, she said. Cause I am.

That's what I figgered.

They dozed off then and when they awakened the sun was coming in the window through the blinds. He lay on his back watching the dust motes float through the room from one narrow band of light to another. He tried to follow only one but could not. They kept getting lost in the shadowed strips in between.

You ever been married? he said.

She curled up under the sheet with one knee touching his thigh. My kids' daddy, she said. We was common law.

Where is he?

I dunno. Oklahoma, I think. He ain't in touch.

He don't see them kids?

He claims they ain't his.

Sonofabitch, Eddie said, that ain't right.

She nodded. Well, he never was. He had a bad temper and lacked patience. I don't know why I ever took up with him. Love I guess. Only it wasn't mutual.

He hitcha?

Just once or twice. When he was drunk. She reached up and touched her left eye. The swelling was down some but it still hurt to feel.

Eddie watched another dust mote disappear into shadow. Saying, I tell you one thing, I ever see him I'm gonna kick his ass back to Oklahoma.

Why ain't that sweet. Della sighed. She put her head over and kissed him on the shoulder. I never had no offer like that before.

Well, here's another'n, he said. I wanna marry you.

Marry me? Good lord, you really are sweet. She kissed him on the shoulder again. You are just full of surprises.

Well then?

It's kinda fast, Eddie. Can I think about it?

If you gotta. He sounded disappointed. But from what I know everything's fast.

She put one hand on his chest and fiddled with his nipple. It was small and hard, like the flange on a .22 short. She saw the blue tattoo above it and drew up a little to make out the lines and musical notes. That's a nice tattoo, she said. You a musician?

Not anymore. That's what I mean, though, about everything moving fast. How life is. When sumthin good comes along you better grab on tight while you can.

Well, that sure makes sense, she said, it really does. Is that your philosophy?

Eddie raised his head and turned it to one side so he could see her face. Then he laid it back down on the pillow, looking at the ceiling. Saying, I ain't got no philosophy, I'm too busy living.

16

He drove downcountry through bluegreen morning hills, the sun swimming low out of the east like a swollen globule of red molten iron. Dewsparkled fields lay against stands of longshadowed pine, beneath spreading oak. Meadowlarks spun arcs calling day into pasture. Cattle had come down into the fields from the night.

He bridged the winding bluegray current of the Colorado for the third time at LaGrange and by the time he crossed it the final time just north of Columbus the sun hung midway to the meridian. A pupil of white light pinpointed with heat, peering from a broad curved countenance of paling blue. Early May yet, but it was going to be a hot one.

The Diamond Shamrock sat outside town by its lonesome. A ways farther on the state highway curved eastward around the town and merged with the interstate. But here midst the outskirted meadows and farms nobody would stop but the southbound low on fuel. Or somebody looking for an isolated mark.

They'd found it.

The station was shut down. Parked in the drive between the pumps and low glass storefront sat a dark brown Ford with a Colorado County Sheriff insignia. Rule drew up behind and parked. A small bandylegged man got out of the Ford wearing a smartly ironed khaki uniform with a gold star and wildcatter boots and an oilman's special with a boomtown crease. Late fifties, short, thin face and shoulders. A Colt Python magnum revolver with a barrel almost reaching his knees hung holstered to his side.

He came up crabwise and curious. Howdy. You the Ranger?

That'd be me.

We ain't met.

The sheriff introduced himself. Said he was newly elected, done vacated the natural gas distribution business for law enforcement. Said it seemed to him like the other feller had got kinda slack. He laid one hand along his holster and hooked a thumb toward the low concrete building. Stuff like this going on, folks ain't used to it, nossir. So I volunteered, cleaned out the department, got new deputies.

Rule straightened his Stetson and nodded. Almost said the sheriff had made a damn good start if dressing the part was a start. Then let it go.

The sheriff slapped his holster. Course we ain't up yet on investigations like we ought to be. He sounded rueful. Plan to get some fellers up to school in Austin here pretty soon. But we don't draw much water, budgetwise. Glad you can be of help.

Well, I figger it's a coupla ol' boys I'm looking for, said Rule. I need to look around.

The sheriff backed up a step. Yessir, help yourself. We ain't done much. Moved the body down to the funeral home's all.

Rule gazed out on the highway watching a diesel pass hauling a sixteen wheel trailer loaded with heavy equipment. Sunlight glinted off the yellow hulls and he squinted. Heat rose off the pavement of the drive dosed with the smell of transmission fluid and oil. He turned back to the sheriff.

Got anyone on ballistics?

Nossir, we don't. He paused. Well, I say we don't. Doctor pulled the bullet outa Henry's chest. Got it down there in that half-ass lab of ours. My nephew Grover—Deputy Grover, one of the new boys—he's takin a looksee at it. He got him a microscope from the high school. I told him not to mess it up.

That's good advice, Rule said. Our boys'll handle it.

The small man propped a hand on his gun butt and nodded. We heard about that thing down in Brookshire. Deputy's wife. Ain't nobody safe no more. He wagged his head, tongue clicking noisily. But we'll get that bullet to your people. Just say where.

I'll let you know.

He went back to his truck and opened the door to get his evidence kit. The sheriff followed, watching. He ran his hand down the red fender of the pickup, a Dodge Ram 2500 with a V8 magnum. Unmarked, no state insignia. You got a nice rig here. All you Rangers got one?

Rule grunted.

The sheriff stood by the open door and tipped back his hat and peered inside. The equipment was packed in tight. A Remington twelvegauge pump tucked below the sixtyfour channel radio, a Nikon camera case, binoculars, Kevlar vest and helmet, first aid kit, heavy duty threefoot boltcutters, a high-intensity light. A Toshiba laptop computer lay on the seat next to the cellular phone.

Well, I'll be a monkey's uncle, the man said. Would you look at that. He whistled low.

Rule put the cellular in his shirt pocket and backed out with the evidence kit. He shut the door, glanced at the storefront. Wasn't any video, I'm told.

The man didn't answer right away. His eyes were turned inward as if memorizing what he'd seen, making a list to remember later. He blinked twice and jerked his head. Say what? I missed that.

No video security?

Nossir, there weren't. A crying shame too. That's one of the first things I'm gonna see to in this county. All them stores oughta have it.

Well, it'd help, Rule agreed. He leaned to one side and spit. That and armored vests and fulltime security guards.

The man touched his hat brim and pursed his mouth doubtfully. I don't reckon we'll get all that, nossir. Knock gas up a nickel a gallon.

I don't doubt it.

People wouldn't put up with it.

Naw, I suppose not, Rule said. Funerals is cheaper.

The small man looked stunned, then offended. Well now, that ain't what I'm saying. The thing to do is to catch them boys.

That's right.

Put 'em away, outa our misery. Put a needle in 'em.

Rule allowed that was a good idea. A right goodun. Said he'd even bought stock in a needle company but was waiting yet for the dividends. Said defense lawyers might put the needlemakers outa business for all he knew. Might lose all his money. In the meantime, he said, we gonna be going to funerals.

The sheriff narrowed his eyes and waited for him to finish. Said then, You don't sound too optimistic.

Nossir, I don't, admitted Rule. I surely don't. But that's life. That's the one we made.

Well, said the sheriff. Don't put me in it.

You breathing, you in it, Rule said.

All right. What else?

That's it.

That simple.

Well, it ain't complicated. Rule looked off. We got fellers gonna

do bad things and we got fellers gonna catch 'em. Then we got
fellers to defend 'em, and more to turn 'em loose. It ain't fancy but
it's what we got. He shifted the evidence kit to his other hand. I
better get to work.

He worked the scene inside for an hour. He worked fast but he
worked careful. The sheriff stood back watching. Rule saw him
pull out a small spiral notepad twice and write in it with a ballpoint pen. When he finished and packed up his case the man said,
We got anything?

Well now, that is always the question, Rule replied. It surely is.
Problem is we usually got too much. Can't figure out what
counts.

Ain't there a method?

Yes there is, said Rule. We got your forensics, ballistics, your
serology and toxicology. Even got that hightech DNA, track down
folks in the shallow end of the gene pool. We got machines to cal-
ibrate machines and computers to decipher computers. It's scien-
tific as hell, with a bureaucracy to support it. Behind every
lawman with a gun you got a dozen civilians in lab coats turning
dials and crunching numbers.

Rule paused. The sheriff listening close, nodding, his face serious.

Only a fella like me in the field's still gotta think, Rule said.
Cause a machine ain't gonna find them bad boys and it sure ain't
gonna throw on the cuffs. That's for me and you. For which we
got even more methods. We got inductive, deductive, intuition
and trial and error. Add in guesswork. Throw in plain ol' back-
bone and gut. Yessir, we got methods aplenty. 'Scuse me.

The sheriff followed Rule out to the truck holding the long
leather holster and hawgleg Colt against the length of his thigh.
Saying, I sure heard that. Method's one thing but what we want's
results. Find any fingerprints?

Enough to start you a new filing cabinet.

The man whistled. I'll be dawg. You want us to carry 'em up to
Austin?

If you don't mind. I need to head on to Brookshire.

Nossir, I said we would.

All right. He handed the man a thick manila envelope. Don't expect this'll amount to anything.

You sure?

Rule rubbed his jaw. Well sir, I ain't sure of but two things. Not in this life. He paused.

Death and taxes?

Nope.

The sheriff reached into his pocket for the small spiral notepad, clicked the penpoint open.

First thing, Rule said, is when you're working in close on a woman don't hand her a limp dick. He winked. Second thing, the size of a man's pecker lies in direct inverse ratio to the size of his gun. He grinned as the sheriff slid his hand away from the notepad. The man's face was dark red.

Rule climbed in the truck and started it. He laid the Stetson on the seat to the side. He rolled down the window and wiped his forehead along one sleeve, looked at the sheriff. Saying, Make that one more thing I'm sure of.

Suspicious, the sheriff drew back his head and waited. He passed a hand over his mouth as if wiping something away. Like he was waiting for a punch line he might not like.

It's gonna be a hot one, Rule said. That I'm sure of. Damn hot.

The man grunted. He visibly relaxed at this sudden and unexpected congress. Saying, Yessir, it is at that. He peered up at the sun, eyes half shut, then back. He wore an expression as if deciphering an intriguing but inscrutable puzzle. You the first Ranger I ever met, he said.

Rule grinned. Well, they say we're something special. That's PR mostly. Deep down inside, I'm the same as anyone else.

The sheriff hooked his thumbs in his gun belt. Nodding thoughtfully at the apparent sagacity of that remark, at its implied candor.

I'm a regular sonofabitch, Rule said. Why I work alone. Nobody can stand me.

With that he let off the brake and rolled on forward and out the drive. When he pulled onto the highway he glanced into the rearview mirror and saw the man still standing there. He was hunched over, writing in the small spiral notepad.

17

She didn't have anything in the kitchen but Fruit Loops and Cap'n Crunch and the milk in the carton was sour. They sat at the small round table eating dry cereal from boxes while she phoned her mother. They chewed with the enthusiasm of eating sugared cardboard. Which wasn't far off the mark.

They sat at the table and chewed, listening to her argue. Leaning into the receiver, she'd say one thing and wait a second, then say something else. Back and forth. Hit and run, parry and thrust. Moving in and out of some familiar perimeter. Tone rising in offense, falling in defense. Volume in inverse ratio.

Saying, Well, if you don't want 'em just say so.

Saying, I am *too* trying. I am *too*. It's just hard and you don't know.

Saying, Some time for myself, that's what I need. Every mother needs *that* much.

And so on.

Eddie listened and filled in the gaps. It didn't take much imagination. Della needed some time to get away and relax and the old woman wasn't helping. Old folks, a pain in the ass. Always crabbing, wanting sympathy. Trying to squeeze out every drop from a life not worth living. Nuthin to live for but an iron will to live. Making sure you know all about it, too. Then they bitch cause you stay away. Man oh man. Old folks.

He pushed away the box of Cap'n Crunch and picked up the Fruit Loops. Reading the offer on the back. Three boxtops and a dollar gets you a genuine colored poster of a Guatemalan toucan. Whatever that was. Greatest offer of all time, what it was, according to the offer. Thinking about all those posters in the kids' room. Halfway listening to Della.

You stopped taking your iron, she was saying. Tone rising, volume falling. *Yes* you did. You did too. *That's* why you're tired. Cause you quit. It is too.

Eddie shoveled in a mouthful of Fruit Loops and wished he had something to wash it down with. Something besides water. A beer maybe. Coke at least. Ray Bob had done give up. Pushed the box away. Saying, Ain't this some shit?

Well, I had more substantial, admitted Eddie. He wiped his forehead along the back of his arm. It was hot in the apartment, and stuffy. The place had seemed large enough the night before, but now it felt tiny, like it was closing in. Smelled bad too, with a single small window in the livingroom that didn't even open. It was stuck shut, the sash swollen from humidity. The offwhite walls were streaked from water leaks, the brown shag carpet worn to the pad in paths where everyone walked. He wondered what sort of rent she paid.

After a minute Della said, That's right, don't worry, I'm going to. I'll bring by some clean clothes. I *said* I would. And make sure Randy takes his medicine. You don't want him sick. Is he coughing? Well shoot. How about Waylon? Good grief. Okay, give them two spoonfuls. I *know* what it says, give two anyways. And make sure they swallow.

She hung up the phone and blew a noisy breath upward, ruffling her bangs. She was barefoot wearing bluejeans with a red and blue checked cotton blouse tied in a knot at the waist. The skin beneath her left eye was dark red and blue.

Della said, I swear she's getting more and more *difficult*. Like I got three kids.

That's how they are, said Eddie, just like a kid. You know your eye matches your shirt?

Well, that's just luck, I didn't intend it.

Ray Bob didn't say anything. He got up from the table and went into the livingroom on the other side of the Formica bar and stood staring out the small second floor window overlooking cars parked along the street. He lit a cigarette.

In the kitchen Della said, Anyway, it's settled. She's gonna keep 'em. Plus I got this idea. She smiled and waited. When Eddie didn't reply she said, Why don't we go to the beach?

Beach? said Eddie. Which one?

Crystal Beach.

Where's that?

Other side of Galveston. From Galveston you take the ferry over to the Bolivar Peninsula. Over there somewhere, Crystal Beach.

Man, them beaches up there is muddy, Eddie said. All that river silt and oil washing up, and trash. Just like Louisiana. Them's dirty beaches.

Well I know that.

Della frowned while she took the cereal boxes off the table and set them on the counter by the sink. Something to do, staying busy. Then said, My friend Ruby's boyfriend LD, he's a contractor, has a beach house over there and we could use it.

They ain't there?

They went to Las Vegas, she said. She picked up the Cap'n Crunch box again and shook it and then put it in the plastic garbage can beside the refrigerator. Saying, LD likes to gamble. He's been filthy rich three four times. Ruby says he's addicted. It's a nice beach house, I know where they keep the key.

Eddie considered it. He liked trees himself. Trees and rivers and creeks. Something to look at, hold your attention. Never was much of one for the beach. All that sky and sand and nuthin in between. Just heat and humidity and sand getting everywhere. In your boots, between your toes, sand in your eyes and teeth. And people. Fat people smeared with oil laying around on towels, baking in the sun. Or standing there sweating like a ditchdigger holding a beer staring out at the waves. Just standing there watching. Like they was something to see. Like something might happen they stood there long enough.

You seen one wave you seen 'em all, Eddie said. He wiped his forehead again. He was perspiring. Ain't it kinda warm in here?

My air conditioning's broke, Della said. It only works in winter. That's when the heater breaks. They don't fix a thing here. Which is why I'm in the process of relocating. She propped one hand on a hip and twisted the knot in her blouse with the other.

Saying, At the beach you could relax, you know, and I could work on my tan.

Eddie looked across the room at Ray Bob standing by the window, staring out. Acting funny. Not saying anything.

For how long? he asked.

Della glanced at the plastic smiley-face clock hanging on the wall. Thinking they'd probably found Mister Dreamboat by now, stiff as a board. After that they wouldn't fool around, you could bet on that. Her twelve hours were about up. With both hands she twisted the knot in her blouse tighter and said, How long? I hadn't thought about that. You can't figure everything out at once, you know. Sounding kind of defensive. Anyhow, I just need to get away, I need a break. The sooner the better too. I'm gonna pack a bag while you think about it. She went down the short hallway to the bedroom.

Eddie stood up from the kitchen table and lit a cigarette. He went over and joined Ray Bob by the window. Looking out. A flock of blueblack grackles swooped down from the roof of a building down the way and landed in the narrow yard between the apartments and a sagging redwood fence along the street. They strutted over the short Bermuda grass like they were hot shit. Pecking for food, necks bobbing up and down.

What you think?

Ray Bob shrugged.

What's with you, man? You don't like her?

Ray Bob looked up at Eddie with his small graygreen eyes hard and flat in the square freckled face. I think she's trouble.

Eddie drew on the cigarette. Course she's trouble. She's a woman ain't she?

She ain't tellin the truth.

Eddie didn't bother with that one. Said, Neither are we. Not exactly.

What did you tell her?

Nuthin. Just what you heard. We robbers. We on the run.

What else? Ray Bob staring out the window again. While you was fucking her. What else?

Nuthin, man, I said nuthin. Jesus. She was doing all the talking. Eddie hesitated, tugged at his earring. Only I did ask her to marry me.

Motherfuck. Ray Bob shook his head, disgusted. What a moron. You a pussywhipped motherfucker.

Says you. Maybe I know a good thing.

You don't know shit, hoss. A good thing, that's what we had. Me and you, runnin buddies. Ray Bob took a final hit on the cigarette and dropped the butt to the carpet. He ground it out with a boot heel. Now you done expanded the business, dickhead.

Well, yeah. I guess I did. Eddie drew up his mouth and rubbed his eyes with thumb and forefinger, rubbed hard. You right, I shoulda asked.

Ray Bob grunted. I'd a said no.

I figgered that. Reckon that's why.

They watched the grackles grubbing for breakfast down in the yard and didn't say anything while they watched. Then Eddie said, What if it was you fucking her?

Coulda if I wanted. Was just showing you some respect.

That ain't what I asked.

She wouldn't be packing no bag, Ray Bob said. Said it right back, no hesitation.

Eddie nodded. Yeah, she'd probably be dead.

Might be. Ray Bob scratched a thick forearm with his knuckles. Sure might. It ain't too late neither.

You guys ready?

They turned to see Della standing by the bar holding a nylon overnight bag and leather sandals in one hand and a small canvas Lone Ranger suitcase in the other. She'd put on a pair of flaming red highheeled pumps. The heels made her ass poke up.

Yeah, it is, said Eddie. That there's my fiancée, pardner. We'll just have to wing it.

18

Rule crossed the Colorado one more time east of Columbus and ran the truck hard eastward over the interstate through the smooth hills and flatlands. The sun bore down on the pavement, bounced back flashing. He put on his sunglasses and dialed Moline in Austin.

Dana called me, Moline said.

Rule shifted the cellular to his other ear. That ain't why I'm calling, Moline. What we got?

Not much. I'm still waiting for those pictures from Brookshire.

Where I'm headed, Rule said. He told him to expect the envelope from Columbus with the slug and prints. Check the ballistics against Bernie and that Indian fella too. They been compared yet?

They don't match, Moline said. Two shooters. Two guns anyhow. Them ballistics from Columbus and Brookshire get here we'll run more tests.

Keep me posted. Still nuthin on the computer?

Nuthin on DeReese we didn't already know. Small stuff. He's playing in a different league now. No ID on Redhead.

All right. Call me if you need me. He started to punch the button but heard Moline talking.

What?

I said Dana said she saw you last night.

Rule didn't reply. He veered left to miss an armadillo crushed in the road and then the highway scooted over the low bridge spanning the dry riverbed of the San Bernard. Thin green willows leaned over the rocky banks thirsting, their spindly shanks rustling in the breeze. He heard Moline breathing on the other end, waiting.

That what she said?

Yeah. Moline paused. You didn't mention it this morning.

Rule said he forgot. Then he said it was early when Moline called. Then he said he hadn't thought it mattered one way or another anyhow. I ain't no counselor, he said. I ain't getting in the middle, leave me out.

I'd a thought you'd be on my side. Moline sounded peeved. When Rule didn't respond he said, She said she saw you at the Broken Spoke.

Rule cleared his throat. And I suppose she told you we spoke to each other. Then we had a dance or two. I bought her a beer and told her she looked real nice. One thing led to another. That what she said?

No.

Give her the divorce, Moline. I gotta go. Keep me posted.

He hung up the phone and laid it in the seat. Then he picked it up and dialed his nearest neighbor, Elmore Westland. Elmore, a retired assistant state attorney general, owned the section of hill country adjacent to his own about fifteen miles southwest of Austin. Elmore answered the line. They talked rain or not, agreed they were in for some heat. Then Rule asked him to go over and feed Lefty for a day or two. Saying, I might be gone.

Who you hunting? Elmore asked.

Coupla bad boys. Headed down toward Houston way.

Well, you nab them sumbitches, said Elmore.

I aim to.

All right.

Rule punched the disconnect and called Katie's number in Austin, apartment off Speedway near the university. When her machine kicked in he listened to her voice, hesitated, hung up without leaving a message. Not sure what to do. Used to be so close. When she was younger, before the divorce, and after. But not lately. Always seemed mad at him. Didn't know what had happened. Worried him. Only child, and she was slipping away.

He spanned the Brazos just after noon. The road shot over the wide plain straight as a carpenter's level, bubble on dead center. His stomach growled. He ignored it. He missed many meals and did not think much of it anymore. He watched the country pass, the flat green fields stretching away into more flat green fields, boundaries indeterminate but for sparse stands of cottonwoods along creek banks sometimes having that meaning and sometimes not. Shortly he drove up on Brookshire.

The town tumbled away northward from the freeway as if it held no interest in interstate hustle or bustle, had meant to avoid it and had. He rolled off the exit and down the access to the intersection of the road leading back into town. The near entrance to the Exxon convenience center was blocked off by a city patrol car. He pulled past and turned into the exit drive and parked by the pumps. A green wrecker truck with a hoist sat around the side.

He was met by Chief Wharton and a man wearing a pair of gray Dickies coveralls. Wharton was a former highway patrolman who'd got bumped on too many complaints and Rule knew him from that time. They shook hands. The chief looked mean and acted tough and all of it was true. A dark red scar ran the length of his face from the right temple to the jawline. He cocked his head toward the other man.

This here's Harvey Lomax. It's his wife was working.

Rule looked the man over. Coarse features leathered outdoors, tall and wiry, big roughskinned hands with scabbed knuckles. His frayed sleeves short above bigboned wrists. He was probably forty but looked fifty and his eyes were swollen and red.

We gonna get 'em, he said, voice cracking. More question than statement, one he answered himself. Gonna get 'em, all right. You bet. Ain't never gonna make the jail. He rubbed his mouth with the flat back of one wrist.

Harvey's on auxiliary with the county, Wharton said.

Rule nodded. I'm sorry about your wife.

But Lomax wasn't listening. He was off somewhere, back down in his grief, seeking solace in revenge. He mumbled some incomprehensible thing. Then, more clearly: They never seen Waller County justice. Nossir. The Almighty's justice neither. But they gonna learn.

Rule turned to the chief. Maybe I oughta take a looksee inside.

They went through the front door and Rule studied the layout while Wharton described what he'd seen on the security video.

The pictures is clear, he said. They already on the way up to Austin. Ballistics, too. Looked like a thirtyeight auto on the screen, you ask me, maybe nine millimeter. Wharton crossed his arms and hooked both hands in his armpits. I hear one a them boys is ID'd.

DeReese Ledoux, said Rule. The ponytail.

The chief leaned forward onto the balls of his feet, bounced on his heels, one two three. Saying, Well, it's the other'n we want.

I want 'em both.

Just a matter of time. Boys like that ain't going nowhere. He took a pouch of Red Man from a hip pocket, tucked a wad in his jaw. The red scar bowed over his cheek. He arched one eyebrow. Yessir, ain't goin nowhere but hell. We'll help get 'em there sooner or later.

Well, I'm more interested in sooner, Rule said. We got anything here that might help?

The chief jerked a thumb toward the back. Might check the head. Video shows him walking out with the key. Can't find it now, reckon he ran off with it. Didn't flush the toilet either. Fucking animal.

Wharton stepped to the door and opened it a crack, hawked a dark blob of tobacco juice onto the drive. He wiped the corner of his mouth with a knuckle, saying, But I reckon if he was in there he had to turn the door handle. Worth a check. You never know.

No, Rule agreed, you sure don't. But it's a public restroom. Wouldn't get my hopes up.

Ain't me, Wharton replied. I been in this game too long. Hope ain't what catches bad men, never did and never will. You just dawg 'em down, whatever it takes. Nossir, hope never meant nuthin to me one way or the other. Mainly it's for pore folks and religious nuts.

He leaned a forearm as thick as an oak bough against the front door glass. Take that feller out there now. Wharton pointed his chin toward Lomax standing in the drive. All his hope gone, a walking time bomb. Drives that wrecker out back, reads the Bible. We don't ride close herd on ol' Harvey, you gonna have his wrecker in your rearview. Done forgot about jurisdiction. He's justice incarnate, and I mean the Old Testament kind.

Need me to talk to him?

The chief wagged his head. Wouldn't do no good. Only person Harvey ever listened to was his wife, and she's dead.

Know anything about police work?

Naw, hell no. Harvey's auxiliary. They ride around, carry a badge, get to tell folks they a lawman. Call each other deputy, help get the sheriff reelected. You know how that is. He stood at the door watching the man through the glass. But I'll tell you what ol' Harvey does know about. Guns. He knows about guns.

Rule went over and stood by the sheriff. Out on the drive, Lomax appeared to be talking to himself, or to someone no one else could see. What's he carry?

Shit. The chief tilted his big head sideways and down with one eye closed. Harvey? He carries anything that ain't too heavy to haul. Harvey's a one man walking arsenal.

19

They dropped the Lone Ranger suitcase off at Della's mother's in Missouri City. The small clapboard house sat on cracked concrete-block piers facing a potholed street lined with other clapboard houses set on crumbling piers just like it and ditches and seedy overgrown yards with junked cars set up on axles and rims among the weeds. A working class neighborhood working its way into white trash status. Della's mother's house leaned a little to the left, as if it was tired but couldn't decide whether to stand or fall.

Nice place, Eddie said.

You think so?

Oh yeah, real nice.

Well it was, said Della, before it went downhill. Now the whole neighborhood's a dump. Tornado could hit and cause major improvement.

They were parked on the street alongside a shallow weed-infested ditch with standing runoff. The murky water excreted a strange reek, mixture of warm rotten eggs and mud. Della got out with the child's suitcase on the street side and went down the short oyster-shell drive around a battered Dodge Dart, her legs weaving and bobbing as the sharpheeled pumps sought purchase among the shells. She wore a pair of big-lensed sunglasses to hide her bruised left eye.

Don't seem like a dump to me, Eddie said. Shoot, reminds me of home.

Not mine, said Ray Bob.

Didn't know you had one.

Well, there you are.

When Della climbed the two-by-eight wooden steps onto the sagging front porch two kids came out running and threw their arms around her legs. She grabbed the bigger one by the ear and shook his head side to side, his eyes bulging. Eddie and Ray Bob could hear her.

You take your medicine, Randy?

The kid put a thumb in his mouth and nodded.

You swallow it?

He nodded again, still clinging to Della's leg with the other hand. The second child began sucking his thumb too. Della slapped him hard on top the head, he flinched. All right then, she said, and y'all better be behaving. You hear me?

Reckon they better, Eddie said.

The screen door on the porch opened then and a woman put her head out. Her dry turtle face was drawn and pinched, deeply furrowed with cracks. She wore a long terrycloth housecoat held shut at the throat by one worried hand. The woman stared at the Caddy in the street with close-set sharpshooter eyes. She had short curly hair dyed just shy of screaming Mercurochrome yellow.

Now that there's a wig, Eddie said.

Where?

There. On Della's momma.

Looks like hair to me, said Ray Bob. Ugly old bitch.

You betcha.

That's some tired looking shit.

She don't take her iron.

What's that got to do with the price of rice in China?

Eddie shrugged. He flicked an ash over the side into the ditch. Saying, Anyhow, it's a wig.

Bullshit, Ray Bob said, five bucks says it's hair.

You got it.

The woman stared at them a moment longer, then sucked her head inside, tortoiselike. Della and the kids followed. The screen door screeched open again almost immediately and Della waved. I'll be right there, she called out.

Eddie smiled and waved back.

Ray Bob rested his arm on the car door and lit a cigarette. Looked over at Eddie, looked off down the street. Said shit. Said pussywhipped. Said, That musta been some good stuff, hoss. Finally asked, How was it?

All right.

Better'n that cow?

I ain't never fucked a cow, said Eddie.

Said you did yesterday.

No I didn't. I asked if you did.

Ray Bob frowned, trying to remember back.

Your problem's you don't listen good, Eddie said. Why you end up shooting people.

Della came out on the porch and sideways down the steps, moving quickly but carefully across the yard, dodging mud crawfish towers. Terra firma soggy. The red stiletto heels sinking into waterlogged ground. She held her arms up to keep balance and made it to the far edge of the ditch, lifted the sunshades and rolled her eyes, exasperated.

You got ten dollars? she said. My momma ain't got anything to feed them kids with.

Eddie reached down under the seat and pulled out the plastic bag. He opened it and felt around, brought out a roll of dimes and three rolls of nickels. He tossed them airborne over the ditch one by one while she caught them, small bonehard cylinders spinning in space, a coin roll odyssey.

There's eleven.

Thanks, Eddie. She smiled and turned, took a step and sank to one side. Dammit to hell. She took off her shoes and went on, saying over her shoulder, Don't go nowheres now. I'll be right back.

They watched her go back inside carrying a shoe in each hand.

Don't even say it, said Eddie. It's outa my share.

Pussywhipped.

Better'n a watermelon.

Fuck you.

Up yours sideways.

Up yours inside and out.

Eddie started to say in your momma's mouth but decided against it. Said instead, Case you ain't noticed, we running short of money.

We gonna fix that. Ray Bob tapped the fuel gauge. Plus we gonna get a little discount gas while we're at it.

Not me.

You either out or in, hoss, ain't no in between.

Della came out then carrying her shoes, minced across the weedchoked yard and jumped the ditch behind the Caddy. She climbed into the backseat. Eddie told her she could sit up front but she said it was too crowded up there and she didn't mind. The kids appeared on the front porch watching. Both sucking their thumbs. Della waved and told them to go back inside. They didn't move. Go back inside! she hollered. Ray Bob started the motor and pulled away.

Eddie swiveled in the seat half a block down and looked back. The two kids still standing on the porch there staring, both hand to mouth, sadeyed snotnosed mannequins from a community service ad. He said to Della, You need to break 'em on that thumbsucking.

I know it.

Rot a kid's teeth out, Eddie said. My cousin Earl rotted all his teeth out and couldn't eat nuthin but oatmeal. He was a skinny little bastard. Nervous too.

Well, they only do it when they're nervous, Della said. That's why they do it.

What they nervous about?

You looked at the world lately, Eddie? All you gotta do is watch the news.

He thought about that, said, Sure you don't wanna sit up here?

Della said no, thank you anyway. You wanna get back here?

Eddie closed one eye and made a face. Naw, that would look kinda funny. Like we was renting a limousine or something. Don't wanna draw any attention.

Well whatever, she said, you the experts.

Della took a brush from her bag and removed the red elastic band from her hair and brushed her waves back, then replaced the hairband. Saying, My hair's a total mess in all this wind. She brushed her bangs down. I'm gonna miss my kids.

Yeah, Eddie said, they real cute. Your momma wear a wig?

Della giggled. I ain't gonna tell her you said that.

Don't then.

I sure won't. She's sensitive about her hair. Anyways, I did it myself. That's professional work.

Della's voice dropped. She became quiet for a minute, saw Ray Bob peering at her in the rearview. Looking suspicious. She moved to one side, out of his line. Saying, See I didn't tell you before but I went to beauty school. Only that was just to fall back on. Like insurance. In case my modeling career didn't take off.

That was a right smart idea, Eddie said. He bent over and took a five-dollar roll of dimes out of his plastic sack and passed them over to Ray Bob. Saying, Good thing it took off.

What you mean by that?

Nuthin.

You sure?

I said I was.

Sounded like you meant something.

I can't help how it sounded.

Cause I can tell what a person's thinking.

Okay, tell me.

I'm not sure you wanna know.

If y'all would shut the fuck up a goddamned second, interrupted Ray Bob, then somebody could fuckin tell me how the fuck
to get outa here.

Good lord, said Della, you sure know how to talk. Just go right
up here and left and then take another left a ways up on the highway. That's the Alvin Sugar Land Road.

All right, said Ray Bob. They any fuckin gas stations on it?

Oh yeah.

She took out a tube of red lipstick and stretched her mouth into
a big O.

Lots.

20

Rule had finished in Brookshire and Chief Wharton had agreed
to run the prints up to the lab in Austin when the cellular rang. It
was Moline.

Yeah?

They hit again.

All right.

In Manvel.

Down by Corpus?

Naw, that's over south of Houston. Not an hour ago.

Do tell.

Rule stood on the apron of the Exxon near Chief Wharton and
Lomax. He shook his head their way to mean it wasn't important.
Nodding and saying uh-huh he sauntered away and stood to one
side with a view of the storage shed out back and the farmland
and pasture beyond. Heat rose above the pale green lea in rippling
waves, off black furrows of plowed fields.

Manvel, he said. Where's that exactly?

Just above Alvin. Highway Six.

They cutting around Houston then. Rule paused. Headed toward Galveston.

Maybe.

That's good. Corner 'em on that island.

Maybe, maybe not, Moline said. They could cut back, go down the coast.

Tell me what you know.

Moline said he'd just received a call from a state trooper in Brazoria County. Officer heard some commotion on the radio so he went down to see. County was already there. Said it's a Mobil station hooked up to a Taco Bell. They took out the clerk. A kid this time. Couldn't a been more'n sixteen.

In the station or the Taco Bell?

The station, Moline said, the taco joint ain't open yet. Under construction. The workers were down the road having lunch. In a bar.

Damn.

That's right, not a single witness.

But you know it's our boys.

We got 'em on video again, said Moline. Audio, too, this time. Owner's trying out some new state of art security system. Don't trust his own people. Trooper gave me a blow by blow. It's them.

Rule squinted into the sunlight reflecting off the side drive of the service station and the landscape beyond. A crow flew over and away, black wings curving gracefully on air. He watched it glide down into a plowed field, disappear against the charcoal furrowed earth.

So how'd it play out?

From what I understand, Moline said, DeReese goes in and buys a sixpack, asks how's business, shit like that, small talk, then goes out. Tells the clerk they're filling up on pump three. Coupla minutes later Redhead goes in. He looks around, pulls a gun from a boot and sticks it in the clerk's face. The kid about shits. He's stuffing money in a bag babbling about the weather and baseball, nonsense like that, scared as hell, and our boy still ain't said a word. Smiling though. Enjoying it, watching the boy sweat. The kid hands him the bag and Redhead asks how far it is to Corpus Christi. The kid says he don't know, never been there. Our boy says that's too bad, he heard it's a good place. Clean beaches, pretty women. The kid agrees, says he heard that too, he'd like to go someday. Still shitting in his pants, ready to cry. Our boy says, C'mon, you can come with us. Still grinning. Kid's shaking his head. Can't do it, his parents'll get mad, he'll lose his job, thanks anyhow. Our boy says he admires the kid's spunk, his loyalty. Says he has a damn good work ethic. Says he's sorry the kid can't make it so he'll do the next best thing. He'll send him a nice picture postcard from Corpus, show him what it's like. A girl in a bikini maybe. The kid thanks him. No problem, Redhead says, no problem at all, glad to do it. Says he'll send it care of the cemetery. Then he fires off two quick shots right in the kid's face. One in each eye.

Goddamn, said Rule.

Yeah, it was a mess. Gonna be closed casket, count on it. Fucker was standing directly in front of the camera, too. Looking right at it, winking and mugging. Guys watching the tape said he acted like he was putting on a show.

You sure?

What they said. Like he was aiming to get on TV.

Or sending a message, said Rule.

Such as.

Such as they headed to Corpus. Meaning they ain't.

Maybe not. Who knows? This goombah's hard to read. Could be they are. Could be he wants us to know. Moline paused. Or they could be going back into Houston. Big city, easy to disappear. That's what I'd do.

Rule pondered it. I don't think so. These guys are on the move. They going somewhere.

Well, all we know now is where they been. That ain't hard to find.

Any word on what they're driving?

Nada. Hard to believe. And here's something else. There may be a woman with 'em now. Can't be sure but it looked like she went in and out with DeReese. Big head of hair. Not a bad looking gal they said. Lotsa hair. Kinda longfaced though.

Rule frowned. You mean unhappy?

No, I mean her face is too long. Throws off her looks. But they're pretty sure she was with DeReese in there. First he got one kind of beer. Then she said something and he put it back and got another.

All right. Run her picture too. Anything on those ballistics?

Rule heard paper shuffling in the background. Moline came back saying, We think maybe we got a match on Bernie Rose and the Columbus shooting. Only the slug's screwed up, the one from Columbus. Somebody mess with it down there?

Rule stepped forward and kicked a pebble over the pavement, watched it bounce into the far grass. Said, Grover.

Grover?

Deputy Grover. Sheriff's nephew. Got hisself a microscope.

Well fuck him.

Kiss him for me when you do. Listen, Moline, just do your best. I'm still in Brookshire. You got some more prints coming up.

Man, I'm up to my asshole in prints.

And run that gal's pic through the system. Maybe she's hooked up.

You know, it's not like we ain't got nuthin else to do, Moline said. Pretty soon we gonna be running checks on half of Texas.

They'd probably turn up positive. Quit complaining, you need the overtime. I'll check you later.

You headed over to Manvel?

Rule hesitated. Thinking about it. Then made a decision. Nope, he said, I'm gonna roll south. Down toward Lake Jackson and Freeport. They going to Corpus, maybe I can cut 'em off.

If they headed that way.

I think maybe you're right, Moline. Some reason or anuther they want to get caught. Either that are they threw a double reverse. I can't tell, ain't able to get in their head yet. But they ain't stupid.

Maybe not. But they mean.

Rule grunted and hung up. The noon heat bounced off the pavement. Not a cloud in the wide upland sky. His feet were sweating in his boots. He pulled out his handkerchief and wiped his face, the back of his neck, looked over toward Chief Wharton and Lomax. Thinking he was beginning to feel pretty mean himself. Not as mean as Lomax, though. Lomax looked like death warmed over, all that crazy vengeance in his eyes. Guy a ticking bomb if Wharton was right. Which he usually was.

Rule put a hand down, adjusted his nuts through the khakis. Only thing worth feeling good about was Moline hadn't mentioned Dana.

21

The top was back and dazzling light and heat flamed downward from above as from a blowtorch. The hot wind whipped over the windshield and down, the Caddy swept over the flat coastal prairie. Flying through broad grassy fields with grazing cattle, through wetlands and swamp toward Galveston. In the front seat Eddie and Ray Bob drinking beer, watching the wide sweep of ken—

Vast stretches of land to a horizon unbroken save for lonely trailer homes perched queerly in the stepped greenbrown expanse, as if dropped there from the sky as an alien afterthought. In fields among roving longhorns and cattle egrets, great iron hobbyhorses pumping oil, the smooth seesaw motions like colossal black birds endlessly dipping for a drink, remorseless in their crude need and want. An occasional drilling rig.

They watched it pass.

Della, meanwhile, huddling in the backseat. Thinking, remembering. Almost done with the crying now. She couldn't believe it. Just could not *believe* it.

Eddie looked around and tried to hand her a beer over the seat but she turned her head away. He told her something. She didn't hear. He leaned farther over the seat and repeated it. Said, I told you.

She looked at him briefly, then away.

I told you we was robbers, puddin.

She sank down farther into the corner of the upholstery and leaned an elbow on the armrest and put one hand over her face.

That wind bothering you?

She didn't answer.

He swiveled back in his seat and glanced at Ray Bob. I think she's upset.

Ray Bob grinned, bottomed up the can of beer and swallowed. He pitched it sideways over his left shoulder, saw it tumbling forward back down the pavement in the rearview, skidding end over end until it blew off the road. He stuck out his right arm, wiggled his fingers.

Gimmee anuther.

Eddie pulled a cold Bud from the plastic ring, can dripping with condensation. He handed it over, saying, You kinda gettin in a rut, bud. Ever see them old movies where the guy just goes in with a gun and robs a place, walks out with the money?

Ray Bob rubbed the cold can against his shirtfront, said, You trying to make a point?

You gonna shoot everybody?

I might. Ray Bob grinned again. That might not be a bad idea.

Take a while, said Eddie, and at this rate, I don't think we got that much time.

Ray Bob popped the tab, drank down half the beer. I ain't in no hurry.

Act like you are. Jesus, you act like you got snakes in your head.

What you know, hoss? You never been in there.

Eddie admitted he hadn't. Said he didn't think he wanted to either.

Then stay out, Ray Bob said.

All right, Eddie said. I ain't much of a psychologist anyhow.

Well, I met some gooduns, believe you me, in prison. Ray Bob took a swig of beer, pulled back his lips over clamped teeth. Saying, Ahhhh. Saying, Those pastyfaced suckers had certificates all up and down the wall, only I never met one what could explain me. They listen and nod, say they *empathized*. Get paid for that shit. They all give up.

Well then, Eddie said, I guess you won.

Said I was smart though, Ray Bob went on. Which I already knew. Always giving me these IQ tests? I passed 'em. That's why I told the video back there we was going to Corpus Christi. They gonna think I was trying to fool 'em into thinking I was tryin to fool 'em.

Eddie squinted one eye and made a face.

See there? Ray Bob grinning again. I done fooled you too.

Eddie tugged at his earring and shrugged. Man, all I can say is I'm glad I ain't in your head.

You got that straight, hoss.

In Hitchcock they pulled off the road where fastfood joints and convenience stores stood asscheek to asscheek and entered the drive-thru at a Burger King. Della said she wasn't hungry.

Better eat gal, said Ray Bob. Him staring at her in the mirror.

Said I wasn't.

Least she's talking, said Eddie.

They waited in line behind a twin cab pickup hauling an over-sized sump pump. The wind shifted and an acrid aroma swept over them from inland. The rank odor brought tears to their eyes. It smelled like someone had cracked open a cesspool.

Ray Bob made a sour face. Shit, hope that ain't our lunch.

Eddie said it was Texas City. Said it was the smell of money. He pointed northward over the marshes to where a tangled line of vertical smokestacks black and gray lipped the far seagrassed scope. Them's oil refineries and petrochemical plants, he said. Where everybody works.

Let 'em, Ray Bob said. They all morons. I wouldn't work in one of them places. Toxic waste dumps. Can't even smell the worst part.

They pay good. Della in the backseat, speaking quietly.

Not that good, said Eddie. He looked back at her. Get cancer in them places. Get it bad. You want the cancer?

She didn't say anything.

Well, me neither. No way, uh-uh. Eddie shook his head. My old man died from cancer. Shriveled up like a worm on a hot sidewalk. He wasn't a big man but he was a strong man and that chemical shit eat him away to nuthin. Didn't take no time neither, once it got going. Started in his guts. Said he could feel it gnawing away. Felt like rats in there.

Ray Bob inched the Caddy forward in the line. Eddie lit a cigarette. Said, That's right, big ol' hungry rats. He looked back to Della. Sure you don't want a burger?

No thank you, she said, I lost my appetite.

Well, Eddie replied, if you find it just say so.

When they pulled back onto the highway, they followed it on down to where it angled into I-45 and merged, heading toward Galveston. Soon after the interstate began to ride up on piers above bayous and tidal sloughs and the cobalt green swamps ran off and away to either side below a bright transparent sky, and though they could not see they knew there was open water beneath them the way lighted space hung there floating over the proximate outscape. Then the roadbed inclined upward and the azimuth dropped away and they could see the water closing in on the spit of land they were leaving. Another upward pitch in the pavement and they were crossing over West Galveston Bay on a stilted causeway. They craned their necks to watch an oil tanker spewing smoke. It burrowed through the bay upcoast riding the Intracoastal Canal, the dredged channel buried beneath the surface. Their nostrils filled with the tang of brine, their ears with the sharp cries of gulls gyring the bluegray waves.

Eddie stared at the broad reaches of the bay east and west and the narrow uplifted roadbed reaching toward the outranged broken skyline of Galveston Island. He slowly shook his head. Saying, I don't like it. Ain't but one other way off this island.

Two, said Ray Bob. They got a ferry the other end, way we headed.

All right, two. I still don't like it. Too much like a trap.

Three, Ray Bob said. He grinned. We could swim it.

Good luck. Them swamps full of gators. Ever tied it on with a bull gator?

Naw, but it sounds like fun. Tell me about it.

Ain't much to tell. But I seen one cut open that swallowed a kid. He was in there all right. What was left. Some pieces of bone and shit, part of a leg. Along with a big nutria and some angle iron and half a crab trap.

Angle iron, Ray Bob said. They ain't particular, are they.

They'll eat you, that's what I'm saying. Remind me to tell you this joke I know. About a gator with a loose tooth and a prostitute.

Eddie felt a hand tap his shoulder and leaned back over the seat. You see a restroom, Della said, I need to stop.

They came off the causeway curving downward onto the island and the highway ran out into Broadway, its capacious esplanade lined with palms. Forlorn storefronts stood hip to joint alongside weedy car lots and old twostory wooden homes. Old-lady houses. Houses adorned with French Quarter filigree and scrollwork, faded and worn by relentless gulf winds. Windows and doors pushed off square by gravity, by storm. Neglected by owners and time itself, the houses leaned lazy and cantwise from the sandy soil but through some inscrutable act of exertion had not yet fallen.

Eddie watched the houses pass. Them's old, he said.

Della pointed. Said, There's a restroom.

Ray Bob pulled into a McDonald's, backed into a curbside slot under the sprawling shade of a live oak corkscrewed into the ground. She put on her red high-heeled pumps and got out but came back after crossing half the lot, saying, Don't get no ideas.

We full of ideas, said Ray Bob.

That's what I mean, don't get none.

She went inside, her ass rolling high in the jeans. They waited in the lot with the car in idle. A slight breeze stirred the parboiled humidity. Felt like an overheated greenhouse.

Bossy bitch.

She ain't perfect.

Got a nice ass.

It's a hot motherfucker.

Eddie pulled up his shirttail and wiped his face. Della came back carrying a sack and a large drink. Whatcha got? he asked.

A fish sandwich and fries.

Thought you was broke.

I am, she said. Almost. Move over.

Want to sit up here, Eddie said, you gotta sit in the middle. I ain't lookin like no queer.

Never mind then. She got in back.

Ray Bob grinned at Eddie. She don't like me.

Don't seem like y'all are trying very hard, Eddie replied, neither one of you. Least you could half try, he added. Wondering why it was the two of them had got off on the wrong foot.

Ray Bob pulled back onto Broadway and they rode up to the east end of the island and the ferry road and waited for the ferry in the blistering heat. They watched purpleblack cormorants perched stiffly on raggedy piertops, the gulls winging past in chaotic sunlit formations. Then they drove onto the swaying metal deck and parked. The boat blew its horn, pulled from the loading ramp into the bay, began the rolling three-mile trek over the Bolivar Roads between the island and peninsula.

Della said she wanted to stand in back and watch the seagulls feed in the wake. Ray Bob wasn't interested. The other two walked sternward over the metal plated deck vibrating from diesel engines below. The soaring gulls shrieked and dove head first into the wake, splashlanding briefly before rising to circle for another run at the menhaden and shrimp boiling to the surface. The onyx-eyed birds dipped and tumbled in crowded airborne clashes of squabble and screech.

Eddie watched the low form of Pelican Island slip past portside. Old leprosy colony, now a tourist attraction. Off starboard a dozen tankers and freighters anchored in deeper waters awaited pilots to guide them through the cut and across the bay into the Houston Ship Channel. The hot brackish wind off the gulf smelled like fish, smelled vaguely of putrefied crude. Overhead a lone pelican wheeled and turned a half roll, plunged into the bay, disappeared to reemerge with the pouch of its huge scooped bill extended, water overspilling the corners.

Man, Eddie said, it's an oven out here.

My lotion's in the car. I'm gonna get burnt.

They went upstairs to the enclosed deck to get out of the sun. In the bay to either side dolphins sluiced through the waves. Straight ahead they saw the tall dark obelisk of the defunct Bolivar lighthouse rising above a grayhazed point of land. The Bolivar Peninsula. Where they were going. The far northeastern extension of the low barrier islands that ran the whole length of Texas. A slim pencil of land dividing the east bay from the gulf, a sparsely populated ridge of sand and mud verging the shore upward almost thirty miles to merge with the main body of the state at Port Arthur, just downcoast from Louisiana. Where Eddie was from.

He put his arm around Della's shoulders. First time they'd been alone all day. He squeezed and pulled her close. But she did not lean into him and she held her shoulders stiff. He bent forward and sideways to look at her, eyebrows raised in question. She just looked straight ahead. Then said, And I thought you was nice.

I am, Eddie said, honest. Least I try to be.

You won't be long, she said. Not with him you won't.

He looked out at bluegray waves rolling under the ferry bow in momentary surrender, disappearing beneath the hull only to reappear behind in the veed wake, reforming and rolling onward with the immutable force of an indomitable motion.

How you know that? he asked.

Cause, Della said. Cause you can't be nice if you're dead.

There was nothing to do but wait. He had come down over the llano from Brookshire between the Brazos and San Bernard rivers, broad prairie unfurling to either side, truck roaring over a narrow strip of asphalt cleaving the green expanse. He watched the tall grass reeling drunkenly in the heat as he came down into the Brazos floodplain. By then he'd called Moline twice and twice learned nothing. Nothing on the computer and no ID and ballistics still uncertain.

There was nothing to do but wait.

He had learned long ago how to wait, was good at it. When there's nothing to do then one does nothing. Simple as that. An older man's wisdom. Knowing there's no gain in acting if its sole purpose lies in motion. If its single aim lies in discharge. Because the hunter who cannot hold vigil will not hear, will not see. Aimless waste therein. A young man's careless need. Resolved by a certain self-possession: One learned how to act by learning to hold still. Learned when.

So he waited.

He drove down through the towns sustained by the mouth of the red mudstrewn Brazos, towns feeding there on the broad heaving current. Lake Jackson, Clute, Jones Creek, Freeport—rough settlements joined by industry and oil, clinging everywhere to water in any form, intake or outflow.

He drove slowly. Watching, listening. Waiting.

Except for one more phone call to Katie. Machine again. He left a message, saying he was working a case down the coast, near Freeport, she could reach him on his cellular if she wanted. If she felt like talking. Or just to say hello, that'd be fine. Hoped she was all right, that her classes were going well. And don't be a stranger. Whatever the hell that meant.

He knew what it meant. *Call.*

Not likely though. He wanted it too much.

In the late afternoon, on the coast above Freeport, he took the Surfside bridge over the Intracoastal Waterway and drove up the low barrier island. Follets Island, a narrow spit of sand pushed downcoast by the longshore drift. The windward beach and surf there surging inward without pause, the moonripped tide. Leeward lay shallow lagoons or the paltry southern reaches of the west bay. He was accustomed to green hills and limestone outcrops and this land seemed to him a vast waste that could not interest anyone. Though people lived here, called it home.

He finally stopped before a windweathered clapboard beer joint topping the upper tip of the island, last building before San

Luis Pass. He stood on the lot among sharpedged venus shell hash and ligamented weeds and gazed out over the cut toward the southern point of Galveston. He cocked his head, listening.

After a moment he turned to scan the tavern's edifice, at the remnant of a warped sign spelling BOOMER'S PLACE. Smashed windows, a broken bower anchor with rusted flukes abandoned by the front steps. Painted on the door: *Closed*. Boomer gone for good.

The searing late afternoon sun stabbed his eyes and he blinked away sweat, pushed back his hat and wiped his face on a shirtsleeve. Heat like a furnace, damp salty smell of the sea. Windborne sand brazed his cheeks, clung to his teeth. He gazed once more across the cut toward the near tip of Galveston Island. Thinking, Could've gone that way as easy as this way, they sure could've. Might have.

He looked at the far shore, squinting. The water in the pass chopped the surface in short gray pyramids lipped with froth. From overhead in the glare he heard the sharp cries of gulls. He stood still. He was having a feeling. He had them now and then and sometimes he listened and sometimes he didn't. It all depended. Just now he didn't know. Wasn't sure.

So he got in his truck and drove back south along the slip and over the bridge back into Freeport where he checked into a motel for the night. That would be as good a place as any to wait. Which he was good at.

Although sometimes it got kind of old.

23

The Caddy tires wharumphed the joint between ramp and road and they came off the ferry headed northeast along the pitted state twolaner riding the low flat finger of the Bolivar Peninsula. Grass flats to either side, oyster grass and wire grass and weeds. Salt marsh shortly beyond to bayside, where mud flats and oyster beds seethed in shallow shifting waters. Across a fringe of tough thistled fields gulfside lay a line of low rounded dunes and the scant tidal slope of the beach. Bay and gulf, each crowding the slender strip of land, the entire length and scope of the peninsula a tenuous compromise broken at periodic impulse by hurricane and storm.

All the way up to Crystal Beach, Della said. That's a town, sorta. We gotta go past it.

They advanced in silence beneath the immensity of the skywheeled blue and bonewhite clouds as large as mountains without weight. Accompanied by a late afternoon sun fallen large in the west. A great lemon-yellow circle without circumference, unrelenting in its heat. Overcome by that, they rode on, and the emptiness.

Save for birds. Blackbirds on the lines, blackbirds on the poles. Kingfishers and doves by pairs perched along the drooping arcs. Suspended there, dazed by heat. Hawks gliding over the grass and egrets in the fields, coiled necks flashing white.

They watched without speaking and then came a beach house and sandy roads leading left and right flanked with more and then low disheveled buildings strewn roadside, devoted to commerce of one kind or another. Always the oyster shell lots with weeds renegade and rogue, and the salty sweet odor of decay, as if on this seasoaked ground where fertility and death were twinned the very construction of any building called for its selfsame demise, had entered into its very design.

The so-called town stretched along the road for miles, a vague scattering of rundown stores and taverns tossed among grasslands and marshes. As though the residents had never agreed where the town should be. And so it was nowhere and everywhere and in truth did not even exist, was merely called so for convenience. They passed a service station and on into emptiness once again but for wooden houses on piers set toward the tidal flats off the beach.

I think maybe we come too far, Della said. I only been here once.

You sure?

No.

They drove on and they came to a place called Gilchrist and crossed Rollover Pass where the gulf washed through a roiling cut into the east bay, banks reinforced with steel plates to counter erosion. They spanned the pass on a low concrete bridge and turned around. Ray Bob pulled into the shell lot of a bait camp and parked. Saying, Gonna get us some directions.

I know where we are now, said Della. We just gotta go back.

Fuck it, I want some beer. He got out.

Don't do nuthin stupid, pardner. Eddie talking now. Ain't no place to run to.

Do I look stupid?

Eddie closed an eye, scratched his chin.

Never mind, dickhead.

Ray Bob strode off toward the front door. The bait camp was a windowless plywood shack with a rattling air conditioner hung on one side. Metal beer signs were nailed to the front wall, along with a crudely lettered board sign with the owner's name: MOODYS. Other such painted boards promised snacks, sodas, live mud minnows. Ray Bob went inside and slammed the screen.

They waited.

Della took a small mirror from her purse and checked her face. Saying, you ought not let him talk to you that way. She turned her image right and left in the mirror. My lord, I'm getting burned already.

What way? asked Eddie.

That name.

What name?

Good grief, Eddie, the one he called you. Weren't you listening?

You mean dickhead? Eddie smiled. That's just the way we talk. Don't mean nuthin.

Not where I come from. Della fished in her bag for the lotion. Where I come from, it starts fights.

That all depends on who's saying it. Eddie lit a cigarette. Also when and where. It depends on the *way* they saying it. Whatcha call the *noo-ances*.

Well, you musta been listening closer than me then, Della said, cause all I heard was him calling you a name which in my opinion wasn't very nice. But that's between you and him, leave me out of it.

Well, I'm trying, Eddie said. He pulled a comb from his back pocket and unloosened his ponytail and combed it, then put the elastic band back around tight. Saying, It's just buddy talk anyways, like I said. You never been around guys talking without women.

That'd be hard to do, she said. If I was there.

What I'm saying.

She put the mirror away, snapped her purse shut. Well, I'm certainly not gonna argue about it.

Me neither, Eddie said. I don't like to argue.

You coulda fooled me.

I don't. Ain't no good at it.

Maybe, she said, maybe not. She folded her arms and stared away to one side toward Rollover Pass. Two black men stood along the hiphigh steel plates banking the channel holding casting rods. They laughed and slapped skin, highstepped in place like someone had just cracked a good one.

Eddie said, Look at 'em laugh.

Della made a small harumphing sound.

I used to laugh like that, Eddie said. They musta told a joke.

Della leaned down to swipe a bug off her foot, saying, Maybe it's the one about that alligator and prostitute. The one you wouldn't tell in front of me?

No kidding, Della, Eddie said, I sure wish you wouldn't be like this.

Like what?

Nuthin, forget I said anything.

Well I will, she replied, if I can.

Much obliged.

You're welcome.

After a minute, she added, Anyways, I'm not gonna argue with someone I just met.

Tell you what, Eddie muttered, feels like I *always* known you.

Della didn't say anything. She folded her arms again, watched the black men laughing. It was true, though, what he'd just mentioned, about it seeming like they'd always known one another. Wasn't that strange? Then she said, Well, you haven't.

Eddie sat in the front seat tugging at his earring waiting for Ray Bob to return. Thinking anytime would be just fine. Then the front screen door flew open and he came out carrying a sixpack of Coors, already drinking one. He tossed the others to Eddie saying, That ol' Moody is one strange dude. You know he's blind in one eye and missing a leg? Said a shark got it. A fuckin hammerhead. Right out there. Ray Bob pointed beyond the bait shop at the curling spit of beach mouthing the pass.

Them hammerheads is bad, Eddie said, you can depend on it. Got terrible dispositions. And stubborn.

Ray Bob got in behind the steering wheel, crushed the empty beer can in one hand. How'd the fuck would you know? he asked.

Man, don't you start.

Ray Bob backed out and pulled onto the road recrossing the pass going south, telling about Moody and his parrot named Jim. Sounding excited—

Parrot's named after some kid in a pirate book, Moody said, story about buried treasure. Said there's buried treasure around here somewhere, too, from a French pirate named Feet. John the Feet. Fuckin weird name. Moody almost found it, only it was a dead man in a casket. Guy'd been missing for a year from a cemetery in Galveston. Believe that shit?

Believe almost anything, Eddie said. Life ain't nuthin but surprises, you ask me. Surprises and fuckin bummers, a regular rollercoaster ride.

Ray Bob looked at him. Said, What bug crawled up your ass, hoss?

Eddie waved him off. Just the heat, I reckon. He watched the flat sandylands passing to the right, the light tan terrain shifting over waving tufts of grass. Watched the sandy dunes lifting to the left between the road and beach. Man oh man, sand everywhere he looked. He could hardly wait.

A few minutes later Della leaned forward and pointed at a sign advertising the Stingaree Marina and Restaurant on the bay. There, she said, but go left toward the beach. They turned into a narrow sandy lane and passed several beach houses with the faded paint and shuttered windows. The road soon culverted over a small lagoon of stagnant standing water fringed with cattails and reeds. She pointed to the last house, said it was LD's. It rose from the gritty soil on tall pole piers coated with tar and stood perched by itself, a rambling palepink house with a deck wrapped around three sides. Ray Bob pulled the car onto the cracked concrete slab under the house between the piers.

He put the Caddy in park and let the motor idle while he sat behind the wheel sipping a Coors. He lit a cigarette. The others watched, waiting.

What? asked Eddie.

Ray Bob leaned his head to the right, giving him a sideways look. Tell you what, pardner, I ain't staying here long.

How long's long.

I dunno. He turned off the motor. But I'll tell you when I reach it.

You guys, Della said, I can't believe you're talking about leaving. We just got here. Sounding enthused now. She climbed over the side gripping her nylon bag and opened Eddie's door, pulling on his arm.

C'mon inside, now, the both of you. You'll like it.

24

The motel was situated on Highway 36 where it bridged the Brazos just outside Freeport. The delta there lay flat and humid beneath an atmosphere of lazy expectation, as if the river had already surrendered to the gulf, as if the land hoped to profit from the loss. An expectation like so many, inferior to need and heedless to cause.

Midst this addled confusion, the motel. The Brazos Motor Inn.

He might have stayed in a better place. His expense account permitted more but he found the vintage motor court with the shabby brick cottages comfortable, as an old flannel shirt reassures the skin in the way a new one cannot. Each room a freestanding cottage. Each cottage its own carport and kitchenette, a window unit rumbling and lurching in the frame, television without cable. As good a place as any to wait.

He put his gear in the room and called Austin once more. Moline had left early. The lab tech reported no news save for the ballistics from Brookshire matching those of Bernie Rose. They were working the Manvel evidence now.

Rule told the technician, a young woman he'd never met, to call him when they got it. Asking, What happened to Moline?

Moline? He felt dizzy and threw up. Said it might be the flu. The tech hesitated, then continued. Actually, I believe his wife called right before that. I think they may be having problems.

You reckon?

Rule hung up the receiver, took off his shirt and boots, loosened his belt and laid on the bed. His lower back ached, all that driving. He awakened half an hour later from a dream he couldn't remember with the phone ringing. Over there on the chair, the cellular in his shirt pocket. He rolled off the bed and answered. Expecting the lab tech but it was Dana.

Rule, you mean thang, where are you, honey?

How'd you get this number?

Your work. Told 'em I was with the FBI, a secretary in the Houston office. Is that bad?

Where are you?

Home.

Where's Moline?

He's back in the den with a bottle. Don't worry, I'm in the kitchen.

Rule pushed the disconnect button and dropped the phone to the bed beside him. A moment later it rang again. He picked up. Yeah?

Dammit, don't you hang up on me, Rule. That's a—

He punched the button again and turned the phone off. He laid with one arm over his face and tried to recollect the dream, remembering it in glimpses, connecting the pieces. He was in Nam under a full moon playing poker on watch. Eating beans and motherfuckers on the side. Him and Slide Henderson playing stud poker and shooting the shit, laughing. Moonlight so bright the face cards were squinting. Then the dream abruptly stopped, frozen in the frame.

He got up and took a shower. He pressed his hands against the tiles under the nozzle and leaned forward, hot water streaming down his back. He closed his eyes, kicked the frame into motion, remembering. Nam still. But him a brown-bar lieutenant now, no longer laughing. The moon either full or not, you can't tell because of monsoon clouds and rain falling thicker than oil. On night patrol. So dark you lose balance. So dark on the trail you're holding the shirt of the guy in front and the guy in back's holding yours. Not to get left behind, not to get lost. The elephant grass brushing your face. Grass taller than a man. VC in the grass, waiting, listening. And some unthinking boot in back panics and hollers, Sonofabitch! Where you guys at! Everyone freezes. Then a flash and a sickening explosive pop, and the frame stops again.

Hell of a dream.

Rule stood with the water steaming down his back, feeling the rain, the night, the grass against his face, the sheer terror of it all. One of those dreams where you're on the verge of losing your nerve and you know it.

Only one problem: He'd never been in Nam. Slide Henderson, either. Slide was a professional gambler from Fort Worth, a poker player. Knew all about odds. No way he'd've gone to Nam.

Hell of a dream though.

Rule shut down the water and toweled off. Standing bareassed in the room with the towel around his neck, he called the lab on the cellular. Standing there lifting his nuts, one by one. They were drying up, no doubt about it. Not a good sign.

The lab answered on the fourth ring. Same technician. She sounded competent enough, all these young kids now with degrees in criminology and chemistry and genetics, it was a different world. Proving cases with evidence you can't even see, like a science fiction movie. And here he was sniffing down a trail like an old hound dog, looking for a lead, the old way, not even basic police work really, just intuition. Experience and a sensitive nose. Couldn't teach that in college.

The ballistics from Manvel were done. Same gun for Bernie, the Lomax woman and the kid. Nine millimeter automatic. Probably the case with the old man in Columbus but that forever uncertain since the slug had been damaged by someone at the Colorado Sheriff's Department.

Rule said, Grover.

Who?

Grover.

She said, Oh, then continued. A consultant from the school for the deaf had come in, looked at the first video, one with Abraham Krishna. The photographic section sped up the tape from five frames a second—store saving money, running a twentyfour hour loop—got it closer to real time. Argument over the cigarettes, the shooter a penny short, clerk wouldn't let it go. Nothing helpful on the prints though, none of them. And no more sign of the bad boys. There'd been several convenience store robberies in the Houston area since midafternoon, a routine day in 7-Eleven Land, but none of them our guys.

Rule said thanks and hung up. Thinking the gal had the lingo down, that was for sure. You'd think she was on *Law & Order*. Thinking Abe Krishna had taken his job just a tad too seriously. World full of nuts. Some of them with guns, one brick short of a load. Or one penny. Jesus. Thinking about five people dead, at least. Two of them, Abe and Bernie, over a missing one-cent piece. Dead and gone. Wondering how the actuaries would work that into the equation.

He got dressed and went out to eat.

The sun had set. Twilight lay over the landscape, the lights on the motel sign turned on, cicadas in the trees. The air smelled acrid, like creosote and sulphur. He didn't feel like driving so he crossed the road to a truckstop cafe that didn't seem busy. He took a corner table, ordered a chicken-fried steak with mashed potatoes and blackeyed peas and cornbread instead of rolls. A beer while he waited, another with the meal. A couple of local cops came in while he was eating and tried to strike up a conversation but he didn't feel like talking. They moved away, glancing back. It irritated him, the way cops thought of all law enforcement personnel as some sort of brotherhood. Like belonging to an Elks lodge.

Afterward he walked next door to Jack's Lounge, a small brick building, generic. The place inside was quiet, oilfield hands taking the edge off the day, the jukebox turned down low. He drank at the bar listening to George Strait and Alan Jackson until he got tired of standing and took a table to one side beneath a Busch sign lighted with a moving waterfall. He'd never seen anyone drink Busch but the signs were everywhere. He watched the water tumbling over the boulders while he drank. He'd been in the mountains in Colorado once and the sign reminded him of it.

It's pretty ain't it?

She stood beside his table holding a Tom Collins wrapped in a cocktail napkin. She wore a starched white blouse and pressed limegreen jeans and penny loafers, in her midthirties with short light brown hair and a wide face with large green eyes. Dressed casual but very neat. Nothing about her by accident. She motioned to the waterfall. Saying, I grew up there, in the mountains. And I still miss it. Can I join you?

Rule raised a hand palms up across the table, above the red glass globe in which a candle burned low. Part of Jack's generic decor. She sat down.

My name's Jan. She put out her hand and he took it. Her skin was soft but the handshake was firm. Making a statement. She could take care of herself.

Rule, he said, pleased to meet you.

Likewise. She smiled.

An hour later they were in his room in the bed but his heart wasn't in it. His prick was barely hard. Not limp exactly, but it bent if he wasn't careful so he was careful and he kept moving. He was working in close, thinking about his smartass advice to that sheriff in Colorado County. Thinking about his nuts drying up, thinking about himself. But he kept on moving, what you had to do. Watching her below. Face turned aside and eyes shut, she was moaning and she seemed sincere. Her thighs laid wide open, calves turned inward, heels resting on the backside of his knees. Meeting his every movement in kind, making it easy. Like she knew what she wanted and how to get there. Like she meant to come, no problem, and might get there soon. But the whole thing bored him, he was just going through motions, he'd been there before, too. Another rerun. And because there was nothing to it that would have caused him to offer more or even care if she asked for it, he soon quit trying and brought himself to a head and shot off, her reaching down to stroke his balls when his back arched. He rolled off and she laid alongside draped over him, sighing. She said it was good and he agreed. She said it wasn't like that every time. He allowed that was true, it was never the same way twice. Then he told her it sure had been fun but he needed to turn in. That he'd offer to walk her to her car but it was right across the road.

She didn't say anything when she got up to dress. She covered her feelings pretty well, he thought, which was a relief. But when she put her hand on the door to leave she turned and said, I won't offer to give my number.

Rule said, All right. Thinking, Here goes.

She said, You don't seem to want it.

He said, Don't get down this way much.

Yes, she said, I understand. You'd need a good reason.

I reckon.

Well, the picture's pretty clear. Still standing there with her hand on the doorknob, looking neat as a pin. Saying, You don't know what you're missing.

He figured he did and didn't feel like discussing it anymore so he told her to be careful and to keep it between the ditches. She didn't say anything after that and left with her head up.

He was glad she was gone but it was early yet and he couldn't sleep. He got up and dug into his overnight bag and came up holding the little book Katie had given him for his birthday. The one he always carried on out-of-town trips. A book of quotes, one for each day. He'd promised her he'd read it every morning or night, like a ritual, but hadn't for days. Maybe weeks. It occurred to him then that he ought to ask Katie about the dream. She was big on psychology, was studying it in school. Been reading a lot of women's stuff, she'd mentioned that much, about sex roles and self-image, about what men were up to. Something about power and control. That part mentioned with a disapproving frown. She kept a dream journal though. Maybe he'd ask.

If she ever made contact.

He missed her then, recollecting a time when she crawled into his lap every chance she got. When she was little. Cuddly little thing. He smiled, thinking about it. Katie in his lap, her mother next to them on the couch, cuddling too. Then he saw his ex standing in the bedroom doorway, crying, telling him she couldn't take it anymore. Telling him she'd tried. Saying, And the sad truth is, Rule, you didn't. You're a selfish sonofabitch.

He reckoned she was right.

Course, she'd been mad when she said it.

He lay on the bed and opened the book, turned through it looking for the last quote he'd read. He couldn't remember. Problem was, some of the stuff was pretty dense. It wasn't easy going. Seemed like most the quotes'd been culled from longer pieces that might've provided a little context, given it more sense. Sure wasn't like reading those Quotable Quotes in *Reader's Digest*. Those were to the point, entertaining.

He finally settled on reading the pages for the past three days. The first quote seemed overly sunny and the second made no sense one way or another. But the last one talked right at him. He read it twice. It was from some writer named Nietzsche. No idea how to pronounce it. Funny German name, a philosopher. He saw then the editor's note saying the guy had gone mad, died in an insane asylum.

He read the quote a third time:

"An image made this pale man pale. He was equal to his deed when he did it, but he could not bear its image after it was done.

Now he always saw himself as the doer of just one deed. Madness I call this, the exception having become his essence."

He thought about that. One deed. Damn right, that was all it took. He thought about it, and for a while forgot he was waiting.

25

Della washed up after supper and tracked the clock, intending to watch the ten o'clock news. There'd been nothing on the early shows. Sat there watching every word, too, mostly bored out of her mind except for the segment on summer bathing suits, how thong bikinis were back in. Watched *Live at Five* and then the *Six O'Clock Report*. Nothing.

A mention of the Mobil killing in Manvel was all. On both shows. That sure caught her attention. The reporter—a young Latino woman named Maria something or other, with an accent, real cute, and with eyes set a little too close, Della noticed that right off—said certain inside police sources had confidentially confirmed for this exclusive report that the Manvel robbery and murder—good lord, *murder*—fit in with a pattern of similar heinous crimes being perpetrated along a tragic trail between Austin and the Houston area, apparently by the same persons.

No, not persons. *Assailants*, the reporter had said. And not just assailants either. *Brutal* assailants. Brutal assailants on a wild crime spree across Texas marked by violence and death. Della had sat bugeyed and watched, saying good lord, good lord.

Now, arms to elbows in dishwater, she closed her eyes and spouted air, ruffling her bangs. She still couldn't believe it. Just couldn't. Didn't want to. Good grief, Ray Bob had shot that boy in each *eye*ball. Pure meanness, all that was. And him sitting there in front of the TV bragging about it. About getting that second shot off true while the boy was falling, a moving target. It turned her stomach. No way she could keep quiet.

Well, that don't impress me none, she'd told him. And he'd said, Yeah? You try it then. And she'd replied she didn't care to, she wasn't that kind of person. Well, what kind are you? he'd said. She'd told him then she was a different kind of person. She said she had goals in life, and that becoming a brutal assailant wasn't one of them. That shooting young boys in the eyeballs wasn't her idea of a good time. That wild crime sprees across Texas weren't up her alley. He'd replied he wasn't so sure about that, and then he laughed.

Eddie just sitting there not saying one word in her defense.

She stacked a red plastic plate in the drainboard, her eye roving to the clock above the refrigerator, hanging cockeyed on an exposed two-by-four stud. Almost ten o'clock. If they didn't say anything about Mister Dreamboat on the news she'd buy a paper tomorrow. You'd think it would be on the TV, though, the way they reported. If it wasn't for murders and fatal accidents, there wouldn't hardly be any news. Plus him being Mister Fortune Five Hundred, which ought to mean something. He'd sure thought it did.

Maybe he lied.

That gave her pause. She hadn't thought about that. But the guy must've been important somehow, way he was dressed, the way he acted. He was *some*body. And being discovered naked in bed with a knife in his chest? That should've been news no matter what. Assistant manager of a Taco Bell gets found like that, it's on the news. TV all over it, as if the president'd been shot.

She wished she'd bought a newspaper. They were more thorough, had more space. *Houston Chronicle* thick as a Wards catalog. She'd've bought one earlier but they were in such a rush she wasn't thinking straight. No wonder. It wasn't easy trying to think of everything you had to think about when you were a wanted criminal.

Which she had to assume she was.

Plus now she was consorting with a couple of *real* criminals, wanted all over it looked like. Well, one anyway. Eddie she wasn't sure about. But Ray Bob wasn't nuthin but bigtime trouble. Think the police weren't hot on their trail? They didn't even seem that worried. And here she was right in the middle. It was some kinda way to try and escape notice. Like jumping from the frying pan into the fire. Might as well be wearing a T-shirt with big letters saying: WANTED CRIMINAL, HERE I AM.

Five minutes to ten.

She scrubbed the aluminum pot and rinsed it, put it on the drainboard. One lonely pot. Not even a skillet in the kitchen. You'd expect that of LD but she thought Ruby would've done something about the situation. A single pot to cook a box of macaroni and cheese, wash it out, cook a box of chicken-flavored Rice A Roni, wash the pot again, and finally heat up some canned ravioli. What a hassle. Took forever practically. And then Ray Bob griping because the macaroni and cheese was cold. Cook it yourself, she'd told him, think you can do better. I'm not a woman, he'd said, like that was some kind of argument. There was about a hundred things she could've replied to that, but all she said was, Eddie liked it.

Eddie of course saying nothing.

She snorted and dried her hands, then straightened her hair, went around the kitchen table and the opening in the floor for the downstairs stairwell to the TV spot. The house was big enough but it wasn't divided into rooms with walls like a normal house. Not one wall in it. The stairs came up in the middle from the concrete slab below, like steps coming up from a cellar, and then nothing but one giant room. Tall screened windows with open shutters running the length of every wall. Beds off in the corners as if that offered some kind of privacy. Like a kid's oversized playhouse. Or a hunting camp. The bathroom no more than a toilet bowl and rusty halfplugged showerhead behind a plastic curtain. The curtain hanging from pieces of plastic plumbing pipe with elbows, fastened to exposed studs beside the refrigerator and stove. Bathroom right in the kitchen, some kind of planning. Sit down to potty and people eating at the table hear everything. What kind of privacy was that? Another thing Ruby fell down on.

And no telephone. She'd forgot about that.

Only good thing about the situation was, she wasn't sitting around back home in Sugar Land waiting to get arrested.

Della sat down in an old La-Z-Boy recliner that LD must've brought to the beach after he wore it out back in Houston. It fit in with the rest of the furniture though. Beat up and shapeless. Eddie and Ray Bob were sprawled on the floor in front of the TV. Watching some special report with Ed Bradley exposing abuses in the chicken farm industry. The only other choice being a *Three's Company* episode on the second channel. Ray Bob had said no way, he wasn't watching John Ritter, guy was a pussy.

She listened to the TV. Ed Bradley talking now about chicken farmers, what they did with all that chicken shit. Man, I never thought about that part, Eddie was saying over Ed Bradley's voice, that's a shitload of shit. Ed Bradley, dressed up in a khaki jacket like he was on safari, summing up now, saying, Whether the farmers and regulatory agencies come to some agreement remains to be seen. It's a story we will continue to follow. For now, the two sides are far apart, and neither appears willing to compromise in this game of chicken.

Ray Bob, lying on his back with his arms under his head, said, Man, that's real cute, listen to the jigaboo talk. I could write that shit. He rolled to his side and reached up scratching an armpit. Saying, Can't believe you can't get but two fuckin channels here.

After about five years of commercials, the ten o'clock local news came on with a fanfare. The anchor team, a guy dressed like a new-car salesman with coiffed hair and a woman who looked maybe half Mexican and half Chinese, said there'd been another Indian massacre in Mexico and a major mud slide in California. Also, a fatal car bomb in Tel Aviv. Many deaths, lots of footage. They also promised a stunning report on how to get more for your money buying automatic garage door openers. Plus a special segment on buying supermarket chicken while avoiding bacteria. They didn't mention Ed Bradley's report. Then they cut to more commercials.

Think we'll be on? Eddie asked.

Naw, Ray Bob said, we already been on it twice. Want on it again, we gonna have to shoot somebody new.

I just as soon you wouldn't, said Della. I'd like a little peace and quiet.

You want peace and quiet, Ray Bob said, move to Iowa.

Della said maybe she would.

Ray Bob said they could put her on a bus tomorrow.

Della said she would schedule her own life, thank you.

Eddie said, Hey guys, how about some cards? Yanking on his earring, he picked up a deck of cards off the TV stand, began shuffling them fast. Maybe some three-way rummy?

Ray Bob said he wasn't interested. He went out the screen door onto the deck facing the beach and sat on the rail smoking. The crescent moon was up but a reef of highpiled clouds moving in off the gulf snuffed it. The breeze stiffened and smelled like rain. His nostrils prickled with ozone. Within minutes the first drops fell, large marshmallow spheres that splattered on the deck and rail and drove him back under the narrow eaves. The rain cut the heat and salt from the air, cleared his head. He thought about the kid at the Mobil station, pictured the second bullet hitting the bull's-eye, the juice squirting out. Even now, remembering it for the umpteenth time, it surprised him. He'd never been that good a shot, least not with a handgun. He smoked and watched the rain for a while, then thumped the butt into the wet darkness over the deck rail and went inside.

On the TV the weatherman was promising overnight showers and cloudy skies clearing by sunrise. Colored maps and satellite pictures, a tidal schedule, barometrics and dew points, more weather than you cared to know. Then came sports and some guy waving his arms, yelling about the scores.

Della said, Well, it wasn't on there. She sounded disappointed.

I figgered you'd be glad, Eddie said. He sat crosslegged on a frayed piece of outdoor carpet—LD's idea of a rug—playing solitaire, frowning. Said, I think this deck's missing a king.

Ray Bob stood just inside the door with his thumbs hooked in his back pants pockets. They any beer joints near here?

Della said there were beer joints all up and down the beach road. You didn't see them?

He didn't reply. After a minute, he disappeared down the stair-well. They heard him below trying to get the top up on the Caddy.

He yelled a couple of times, cussing, then made some banging noises, and then silence. He reappeared shortly and went to a bed in one corner and stripped down to his shorts and climbed in it. Della watched sideways, shifting her eyes away when Eddie looked up.

They turned off the TV and lights after Letterman's opening monologue, went to bed in the far corner from Ray Bob. While they were undressing, Eddie said, I never could understand why folks watch that guy, he's a smart aleck.

Della told him that's why people watched. She said, David gets to say stuff in public you can't. Eddie replied that he could if he wanted to, only the things he really wanted to say didn't occur to him until it was too late, usually. Della said, Well, that's another reason.

They lay naked on the sheet which was damp and cool next to the screen window and listened to the raindrops fall against the roof. It was dark without moonlight, without starlight. The steady random patter was soothing, hypnotic. After a while, Della said for another thing the show was taped ahead of time and he had writers. Eddie observed that was cheating but it didn't surprise him to hear it. She said everyone cheats, even in the modeling business, it being part of the fashion industry. Though their voices were low, almost whispers, the sounds seemed to violate the low murmuring lilt of the rainfall in darkness, and they soon quit talking.

Della lay there wondering how Eddie might look in a nice Ralph Lauren suit. Eddie thinking about the kid in Manvel, the girls up in Austin, all the rest, the A-rab. Feeling limp down there, wondering if the forgiveness thing had been a oneshot deal.

After a while, Della reached over and laid her hand on his belly. He let it abide there, feeling the softness and the heat from her hand rising and falling with his breathing. Then he began to stir, and then he rolled over smoothly and she took him between her legs.

She was careful not to make noise, did not move much. Nor did he. They took a long time and when they were done they did not talk about it. They lay on the bed with the breeze silting through the screen and the rain subsiding, falling gently now.

And they passed into sleep.

Across the wide room, in his bed in the darkness, Ray Bob lay listening.

26

Sunrise found him in the truckstop cafe across the road eating venison sausage with hash browns and fried eggs and a side of homemade buttermilk biscuits he dipped in Steen's sugarcane syrup. Washing it down with steaming mugs of black coffee. Watching truckers and roughnecks doing the same before a long day on the road or in the oilfields.

He sat at a table by the front window. Showers had moved through during the night, and the sun rose bleeding in the east through jagged scraps of clouds, detritus abandoned by the front. Puddles in the oyster shell lot lay under the quickening sky like dark pools of blood.

Shortly after he was rolling west on a narrow ranch road as the sun topped the horizon, a fat red globule in his mirror. He rode up over the flatlands leaving the delta behind and the coastal marshes, climbing the imperceptible uplift of the ancient seabed into grassy prairies. Near Danciger he cut back east toward the San Bernard River, then pulled into a dirt lane across a cattle guard. He stopped before a small woodframe house with an oleander hedge lining the yard to one side, the slender blooms magenta starbursts, and a trellis of flowering jasmine shading the front porch. He got out.

An old man using a cane came out onto the porch. He was a short and angular man, with wide shoulders bent forward over a sunken torso and bowed legs above muleskinner boots. He wore khakis, a faded flannel shirt. His gaunt nutcolored face was furrowed and cracked by the tributaries of many years, the story of his life written thereon. He waited, head cocked aside, squinting with milky gray eyes until the visitor came striding into the yard.

Rule Hooks, he said.

That's right, Jedidiah. You still know how to listen.

Right foot's heavier than the left, the old man said, always was. Guess it always will be. He turned and sat down on a wood bench set back against the wall. You had your morning mud?

I did.

Have a seat.

Rule shook hands with the old man, then sat on a cowhide chair facing him. Jedidiah Comfort, who had brought none of that name to uncounted others wanted for one reason or another by the law during his fortyfive years as a Ranger. He'd killed a dozen men and shot many more, been shot several times himself and knifed more than once. Most of that from horseback. When his last ride got nailed and rolled him under, the force retired him crippled. A ceremony in Austin with the colonel presiding, then he returned to the family homestead to live alone, a widower twice over.

You looking fit, Jedidiah.

Can't say as I noticed. Mostly go by hearing and smell now. What I hear's got three legs and smells a little ripe.

He chuckled and rested the cane—a smooth length of ironwood with a rawhide knob, a used twelvegauge shotgun shell for the tip—against one thigh. The old Ranger rubbed the thigh through the khakis, the dark leatherskinned hand twisted by arthritic fury. He waited a while, until the silence was primed, then snorted. Said, Ever wonder why they call it the golden years?

Reckon I ain't.

Well, you will.

He leaned sideways and spat into a brass spittoon beside the bench. Shortly, a saddlebacked Walker hound came round the side of the house and padded up the porch to lay at his feet. Jim Dandy, sire of Lefty.

Rule said his name and the dog looked. He said his name again, Jim Dandy, then said, Your boy Lefty's doing fine, thought you'd wanna know. Coming right along. The hound flicked an ear and slowly laid his muzzle in his paws.

Jedidiah said, If Lefty takes after his daddy he's a goodun. He grinned. When he takes a mind to, I mean. The momma now, she never had much get up an go. You after them boys?

I am.

The old man nodded. I heared it on the radio. They leaving some spoor.

They are at that, Rule said. He took off his hat and laid it over a knee. Only it ain't telling me much. Not yet.

It will.

I know it.

A meadowlark whistled in the field and they listened. Sunlight fell through the jasmine trellis in tatters over the porch. The day was well up now, the dew off the grass. The sweet aroma of jasmine lay on the air. Rule looked out beyond the yard at the green fields spotted with scrub oak and mesquite, toward a pasture in which a single Hereford grazed.

Only that's not all that's on your mind.

Rule said, No, it ain't.

Jedidiah rubbed his mouth with the back of one hand, wiped it on his trousers. Said, Hard for a man to track when his mind ain't clear. Don't hear good, smells get past him.

I know it.

The old man closed his eyes. He picked up the cane, gripped it upright between his legs, his thin lips wrinkled in a smile. Said—

Recollect a time I was tracking a Mex'can down in Zapata County. Working outa Company D, based in an adobe shack down near Bustamante. Trouble with rustlers pushing those longhorns across the Rio into Old Mexico. So I pegged a trail. There I was, down in that desert up some arroyo. Red sand, prickly pear and ocotillo everywhere you looked. On foot, leading my horse. So hot you couldn't breathe. Nuthin moving but a lizard's eye. The devil's country, it was, still is if it ain't changed, a taste of what's to come, I reckon. Two days in, I can't turn back, done run out of water. My tongue swole up like a snakebit foot and it's about all I can think about. A big old glass of wet water, what I was thinking about. And that's when he raised up behind a prickly bush and put one in me. Right here.

He reached up a wad of gnarled fingers and touched his right collarbone. Said—

Man, that burned. Bounced off the bone up instead of down though, I was lucky. Hit the ground grabbing for my Colt with the wrong hand. He had an old Mauser Ninety-eight and the bolt action jammed. So I was lucky twice and that's more'n you can expect. I got my gun in the right hand and shot him in the head once, then shot him again cause I was mad.

He bent sideways and spat into the spittoon and wiped his mouth.

Course it was my own damn fault. Sure you don't want some coffee?

Rule picked up his hat off his knee and held it. Thanks, Jedidiah, but I better be moving along. It's good to see you.

They both rose then and they shook and Rule went down the steps into the yard. He turned and looked back. Jedidiah stood on the porch with the cane in front, leaning on it with both hands, Jim Dandy heeled beside him.

The old man nodded. Appreciate your stopping by. How's the daughter?

She's fine. Enrolled at the university, don't see her much.

She's growed up.

That's right.

Well, it happens. Come for dinner next time.

I'll do that.

Rule started to put on his hat but instead held it by the brim with both hands and said, Tell me something, Jedidiah. You ever lose your nerve?

The old man tapped his cane against the porchboards three times. Thinking, remembering. Staring off into whatever range or circumference that held what he yet could see, face impassive, his cloudy gray eyes nearly shut in that nutbrown terrain.

Nossir, he said finally, I haven't. But I got the feeling I'm going to.

Rule put his hat on. I doubt that.

Well, that might be, Jedidiah said. He lifted one hand up and forward as though pushing away a fly. Yessir, it could go that way too. Like I said, I been lucky.

You been more'n that, Rule said. A good might more. I expect it'll hold.

It surely will—if it does.

Rule started his truck and drove away down the dirt lane across the cattle guard toward the county road. The last he saw of Jedidiah in the mirror the old man was still standing on the porch with Jim Dandy at his side. Standing there waiting. Listening. The soft call of the ferryman in his ears. A faint scent of the eternal river in his nib.

27

Harvey Lomax awakened on the front seat of his wrecker. He lay twisted on his side, left shoulder crimped beneath his weight, socked feet jammed against the inside passenger door panel. He ached all over, the sun hurt his eyes, his socks were still wet.

He sat up.

An altogether miserable night. Late in the evening, he'd parked his wrecker behind the motel where the Ranger wouldn't see it. Spread an old bumper quilt on the ground beneath the hoist and tried to sleep there. The mosquitos like some plague the Lord brought down on Egypt. He rolled up in the oily quilt, head tucked inside, smothering. Comforting himself with the reminder that this ol' world was nothing but toil and trouble. This life nothing but torment.

Then came the rain.

It drove him under the truckbed. Right after came the water, washing over him in rivulets, soaking the ground. It chased him into the cab around midnight. Like a sauna in there. The seat short and narrow, him curled up like a fetus in his coveralls.

Sometime during the night the rain let off and he took off his boots, stretched out on the seat with his feet out the open window. The mosquitos returned. He rolled up the windows and resigned himself to misery.

He sat in the cab now, thinking. It had been a test, what it'd been. The Lord testing his commitment.

Well, he'd passed.

He ran a big roughskinned hand over his face and opened the truck door. The heat of the morning washed over him. The sun stood at eight or nine and he quickly pulled the scarred leather workboots over the wet socks and waded through the damp grass around the side of the motel and checked the Ranger's cabin. The pickup was gone. He knew then he'd lost him again.

The first time being yesterday.

Back at the station in Brookshire he'd heard the Ranger tell Chief Wharton he was heading toward Freeport. So he'd followed. Followed after the chief had told him to go home, take a shower, get a nap, maybe pray a little. A little? A *little*? Lord, he hadn't stopped since those boys shot Maxine, killed her dead, right there in the Exxon, behind the counter, a cigarette in her hand. Shot down like an animal, like some heathen dog. Nothing left for him now but torment, but grief. And the chief thinks a little prayer's gonna cure that?

So he'd promised the chief, drove off in the wrecker toward home. Then circled back, followed the Ranger. Because the other promise was higher. Vengeance is mine, saith the Lord. Romans twelve and nineteen. The Lord shall take vengeance on his adversaries. Nahum one and two. For the day of vengeance is in mine heart. Isaiah sixtythree and four. And my heart is his heart and his vengeance mine. The meaning being clear: I am His vessel and His tool. His weapon. The Lord's work will be done, and it is upon me to do it. Which I will.

As he'd promised.

So he'd come down over the flatlands in pursuit, pushing the wrecker so hard he feared his heart might burst. The motor wound so tight he dared not push harder. And yet he had. Coaxing it, urging it onward. The tall grass beside the road passing in a blur, the green fields one like the other, peripheral nothings outside the existence of the narrow asphalt surface rushing beneath the onslaught of the wheels, the motor, his heart, his promise.

And in that way caught him. Just north of Brazoria the Ranger's Dodge pickup appeared ahead in the gray range like a mirage suddenly thrust upon him, and he backed off the speed and trailed it down into the delta through Lake Jackson into Freeport. Then lost it near the Surfside bridge. One moment it was there and the next moment not.

Gone.

He had despaired then. Had parked the wrecker beside the road and wept. And then found renewed strength through prayer, through faith. Loss of hope being a sin. A voice speaking to him, saying the Ranger would return if he waited. Become the virgin in the garden while the bridegroom tarries. Sleep not, hold the faithful vigil. The voice saying: Let not the lamp go out. Which he had not done. Nor had the voice been wrong. An hour later came back the red pickup to his tendered belief and he followed it again until it drew into this motel near the Brazos. Where the Ranger took a room.

And again he waited, watching. Crouching alongside the motel in the shadows, as vigilant as a predawn passing of time in a deer stand. Alert, wary, patient. For some time nothing, then the tall Ranger crossing the road to the truckstop. Supper in the cafe, dessert in a beer joint. Returned to his cabin with a woman. Who left sometime later, weeping. The light in the cabin remaining on for a while, finally extinguished.

Then he laid his quilt on the ground behind the wrecker but could not sleep. Mosquitos and rain only a part of it. Yet another torment: Wondering what sort of wretched man was this Ranger who in his sacred duty to enforce the law found time for food, for drink, for women. Who besmirched the purity of an inviolable task with the casual transgressions of a reprobate. This question plaguing his aching brain more than insects. Him wrestling with this demon in the rain. Moaning. Praying. Begging for an answer. Then getting it. Came the voice again, saying the moral depravity of the Ranger was beside the point. The Ranger merely a tool, but a guide. Leading him, Harvey Lomax, toward a higher goal. A divine if impure polar star for a truer vengeance and for a truer heart, his own.

And now he stood in the morning heat knowing he had lost him again, the star faded into daylight, disappeared. He had slept too long. The lamp run out of oil, the vigil failed. Once again the despair came over him. He had not passed the test after all. Weak flesh, weak flesh.

Lomax stared at the cottage where the Ranger had been and now was not, then beat himself on the head with his fists. He fell to his knees and wept, then prayed. Then finally he arose and strode through the weeds to the front of the motel into the office. The clerk behind the desk, a short heavyset woman, dark skinned, gazed at the fierce coarse-featured face beneath the disheveled hair and took a step backward holding a ballpoint pen with both hands like a cross.

Yes, she said, I help you?

I'm lookin for a feller with a red truck. That Ranger.

The woman blinked, gripping the pen. *No esta*, she said. Is gone.

He check out?

No, *senor*.

All right.

Lomax turned abruptly and went out across the road to the cafe. In the restroom he washed his face with cold water. He pulled the Dickeys coveralls to his waist and splashed his knotted arms and shoulders, the pale chest, toweled off with handfuls of toilet paper. Then he sat near the front window and ate a bowl of oatmeal and drank black coffee. He lingered so long the waitress twice asked if he was finished. He heard the meaning in her voice so ordered another bowl of oatmeal and ate that too.

Sometime late midmorning the red pickup appeared on the road and turned into the motel. Lomax watched the Ranger get out, go into his cottage. He paid his bill and loped across the highway down the backside of the motel to his wrecker. *Waller County Wrecker Service* painted on the door panel in white cursive letters. Below that: IN GOD WE TRUST.

He started the motor, moved the wrecker forward until he could just see the back end of the Dodge pickup, shut down the engine, opened the window and waited. Crickets in the field, humming. The sun blazing overhead, the air hanging heavy and humid. By noon he was nodding off so he got out and walked around the truck several times and stretched.

He leaned against the front fender, lamenting that his own sanctified mission should be subsidiary to that of a man who would hole up in a motel room while killers stalked the earth. That he should receive a guide who suffered neither the ardency of justice nor its urgency. He recognized then the doubt coherent in this lamentation and he felt remorse. Kneeling to the ground beside the wrecker he asked for forgiveness and for patience and it came forthwith and he cried. Head in hands, he leaned against the fender and wept for his weakness and for a suffering that approached not near what his beloved wife had endured in her own recent calamity. The sin of self-pity.

Afterward he felt cleansed. And in such revived state he returned to the cab of the wrecker and waited. The sun beat down, nothing moved. Not even the wind, not even the eye of a blackbird. Yet he did not doze or sleep. He reached into the pocket of his coveralls and removed the small scrap of paper on which he had written the name Chief Wharton had cited. He studied it.

Darees Ledoo.

He did not know what sort of name it was nor did he care. Only that it was the name. And with it the man. And in that man's heart born of flesh the evil that all men carry. But this one's lately made manifest. His fate now decided.

Lomax stuffed the paper back into his coveralls pocket and leaned over to partly unwrap what lay folded in a blanket on the far floorboard. He examined what was there. An immaculately cared for bigbore 460 Weatherby with a 3.5-14X Leupold Premium Scope. Something to bring down rhinos. And a German .357 Sig Sauer, spotless, gleaming with a slight sheen of oil.

That was it. A rifle, a pistol. They were all he'd brought. That and the small New Testament he kept in the glovebox. But they would do. For so much as the Holy Word, so did the rifle, the pistol speak. They said: Lord, behold, here are two swords. And he said unto them, It is enough.

Luke twentytwo and thirtyeight.

28

Saying—

Even as pharaonic Egyptians carved prosaic hieroglyphs upon stone, the primordial sea embraced rushing rivers here, where we stand, and left the distinctive signature of an uneasy treaty, the barriers islands, of which this peninsula is a part.

Saying—

An uneasy and provisional treaty inscribed on sand. Each grain an ancient survivor, immortal, witness of the Cretaceous, Jurassic, Triassic, Permian, and Carboniferous. A witness to the ages. Let us listen, for example, to this single voice.

The bearded man with glasses bent down to the beach. Fiftyish, heavyset, thick blackhaired legs exposed between khaki shorts and hiking boots. He rose with an arm extended, a clenched overturned hand. Protruding from the hand one stubby forefinger. A solitary grain of sand presumably resting upon it.

Saying—

This single peripatetic grain began its life one billion years ago. A thousand incarnations since. Resting on Cambrian seabeds, buried deep within the bowels of the earth by spectacular tectonic events, thrust back upward by certain others. Fused in great metamorphic mountains, exposed by erosion, methodically ground from its nomadic tribesmen, separated, then released back to primeval sea. Abandoned thereafter as the great waters retreat, windblown and crushed by heat, by ice, washed downward by rivers, into the sea yet again, then cast back on the rolling surge of longshore drift. Gathering finally in the communion of islands, peninsulas, the planar barrier shore. All that, my friends, recorded on the surface of this single fugitive grain of quartz. Let the Egyptians surpass that!

The students gathered round the man leaned forward, frowning, notebooks clasped to chests, staring at his outstretched finger as though they might indeed find written on that minuscule blond particle the very story he had told.

A protracted silence.

Then, said one, I don't see nuthin, and the others giggled.

The professor, unsurprised, looked at the boy. He flicked his finger with disgust, wiped it on his shirt.

Saying—

A failure of the imagination, as usual. Science is an allegory of fact bound by theory, circumscribed only by the limits of the human mind. Yours, unfortunately, is limited in every respect, Rusty.

The boy shrugged indifferently, the others grinned with malice. Then the professor stalked away, the clump of students following him up the beach.

Eddie watched them go. From some college in Beaumont, on a field trip. He'd followed for a while, curious, listening to the teacher describe tubebuilding worms that lived beneath the beach, ghost shrimps in subterranean silos, mucus-secreting mollusks and weird snails that sucked the juices of clams. The guy could really talk. The students, though, were morons. Making cute remarks, yawning, exchanging eyerolls.

They disappeared behind a low grassy dune and Eddie picked up a piece of driftwood. He wrote his name in the sand. A wave rolled over, the water rushing forward to obscure it. Several more surges and his name disappeared. Gone. How it went, him and everybody. No choice, except maybe when, maybe how, if you call that a choice. You be, or not be. Try to understand: not being. Too big to grasp.

Eddie thinking about that clerk up in Austin, the A-rab or whatever he was. Here one minute, gone the next. There, then not. Dead, man. Just like that. Guy probably had people missing him, grieving.

Cause he killed him.

Gone.

He tossed the stick aside. It landed on a gooey patch of oil stranded on the beach. The brown beach was densely strewn with such patches, and with plastic jugs, pieces of nylon rope, glass bottles, garbage. Most of it discards from offshore rigs and boats. Eddie standing there thinking he couldn't read a grain of sand, but he sure could read a beach. Jesus. Letters ten feet high. People were filthy.

He turned his gaze toward the horizon, toward the waves, the near heaving surface and silty surf. Here comes one. Whoops, there's another. Wasn't this fun? Staring at the waves with a beer in his hand. Like they was something to see. Like something might happen if he stood there long enough.

And it did. The beer got warmer, the wind more hot and humid. He was sweating. Sand between his toes, sand between his teeth. A sea of sand. Thinking, No goddamn joke, one fuckin wave looked like any other. Thinking you'd *have* to be a professor to find this shit interesting.

Then thinking about that A-rab again. And the girl up in the park, weeping. Lying on her side by the creek, shaking. Terrified. Man oh man. All that pain, all that grief. Cause of him. Made him feel . . . what?

Regret.

He swallowed the last of the warm beer and tossed the can into the surge, watched it float out on the ebb, and back, then out again and back. It wasn't going anywhere so he turned and trudged up the dirty rutted incline between low windtossed dunes where cars drove onto the beach. He saw Della lying on the deck of the beach house sunning. The Caddy was gone. Ray Bob running the beach road, hitting the beer joints, searching for the coldest beer. So he'd said.

Eddie went under the house and up the steps inside, then out on the deck. Della lay facedown on a large striped towel, skin smeared with tanning oil. Her head propped up, reading the *Houston Chronicle*. The Gideon Bible lay next to her.

Eddie said, You bring that Bible?

Della said she'd put it in her bag without thinking, but it was good to have. Just in case.

You been reading it?

Well, I've been *looking* at it.

Eddie observed that's how most Bibles got read, far as he could tell.

That's not what I meant, Della said, opening the comics section. I been reading the parts in red letters, where Jesus is talking.

What'd he say?

He said try to be nice to people. Like if you was to put some more oil on my back? She reached around to unfasten the strap of her twopiece. Saying, You know I just bought this thing last year and already it's out of style.

What's wrong with it?

How big it is. I need me a thong.

Eddie said she might as well go naked. She said that wouldn't be very nice, then he straddled her thighs and slathered on the tanning oil while she read the comics. When she laughed, he asked what was funny.

Garfield. He's so *cute*.

He leaned forward to see over her shoulder. Who?

Garfield. She pointed. You don't know Garfield?

Eddie looked at the drawing. That a coon?

A cat, silly. Della said madeup characters never looked exactly like the real thing, that's why they're called characters.

He does. Eddie pointing to Dagwood. He closed the bottle of oil and wiped his hands along his arms, scooted over the deck until his back met the wall, in the shade beneath the eaves. Saying, Looks just like my old man, the way his hair pokes out.

Della said that made twice Eddie'd mentioned him, his daddy. She lifted her calves vertical and wiggled her toes. Her toenails were painted green. She said, You musta loved him.

Eddie looked out over the near dunes and beach and the rolling gulf beyond. Smelling the breeze rising off it, brackish and hot, the faint aroma of crude oil and seaweed. Wondering, trying to remember.

Saying—

He was alright, a little crazy. Tough old geezer. Drank a lot. Didn't have much education, grew up down in the swamp, quit the third grade. Trapped nutria and gators til he was nineteen and discovered dry land. Said he didn't know until then most folks lived without mold between their toes. Give his pirogue to his brother and moved to Lafayette, hired on as a pipefitter, got married. Never could keep up, though, moneywise.

Saying—

His paycheck gone before he got it. Rent, kids, groceries, you name it. Living on the installment plan. Everything on discount or layaway. Still falling behind. And everybody calling it progress, that part confused him. Bill collectors come round, he'd get that crazy look and head to the beer joint and tank up, get in a fistfight. Didn't matter whether he won or lost, though, them debts still there. How poor folks, working people live. That's their life, fighting to catch up, drinking to stay alive. Some things never change. You can write that down in stone.

He set an elbow on a knee and shaded his eyes with one hand. The sunlight reflecting off the distant water and a sky clear as glass hurt to see. But remembering.

Saying—

One thing for damn sure, he could play that fiddle. It was old and beat up, looked like shit, but he could make it sing. Sit in with the boys on Saturday night and play that Cajun twostep, arms a flying like a little banty rooster, bringing down the house. Only time I ever seen him happy, that fiddle under his chin, making music. Most the time he was busy feeling guilty, what my momma said.

About what?

I dunno. Everything, I reckon. Don't you ever feel guilty?

Oh yeah, Della said, all the time. I think it's normal.

My old man never seemed normal.

Well, you have to talk about it. If you keep stuff inside it makes you crazy. That's why there's more unstable men than women. Women talk more.

You read that somewhere?

In a magazine, Della said, *Redbook* I think, they run good articles. But I already knew it. Women are smarter too.

Eddie said he wouldn't know about that, he didn't meet too many smart people, one way or the other.

That might be because of the circles you run in.

He allowed that some of the smartest people he'd ever met were in prison, and they didn't talk hardly at all. And the crazy ones talked all the time.

Della said that didn't sound right.

Eddie observed that wasn't his fault. Said, So what you got to feel guilty about? You got a secret?

Della laid her chin on her hands. Maybe.

What is it?

You tell me one and I'll tell you mine.

Eddie gazed up the beach. He saw the professor and his gaggle of students emerge from the dunes. They strolled along the waterline, scattering sandpipers and plovers, the bearded man gesticulating dramatically. The students lagged behind, strung out in a broken line of sulky draftees on patrol. Eddie thinking you can lead a horse to water.

All right, he said, tell me.

Della saying, No, you go first. Only it's got to be a real secret. It ain't one if Ray Bob knows.

He don't know.

Okay, what.

He started to say take your pick, I got plenty, then said, My real name ain't Eddie.

Della giggled. Really?

That's right.

What is it?

Wade.

She curled her mouth and squinted at him skeptically. You don't look like no Wade.

Well, that don't matter. It's my name. Was named for my mother's brother Uncle Wade. Only keep calling me Eddie, okay?

Okay.

Your turn.

Della frowned, thinking, trying to choose. There was Mister Dreamboat, for starters, and not one friggin word about him in

the newspaper, either. She'd looked on every page, even the business section. She couldn't imagine what the problem was. Mister
Busy Executive dead and not one mention anywhere, like it didn't
even matter.

You must have a lot of secrets, Eddie said, take that long.

Well, I'm trying to remember one, Della replied, on account of
I'm a woman and we don't keep secrets much. Okay, I got one.
Ready?

All ears.

Okay, remember how I was telling you about my modeling
career? She waited, scratching one thigh, looking at him.

When she didn't say anymore Eddie said sure, okay, he remembered. What about it?

Well, that's not exactly true.

All right then. Eddie shrugged. You ain't a model?

Della said, Of course I'm a model, Eddie, but I didn't just start.
What I meant is, I been at it a while. To tell the truth, I started in
junior high.

Is that right?

Yeah. Then I got kinda heavy and quit. Now I'm in my second
phase.

No kidding.

Well, I realize it's not much, Della said, a little disappointed.
But it's sumthin you didn't know.

You right, Eddie said. What else you fib about?

29

Rule was on the cellular with Moline when the telephone in the
motel cottage rang. It was the desk clerk saying there'd been
someone by the office asking about him. He told her he'd call her
back, returned to Moline.

Come again?

A nine millimeter Walther, Moline said, Model P-Ninety-nine most likely. That's what Redhead's using. Doing all the shooting now, too. He's the badass.

Rule said that didn't surprise him, what he expected. Only the boys were running together, both bad, one just worse than the other. Or maybe DeReese was taking a breather. Hard to say.

Well, that's all we got, Moline said, and I been scratching. Still no ID on Redhead or the girl. Fellow down at HPD said he thought DeReese was in the Houston area but there's no listing and the file's out of date. He was on parole but they cut back staff, terminated him early. Saving them tax dollars. What happens when you got a governor wants to be president. But the guy promised to ask around.

All right. Thanks, Moline. That it?

Rule got up from the vinyl upholstered chair and spread the venetian blinds with two fingers. He looked through the bright sunlit crack. Hot as a firecracker out there. Inside the room with the air conditioner it was cool. The lights were off and the room was dark. Rule was in his undershirt.

Moline said, That's it. What're you doing?

Only thing there is to do. Waiting.

Rule shut off the cellular and sat down in the dark, pulled his boots off. Then reached for the room telephone and called the front desk. The clerk told him a man had come in asking about him. A man who seemed maybe strange. The clerk said, I tell him, no is here, no no, maybe later. I call, warn you. Because he look *poquito loco*. He don't leave a name.

Then, almost as an afterthought: I am sorry to make offense, *senor*, if this man is your friend or like that.

Rule told her not to worry, to describe the man. Had to be Harvey Lomax. He thanked the clerk and told her to call if the man returned. He'd no more than hung up when the cellular rang again. He answered it.

Yeah?

Hey there, what're you doing?

Playing like a fuckin phone operator.

Well, no need to get nasty.

When he didn't reply she said, Sounds to me like you need a backrub. Where are you?

Freeport.

Way down there? What for?

Waiting.

All by your lonesome? In a lonely ol' motel? Using her kitten voice.

Maybe.

I could come down and wait with you, help pass the time. Purring now.

Might get crowded.

For a moment she was silent. What, you got someone with you?

Rule said you never know. Said he had to run.

Why you being so *mean* to me, Rule?

We done been through that.

You know I miss you, hon. Purring again.

I gotta go.

He punched the button and turned the phone off. He stripped down and took a long shower, then stretched out on the bed. Wondering where they were. Thinking maybe they'd headed north into Galveston, after all. Maybe that feeling had been right. Maybe they'd done gone up the coast to Louisiana, skipped jurisdiction. Or maybe not. Maybe they were holed up in Houston. Maybe, maybe, no telling. It was goddamn guesswork until they hit again or something turned up. In the meantime, nothing to do.

But wait.

And he realized then he didn't much like it anymore. After a while it seemed like even the things you were good at got old. Either that or you did.

World he'd made, though.

In the dark room, though it was not yet noon, he dozed off, drifted into the dream. Back in Nam, in the monsoon darkness on night patrol, leading the boys through a jungle, can't see a damn thing. The heat and humidity forgotten for the fear. When someone hollers, cursing. Then the explosion. And gunfire. All around, blinding flashes. Screams. And him running, running . . .

He awakened sweating in the dark cool room and got up and

cracked the venetian blinds. Still daylight. He checked his watch. Barely half an hour had passed. He sat on the chair rubbing his eyes. Then remembered the conversation with the desk clerk. So he dressed and put on his gun belt and hat and went out the door.

30

When he saw the Ranger striding through the weeds toward the wrecker, he reached out a boot and kicked the blanket over the guns. Then laid the New Testament on the seat to the side, open to the twentythird chapter of Luke. Fortysixth verse where the crucified Jesus cried out in a loud voice. Saying, Father into thy hands I commend my spirit!

What he imagined Maxine had cried in her final moment. Or would have, given a chance.

He did not get out but sat in the cab behind the steering wheel, a sour taste in his mouth, his rough hands spread over his thighs, and stared out the side window over the field toward a stand of tallow among the blackberry. Grackles in the limbs, ruffling coal-black armor.

Rule drew alongside the door and stopped. He pushed his hat back. The man inside did not look at him.

Afternoon, Mister Lomax.

Harvey Lomax turned, his eyes focused on a point just left of Rule's shoulder. His face was damp with sweat. A smashed mosquito clung to one leathery cheek, his short uncombed hair shot wildly in every direction. Dark gray eyes like lead, the skin about them swollen, his eyebrows two thatches of unkempt wire. He nodded.

Ranger Hooks.

Rule's gaze drifted away, off across the field, out toward the highway. His eyes squinted in the late afternoon glare.

Hot day we got.

Lomax nodded again. It was at that, he wouldn't argue about the heat. Though the fires of hell were seven times seventy times hotter.

I appreciate your interest Mister Lomax, but reckon I can do my job better without the help. Rule still looking away.

Lomax slowly lifted his hands, spread the scarred knuckles over the steering wheel, gripping it tightly. Thinking the man hadn't done much of a job at all, far as he could tell. Eating and drinking, consorting with libertines. Debauchery and lust, wallowing in flesh. His spirit unclean, the natural carnal man. But that was on the Ranger's soul, not his.

So Lomax stared off in the direction of Rule's gaze, as if by unspoken mutual consent each had agreed it was better not to look directly at the other.

I'm told it's a free country yet.

Rule crossed his arms over his chest, leaned to one side to spit in the grass. Yessir, it is, he said. It surely is, more or less.

They did not speak for a while. The crickets in the field began to chir, the hum rising and falling in waves. Trucks passed along the road. The sun hovered midway overhead, a glowing torch of white heat in the pale blue expanse. In the silence both men considered what might be said and the lack of any necessity in saying it, yet in the end they both knew it could not be dismissed. There was no going around it. When it could be put off no longer, Rule started.

Thing is, Mister Lomax, that freedom ain't free.

No, it ain't.

That's right. It comes at a cost.

Lomax glanced sharply at Rule, then away, the gray eyes molten with heat. As if to say, What might you teach me about cost?

Rule took a deep breath, continued. What we got, Mister Lomax, is some rules. That's the cost I mean. Rules to protect my freedom against yours, yours against mine. Some big ones have been broken. Them boys broke 'em. They some bad boys, Mister Lomax, and now it's my job to set things straight. I can't have you interfering with that. That's another rule.

The man replied, Don't believe I've broken that one.

Rule rubbed his jaw. No, you haven't. But I believe you intend to.

The two men looked at each other directly, briefly, then turned away again, both gazing toward the highway like it offered some sort of mediation, as if they waited long enough it might intercede, provide a solution.

It was Lomax who finally spoke, his voice matter of fact, brittle. I suppose you'd call that a warning.

Yessir, it is.

All right.

After a minute Rule touched the brim of his hat and said, I'd best be moving along. I wish you the best, and I offer you my sympathies, sir, for what they are worth. He turned and strode away, but after several steps stopped and turned. Saying, I'm not one to preach, Mister Lomax, don't reckon I qualify. But I'm told you're a Christian man. You're also an officer of the law, at least up in Waller County. You took an oath to uphold that law. I expect you'll want to hold on to that. Expect you'll be glad you did.

Lomax gripped the steering wheel more tightly. He spoke low, his rough voice rising in singsong recitation. Saying—

The law, Ranger Hooks, is not made for the righteous man, but for the lawless and disobedient, for the ungodly and sinners, for the unholy and profane, for murderers of fathers and murderers of mothers, for manslayers. And so it was written, Paul to Timothy.

Rule dropped his head, pulled at one ear. He stepped through the tall grass closer to the wrecker, laid his hand on the sill of the driver's window. The metal was hot. He saw the small New Testament lying open on the seat.

He said, I don't reckon Paul ever studied the state code of Texas, Mister Lomax. Don't know that you have. But it does say the law applies to all of us, says it clearly. I don't recall any exceptions. So maybe we ain't talking about the same law.

Lomax stared straight ahead.

Is that the case, Mister Lomax?

The man observed the Ranger. It might be.

Well then, we got a problem. Rule patted the metal door sill several times. Said, Mister Lomax, how much you know about these boys?

The gaunt man pulled a scrap of paper from his coveralls and thrust it out the window. Rule read it: Darees Ledoo.

That's not the man who shot your wife.

He was there.

Yes, he was. What else you know?

The other feller was redheaded.

Then you know as much as we do.

Lomax returned the paper to his coveralls pocket, saying, Then you don't know much.

That's right, not yet. So I suggest you go on home. If we need you, we'll call.

Lomax eyeballed Rule, a thatched eyebrow quivering. You ain't gonna learn nuthin laid up in a motel room.

Rule grunted. You ever hunted deer, Mister Lomax?

I have.

Then you know about waiting.

I know about hunting.

You think I'm going about it wrong.

The man turned away, his face impassive. Like you said, that ain't my concern.

Mister Lomax, I wish you meant that. Let me tend to these boys. That's my job. I aim to do it.

Go right on. I'm told it's a free country yet.

Rule nodded once, then turned and strode back across the field toward the motel. Lomax watched him go. Thinking the man was a Ranger, maybe he had his own way of working. Some peculiar way he did not recognize. But recollecting he'd seen more than one government bureaucrat wearing lawman's clothes toting a gun while he sucked off the taxpayer's tit. Thinking, I'll be paying for it come tax time, too. Just like I'm paying for that red Dodge pickup. And Lord only knows what else. That motel room, for instance.

He wondered if he was paying for the whore the Ranger'd brought there, too.

Lomax watched the tall man pass from sight. Thinking, There

was laws, and then there was laws. Thinking, There was oaths, and then there were oaths. Duty to one and duty to the other, and if they should coincide, that was fine. But if they should fall into dispute, no doubt in his mind which held precedence. It was right there in writing: But if ye be led of the spirit, ye are not under the law.

Galatians five and eighteen.

31

The Shipwreck squatted just off the beach highway in an overgrown treeless field. A generic cement block building, lowslung, windowless, with peeling whitewash. Otherwise without character, as though its single utilitarian purpose lay in providing walls and roof to deflect sun, wind and rain off the trade inside. The trade being straightforward—cash for the immediate means of forgetting or dreaming, for remembering how it once was or how it might have been if not for bad luck, miscalculation, or the malicious intervention of others. In this existential purpose the Shipwreck succeeded, then prevailed in nothing beyond: a beer joint.

What it's for, said Ray Bob, almost hollering. Cold beer and a good time. Got the coldest fuckin beer on the beach. It'll make your teeth hurt!

Well, that's certainly a great recommendation, Della said.

Who asked you?

In the backseat she did not reply. Wasn't sure why she'd spoken. She was still smarting from what Eddie had said to her earlier. Calling her a fibber, a liar. Open yourself up to someone and what do they do? Rip out your guts, that's what. They wound you. It had hurt, him saying that. A deep hurt, right in the heart, in its most sensitive place. She wasn't sure she'd recover from it, to tell the truth. A thing like that sets you back, damages your trust. She'd hardly spoken to him since, giving him the silent chill. As

Ruby always said when LD stomped on her feelings, let the motherfucker rot in hell.

There he was now, Eddie sitting up in the front seat, chatting
with Ray Bob. On their way to this beer joint Ray Bob found. She
wouldn't even have come except she was bored. But she had certainly let Eddie know it wasn't on his account.

Well, you said not to keep things bottled up, he'd said, didn't
you? You told me to talk about things, honeybunch, say what I
felt. Keeps a person from getting crazy, ain't that what you said?

Like that was an excuse for injuring someone.

He turned around now and looked at her and she looked away,
stiffing him. He shrugged and faced back to the front, lit a cigarette and joked with Ray Bob. Cold motherfucker. Kinda cute
though.

So after listening to that dumb excuse she'd told him—breaking
her rule of silence for a second, making an exception on account
of she needed to defend herself—she'd told him the importance of
talking didn't mean you had to say *everything*. She said, If everybody said everything they felt, could you imagine the trouble it'd
cause? You have to use judgment.

And he'd replied that's what he did, usually. That it'd seemed to
work just fine, too, before he took her advice.

So she'd had to make yet *another* exception to explain about
the little black box. That's the thing you use to make bad feelings
and thoughts disappear, she told him. You just open the lid and
shove a feeling in there, or a bad thought you ought not say, and
shut the lid. Then it's gone, it just disappears. And you go on
about your business. Nobody gets hurt.

Where you keep this box? he'd asked.

Good grief, what a question. So she'd explained it wasn't a real
box, it was imaginary.

He'd grunted, like that wasn't a good explanation. Then asked,
You get that from *Redbook* too?

Did it matter? Then she'd remembered. No, from *Family Circle*.

Well, did the article tell you how to know when to talk and
when to use the little black box? he'd asked. Cause that seems
kinda tricky, knowing the difference.

She'd told him—speaking patiently, like talking to a halfwit—
she told him it all depended on the circumstances, there wasn't no
rockhard rule. That's what she meant by *judgment*. Which he was
lacking in.

And then he hadn't said anything, just frowned and went off. A
good thing, too, as she was tired of making exceptions to the
silent treatment she was handing him.

Not that it seemed to bother him much. Sitting up there now
laughing at something Ray Bob said. Like she wasn't there in the
backseat, suffering. She watched him laugh. When he threw his
head back that way, it sort of reminded her of that real cute guy in
Aerosmith, the singer, Steven Tyler. Only Steven's lips were bigger,
like Mick's lips. Eddie's lips weren't quite as big, but otherwise,
yeah. Also, he was pretty good in the sack.

Maybe she'd let him off the hook at bedtime.

Ray Bob turned the Caddy off the dark beach road into an oyster shell lot and parked between two pickups. Twilight had settled
over the peninsula and a brisk offshore breeze cluttered the first
stars with a flotilla of fastmoving clouds. It was still very warm,
the sounds of insects everywhere, and the air felt heavy on the
wind. Like maybe it was going to rain later. Eddie got out and
pushed the seat forward for Della.

The Shipwreck, he said. They got music?

Ray Bob said, It's a beer joint ain't it?

I mean live music.

Goddamn, I said it's a beer joint. They got a jukebox.

Eddie waved him off and tucked his T-shirt in his jeans while
Della brushed her hair. Ray Bob went on in the front door. Eddie
watched Della arrange her bangs in the side mirror of a nearby
pickup truck. Mosquitos descended in a stinging swarm, he swat-
ted at them.

C'mon, Della, these skeeters are bad.

Just a second. She smoothed her cotton blouse and straightened
the collar. Just because it's a dump doesn't mean I want to look
like a tramp. They do have some nice places, you know, here at
the beach.

Thinking then, Well, it looks like I'm gonna talk. But if he takes it for granted he's got another think coming.

Eddie saying, Like where? They all looked the same to me.

Della poked out her bottom lip. Said, Well, nicer than this one. It looks rough.

Inside Ray Bob was already standing at the bar with a beer. On either side stood shrimpers and crabbers, men young and old wearing white kneehigh rubber boots and grimy jeans, sunbleached shirts and gimmee caps. Their skin was burnished dark brown. When Della and Eddie came through the door they all turned to watch.

Good lord, Della said, let's find a table.

They passed several empty tables and took one pushed against the far wall near the jukebox, away from the bar. Eddie said there wasn't a waitress, asked Della what she wanted.

A Tom Collins.

Eddie hesitated. They might not have that.

Well, you could at least ask.

All right.

While he went to the bar she lit a cigarette and observed the interior. A concrete slab floor, rickety tables with molded plastic chairs, neon beer signs and beach trash decorating the walls: driftwood, mooring ropes, scraps of fish nets, broken buoys. A sixfoot hammerhead shark mounted over the bar. An even larger one hanging on the wall by the pool tables in the back corner. And customers to match. A classy place if your taste ran to rednecks reeking cutbait.

Eddie returned with two cans of cold beer. Saying that's all they had. Apologizing. Della rolled her eyes. You ever seen so much white trash in your life? she said.

He popped the tabs, saying, Not since my last family reunion. He pushed a beer across the table. There you are.

Well, that don't mean you're stuck with it, she said. Your family, I mean. There is such a thing as working your way up. Don't they have any glasses?

I dunno, maybe. He returned shortly with a glass and put it on the table in front of her, then went over to the jukebox. What kinda music you like?

They have Mariah Carey?

Eddie went through the selections, drumming the sides of the jukebox with both hands. After a minute he said, Naw, but they got some good stuff. He dropped in several quarters and punched buttons. Johnny Copeland came up singing "Down on Bending Knees," his bluesy voice pleading with his baby over a groaning litany of saxophone licks. Eddie sat down smiling, said he couldn't believe the number of R and B and soul tunes on the box, especially considering there wasn't a black soul in the place. They listened to T-Bone Walker, Percy Mayfield, Junior Wells, with Eddie explaining the background of each.

They aren't exactly my favorites, Della said, sipping her beer, but they sound sincere. I never even heard of 'em.

Eddie grinned. That's the history of rock 'n' roll you listening to. Most white people don't know it cause they ignorant, always putting it down. I seen more fights start that way. Just watch.

He looked across the dimly lit room and saw Ray Bob leaning against the bar, looking at them. Eddie cocked his thumb and shot him with a forefinger. Ray Bob shook his head and finished his beer, turned back to the bar. One of the shrimpers, a heavyset bearded young man wearing a blue denim workshirt with sleeves rolled above the elbows, moved over to say something. Ray Bob shrugged.

Eddie told Della to look at the shrimper next to Ray Bob. Just watch, he said, I bet he's the one.

Percy Sledge came on with "When a Man Loves a Woman" and Eddie mouthed the words, beating out the rhythm on the table edge with his fingers. Della said she'd heard that one, of course, everybody had, although she doubted any man could love someone that much. Della said, I think what he really loves is the idea of her, especially now that she's gone. Because he's lonely. But if she was to go back he'd treat her bad all over again, most likely.

Eddie raised his eyebrows. You think so?

Oh yeah, Della said, that's why he misses her. But it's still a sweet song, real sad, even if he is full of it.

He was about to ask if she'd ever heard ol' Percy do "Cover Me" when the song ended and in the silence before the next selection someone yelled, Who's playing that nigger music? Eddie looked over toward the bar, saw the glazed eyes of the heavyset bearded shrimper roving the room. The guy hollered again, more loudly, his jaw thrust forward belligerently: I asked, who's playing that nigger music!

Eddie said, What'd I tell you?

Then the jukebox kicked in with the Boogie Kings singing the "Harlem Shuffle" and Eddie turned back to Della. Listen to these guys sing, he said, this shit is straight from the swamp. He was describing how he grew up knowing two of the band members when Della stopped paying attention. She was looking up over his shoulder. Eddie twisted his head, saw the shrimper standing close behind, Ray Bob alongside.

Ray Bob said, This dude wants to know if you're playing those songs. I told him it was but he wants to hear it hisself. He grinned maliciously.

The shrimper nodded and threw his head back, taking a long swallow of beer from the can enclosed in his enormous fist. He stared at Eddie, his eyes slightly out of focus, saying, That's right, cause I can't believe no white boy'd spend money on this shit.

Eddie observed the guy more closely. His gut hung over his belt and he was overweight, but he was built to carry the weight and underneath the fat the muscles were big. His legs rose from the tops of white rubber boots like thick treetrunks, his sunburned biceps almost split his denim shirtsleeves. A black gimmee cap advertising Bolivar Barge Company sat above a wide forehead and eyes like glassy brown marbles. He was big and knew it and he liked it. He outweighed Eddie by a hundred pounds.

The guy said, That your quarters?

Eddie leaned forward, set an elbow on the table, flipping the top of his Zippo lighter open and shut in one hand. Snap, snap. You mean this song here?

The guy nodded. Yeah, that shit.

Well, that's the Boogie Kings, Eddie said, they're white boys.

A bewildered expression gathered on the guy's face.

Yeah, they're from Louisiana mostly, Eddie continued, over in them swamps. Or they were. And a couple come from Port Arthur, just up the road.

The guy frowned. You telling me that ain't nigger music?

No, I'm just sayin they ain't niggers is all. They white.

For a moment the man seemed to deflate, then his small eyes narrowed to slits in the wide sunburnished face. He shot back, You telling me all that music you been playing is by white boys?

Naw, Eddie said, just this one. Top of his Zippo going flip, flip. Them others was niggers, all right.

Ray Bob nudged the guy with an elbow. See? What'd I tell you?

The bearded man seemed confused again. Then he raised the hand wrapped around the beer and crushed the empty can, his face flushed with anger. Saying, What I think is, I think you guys are fuckin with me. And I better not hear no more nigger music. His voice strained, an octave higher.

I hate to disappoint you, Eddie said, but I think some more's coming. Because I played an Albert Collins and we ain't heard that one yet.

Well, I guess you aren't here for a crosscultural experience. Della talking now.

The others, all three, looked at her, surprised.

She was sitting up straight with her hands folded in her lap. Now, if you ever watched *Oprah*, she continued, speaking to the shrimper, you'd see why it's important to expose yourself to other subcultures. It's part of understanding and appreciating the diversity in American life.

The shrimper winced, looked first to Eddie, then to Ray Bob. What the fuck's she saying?

Eddie shrugged, Ray Bob grinned. Della continued, saying, Or maybe you just come here for the cold beer. Does it hurt your teeth?

The man raised his arms and took a step backward, his unfocused gaze pointed somewhere in the vicinity of Della. He said, I don't know where you people come from but I think you'd better go back. And he turned and strode half staggering back to the bar bellyup.

Ray Bob sat down at the table grinning. That was pretty good.

Della fluffed her bangs. Saying, I wasn't born just yesterday, big ol' blowhard like that.

You know that ain't the end of it. Ray Bob still grinning.

No, it ain't, Eddie agreed.

Well, Della said, I think you two are just cruising for a bruising.

An hour later, when they left, the shrimper with two of his friends was waiting in the lot. The sky had clouded up with large black bruises, rainclouds obscuring starlight and moonlight, but the watery electric light mounted on a pole outside the Shipwreck cast the figures of the three men in pale countenance. They drew up in a tight semicircle just as the others reached the Caddy. All three wearing gimmee caps and dirty jeans with white rubber boots. One could have been the twin of the first, a bearded hulking grizzly with angry eyes. The third was short and lean with long hair and ropy muscles that looked like seasoned rawhide. He held one hand behind his back. When he brought it round, the long thin blade of a filet knife glinted in the low light.

Eddie helped Della into the car, moving fast, and turned around to face the three men. He put up his arms and said he didn't much feel like fighting, thanks all the same.

Ever how you want it, the first shrimper said, it don't matter to us. We're taking you down anyhow.

Eddie said it again, he wasn't interested.

The shrimper smiled in his beard.

Ray Bob said, Sounds fine to me, I'm in the mood.

The slender man with the knife motioned with his arm. Said, Then c'mon.

During the next few minutes, Ray Bob, with a roll of quarters clinched in each fist, sidestepped the thrust of the knife and took out the ropymuscled guy with a wicked blow to the side of his head. Then got inside on the first bearded shrimper and rabbit-punched him twice, rammed a knee into his groin several times, grunting, and laid him out with a short uppercut to the jaw. The third shrimper was bent over pulling a gun from his rubber boot when Ray Bob swung his leg upward, hard. His leather boot toe made an ugly crunching noise as it jammed the guy's nose somewhere up between his eyebrows. All three lay among the oyster shells in the lot, the slender one with a dark stream of red oozing from his ear, the third with a fountain of blood spurting above his disfigured upturned face. Ray Bob took the filet knife and crouched by the first guy, working the blade down by his ear. He stood up and tossed the knife and what appeared to be a small morsel of flesh into the weeds. Then he pulled out the car keys, took a moment to study the three prostrate figures, slid behind the wheel and cranked the motor.

A minute later, cruising down the beach road back toward the house, with the first sparse raindrops falling, he glanced up into the rearview mirror at Eddie and Della in the backseat, Della with her face in her hands in Eddie's lap, shoulders quaking, Eddie jerking at his earring, and grinning, saying, Pardner, now did I tell you that was a fine beer joint or what!

32

Rule spent the evening in the motel cottage. Sitting in the chair by the air conditioner's hum, trying to crawl inside the heads of those bad boys, figure out where they went.

Frustrating. Especially Redhead.

He'd get halfway in, start having a feel for it, get kicked back out. Crawling into dark places wasn't the problem, he'd been inside some ugly heads, that was a fact. But with these guys, he couldn't find the right angle for entry.

About nine o'clock he got up and stood outside the cottage door. He saw piles of marineblue and black clouds gathering in the east, coasting inland, booming warships loaded with thunder and rain. He could feel it in the air, smell it. Lomax still sitting out there in his wrecker, not bothering to hide anymore. Now there was a head he didn't need to crawl into, it was written all over his face. An avenging angel. He wondered what kind of gun the man was carrying. Or guns.

Inside the cottage, he took a shower and laid on the bed.

If it was him, he'd go into Houston and fade into the woodwork. But these boys were something else. Redhead playing games with him, taunting. DeReese in over his head most likely. Maybe some gal along for the ride now, juicing off the guys, excited, some kinda offbeat foreplay.

Redhead was the key, though, he was sure of it. No name, just a Model P99 Walther automatic. Nice gun, expensive. Plenty of power.

Galveston probably where they were.

It was only a hunch. Based on a vague feeling. Standard police work method, half the time, you got right down to it. Like knowing Redhead was the one. The alpha dog. Don't worry about DeReese's head, crawl into Redhead's.

Man, that was a dark place, kept kicking him back out.

Bound to have a record, though. Boy like that don't come outa nowhere. Leaves scent everywhere he goes.

He saw lightning flash through the venetian blinds, heard the first rumbling thunder overhead. Here it comes. Lomax gonna have another bad night.

Thinking he'd better get to those boys first. Before Lomax, the one man vigilante squad.

He went over to the TV and turned it to Letterman, laid back down. Dennis Hopper sat by the desk in front of the Manhattan skyline, explaining what happened. Letterman fiddling with a pencil, silly smirk on his face. Something about Hopper being stoned, the audience tittering. Letterman gives a deadpan, throws the pencil through the glass. A crashing sound, the music starts and the camera cuts to the bald guy on electric piano, grinning and rolling his head like Ray Charles. Cut to commercial. Big mattress sale at Quality Discount, come on down.

Rule not paying attention. Thinking if it was him, he'd be in Houston. Except the feeling kept saying Galveston. Only Redhead had said Corpus. No telling. If he could just find the angle, get inside his head. Hell, Redhead might not even know where he's going. Wouldn't be any surprise, boy like that moving on instinct.

He sighed and bunched the pillow under his head. Heard the first raindrops hitting the cottage roof, large and random, then faster, a steady peltering drone. Across the room, some comedian on the tube now telling lightbulb jokes. He wondered where that got started, lightbulb jokes.

Thinking that if nothing turned up tomorrow, or day after, he was heading back to Austin. When a trail gets cold there's no use tracking it. When it runs out, head to the house and wait for fresh spoor. Go home, cut the grass, hang loose with Lefty. See if Katie's interested in lunch, take her to one of those organic places. If he could reach her. If she was interested. Maybe tell her about the dream. If Dana calls, tell her to stay away. Then fuck her when she comes over. And listen to Moline whine.

What life had come to.

Meanwhile, you listened to lightbulb jokes, laughed if they were funny.

Haw.

Interlude

Eddie and Ray Bob were inside the Gulf Coast Market on the beach road, doing the grocery shopping because Della needed to make phone calls. The telephone hung on the outside wall near the store entrance, in the open, not a lick of shade. Noontime on a hot day, sun directly overhead, no wind, high humidity. She stood melting in the heat with two rolls of quarters Eddie'd given her.

Della made four calls.

Call Number One:

She got the number from information for the *Houston Chronicle* and called the newsroom, asked to speak to the reporter who covered crime. Big crimes. Murder and that sort of thing.

You mean the police reporter, the voice said, just a minute.

Three quarters later a man picked up the line saying, Yeah?

Yes, Della said, I'm an interested reader of the *Chronicle* and I saw something on TV that I didn't find in the paper and I wondered why. I wanted to read about it. You always give more details and all.

What was that? The guy sounded bored.

Well, it was a murder out at the Holiday Inn, the one out on Interstate Ten, I think, out past the loop.

When was this?

Della counted. Maybe three nights ago?

The reporter spoke away from the phone. Talking to someone on his end. She listened to the murmuring sound of his voice. Then he returned, saying, I'm not aware of it. Neither is the guy who covers nights, he's sitting right here. What can you tell me about it?

Della paused. Good lord, here she was, cutting her own throat.

Like some criminal returning to the scene of a crime nobody knew.

Well, she said, I don't *know* that it happened. That's why I called. I probably just misunderstood, I was in the other room and didn't hear good. Thanks for clearing that up.

I believe you said the Holiday Inn?

Lanes, Della replied, lanes. Holiday Lanes, the bowling alley? Only I made a mistake. It wasn't important anyhow, I was just curious. Whoops, there goes my doorbell. Better run. Thanks, bye.

She hung up. Damn.

Call Number Two:

She called information again and got the telephone number for the Houston Police Department, homicide division. A Sergeant Eastland answered and she told him she was a reporter with the the television news.

Which one?

Della squinched her eyes, thinking quick. KPRC, she said.

What's your name?

Stone, Della said. Stone . . . Waters. She winced.

That's a funny name, said the sergeant. That a TV name?

Della said, I'm from New York.

You don't sound like it.

I grew up in Minnesota, way up there.

Sound Texas to me, Eastland said. What's your real name?

Della paused. That is my real name.

The sergeant said, Never seen you on TV. I watch that channel. But I suppose you're new. Just in from New York.

That's right, Della said, I just started this week. Hot down here, too. Whew!

Ain't it so? Well, I tell you what, Miss Waters, I'm neck deep on a homicide right now, body from down on the ship channel, Vietnamese guy, so unless this is an emergency, why don't you just let me get back to you soon as possible. How's that sound?

Della blew out her breath, wondered what a real reporter'd say. Probably ask about that body. Occurred to her then the guy probably knew. He was just screwing around.

What's your telephone number, Miss Stone?

Never mind, Della said curtly, if you don't care to talk to the TV news then I'll just call the chief's office. Maybe *he'll* have time.

She hung up. Damn.

Call Number Three:

She dialed the beauty shop in Sugar Land and LeeAnne, the second chair, picked up.

Clippers and Curls.

LeeAnne, this is Della. Can I speak to Ruby?

Della, where *are* you girl? Just a sec.

She heard LeeAnne clunk down the receiver and tell Ruby the telephone. Telling her it's Della.

A moment later Ruby came on saying, I'll be a Chinaman, I done thought you was dead, girl. Where'd you disappear to?

I wasn't feeling well, Ruby. I had this boyfriend you didn't know about? And he dumped me for nuthin and it just knocked me flat. I tell you, I been in bed feeling *sooo* bad.

Well, that shitass. What's his name?

Never mind, Ruby, he's history, don't you worry.

Why didn't you answer the telephone? You know I been calling, honey. I been worried sick.

I just wasn't up to it, Ruby. That's why I'm calling. I need some more time off. And I was wondering, you think I could go over and use LD's cabin a few days? I need some time to think.

What about them kids?

My momma has 'em. Lord, I don't know what I'd do without her. They run me ragged. You think LD'd mind?

Naw, honey, he don't care about that cabin. Only reason the pissant goes over there's to get away from the phone and drink. Only he can forget that. He was at the doctor yesterday. You know his blood pressure was oneninetyfive over onefifty? Surprised he ain't keeled over. LD's off the sauce. How come you never told me about that boyfriend?

I didn't want to get your hopes up. Like mine was.

That shitbird.

So you don't mind? Della said. About me taking off a few days?

Naw, go ahead, we ain't that busy. Plus LeeAnne wants extra hours, she's planning a trip to Cancun. Thinks Carl's gonna pop the question down there. Told her not to count chickens, she don't listen. Know where the key is?

Della said, Up under the stairwell?

That's right, honey. Don't forget your sun lotion. You don't want no skin cancer.

For a second Della wanted to say, Ruby, remember that knife you give me, the one from Nuevo Laredo? Just joking around? Well, you'll never guess what happened to it.

But instead, she said, All right, thanks a gazillion, Ruby. I'll call you soon.

She hung up. So LeeAnne was getting engaged. Damn.

Call Number Four:

She called her mother in Missouri City. Randy picked up the receiver, or maybe Waylon, she wasn't sure which, one of them just stood there breathing on the line while she kept saying this is your mother, go get Grandma. Wasted four quarters that way, she was on the second roll. Finally her mother came on.

Hello?

Well, I thought you'd never get here, Della said, it's me.

I was in the other room watching TV, trying to rest up. Oprah has this boy killed his momma. Didn't even hear the phone. Did it ring?

Of course it rang. Who was that on it?

Waylon. Did you talk to him?

Well, I tried. All he'd do was breathe.

I think he misses you, he don't hardly talk. All he does is stand around, sucking his thumb raw.

Tell him to stop, Della said. My lord, that'll ruin his teeth. He's just nervous.

I think they both are. You know they still wet the bed? Randy's been coughing.

You giving him his medicine?

Well, I try, her mother said. He don't like it. They sure are tiring me out. When you coming back?

I don't know yet. It's only been three days, you know. I just now got relaxed. Has anybody called?

She listened to her mother thinking. Then, Who's gonna call you here?

Della said, I don't know. For goodness sake, *some*body might. Maybe the finance company, about my car. Just take a message if they do. Tell 'em I'll get back.

All I can do, her mother said, unless you say where you are. What if there's an emergency?

Call nine one one, that's what. I don't have a phone where I am. Anyhow, negative thoughts just cause things to happen. Think positive.

Her mother made a small sucking sound with her mouth. Said, I don't see how you can live without a phone.

You'd be surprised, replied Della. Listen, I got to go, I'm running out of quarters. Kiss Randy and Waylon for me. Tell 'em I said Mommy loves 'em.

Her mother was silent, not letting go. Then said, Randy's been picking on Waylon, pore little thing.

Well, give him a good smack then, and stick him in the corner. I don't want no bully.

He kicks back.

Then get out your belt. Good grief, you know what to do, Momma, you raised four kids.

Why I'm so tired.

I got to go, Della said. I'll call later. Bye.

She hung up. Damn. Forgot to remind her to take her iron.

Della stood in the heat by the telephone waiting for Eddie and Ray Bob, thinking about Mister Dreamboat, wondering what happened. Didn't make any sense, the newspaper not knowing. Didn't get a chance to ask that detective, Sergeant Eastland, he was kind of a smartass, ask her opinion. Maybe they were keeping it a secret, Mister Dreamboat being such an important executive. Something to do with public relations or such. Big corporations could get away with murder, seen that on *Dateline*. Whole thing was driving her cuckoo. At least it was fixed up with Ruby, about the cabin. And missing work. Not that she was gonna get *paid* for missing work. Come the end of the month she'd face that little problem. A day at a time. She wondered where the Hyundai was. She thought about Waylon sucking his thumb raw. Boy, there just wasn't any end to it. If it wasn't one thing . . .

She heard Eddie calling her name and saw that he and Ray Bob were already in the car. Out there in the lot, drinking beer. Doubted she should even get in the car with them. Just walk home. Ray Bob being halfstewed already when they drove over, Caddy drifting into the far lane until she hollered. Pissed him off. They'd called each other names, Eddie sitting in the front seat quiet as a mouse. Like he didn't want to take sides.

No way she was gonna walk in this heat.

When she climbed into the backseat among the grocery sacks Ray Bob glared at her in the rearview, an unlit cigarette between his lips. Still mad, the pisspot. Without turning around to face her, he said, The goddamn dashboard lighter's missing. You take it?

What a question, Della said. I ain't no thief. But if you happen to find it just stick it up your butt. She folded her arms and stared out the side. Adding, to herself, And pardon my French.

Ray Bob, still staring into the rearview, said, When habitual liars are accused of small things they didn't do, they get more defensive than ordinary people would.

Is that so, Della muttered.

According to Dashiell Hammett it is, said Ray Bob, lighting the cigarette with his pocket lighter. He wrote it in a book.

Della said, Well, give him the prize.

Ray Bob peeled rubber turning the Caddy onto the beach road. Eddie braced himself against the dash so as not to spill his beer. When the car straightened out he reached up and tugged his earring. Man oh man, he sure did hate it when Della and Ray Bob argued. Wasn't like they was kidding around. All that anger put a knot in his belly.

He leaned his head to the side into the wind, closed his eyes. Thinking it seemed like he'd heard that guy's name before, one who wrote Ray Bob's quote. Hamlet. Pretty sure he'd heard of him.

He swung around to ask Della if she knew who he was, way to make conversation if nothing else. When she didn't answer he asked if she'd had enough quarters for the phone, still trying. She wouldn't look at him, so he finally asked if she was worried about her kids. She replied to that one.

Said, Whaddaya think, you shitass?

Part 2

33

On the seventh day God rested, then never returned to work. Not Ray Bob. Sitting around watching, waiting, it drove him up a wall.

Difference was, God started with a plan. Gave it a push in one direction, kicked back to watch, hands off, see what happened. Whereas Ray Bob lacked an overall design, unless unsated need should offer purpose. It was all he had: need, urgent and unsated, insatiable. A need to move, to get going. Nowhere in particular, motion being enough. Movement in the void, heedless to cause, effect inconsequential. Backward, forward, who gave a shit? Wasn't his problem.

It was a simple cosmogony: Creation having come from nothing, nothing was Ray Bob's aim.

So on this day of reputed rest he stood on the deck of the beach house overlooking the gulf, smoking a cigarette. Midmorning and the sky clear as bluetinted windowpane, the air yet light, almost brisk after the rains. Something in it, the air. Something suspended there, an energy, perceptible, invigorating. Causing the distinct conviction he might live forever, might want to. A routine day for a kid, that was a fact, but at his age such days occurred more sparingly, so Ray Bob inhaled it, breathing deeply. Grabbed it and ran, smiling softly.

Thinking this was the day, no doubt about it.

After a while he went inside, paused by the door sniffing the residual aroma of fried bacon and eggs. The large open room lay in faint shadow, morning sunlight filtering through the screened windows all around. He stood there, watching. Della in the La-Z-Boy going through the *Chronicle*, frowning. Not a bad-looking chick. Eyes set too close, otherwise passable. But what a bitch. Christ, he'd a killed her after one go around. Not Eddie, though. His runnin buddy a pussywhipped motherfucker. Sitting on the edge of the bed over there, plucking on a guitar, moving his lips. Not bad on it either, better than he'd expected, only playing old nigger music, some bluesy shit.

He walked to the far corner and picked up his duffel bag, started stuffing in his spare jeans and shirts, laid in a box of 9mm Federal ammo. The guitar stopped. He could feel Eddie watching.

What you doing?

He didn't answer. Sniffed a T-shirt, jammed it in the canvas duffel. Unwrapped the Walther from another shirt, put it down his boot. He heard Eddie lay the guitar aside, heard his footsteps approaching over the linoleum floor. Standing next to him now.

What you doing, man?

He didn't look up. Said, This is it, hoss, I'm splitting.

Eddie didn't say anything.

He shook the duffel down, stood it on end on the mattress and pulled the drawstring tight. Then looked over at Eddie, eyeballing him. Said, You in or out, pardner? Ray Bob talking evenly, laying it on the line.

Eddie said, Shit, man, nuthin wrong with this place. This is a good place, let's lay low for a while. Eddie playing for time.

Ray Bob said, You laying all right, why you wanna stay. Pussy on the brain. Vacation's over. You in or out? When Eddie didn't answer, he added, And I mean you, hoss. Not her.

Eddie glanced over at Della, her nose in the newspaper, not listening. He lowered himself to the edge of the bed, shoulders hunched, scratching one forearm.

Ray Bob said, I see you still confused. Figure it out, dickhead. I'll be downstairs. You got five minutes.

Shit, Eddie said, you putting me in a vise, man.

Like I said, I'll be downstairs.

Ray Bob slung the duffel over a shoulder and went down the stairs. Eddie sat on the bed, heard the Caddy motor start below. Across the room, Della laid the newspaper in her lap, was looking at Eddie. She said, Where's Mister Hothead going now? Gonna find somebody else to beat up?

Referring to the shrimpers, two of them in Galveston, still in a ward at John Sealy Hospital. Plus a couple others from the last few days, in joints up and down the beach road. Mister Hothead keeping busy.

Eddie said, Naw. Well maybe. He's leaving.

Della squinted at him. You serious?

Eddie tugged at his earring. Said he was. Serious as cancer.

Well thank the lord, Della said, I never woulda guessed. And good riddance, what I say, he has me a nervous wreck. She patted the arms of the La-Z-Boy, blowing her bangs. Saying, Way he looks at me, like he wants to beat me up too, only after doing terrible things first, things I don't even want to mention. Della talking fast. And don't tell me you don't understand, cause you seen it too, Eddie. If you wasn't here I'd of walked back to Sugar Land, just knowing he was in the same vicinity.

Eddie said, You been using that little black box.

Della said he didn't know. Said he had no idea. Said the box was almost full, been stuffing it right and left, she could barely get the lid back on.

Eddie, sitting on the bedside, looking at the floor, allowed that came as no surprise. Between the talking and the stuffing she'd been as busy as Ray Bob. Sounding resentful, undecided. Eddie having to choose.

She caught the tone and banged the recliner down, startled, as if it was the first time the possibility had occurred to her. Her stomach flipped, it made her lightheaded. She pushed the paper aside and stood, swaying, padded over barefoot to him and stood directly in front, her hands on his shoulders. He gazed directly at her belly button, hovering there between the snap on her jeans and her swimsuit top. She undid the snap and unzipped her jeans, opened the fly, pulled his face to her. Nothing on underneath, just soft pubic hair nuzzling his chin and mouth. He closed his eyes and breathed in. She smelled good, like soap, only different. Then she reached down and opened the jeans farther, shimmying them downward a little over her hips, and opened her swollen lips with both hands, fingernails bright pink, thrusting her pelvis forward. A strong musky smell, his head full of it now. He opened his mouth, licked her. She was wet. A slightly sour taste, but good. It made his belly shake. She locked her hands behind his head and pulled him into her, his tongue flicking her spot, playing with it. She groaned, her pelvis beginning to tremble.

Then he abruptly pushed her away and stood up. Wiping his mouth with the back of his hand, saying, This ain't right, I got to talk with Ray Bob. And brushed past, going down the stairs, hustling, taking two steps at a time. Left her standing there like a statue of Eve holding the apple. She tumbled onto the bed, realized it was Ray Bob's, didn't care. Put her face in her hands and wept.

After a minute, she got up and moved across to the other bed, hers and Eddie's, laid down and cried some more, holding on to the Bible. Wept buckets. All alone, abandoned, chased by the police for something she couldn't help, her kids stuck with her mother, not working, no transportation, no money. Stuck in this lousy crapper of a house. And still not one word anywhere about Mister Dreamboat. Thinking of Eddie, her only best chance, down there right now with that snake, that monster. Thinking life wasn't nothing but a pile of shit, you could stick positive thoughts up your ass along with expressing your feelings and that little black box, all that smiley twobit here's-how-you-do-it shit in *Redbook* and all them other magazines wasn't nuthin but cheap glue by which you tried to hold together the pieces while life was trying to tear them apart, and life was stronger, it was gonna win in the long run no matter what you did. Not even love, not even love. Which she had recently tried. Now look at her. And where was he? She began to weep again, sobbing. Down there with his runnin buddy. Down there planning to run off, cooking up another crime.

Though he was not.

He was standing by the Caddy tugging on his earring listening to Ray Bob, who was still talking evenly, but anger burning in there, you could feel the heat, saying, You some kind of fuckin pardner, hoss. First snatch looks your way, you bust up the deal.

Eddie shook his head. Naw, man, that ain't how it is.

How is it?

Eddie still shaking his head, thinking. Finally saying, looking at Ray Bob, You just ain't flexible enough, man, won't let nobody else in.

Ray Bob saying, Oh yeah, I get it, we Butch and Sundance, and that bitch up there's what's her name, the schoolteacher. That how it is?

Eddie grinned. Hadn't thought about it that way, but yeah, he liked it. Said, Why not?

Ray Bob grinned back, teeth showing, eyes steelshot cold. Cause I ain't Sundance, pardner. I'm Johnny Ray Matthews, and I won't sit around with my thumb up my ass watching you and Miss Fancy Pants ride a bicycle built for two singing about raindrops falling, acting like your old asshole buddy don't even exist no more, like you never heard of a genuine one-on-one hope to die runnin buddy deal.

It was a mouthful, for Ray Bob.

Eddie nodded, listening. Then he leaned against the Caddy door, crossed his arms over his chest and smiled. Said, No shit, that's your name? Johnny Ray? Goddamn. Wanna know mine?

But Ray Bob wasn't listening. Still standing there redfaced, holding the car keys in a balled up fist saying, You one hell of a sidekick, hoss. First time I ain't watching my back you stick it up my ass. You dig the ride but you want it for free. You like the juice, you spend the money, but you too much a pussy to take the risk. You paying attention?

Eddie nodded, said he was. Said a person didn't have to take risks to enjoy the ride, though, or to appreciate the juice or even get money. Said hell, this is America ain't it?

Ray Bob stared at him. What the fuck's that mean?

Means what it means. Eddie shrugged. That's all.

You one confused sonofabitch, Ray Bob said, get outa my way. Eddie moved and Ray Bob opened the car door, crawled inside, and opened the glove compartment. He dug around a minute, backed out with a scrap of paper and a pen. Said, What's the name of that shithead that fingered you?

Eddie said, Who?

Ray Bob said, That coonass, one who snitched.

DeReese?

How you spell that?

Eddie watched Ray Bob bent over the hood, pen on paper, waiting. Man oh man, what was he up to now?

C'mon, Ray Bob said, spell it, I ain't got all day.

So Eddie spelled it. Then said, What you want to know for?

Ray Bob stuffed the paper in his jeans pocket, spun the pen into the backseat against the duffel. He got up in Eddie's face, close enough for Eddie to back up a step, and said, Cause I'm gonna take the guy out, show you what a *real* runnin buddy is, hoss. Teach you what *real* loyalty is. Something you oughta think about.

Well now, only thing about DeReese, Eddie started to say, but Ray Bob interrupted, halfway down in the seat behind the steering wheel, pointing a thick finger. Saying, I don't leave unfinished business either, pardner, something else you better think about. You got a choice to make. Cause you ain't seen the last of me.

Okay, okay, but the thing about DeReese, Eddie started to say again, waving his arms now, only Ray Bob already had thrown the Caddy in reverse and backed out, churning sand and dirt as he fishtailed forward down the road toward the highway, leaving a floating trail of sandy dust in his wake. Leaving Eddie standing there to watch.

Which he did.

Stood there watching the Caddy disappear, feeling the sandy grit settle between his teeth, thinking, There he goes.

Thinking, Well, at least he didn't shoot me.

Thinking, Only thing about DeReese was, Ray Bob might have trouble finding him.

34

She lay on the bed with the midnight breeze tickling her nipples, Eddie snoring. By leaning back her head she could look through the screen and see a pearled threequarter moon floating overhead, a sprinkle of milkywayed stars. Clouds here and there, not many. She listened to Eddie's rhythmic snuffle, heard the surf breaking down on the beach. Funny, he hadn't snored before. Or she hadn't noticed. He snorted and turned over.

She would've noticed.

At least Mister Hothead was gone. That had been a weight off, no joke. Guy who shoots kids through the eyeballs, he'd do anything. Ruby said she'd never met a man she couldn't learn to hate. Said it usually to a customer having man trouble. Lots of that, everywhere you looked. Mrs. Patterson with the wifebeater husband, bruises on her neck. Patty who was pregnant but the guy denied he'd done it. Then Mrs. Helms, married to a guy who'd lost his nerve and stayed in bed all day. And LouAnn Groves, now there was a situation. Four kids and a rich lawyer ex-husband who refused to pay child support, LouAnn waiting tables at Bennigan's. Just try and name someone with a decent relationship.

She tried, couldn't come up with one, with the exception of Kim Basinger, she seemed happy with what's-his-name. Alec, the actor. Alec Baldwin. Saw him everywhere except in movies. If he didn't get in a good one soon, that relationship was headed downhill, too, Kim was a big success.

It was true, though, what Ruby said. Only usually it took a while, the hating. In Mister Hothead's case, she'd made an exception. Took her maybe thirty seconds, minute if you stretched it. First time she saw his eyes in the rearview. Sometimes you just know. Guy was a rattlesnake. Past tense, thank god. Hoped the motherfucker rotted in hell, excuse my language.

She leaned her head back and watched the moon again, couldn't find the man in it. Eddie had stopped snoring but the surf was still breaking, steady as a heartbeat. She couldn't sleep. Too much on her mind. The breeze came up a little, made her nipples cold, and she reached down and pulled up the sheet. Thinking back.

Remembering when she heard the Caddy speed away, then Eddie coming up the stairs, finding her on the bed crying, crawling up beside her. Hey now, hey now, he'd said, leaning over her on all fours, you all right, you was just scared's all. But you gonna be all right.

She'd rolled over then and pulled him down. Saying, I need

you, Eddie, I need you bad. And him saying, I need you too, honeybunch, like a flower needs rain.

Now wasn't that sweet?

And then she'd pulled off her pants—them already being
unzipped, that was easy—and she opened his fly and pulled out
his cock. Hard already, and hot. Sometimes that didn't happen
with lots of men you had to work at it. She paused, thinking. Well
not that she'd had so many to know about. Anyway, in this case
she didn't even pull his pants off, just down below his hips, far
enough, and spread her legs and put him right in, she was already
wet. Sometimes that didn't happen either. But there you are, when
you love someone and they love you.

Then they did it for about an hour. Maybe longer, seemed like.
Long enough to get sore. Somewhere in there she realized she'd
never even taken off her top, so she did. He smiled and said she
had the prettiest titties this side of paradise. What about my
ankles? she asked. He told her they were just right, went perfect
with her feet. She said she liked his whole body, especially his
butt. And so on. Them talking like that while they did it. Like
some old married couple. *Did you remember to take out the trash,
honey? Yes, I did, sweetheart, here let me get on bottom. Ohhhh, that
feels good, how about the bag in the garage? You bet, there you go,
whoops, put me back in.*

That was exciting, talking like that, all the time him thrusting
in and out, filling her up, making her feel like a love bunny. Then
for a while her on top, moving her hips back and forth, riding
bareback real fast, his hands squeezing her ass, caressing her belly,
twiddling her nipples, all over her. Then oopsy daisy back over
him really coming at her then, hard, breathing heavy and fast, his
balls whack-whack-whacking her ass, that was a rush, and finally
hollering and shaking like he was having a heart attack, scared her
to death for a second, right before she came too. Came again. In
all, three times, a record. Which made her feel like the Queen of
Sheba. Until she felt something funny beneath her back, reached
under and pulled out a book.

Good lord, fucking on the Bible.

Then she felt like Bathsheba. Or someone like that, she couldn't recall the details. Someone bad anyway.

Eddie paid it no mind so she acted like it never happened. Put the Bible on the floor. Then they lay there on the bed maybe half an hour drifting along before they talked again. Finally, Eddie said, I'm sure gonna miss ol' Ray Bob.

She said, That sure felt nice.

He said, Not every day you find a runnin buddy.

She said, It was the best I ever had.

Or lose one, he said.

At least you're still alive.

He was my best friend.

She said, How long you known each other?

He said, Three weeks.

Now, wasn't that some shit?

35

On his first day back home he got drunk. He arrived midafternoon intending to ask Katie to dinner. Then he picked up the *Austin American-Statesman* from the front porch and saw he'd missed Bernie Rose's funeral. Big headline: COP KILLER TIED TO 7-ELEVEN MURDER. Bernie gone. *Rosie.* Next thing he knew he was halfway through a fifth of Jack Daniels.

He didn't know he was drunk until he tried to get from the kitchen to the bathroom. Floor kept bucking up, twisting sideways. He held on to the wall, sat on the toilet to piss. Reminded him of the time he woke up drunk in the night, got turned around and pissed in a bureau drawer, one with his underwear and socks.

On the way back through the kitchen he grabbed the whiskey bottle by the throat and sat on the back steps. Lefty crawled up between his legs, lay there. Rule twiddled with his ears, rubbed his belly. Said, Howya doing there, Lefty, I seen your paw Jim Dandy, he's doin fine. Lefty rolled one eye, didn't comment.

Rule finished off the bottle just after twilight, when a coolness settled over the dusky hills and nightbirds were calling. He fell asleep on the back steps, then stirred sometime before dawn. The Nam dream again. A jungle, moving through darkness. A voice hollers, Sonofabitch! Where are you! Then the explosion, a scream. His own, it woke him up. His back ached from the steps, he could hardly move. But he made it to the bed, still in his clothes.

That was the first day.

Second day began with a headache and a queasy gut. He tried to work it off cutting grass in the backyard, quit when the mid-morning sun made him dizzy. Took a nap and slept through lunch, awakened in the middle of the dream again. The jungle by moonless night, a monsoon rain. He ate a peanut butter sandwich and drank a beer. It was afternoon. He decided to walk the section, so packed a blanketsided desert canteen and climbed into the low hills of mesquite and juniper to the west, crossed the fence line onto Elmore Westland's place, Lefty roving for scent and sign, heeling when told. They skirted a slanting escarpment shingled with spall, followed a curving path down to a limestone outcropping overlooking pastures to the south, where Elmore ran a few head of Santa Gertrudis. He sat there wiping his head with a bandana, Lefty heeled up scanning the slope. The lower grasslands verged a spring branch lined with scrub willows and wildflowers, widened at one point to make a watering hole for stock. Elmore was down there astride a bay horse and rode on up, said howdy.

Rule thanked him for looking after Lefty.

Elmore said anytime.

They gazed out over the vega, Elmore at the foot of the outcropping, still mounted, the quarter horse grazing the sparse growth. A redtailed hawk drew in from the east, gliding on a current, policing the grassy margins of the branch sprayed with bluebonnets and paintbrushes. A covey of quail blew up and scattered, the hawk passed onward. It was a clear day, and warm, the land indolent and green. Another month and it'd burn brown under dry summer heat.

Elmore leaned to one side and spat. Didn't get them boys, he said. He didn't look at Rule when he said it, wasn't asking. More like observing the sky was blue, water wet. He put his hands on the pommel and shifted, the saddle creaking. He was a small man with short legs and a club foot but he sat the horse well.

Rule unscrewed the canteen cap, offered it down. The older man shook his head. Rule took a mouthful and swished it around, spit it out, then a swallow. He put the cap back on, laid the canteen on the rock.

Just a matter of time.

That it is, Elmore said. Like everything else.

I reckon.

They both studied the pastures below and the hills rising farther south toward the Blanco River, scrub country with limestone chalk mottled in juniper. Above that a pastel lapis sky. In the sky a pale saffron sun arcing westward. Beyond that nothing but weightless vectored space, lacking color or sound, without amplitude or measure. Wherein truth might be found, if it be. Certainly not in words. Elmore took off his hat, a sweatstained Panama with a black cord band, looked down and ran a finger along its crease. Then he put it back on and gathered the reins, turned the bay a quarter and nudged it on down the slope. He lifted one hand in goodbye. Rule watched him go.

An hour later, back at the house, he telephoned Katie to ask her to dinner. When her answering machine picked up he put down the receiver. He opened a can of ranchstyle beans and heated them with a chunk of baloney, ate them with stale crackers. Dana called twice before he was done and he hung up on her both times. Afterward he lay on his bed with the window open to the screen and when the phone rang again he didn't answer. He thought about his first wife for a while, Katie's mother, then his second. He briefly thought about the woman down in Freeport but Dana pushed her out so he thought about her. There was mostly nothing about her he liked, only the one thing, and it held him. Until recently he'd been thinking of getting some of that Viagra but with her he didn't need it. It was a hell of a situation when a man had to despise a woman to hold her. He was still pondering that thought when he fell asleep.

That was the end of the second day.

The next morning he awakened early. He finished the back-yard, then telephoned the lab and spoke with Moline. Still no news. So he called Katie and she answered, he could hardly believe it. She agreed to lunch at the Magnolia Cafe on Lake Austin Boulevard, another shock. He drove in taking Highway 290 and cut up MoPac, crossing the river to the boulevard exit, getting there early. He grabbed a table in the sunroom near a shady live oak. Then Katie arrived on her bicycle late in a bad mood and left in a worse one. Never would say what the problem was, but whatever he said only aggravated it.

Been reading that quotation book you gave me, he told her. It's pretty good.

I'm glad, she replied.

Then nothing, sitting there poking at a spinach salad, frowning. He waited, watching. Her in an Austin Lounge Lizards T-shirt and tight bike shorts, pair of Asics running shoes without socks. Deli-cate hands, stronger than they looked. Curly brown hair chopped short under a blue beret. Weird outfit. And a line of rings and studs running down the outer rim of one ear, pierced half a dozen times.

Him being dumb enough to comment: Not gonna get one of those tongue bobs, are you? Trying to be funny.

A glower, silence.

Him watching some more, her not. Avoidance in action. Fair skin and dark blue eyes. Colored contacts. Freckles almost gone now. Packing a few extra pounds, mostly muscle, all that bike rid-ing, but still pretty.

How's school?

Fine.

Got enough money?

Yes.

More silence. Squirrels in the sprawling oak, chattering away.

Birds whistling off the deck. People nearby talking. Giggles, laughter, everyone eating, drinking. But a heavy scene at their table, like somebody or something had died, the food getting cold. Rule feeling off balance. Tongue tied. Situation sliding away from him. Gotta say something. Let's see . . .

Lefty's doing fine.

That's good.

Deep breath, weak smile. Just say it: I miss you, honey.

She replied, voice gritty: I just wish you'd give me some space.

Space. How could he tell her? Space, you claim. No one gives it. They struggle with you because they care or they walk away, not giving a shit.

Sudden awareness: his very existence crowds her.

Say something: How's your mother?

She throws down the fork, lays it out plain: Mom left because you treated her like some *thing*. Like she was *property*. And she's *human*.

He looked at her, feeling every blow in his bones, waiting.

And she couldn't take it anymore. *That's* why she left. How do you think I felt?

He took a deep breath. Righteous guess: hurt. Only that wasn't it. Old ground, familiar. Everybody gets hurt. Something else. What? Ask.

You think you know *everything*, she shot back. You think you know me. *You don't know me.*

He agreed. No deceit in that, no pride. He didn't, not now. She abruptly stood up, shouldered her backpack.

I gotta go.

All right.

Major disappointment. He paid the check, tried to hug her. She froze, let him, *barely*, gave nothing back. Body language: get it over with. Like some odious duty. He let go, she stepped away.

Goodbye, Katie, it was good seeing you. I'll call you.

Okay.

Then she was gone. Bicycling down the sunlit street, bent over the handlebars, legs pumping. Fast.

Gone.

He got in the truck and pulled away, peeling rubber, back onto MoPac south. Frustration, immeasurable ache. Feeling worse than before. What was going on? Right there in front of him but he couldn't see her. Couldn't see *it*.

Didn't want to.

Shove that one aside. Speculate all the same. Something on her mind, obvious. Could be school or it could be boy trouble. Could be the weather, for all he knew. Only thing he did know was he didn't know his own daughter anymore. If there was anything else to lose he wasn't sure what it was.

Getting old.

Flashback: She was looking more like her mother every day. Remembered then he'd forgot to mention the dream. Had meant to ask how dreams might connect to premonitions. He picked up the cellular to call her and put it down. Let her be.

He slowed down on the throughway, took Highway 290 easy, farm to market even slower. No hurry now. But fuming, anxious. Things slipping past, not seeing them. Past imperfect, future tense. Melancholy.

This father-daughter stuff, Jesus Christ, it was hard. Too hard.

When he turned off the paved road into his long looping drive he glanced back to see the green wrecker following pull onto the grassy shoulder and park. Lomax had tailed him into town and back out, was parked now where he'd been parked since two nights before. On the road shoulder, heavy juniper between it and the house. Rule had passed him on the way out, hadn't even waved. The guy'd lost his nut. If he wanted to live in his truck, let him. No law against it, at least none worth enforcing. Long as he stayed off the property.

He drew up alongside the house and parked next to the blue Buick Regal. Dana was sitting on the porch steps waiting. They didn't speak but he took her inside and they never made it to the bedroom. Right there on the livingroom floor without saying a word. She bit and clawed and called him names and he thought he'd blown his balls off when he came. An hour later they went at it again, this time in the bed, and afterward he kicked her out of the house. She went yowling but she went. Then he showered and

took another walk through the section with Lefty, returned home
at dusk and ate another can of ranchstyle beans and went to bed
feeling tired. He put out the light thinking of Katie, turned it back
on and picked up the book of quotes. He opened it to the day's
page and read:

"Vengeance is mine; I will repay, saith the Lord. Therefore if
thine enemy hunger, feed him; if he thirst, give him drink: for in so
doing thou shalt heap coals of fire on his head. Be not overcome
of evil, but overcome evil with good. Romans 12:19–21."

He put the book down, thinking, Take one generous sonofabitch to pull that off. Then he shut the light and slipped into
sleep. He slept long and hard and did not dream, but was awakened just after daybreak when the telephone rang.

It was Moline. The boys had hit again. Well, maybe not both.
Redhead, though. In Beaumont, at the RaceTrac off I-Ten, a cash
only service station. At least one clerk dead, and this time a witness. Just got a call from the department down there. Thought
you'd want to know.

Rule said he damn sure did, what he'd been waiting for. Said
get everything you can, Moline, I'll call you from the road in an
hour. I'm on my way.

That was the beginning of the fourth day.

36

Ray Bob hit the highway bridge spanning Pine Island Bayou just
north of Beaumont, the big V-8 purring at eighty. Leaving the
coastal prairie behind, heading up into East Texas. Place he knew.
The car radio set on the KLVI morning talk show, couple of early-
bird clowns, fake baritones telling bought jokes. Listening in case
they interrupted their hearty banter long enough to report what
had happened. The robbery.

The fuckup.

Crossing the low bridge, he saw dawn splintering the eastern sky above the cypress and tupelo in the bayou bottom. Amber streaks over a dark green canopy strewn with old widows locks of Spanish moss, white spots of egrets perched low in the trees. The bayou running high, its coffeecolored waters spilling over cypress knees and dense bottom growth, spreading back into wet woods and tangled thicket. Scats of smoky mist floated on the scudding surface. An eerie brooding place, where beauty married death. The air even to the road filled with the odor of rotten mud and decayed vegetation disturbed by the rising flow. He caught it all in a moment, then the pavement spanned out flat ahead with woods crowding the road to either side, mostly slash pine and loblolly.

Ray Bob thinking about the fuckup. Cause he was working alone, what it was. What happens, and why.

He turned up the radio. The guys on the morning show were poking fun at the president, making off-color cracks and whooping, snickering. Talking loud and fast, full of their own bullshit, like that's what folks want to hear first thing they wake up. Radio rolls you out of bed, you get these dumbshits. Ray Bob lit a cigarette, listening, said, C'mon, you stupid motherfuckers, report it.

He was closing in on the Silsbee-Kountze Y when the show broke to the morning newscaster. The guy sounded excited, as if he'd been there. An armed robbery within the past half hour at the RaceTrac on College off I-10, he reported, apparently one person dead, a clerk, another wounded. The lone robber escaped with an unspecified amount of cash. The wounded clerk had given officers a description of the assailant en route to the emergency room at Baptist Memorial, where she was being treated for a gunshot wound to the leg.

Leg! Ray Bob shouted. Fuck!

My goodness, what a way to start the day, one of the morning DJs said, the one named Dan. Terrible, terrible. He asked the newscaster if the victims had been identified. The newsman said names were being withheld until relatives were notified. We do know the deceased is a black male, he added, and the wounded clerk a black female. My lord, Dan the DJ said, a woman. That's right, the newsman continued, and police think they have a lead on the assailant. He fits the description of one of two gunmen who recently hit a number of businesses between Austin and Houston, killing at least five people, including an Austin police detective.

Goddamn leg! Jesus! Ray Bob pounded the steering wheel. Motherfuck!

There was a brief pause, and Dan said, Boy oh boy, folks, what's the world coming to. I'm telling you right now. So this gunman should be considered armed and dangerous? he asked. The newsman fumbled a second, saying, Well, yeah, sure sounds like it, we got a dead person. Then recovered and said, Absolutely, Dan, no question, armed and dangerous. Then he gave the description: A white male with short red hair, about six feet tall and heavyset, wearing jeans and a white T-shirt.

Ray Bob grinned. Six feet, that was good. Probably looked that tall, holding a gun.

What's he driving? the second DJ asked. We oughta warn our listeners.

The newscaster said sorry, the police were withholding that information for the time being. Said there was an all-points bulletin out, though, because the assailant could not have gone far. Said the police apparently knew the make and color of the vehicle but didn't want some citizen attempting to apprehend the gunman.

Bullshit, Ray Bob said.

The newscaster said if he got the information, however, he'd come back on air, pass it on.

Bullshit, Ray Bob said. No way.

In the first place, the clerk who might've seen the Caddy was dead. He knew that for a fact. A 9mm slug in the head, another in the chest, that does not leave someone in shape to describe a getaway vehicle. It was the other clerk who saw him, the one came prancing out of the bathroom after he fired the shots. Back there, behind the soda pop rack, in the short hallway by the pay telephone. Came out in a rush, like she had no idea what was going down, still drying her hands on a paper towel, the stupid bitch. Then ran back inside the bathroom and locked the door before he could squeeze off a shot. Tall skinny gal, skin so black it was blue, all bones and mouth with her hair in cornrows. He stood there, not believing it, then walked back and told her to open the door.

Nossuh.

Open the goddamn door.

Nossuh, I ain't. What you do to my brother?

Who?

My brother Charles.

Where?

He be out there.

He your brother?

Uh-huh.

He be dead, Ray Bob said. Jesus, talking like her now. He raised his voice. Now open up!

Yo a crazy motherfucker, she yelled. Get back!

He lowered his voice, told her to unlock the door or he'd shoot her through it.

She said, Go head, yo motherfucker, it's steel! Go head! Go head! Screaming it, sounding hysterical.

So he did. Fired the Walther six times. Two low, two middle, two high. Door might've been steel but it was light gauge, the slugs went right through. Heard her holler and fall, too. Then silence. He yelled at her to unlock the door. Nothing. Figured she was dead. Squeezed off two more shots low for good luck and left, snatching the bills from the till, didn't even grab the loose change or look for rolled coins, taking too much time.

So she'd seen him. Not for long, but she had. Got his red hair right, and the clothes. He wouldn't argue that. But no way the nigger bitch seen the Caddy parked to the side of the lot. No way. Fucking cops blowing that part out their ass.

Ray Bob took a final draw on the cigarette and flipped the butt over the side, disgusted. Eight goddamn shots and she gets hit once. Maybe more, who knows, they hadn't said. But in the fucking leg? He banged the steering wheel with the heel of his hand. Jesus Christ.

Fucking mess, what it was. What happens when your runnin buddy pussies out.

He came up on the Y where the woods backed off the road and

he turned into the crossover veering left, taking Highway 69 north toward Kountze. A narrow twolaner, major north-south route before the big highways came in.

The pine trees closed back in on the road. The sun stood well up now, casting treetops in bright green, the sky overhead silver-dimpled with puffs of clouds, strung with the doubleveed arcs of spiraling hawks. The wind rushed over the windshield laden with the aroma of pinesap, bathing him in it, the air dense with oxygen and humidity as if he'd entered a tropical land.

A mile farther he pulled off the pavement into a roadside clearing where a log cabin sat beneath a stand of oaks. A cedar sign over the porch said CUSTOM GUNSMITHING in rustic letters. The carport beside the cabin was empty so he parked and got out. He relieved himself behind a tree, then raised the ragtop on the Caddy, tugging at the frame until it released, the electric motor whining in protest. He fastened the cover to the windshield and pulled back onto the road.

Traffic was light going north but within minutes the inbound lane toward Beaumont was busy with early commuters heading into work. Accountants and teachers, nurses and sales managers, bankers, lawyers, librarians, all of them white, in Chryslers and Buicks, driving in from their middleclass brick homes built in country subdivisions beneath the pines, safely tucked away from the blacks and Mexicans taking over the city. Balls enough to run, Ray Bob thought, but not enough balls to do something.

He drove within the speed limit, watching the oncoming traffic, an eye on the rearview. Looking for cops, for highway patrol working the morning commute. But relaxed now. Smelling the woods, inhaling the deep green density, going on up into East Texas, land of endless forests and riverbottom thickets, creeks and bayous and secluded rednecks, meanassed country folks. His people, where he come from. Not the way he'd expected to go, though, that was a fact, even if the terrain was familiar. Houston was where he'd intended. Come up from the beach through Beaumont, circle in the back way, avoid Galveston, already been there. Never reverse on a trail, common sense, someone might be following. Idea was to bag a joint in Beaumont, boogie due west to

Houston. Planning to find that coonass snitch, cancel his ticket. Like he'd promised Eddie. Matter of honor, what loyalty was about.

Until the fuckup.

Shit, he'd known something was wrong, felt it in his bones. Knew that nigger gal wasn't dead. Like some kind of second sight. Had put the Caddy on the freeway headed west, knew it wasn't right, got off at the first exit. Cops be all over that direction, running the interstate, maybe even a roadblock. Too chancy. So he'd turned back north into the woods. Place he knew.

All the while thinking about that fucking pussy Eddie. Get two guns going in a place, shit like that don't happen. Cause he was working solo, was why. What a runnin buddy was for. Cause of that bitch Della. Copacetic setup until she butted in.

Half an hour later the woods opened up and he went through Kountze, little peckerwood sawmill town, a few rundown stores and service stations and nigger shacks along the east flank of the road, Big Daddy's jukejoint and barbecue stands and a fried chicken drive-thru, and then he continued on, in the woods again, past the turnoff to Honey Island. He crossed a swollen branch, then another, the road now straight as a thirtythirty barrel between the dense trees, crows nestled in the high branches and turkey buzzards circling overhead. He knew this country, felt at home here.

East Texas, part of Texas you never hear about. Deep South really. All the way over to Louisiana and all the way up to Arkansas: dark green woods, tangled thicket and vine, baygalls, cypress bogs, sloughs and riverbottoms, where earth struggled with water everywhere. A jungle. A cloistered inward-looking land of damp vegetating heat, of shifting shadows by day and animal screams by night, moonless and starless beneath an impenetrable canopy. Its tenebrous reaches populated by alligator and cottonmouth moccasin, by coon, armadillo, bobcat and panther. And by humans who might've crawled up from the very swamps themselves, either long ago or recently: a changeless place.

His land, his home, his people. Where he was going.

But not for long. Just long enough. Until the heat faded. Then he'd get back down to Houston, take care of business. Then over to the beach, where he'd teach hoss a lesson.

Only he'd start with the bitch.

37

Within half an hour Rule was on the road. Packed an overnight in a hurry, brought Lefty with him. Not sure why, just a feeling. The Walker hound rode shotgun gazing out the passenger window at hills bathed in morning shadow, withers twitching at wings swifting among the juniper.

On the outskirts of Austin, he stopped for a breakfast burrito and coffee to go at a convenience store. When he regained the road Rule noticed what was missing. No tail. Then recalled there'd been no wrecker parked on the road by the house. No Lomax. Avenging angel done took flight. Maybe his luck was turning. Even if it did mean a trip to Beaumont.

The town lay 250 miles southeast, other side of Houston and south of the piney woods, down in bayou country near the Texas-Louisiana border. Where the original Spindletop gusher blew back in 1901, priming the oil boom. Now the city hummed in the middle of the oil refining and petrochemical belt fringing the whole length of coast between Freeport and New Orleans. A polluted little place where bluecollar shiftworkers hustled a buck for Texaco, Mobil, DuPont, a busy money magnet for insurance doctors and sharp lawyers claiming the public interest. Plenty of crime, a matter of civic concern, the bulk of it white collar, so ignored.

Flanking Houston to the north, he hit the East Texas woods, shot through old oilfield boomtowns now derelict villages. He drove fast but felt in no hurry. Back in action, events in motion. The morning lay warm and golden, verdant fields along the roadside sprinkled with wildflowers. Cattle in the pastures and hay in the fields. What May was for, the world unfurled in youth. Lefty curled up on the seat and went to sleep.

When the cellular went off Moline came over with an update on the Beaumont shootings. Was two clerks working, he said, brother and sister. He's dead, two nine millimeters, head and chest. She ducked into the toilet. Redhead shot her through the door. Eight shots fired. Hit her once in the thigh, once in the calf, missed bone. Lucky gal.

Sure it was Redhead?

Oh yeah. I sent down pictures on the computer, she made a positive ID. She said, and I quote, He's a crazy motherfucker.

A psychologist.

What she's majoring in, Moline said. She's a college student. So was her brother. Chemical engineering, straight A's.

Working graveyard shift in a service station?

They black.

Rule grunted. What else?

Moline said that was it.

Bullshit, Rule said. What's he driving? Which way he go? C'mon Moline, I want something I can work with. I want an ID.

We're trying, Moline complained. Christ, what you think we're doing?

I think you got something else on your mind. You ain't paying attention.

Think it's easy? Moline retorted. She stays out all night, drags in when I'm leaving for work. No explanation, nuthin. Like I ain't even there. You know what she's doing.

I know what you're doing, and that's what counts, hoss. Drinking heavy, fucking up your brain.

My woman's out getting drilled. What you want? Moline whining now.

Get an ID on Redhead, Rule said, that's what I want. He punched the button on the cellular, hung up. Lefty was looking at him. Rule reached over and scratched his head, told him he was lucky. When's the last time you got hung up on a bitch? he asked. The hound wagged his tail, went back to sleep.

Ten minutes later the phone rang again. Moline excited now, saying he had good news. They had an ID on Redhead.

All right, Rule said, tell me.

Talked to a homicide detective down in Beaumont, Moline said, name of Kirkland. Grew up in those woods in East Texas, place called Woodville up in Tyler County. Big Thicket country. Ain't that where you're from?

What's the name, Moline?

Johnny Ray Matthews. Kirkland says the boy's from Jasper County, just next to Tyler County.

Right across the Neches River, Rule replied.

Moline said that was right, he was looking at a map. The Matthews clan's well-known to law enforcement up that way, according to Kirkland. Regular clients, you might say. You know 'em?

Matthews all over Jasper County, Rule said. But I reckon I know the family he means. Kirkland figure the boy headed home?

Moline said the detective wasn't sure. Said Johnny Ray hadn't been in Jasper County the past few years. Spent some time in Waco, a stretch in the Dallas area, but most of it in the Texas prison system. A confirmed recidivist.

What's his age?

Twentysix.

Old enough, Rule said. What happened to DeReese?

We don't know. Maybe he dropped out. He wasn't in the security video. Maybe he stayed in the car. Wasn't no woman this time either.

What's Redhead driving?

Still don't know. I'm running a check through motor vehicle right now.

Okay, Moline, here's what you do. Call Kirkland, tell him I'll be in Beaumont in two hours. Tell him I want to see everything he's got on the Matthews boy. Mugs, crib sheet, anything he can find. Contact Jasper County, ask for the paperwork. Sheriff up there is Stace Collins, goes by Buckshot.

Moline said no problem, he'd get it all, including Johnny Ray's high school transcript.

He's a Matthews, Rule said, he didn't get that far.

He hung up and headed into the piney woods cruising the Dodge pickup at seventyfive. At a roadside park he stopped, set a plastic bowl under a faucet and filled it for Lefty. The hound lapped water, then went off into the trees to mark territory.

Rule sat on a concrete picnic table thinking. So Redhead was a Matthews. Why crawling into his head was a problem. He could get in there now but wasn't eager. He'd grown up knowing the clan, or hearing about them. Rough bunch, probably the meanest people in Jasper County, which was saying something. Reclusive and inbred, they were pure East Texas redneck, riverbottom poachers and thieves, violent by nature and ignorant by choice. Kind of folks that thought the Klan was a sanctified activity. The men made their own liquor and drank hard, the women were tougher than the men. Word was a Matthews girl still a virgin at thirteen had to be tough, and fast on her feet. Kind of family that produces a Johnny Ray. Only the Matthews generally stayed put in Jasper County. This one had got loose.

He whistled for Lefty and they returned to the road, the pavement curving gently through the woods. The swaying loblollies crowded the highway, though behind the pines, he knew, the land lay barren, vast stretches of denuded acreage devoted to the clearcut profits of Temple-Inland, Weyerhauser, Louisiana-Pacific. The right-of-ways hid the damage. Out of sight, out of mind, standard corporate policy, good public relations. Everybody knew, no one did anything. One reason he'd left East Texas.

When the cellular rang yet again he almost didn't answer it. He finally picked up.

Change of plans, Moline said. His voice urgent. You need to stop in Houston.

I already passed it. What's up?

We got DeReese down there, that's what.

All right. Rule waited.

He's dead, Moline said.

Rule waited some more.

After a minute, Moline said, You don't seem that interested. Sounding peevish.

Rule said he reckoned it was good news, a fine development. Except Redhead's alive yet. Still shooting people. Let the medical examiner handle DeReese. What happened down there?

Moline didn't have the full story yet. What happened, my homicide contact in Houston called, he got it off the police band. Said DeReese was shot several times, they got somebody in custody. That's all we know. Figured you'd want to take a looksee.

No use in it.

Well, Moline replied, that ain't what the colonel said. He said go down and check it out.

Rule took a deep breath. Said, Why the fuck didn't you say so to start with? You still got your head up your ass, Moline.

What you mean? We getting results here.

Rule said, That's horseshit, Moline. Beaumont cops getting results, Houston cops getting results. Everybody but you. You're playing switchboard. Get your shit together, hoss. Find out what Matthews is driving. Tell Houston I'm on the way.

He shut off the phone before Moline could respond. The order to backtrack to Houston pissed him off. That wasn't where he'd needed to go. Jasper County was where the next play would come. He hadn't crawled very far into Johnny Ray Matthews's head, but he knew that much. Ought to be headed up into those East Texas woods.

He could smell it.

38

How do you rationalize it?

Huh?

Explain it.

Don't reckon I ever tried. Just sumthin I do.

Della and Eddie sitting in the beach house, lunchtime, talking about his criminal career. Or, more specifically, his recent stint as a robber. She wasn't sure where he stood on that, what he had in mind. Eddie wasn't the sort of person who gave much thought to the future. One of his defects.

She said, Sumthin to do.

Uh-huh.

Like going to the mall.

Eddie looked at her.

Like going to Wal-Mart.

He said, Never thought about it that way, honeybunch, but maybe. Listen to this.

Leaning back on the couch, shirtless, his bare left foot propped on the cushion, guitar laid over his belly, he picked out some notes. Frowning with concentration. The musical tattoo perched above the left nipple on his smooth white chest. She watched. All he'd done for days was pick on that guitar, ever since he found it. Cleaned it up, put it in tune, smiling like he'd found a new toy. Pronounced it a Gibson acoustic, a classic, expensive, not the sort of thing you normally find stashed under a beach house bed. Where'd it come from?

Beats me, Della had said, LD don't play.

Finders keepers, he'd replied, and that was that. Only time he put it down was to eat or sleep. Like he'd found a new friend.

Least he wasn't out robbing convenience stores.

Okay, he said, adjusting his hold on the guitar, here we go. Listen up now. It's your basic blues structure, called a progression, which means firsts, fourths, and fifths. You get your pitch inflections, them's the blue notes, African influence. Call and response patterns in the vocals, like a plantation field holler, slaves singing.

She watched as he wrapped his left hand around the neck, began strumming the strings with his right thumb, plucking individual notes in between. Head moving back and forth, one foot tapping the floor. A funny offbeat rhythm. He started singing.

Sitting in the La-Z-Boy with the morning *Chronicle* in her lap, munching on a peanut butter jelly sandwich, Della halfway listened, thinking one blues song sounded like any other. Her gaze dropped to the folded up newspaper. She scowled. Nothing in it on Mister Dreamboat. Again. Not a thing on TV either. Meanwhile Eddie sitting over there, a wanted criminal, not even worrying, playing with his new best friend. While she went bonkers. Every day the same. Get up, make breakfast, read the Bible a bit, or try to, boy was it ever dull, all those *shalls* and *begats* put you right to sleep. Then lay out and work on the tan. Boy, that was exciting. Oprah being the highlight of the day, or Jerry. It was some kind of life. Hiding out at the beach, skipping work, missing her kids, not even sure why anymore.

Thinking, Maybe it'd blown over.

Right, fat chance.

The minute she returned to her apartment in Sugar Land, they'd jump from the woodwork, a whole SWAT team. Throw on the cuffs, yell gotcha! Good lord, she could see it now—

Arms jerked behind her back, the cops all business. You are under arrest for the murder of Mister So-and-so, big important executive with Such-and-Such Company. Here's your rights, etcetera, etcetera. Of which there wouldn't be many, of course. The squad car, ride downtown, being led inside the police station. TV cameras in her face, reporters yelling questions: Why'd you do it? Was it a lover's quarrel? A sex game? Are you a prostitute, Miss Street? Good grief, a prostitute. Keeping her head low, though, not saying a word. Not that it mattered. Getting led inside a police station handcuffed, you gonna look guilty. Then the interrogation room. A tiny table and two straightbacked chairs, stains on the walls, a single bare lightbulb. Sitting there rubbing her wrists, makeup running with sweat. And a fat detective in a bad suit across the table, staring. Another one, skinny, with acne, leaning against the wall. Neither one saying a word, letting the pressure build. Then, finally: Where were you on the night in question, Miss Street? The fat one talking. Who, me? Naw, your momma. Real sarcastic, sneering. What night was that, lieutenant? The night in question. Oh, that night? Let me see. Rolling her eyes, thinking. Until the fat one finally snorts and says, All right, Hank, book 'er, then toss her in the cell with them others. Big smirk. Saying, One night in there and she'll cooperate. Silent Hank grinning, been waiting for this, you can tell. In the cell now. Dirty concrete floor, an open toilet bowl, smells like urine.

There goes a cockroach. Filthy, filthy, with graffiti on the walls: SUCK MY PUSSY. LICK MY STINKY CUNT. EAT MY HOLE. Like that, big scrawly letters, right to the point. Crowded, too. Jesus Louise, just look at 'em. Mexican whores with tattoos, motorcycle mommas smoking cigarettes. Black women wearing curly blonde wigs and hotpants, patent leather highheeled boots. Like straight out of *Dirty Harry*. Plus two bulldog dykes in workboots and flannel shirts giving her the eye. Winking. Oh boy. And over there curled up in the corner with her head against the wall, sobbing quietly, a pretty young woman in a nice pink Laura Ashley dress, double-tier with flutter sleeves, ripped right down the front. Panty hose around her ankles. Hair and face a wreck, bruised, hands thrust between her thighs. Already had her turn, looks like. Guess who's next? Good lord, hold it right there. Stop the picture. The detective was right, I'll talk. Tell you everything I know, tell you stuff I don't know. Holy moley, I'll make up shit. Get me out *now*.

Tell me the truth

Della jumped. What?

Eddie on the couch, talking. Tugging on his earring, guitar silent. He reached over and took a bite of her peanut butter jelly sandwich, talking with his mouth full. I said tell me the truth, sug-arpie, what you think?

Della fluffed her bangs, said it was nice, real nice. She put her hands together, fingers interlocked, and twisted. Thinking about that nice double-tier Laura Ashley dress, torn to shreds. Those things cost money.

Yeah? Eddie smiled. How about that last line? "I'm a tail drag-ger, baby, I wipe out my tracks." Get it? That's Howlin' Wolf.

Della said she got it. Only if they put her in that interrogation room, no way she was gonna play dumb. Not after seeing that jail cell.

Eddie said, It's poetry ain't it?

Della nodded. Nossir, thing to do is admit right off she killed him and claim self-defense, that's what, ask for a lawyer.

Eddie shook his head, said the Wolf was one of the best. Said the Wolf went electric but the Gibson was acoustic. Said if he ever played music in public again, which he was considering, he was gonna play nothing but acoustic blues.

Della figured with a good lawyer she might get one of those plea bargains you always heard about, maybe even probation. If he was a good lawyer. Only most free ones weren't.

Course, it wouldn't be pure, Eddie was saying, on account of me being white. Plus I got too much southern rock and country in my background, bound to have an influence. Only I need me a harp, he added.

That got her attention. Della looked at him, eyebrows squeezed. Sounded like he'd said harp. She said, You mean like angels play?

Eddie said, Naw, honeybunch, a blues harp. Harmonica. A Hohner Golden Melody. What angels *wish* for. He grinned.

It gave Della an idea. If she was gonna get a lawyer, a good one, she was gonna need money. Only if you're in jail, you can't work and get any. Not to mention there was Eddie's future to think about, which somebody had to do. So she said, Maybe you oughta get one. You could learn some songs, kind people like, and get a job playing music. Like in a club. You get discovered that way.

He nodded vaguely, began plucking the guitar.

She took a bite of the sandwich and said, After that you can make records. I read the entertainment business is tops for money, Eddie. Musicians make more money than fashion models. You remind me of Steven Tyler, did I tell you that? And he's richer than Cindy Crawford. Then you could give up robbery as a way of life.

Eddie looked at her. He wondered who Cindy Crawford was. And the Tyler guy, too, for that matter. She sure knew a lot of people. He strummed the guitar, saying, Well, I been thinking on it seriously.

Cause I can tell you right now, there ain't much of a future in the other, Della said. Crime, I mean.

Eddie thought about that. Then he mentioned Robert Johnson who was dead at twentyseven, murdered. King Curtis dead at thirtyseven, also murdered. Then mentioned several others, dead one way or another. Janis Joplin, Jimi Hendrix, Jim Morrison, a long list. Said they'd all gone down early, right in their prime. Said all things considered, he wasn't so sure it was safer, playing music.

Della rolled her eyes.

Or profitable, for that matter, he added. Unless you sell out. True art not being much of an item. He strummed the guitar, smiling.

Della took another bite of the sandwich, said, And just what does that mean?

Well, Eddie said, this is America, ain't it?

39

Rule backtracked, took U.S. 90 down through the San Jacinto bottomlands, swamp buggy suburbs. Going to Houston. Going the wrong way but nothing he could do.

The whitehot sun eased toward its zenith, a high bank of white cumulus clouds floated inland off the gulf. He hit I-10 headed west toward downtown. Lefty lay asleep on the seat.

Traffic into the city was frantic, all day rush hour. Sprinting then stopping, Rule cursing, watching the yellowbronze haze of carbon particulate hovering over the landscape. He despised the place. Fact: Most polluted city in the nation. Cancer capital of the world. Grime, filth, a festering cement dunghill. Too many people, too much noise. Barrios, ghettos, high-rent neighborhoods with security guards and gates. Poverty and wealth cheek by cheek. A mad endless scramble, the excess human roar. A pending distaster: Houston: an outlaw city, the wild west.

Why he lived in the country. A world there outside man.

He passed the Anheuser Busch brewery at the 610 loop, saw directly ahead an upward thrusting hodgepodge of weird geometric shapes refracting through the haze. Cryptic forms rising from a sea of smog. The stone and glass towers of downtown. He picked up the cellular and dialed homicide at police headquarters, asked for Sergeant Eastland. The line crackled, went dead, then the detective came on.

Clint, it's Rule.

My man. Been too long. How's it hanging, pardner?

Seen better. I'm in Houston.

Eastland laughed. Said, Keeps us busy. I'm working one now there ain't no head and both arms missing. Guess why.

Rule pictured his old friend in a cubicle with his feet on the desk, smoking a cigarette. All right, he said, tell me.

Found him down by the Ship Channel. Gators got there first. Had a regular all-you-can-eat buffet. Eastland laughed again, began to cough. He was a heavy smoker, overweight, drank too much. Divorced twice, covering loneliness with wisecracks.

Well, if you can break loose a while, Rule said, I could use your help. He told Eastland about the DeReese shooting. I reckon they're still working the scene, wherever that is. Want to ride along?

Where are you?

Coming into downtown.

All right, I'll get the location, be waiting out front. Homicide ain't on the bayou anymore. Put us in a renovated highrise. We uptown now, baby. Travis and Polk.

Appreciate it, pardner.

You bet.

Fifteen minutes later they were headed east out of downtown on Navigation Boulevard parallel to Buffalo Bayou, a green-banked ditch smothered in outfall and waste. Eastland directed him through turns, then along the Southern Pacific tracks toward Galena Park. The detective patted Lefty absentmindedly with his left hand, waved a cigarette in his right, blowing smoke out the open window. The humid air rushed in and Eastland loosened his tie and opened his collar. Lovely day, he said. Fucking sauna.

Rule looked at him. The detective was heavier than ever, peckerbelly overhanging his belt, straining his shirt buttons. Red-faced, nose splotched with broken purple veins, a rumpled seersucker suit and scuffed Justin boots. White hair curled over his ears and down his neck in tight rings.

You looking old, Rule said.

Eastland grinned. Fuck you and the horse you rode in on, pardner. I am old. Fat alcoholic smokes three packs a day and works too much. I could kick it six different ways tomorrow, no one be surprised. He took a drag on the cigarette. Fifth of Old Crow says I outlive you, though.

How about your balls? Rule asked. They sag?

Eastland laughed, broke into a coughing spasm. Hunched forward, shoulders quaking, he pointed to the right. Rule turned into a side street over railroad tracks, passed a salvage yard, saw a squad car and coroner's van parked in front of a singlestory building lipping the Ship Channel. He parked under a catalpa behind an unmarked motorpool sedan. Farther up he saw another squad car, a wrecker. They got out. Rule told Lefty to stay, put both windows down for air.

They stood in the street, scoping the scene. Gulls shrieked overhead, a steady clanging rang from a distant marine yard. Rule reached behind and pulled the shirt from his back. Thirty seconds outside and he was soaking wet. Eastland took off his jacket, slung it over his shoulder mopping his face with one arm. Lovely, he said.

It was a rundown industrial area, with high chainlink fences sporting NO TRESPASSING signs and overgrown shell lots filled with rusting barge and marine equipment. Trash in the ditches, the pervasive aroma of heatsoaked diesel with the tang of old iron and a hint of swamp rot. The area seemed abandoned but for activity near the solitary building. It was mostly cement block streaked with green mold, partly discolored sheetmetal. A Miller beer sign over the front door announced: LITTLE BROWN JUG.

My kinda place, Eastland said, lighting a cigarette. Exclusive location, quality clientele.

Rule grunted.

There wasn't a crowd and one wasn't likely. A patrolman stood alongside his squad car sipping Gatorade. The rear doors of the medical examiner's van stood open, an aluminum gurney propped against the bumper. A young man and woman sat inside the back, waiting in dilatory shade. A tall beefy man with wide shoulders and a balding head stood in the doorway of the beer joint smoking a cigar, watching.

The body lay in a patch of high weeds to the side of the building. All they could see of it was a pair of bluejeans and brown boots, toes pointed downward. A young slim man with blond hair wearing pleated linen slacks and a beige silk sport coat with a dark shirt and a narrow apricot tie stood in the weeds, leaning over the body.

The fashion plate, that's Charles Phelps, Eastland said. One of our recent additions. Or colleagues, as we now say. He took a long draw on the cigarette and grinned. College educated, psychology, working on a law degree. A procedure nut. Memorizes criminal code for fun. Talks like one of those guys on *Nightline*. Swell guy, just ask him. Only don't call him Charlie. It's *Charles*. Eastland rubbed his swollen nose with a knuckle.

I'll be nice, Rule said.

They walked over to Phelps and Rule introduced himself, told the detective he'd been working a case on DeReese, had been tracking him. Connected to multiple murders, a cop killing.

This guy? Phelps motioned at the body, his narrow face incredulous.

I reckon so, Rule said. If this is him. Mind if I look?

The young man stiffened. He smoothed his apricot tie with one thin hand, pulled the silk jacket back with the other, and put it on his hip. Wearing a lizardskin hip holster with a 9 mm Beretta. The holster matched his belt. The guy wasn't even sweating.

You do understand he's the victim in an apparent homicide, Phelps said. He's in our jurisdiction. I'm responsible.

Rule raised his hands, palms outward. Your tag, sergeant. Just need a positive ID. Make sure he's who he is.

Phelps pursed his lips, stepped back. Okay, but I can tell you who he is. His name is DeReese Ledoux. Had a driver's license in his wallet, his picture.

All right, mind if I see the license?

The detective took a deep breath, put his other hand on his other hip. You realize we're wrapping up here, he said. I already bagged the possessions.

Rule leaned over the body, hands on his thighs, not looking at

Phelps, and said, That's good, son, then you know where to find it. Studying the body facedown in the tall grass. Long dark brown hair, faded jeans, a black T-shirt, sickly pale arms spread out to either side. To one side, in the weeds, Phelp's shoes—fancy woven cordovan loafers, lowcut sides—slowly turned and went away.

This who you wanted? Eastland asked.

Rule didn't say anything. He crouched lower. The head lay right cheek down in the weeds. There was a gold Texas-shaped stud in the left earlobe. We gonna have to turn him, Rule said. Grab his feet. Rule held the head while Eastland picked up the boots and twisted with a wheeze. The body flopped over, face up.

Hoo boy, Eastland said.

Rule counted four entry holes in the T-shirt, all centered within a two inch radius of the midline of the man's breastbone.

Somebody shoots better'n I do, Eastland said.

That ain't saying much.

Eastland chuckled. Naw, it ain't.

Rule's gaze drifted upward. A gaunt face with bony features, sallow skin, no facial hair, the eyes open. Dark brown eyes. High cheekbones, heavy lips.

After a minute, Eastland said, I seen this guy before. Yeah, I seen him on TV, one of them bands on *Entertainment Tonight* or such.

Uh-huh, said Rule, and I'm Porter Wagoner. He pointed to the pale arms splayed out to either side. Needle tracks on both. Guy was a junkie.

Eastland said, Told you he was a rock star.

Rule reached forward and took the bottom edge of the T-shirt between two fingers, pulled it up to the neck. The chest was thin and flat, the pectorals meatless, covered with dark congealing blood. Rule bent his head for a closer look. You got a handkerchief?

Eastland dug into a hip pocket, brought out a crumpled gray rag. He handed it to Rule, who wiped away blood above the left nipple.

Goddamn, Eastland said, that's my handkerchief.

Rule didn't say anything, kept wiping until he saw the dim blue outline of a tattoo. A Harley-Davidson insignia, a jailhouse job.

That him?

I dunno. Rule shook his head. I don't remember about a tattoo. Plus the guy I want wears a ring in his ear, not a stud.

Left ear?

Yep.

Well, hell, it ain't nothing to change an earring, Eastland said. These guys are like girls, got a dozen earrings, one for each outfit.

Rule glanced up, saw Phelps coming back. Walking fast across the shallow lot, one hand on his lapel. His face set hard. He drew up and thrust forward the driver's license. Said, I'm doing this strictly out of courtesy, Ranger Hooks. You should know I just spoke with my lieutenant and he says you didn't clear this through channels. He glanced sharply at Eastland, who shrugged.

Rule peered at the license. Same mug as the body. Name DeReese Ledoux, street address in Dallas. Rule took out his pocket notebook and wrote down the particulars. He looked at Phelps. Said, Fill me in on the rest. Was he packing? You got a perp?

The victim was carrying a thirtytwo caliber H&R automatic, the detective replied stiffly. That's it. You want more, go through official channels. Now, if you'll return the license. He held out his hand.

Rule handed it over. Sure thing, son, show's all yours. Appreciate your help.

He turned and walked away, Eastland on his heels. Then abruptly stopped and spun, cocked his right hand and pointed a finger at Phelps. Saying, By the way, your colleague here, Sergeant Eastland, speaks very highly of you. Thought you'd want to know . . . Chuck.

The detective flushed. It's Charles, he replied curtly.

Whatever, Rule said. Love the way your holster matches the belt.

They turned and left, Eastland shaking his head, grinning. Rule said, Least I didn't call him Charlie.

Hell, that ain't what's funny. I just realized, you do look like Porter Wagoner.

What's so funny about that? Rule pulled up short, held out a hand. I'll be right back. He strode across the oyster shell lot toward the man standing in the doorway smoking a cigar. Interior behind him dark as a cave, musty and damp. Are you the owner? he asked.

The big man nodded silently.

You see what happened?

The man clenched the cigar in his teeth, ran a hand over his balding head. Ain't much to tell, he said. His voice was surprisingly high, a tenor. This fella's inside—he pointed toward the body—another fella comes in, they argue. Then they both go outside. I hear shots, call the police. All I know. He gazed at Rule, shrugged indifferently. Shit happens down here. This ain't West University.

You know the victim?

The man leaned heavily against the doorjamb. He shook his head. Never seen him before. Neither one of 'em.

Rule turned and left. Waste of time, asking questions down here on the channel. No one had a name or a history. No one wanted one, no one wanted to know. He cranked the truck motor and turned the AC on high, left the doors wide open and stood outside while Lefty pissed against the catalpa, sniffed along the ditch. Insects hummed high notes in the grass.

Think you can get me the details on this? he asked Eastland. The detective lit a cigarette, said no problem, get on it after lunch. Which it was time for. Said he knew a place served the best shrimp gumbo and dirty rice west of Lafayette.

Reckon I'm buying, said Rule. The cellular rang in the cab and he reached in, answered.

Was it DeReese?

Moline asking.

All depends. Looks like it. Only he carried a thirtytwo, not a twentytwo.

Probably dumped the other one, Moline said, I would.

Maybe. He ever wear a Texas stud in his ear instead of a ring? He got a tattoo?

Rule heard Moline rustling papers. After a minute he came back saying there wasn't anything on earrings one way or the other. Got a tattoo on his chest, though.

Where?

Doesn't say.

What kind?

Doesn't say that either, Moline replied, just says a tattoo. Man, you'd think these assholes would learn how to fill out a form.

Rule grunted. Anything on Redhead?

No, Moline said, but listen, why I called is someone phoned in a possible sighting on DeReese. Anonymous tip over in Galveston County. Said they saw someone looks like DeReese in a grocery store on the Bolivar Peninsula. Just this morning. Gotta be bullshit.

Rule was silent. Laid the phone on his knee, thinking about Galveston, the feeling he'd had. Then he raised the phone and told Moline to get the prints off the corpse from Houston PD as soon as possible. Told him to go through channels, but push it. Make sure they matched DeReese.

You going on to Beaumont now?

Rule said, I'm going to lunch. Get those prints, Moline, and I mean push it. He punched the disconnect button, frowning.

Fuck it, Eastland said, let's go get some gumbo.

Rule put the truck in gear and pulled into the road, idling down the street between the parked vehicles. He passed the second patrol car and wrecker and stopped. Saying, I'll be damned.

What?

He told Eastland to hold on. He got out and walked back alongside the patrol car, bent forward to see through the glass. The officer behind the wheel was eating a fried baloney sandwich with porkskins. He slowly rolled down his window, looked at the Ranger with a quizzical expression. Rule didn't notice. He was gazing into the backseat at Harvey Lomax.

Mind if I ask this fella some questions?

The officer shrugged and rolled up his window, continued eating. Rule opened the back door, leaned inside.

Mister Lomax.

Lomax stared at him silently, then turned away, his rawboned face inscrutable. His tall frame sat upright, rigid on the seat, arms pulled back and cuffed behind. He wore the same dirty coveralls, the workboots. Bristly hair careening in every direction. Hadn't shaved in days, or bathed. The sour smell of old sweat hung in the air. After a minute, he shuffled his boots on the floorboard and glanced at Rule, chin thrust forward. His leadgray eyes gleamed with triumph.

Well, Mister Lomax, I see you've done the Lord's work, Rule said. Mind telling me how you found him?

Lomax shifted to one side, spoke quietly, his voice quivering with pride. The ways of the Lord surpasseth understanding, and a prudent man concealeth knowledge.

Rule nodded. Well, I don't reckon you've been as prudent as you think, Mister Lomax. You got the wrong guy. Other one was the shooter. I think you'll face charges.

He that keepeth his mouth keepeth his life, the man intoned, but he that openeth wide his lips shall have destruction. Proverbs thirteen and three.

All right, pardner, have it your way, Rule replied. Plead the fifth. But look this one up. Vengeance is mine, saith the Lord. If your enemy's hungry, feed him. If he's thirsty, give him something to drink. That'll dump coals of fire on his head and overcome evil with good. I believe that's more or less correct. Book of Romans.

Lomax flinched, then slowly looked away. Said, Horseshit.

Rule shrugged and shut the door. What could he say to that? Lomax was right, no doubt about that. But the words were in the Bible.

So there you are.

40

In the afternoon Eddie showered, washed his hair, and put on a clean white T-shirt. He combed his hair back tight, used a red ponytail holder. No mirror in the place, so he walked out on the deck where Della was sunning, stood in front of her drumming his thighs and said, What you think?

Della in her twopiece reading the Bible, squinting. She raised a hand to her forehead and looked. Real nice, she said, only your jeans are kinda dirty. I'm getting baked. Did you realize Jews are like Mormons? A man can have as many wives as affordable. Where you going?

Eddie popped his mouth, gazed out at the beach beyond the dunes and the rolling graybrown waves beyond the beach. A humid breeze coming off the gulf, the bright cobalt sky a cloudless glare. Then he went back inside and took his second pair of jeans out of the army duffel and changed. Sliding the white slips off the bed pillows, he put one over each end of the Gibson so they overlapped, tied them down with a string. He stuck his head out the screen door and told Della he'd see her later.

She said, No kidding, Eddie, did you know Solomon had seven hundred wives and three hundred concubines?

He cocked his head. Busy man.

And that's why God punished him.

How?

I didn't get to that part yet, she said. You didn't answer me. Where you going?

To get a job.

Before she could ask about that he ducked inside. She heard him clipclopping down the stairs in his boots. Della put on her sunglasses and lay on the deck wondering what Eddie was up to.

Good lord.

She jumped up and ran inside, opened the canvas duffel, reached one hand in. Felt around, touched it. Jesus. The gun was still there. She took a Coke from the fridge and returned to the deck, breathing hard. Lay there feeling relieved. After a minute, thinking about Solomon again. Wondering how in the world one man could handle so many wives. Filthy rich, for one thing. She felt pretty sure what a concubine was, too. Bible was full of stuff they skipped in Sunday school classes.

Downstairs, Eddie strode up the flat sandy lane toward the beach highway, the slipcovered guitar over his shoulder. Thinking about Solomon's wives. Course, that was back when women listened, followed orders. Acted up, they got whipped. Try that nowadays, you end up in jail, or shot. He pondered Della reading the Bible. Probably a good thing, maybe she'd learn something. Not that he'd noticed.

She sure gave good head, though. Jesus, she could suck. Last night on the beach, a strong wind off the gulf, clouds rushing past the stars, surf crashing, she'd laid him right down in the sand and put one on him. Like some dream, except for the sand in her teeth. Little rough, that part. And the damn mosquitos. Pesky little shits. Worth it though.

He walked on. Hot sun overhead, cattails swaying to either side, redwing blackbirds flitting over alligator weed and oyster grass. Quiet only for the wind over the marsh and the occasional cry of an egret. He broke a sweat. By the time he reached the main road his shirt was soaked. He put out his thumb and a heavyset young guy driving a Southwestern Bell truck picked him up going toward Galveston, dropped him in front of the Shipwreck. The shell lot was empty but for an old Buick Electra parked around the side.

The interior of the beer joint was dark and damp, smelled like stale smoke and warm beer. Momentarily his eyes came around. He saw a man standing behind the bar, arms spread out, palms on the bartop. Eddie went over and said howdy. Said he was looking for the owner.

That's me. The man smiled with a grimace. What you got in the sack, a banjo?

Eddie grinned. That's my ax, man.

The guy smiled again, showing his teeth. He was maybe fifty, wearing tan slacks that hung loose off his hips and a shortsleeved polyester shirt, creamcolored with big yellow flowers. Had a small watermelon belly and wore a thick gold chain around his neck. His pale skin radiated the translucent luminescence of a person either in perfect health or pickled in alcohol.

The man said, An ax. You that guy in the movies?

Who? Eddie frowned.

Never mind. The man shook his head, amused. His face was flat, his hair combed back straight, fluffed up and held in place by hair spray. Looked like George Jones, Eddie decided, back in the early Noshow Jones days. Sounded like him, too, with that country twang.

Eddie held the pillowslipped guitar over one shoulder and set one boot forward, hooked a thumb in his jeans pocket. I'm a musician, he said, and I'm looking for work.

The man nodded, said that's what he figured. Only we don't have live music here, son. Got a jukebox. What you play?

Blues, Eddie said. Like on your box.

The guy made a face. Said, That's my old lady done that. She likes boogar music. Only in here it starts fights. Had one last week.

Eddie said he was sorry to hear that. He observed fights never helped business. Asked what happened.

Can't exactly say, the man replied, wasn't here. He leaned back against a beer cooler and crossed his arms. He was wearing a gold chain wrist bracelet that matched the one around his neck. I was over at my sister's in Houston. But it was a mess, what I hear. Put a coupla ol' boys in the hospital, somebody lost a ear. Up to me I'd clear out that boogar music, have nuthin but country. Real country. George, Loretta, Tammy, both Hanks.

How about Willie?

Willie's a hippie, the man replied, smokes dope. Got long hair. He lifted his pants in back, made another toothy grimace that passed for a smile. Said, I tell you what, though, you might try up the beach at the Stingaree. Fella runs it's an old hippie boy, he might go for it.

Eddie stroked his chin. Where's this place?

Up there towards Gilchrist. The man pointed over his shoulder. You won't miss it, signs everywhere, you'd think he was selling Burma Shave. Old boy calls hisself Bubba Bear.

Well, I appreciate it, Eddie said, and good luck.

Same to you.

He put the guitar over his other shoulder and went out into the parboiled glare. Blinded again. He stood beside the road in the steaming heat and the same young guy in the Southwestern Bell truck picked him up shortly, heading back up the peninsula. The driver lifted his Astros gimmee cap and wiped his wrist over his forehead. I oughta start charging, he said.

Do that, Eddie said, you lose my business.

The guy chuckled. Where you headed?

Eddie said the Stingaree and the telephone repairman said he was going right past it. Said the Stingaree served the best barbecued crabs on the peninsula. Ever had any?

Never been there, Eddie replied. They passed a board sign beside the road saying DINE OVER THE WATER AT STINGAREE. A minute later they passed another just like it. Big handpainted signs he'd never noticed. Eddie lit a Camel and offered one to the driver, who shook his head. Saying, Quit three years now. Miss'em every goddamn day. He patted his belly. I just eat instead. Chow down, brown cow, gonna die somehow.

Eddie said he heard that. Said he planned on dying hisself. Someday. They passed another sign: STINGAREE, DON'T MISS IT. Only I better check out this Stingaree first, he said, looks right popular.

The guy smiled. Said it was, a busy place. Had a good location, plunked right on the bank of the Intracoastal Canal overlooking the east bay. Had a big dining room and bar, outside decks, good food, cold beer. Sit up on the second floor and watch the sunset, see the tugboats pushing barges up the canal, sometimes a cigarette boat loaded with girls in bikinis.

Eddie said it sounded all right.

What I'm saying. Check out those crabs, man.

You know the owner?

The young man shook his head. But I hear he's different. Well, here you are. Right down there. He stopped on the grassy shoulder and pointed west down a narrow lane leading into the marsh. Just go on about a mile or so, it deadends at the canal. You'll see it, a big old place, only thing there besides a boat launch. I'd take you but I'm on a call.

No problem, Eddie said, climbing down, appreciate the ride.

He watched the telephone truck vanish up the road, then starting walking. The ochered red sun lay directly ahead twenty degrees off the horizon, a terra cotta sphere of glowing heat. His feet were sweating in the boots. A blister came up on his right heel. He walked on. Sandpipers and herons stalked the brackish water standing in shallow ditches verging the lane. A pair of pelicans rose in the distance, passed overhead in a wide arc, then disappeared. Gone. He went on, limping, favoring the right foot.

He stopped once to remove the boot, inspect his foot. Taking out his pocketknife, he pushed the blade under the edge of the blister and drained it. He'd pulled the boot back on and started walking when he heard a vehicle approach from behind. He moved over. The low rumbling of the exhaust drew near, stopped alongside. It was a blue Ford pickup, fairly new, mudsplattered, sitting high off the ground on oversized bigfoot tires.

Want a ride?

Eddie looked over. A golden retriever with sad eyes laid his muzzle on the windowsill. He patted the dog and looked inside, studied the driver, uncertain. He was an enormous blackbearded man with shaggy black hair and small dark eyes wearing faded Dickies overalls and a green T-shirt with several large holes. The burnished bulk of his arms stretched the sleeves so tight it seemed they would burst. His great belly pressed forward against the steering wheel, spilled out the sides of the overalls. Eddie's searching gaze came to rest on the driver's feet. There, as if in pure mockery of the rest, the man wore an immaculate pair of custom made Larry Mahan red python boots with sharp pointed toes, riding heels and flame stitching. Major bucks. Eddie stared. Had never seen a pair in real life before.

Them's my workboots, the man said. The voice rose from his broad chest like slow stones rolling over rock. He said, They my shitkicking boots. Then he grinned. Step on in, friend, Walter here'll move over.

Eddie opened the door and climbed into the cab using the sidestep. He stood the guitar between his legs. The dog sat in the middle, leaned his brisket against the driver's heft. The motor revved and the truck leaped forward.

Going to the Stingaree, Eddie said. He pointed a finger and waved his hand straight ahead.

What I figured, the driver replied. Ain't nowhere else. What you got in that sack?

Eddie pulled the guitar closer. He tugged at his earring, frowning, peered out the side at the marsh. My guitar, he said.

Yeah? The guy sounded interested. What kind of guitar you got?

Gibson acoustic.

Why you bringing it to the Stingaree?

Looking for work, Eddie said. I'm a musician.

What kinda music you play? Rock 'n' roll?

Naw, Eddie replied, I play blues.

You mean that nigger music?

Eddie looked out the window. Thinking, Shit, here we go.

Folks around here, the guy said, not waiting for an answer, most of 'em, they like Vince Gill, Shania Twain, that uptown honkytonk music. And Mark Chesnutt, he's big, a local boy. Know what I mean?

Eddie glanced over and gave a vague nod, saw the guy reach down and from somewhere between his vast thighs produce an amber quartsized bottle. He put the mouth in his beard and took a swig. Eddie looked closer. It was IBC root beer. The man waggled the bottle and said, This is some good shit, friend. I'm addicted. Got that ol' time root beer taste. Want a hit?

Eddie raised his hand no.

Anyway, I was saying, folks around here don't hardly listen to nigger music. Ray Charles maybe, but he don't know he's black. What makes you think they'll pay good money for it?

Eddie was silent.

You any good?

He took a deep breath and closed his eyes. Jesus, you go out and look for honest work, you get this shit. Just never stopped, seemed like. He started to tell the guy to pull over, he'd walk the rest of the way, then remembered the blister. So he stared out over the flat green landscape and said, Listen, man, I ain't criticizing your music. Why don't you just let mine alone.

The guy shrugged. Asked if you was any good.

Yeah, I'm good, Eddie said, voice toneless, and I'm gonna get better.

All right then, you're hired.

Eddie dropped his head, shook it, closed both eyes. Man oh man. Redneck was a nut, no telling what he might do. Sure wished he hadn't left his pistol at the house.

The man took another drink from the bottle. Saying, You can start tonight. What's your name?

Eddie opened one eye, looked over. The guy was grinning. He shoved the IBC bottle down between his thighs and reached out an enormous sunburnt hand, knuckles the size of walnuts. Said, Put it there, friend. Name's Guidroz, only most folks call me Bubba Bear.

Eddie stared at the hand, incredulous. Couldn't move, paralyzed. Then shuddered and took the guy's hand, his own disappearing in it. Saying, Shit, this is too much, man. You for real?

The guy laughed, a deep rumbling roar. It's an unreal world, friend, he said, and that's a fact. Most of the time I can't believe it myself. What's your name?

Eddie opened his mouth, shut it. He cupped his hands and lit a cigarette, took a long draw and blew out a stream of smoke. He leaned back in the seat, right elbow on the windowsill, finally spoke. Said, I go by Rufus Slim.

Bubba Bear laughed again and laid an arm over the retriever, pulled it closer. The dog bent his head and licked the man's massive forearm with a long pink tongue.

Well, Rufus Slim, this here's Walter. As in Little Walter. As in Muddy Waters and Willie Dixon, Junior Lockwood and Otis and that whole crew. Cause you see, Rufus, I like my nigger music. Far as I'm concerned, ain't no music like the blues.

Eddie listened, thinking, Man oh man oh man, here I go. On my way. Thinking, I didn't even ask about the pay and he didn't say but that don't matter. Thinking, Jesus Christ I better learn some more songs *quick*.

—three nights a week to start, Bubba Bear was saying, then maybe we can make it more, see how it goes. How's that sound? There it is up yonder.

Sounds good, Eddie said. He looked at the Stingaree up ahead, an enormous twostory wood building sprawled on the canal bank overlooking the east bay. Watched it with his head bobbing yes like a dashboard toy. Sounds real good, he murmured, sounds righteous.

Then it's a deal. The big man put out his paw and they shook hands again. Only got one more little question, he said.

Eddie waited. Christ, he knew there'd be a fucking catch.

Do you believe in reincarnation?

What?

Reincarnation, Bubba Bear said, his voice rumbling. Spiritual concept, from the Hindus over in India.

Oh yeah, that. Eddie thought about it.

Like in former lives, Bubba Bear added helpfully.

Eddie nodded, took a hit off the cigarette. Said, Man, I hope so.

41

The Cajun restaurant, located on South Main near the Astrodome, served greasy gumbo and dirty rice that appeared inordinately dirty. Rule sipped his beer, said he wasn't hungry. Eastland said he was. He mopped his bowl with a crust of French bread and reached for Rule's. What's good about grease, he declared, is it lubricates the valves.

Rule listened to Eastland slurp and watched the traffic pass, the midday sun reflecting off glass and chrome. Thinking the body had to be DeReese, too many obvious indicators. Still, something seemed off. He couldn't pinpoint it. One of those feelings you can't explain. He turned back, studied his friend. Eastland looked bad, and he looked like he didn't care. He'd poured the dirty rice into the gumbo and loaded it with salt.

So happens I got a fifth of Old Crow at the house, Rule said. Reckon I'll take that bet.

You're on, Eastland replied. He wiped his broad red face with a paper napkin and lit a cigarette. Cause folks underestimate the power of genetics.

Old age run in your family?

Hell no, everybody drops dead by sixty. He puffed on the cigarette and motioned the waitress for another beer.

Just a matter of time, pardner.

I know it. Eastland shrugged.

Rule didn't think so. Thinking death was all around but we never look. Knowing someday it'll come looking for us.

After lunch he dropped off Eastland at police headquarters, saying he'd hang tight and wait for the report on the body. Eastland said he'd call soon as he got something. Shouldn't take long. He shut the truck door and plodded across the sidewalk into the building.

But it was late afternoon before Rule got word. In the meantime, he killed time, feeling restless. He telephoned Katie, left a message on the machine: Hey, this is the old man, back on the road. Sorry about the other day. Don't mean to pressure you. Guess we got some things to work out. Call if you need anything. He waited a beat, said, I been meaning to ask you about this dream I been having. Love you.

He hung up, tried to decide if a telephone call was crowding her. Probably. Too late though. No way to erase it now. Past done past. Time flows one way only. A real blur, too.

He drove down Main and stopped at a 7-Eleven, bought a can of beef Alpo, and drove to Hermann Park. He fed and watered Lefty, squatted in the shade, feeling antsy. Thinking DeReese or not, he needed to get up to East Texas, head off Redhead. The boy was on a roll. Bound to get worse, too. Didn't take a weathervane.

He loaded Lefty in the truck and went out Westheimer, found a bookstore specializing in mysteries and suspense. There he browsed the racks and bought two paperbacks by James Lee Burke and Walter Mosley. Both writers had a knack, kept things moving. When he checked out, the clerk suggested something by Elmore Leonard. Sharp ear for dialogue, he said.

Does the good guy win?

The clerk frowned. Well, with Leonard, it's hard to tell who's good and who's bad.

Sometimes how it happens, Rule said. Give me two.

Afterward, he went next door into a discount music shop and bought a Best of Porter Wagoner tape. He was sitting in the truck cab wrestling with the wrapper when the phone rang.

Hey, darlin.

Dana, he said.

Whatcha doing?

Listening to Porter Wagoner.

That old stuff?

He could hear her nose wrinkling. She said, Why don't you try Vince Gill? He's got a new one out. Where are you?

Houston.

When you coming home?

Don't rightly know, he said. I'm tracking someone.

Like an old dog. Then, Why don't you come sniffing around me?

Might get confused, all those strange scents.

Well, she huffed, just what do you mean by that?

Be like nosing a fire hydrant, that's what.

Damn you, stop it. She hesitated, then said, Rule, sweetie, guess what I'm wearing right now. Purring.

He held the receiver to his ear, silent. She asked if he was still there so he said, You wearing me out, that's what.

She giggled. Un-unnh, wish I was though. I'm laying in bed naked as a jaybird. Just polished my toenails bright pink. That shade you like? And my little titties are all swole up. They need a mouth massage.

Rule grunted.

And now I got my legs spread open. Cause I'm thinking about you. Listen to this.

He didn't hear anything. She came back on line. Know what that was?

No idea, he said.

I was rubbing the receiver between my legs. She lowered her voice to a whisper. I'm sopping wet.

He watched people going in and out of the discount music store. Thinking, Jesus Christ she just kept coming. Lust in action, shameless. He could turn her, but at what expense. She was good, that was a fact. Knew what she was doing. He had a hard-on that wouldn't quit.

Of course, I could get dressed, she said matter of factly, and come on down to Houston. I'll shave first. You know . . . down there.

Rule said, I'm all tied up. His voice cracked.

Well maybe that's what I had in mind, she said. Purring again. Or you could tie me up. Whatever works, sugar, you know me.

Sure do, he said, but I gotta run. Call you later. He disconnected and rubbed his jaw. Jesus. No matter what he did or said, there she was. Like a bad weed. Only one way to kill a weed, at the root. He reached down and stroked his pecker through his pants. Big one, hard as a railroad spike. A moment later the phone rang again. He answered right off, saying, Listen, goddammit, why don't you just back off a notch?

Jesus, what'd I do? Eastland talking.

Rule cleared his throat. Sorry, Clint. You got something?

Yeah. This ain't your boy.

Damn. Rule grimaced.

But what's interesting, said Eastland, is he's close. Dude's a Ledoux, sure as shit. Only it's Wade Ledoux.

Rule said, I'll be.

Uh-huh, and if you like that, you'll love this. Turns out he's got a cousin named DeReese. I called a contact over in Lafayette, parish where Wade comes from. He laid it out. Says both boys were trouble, mostly B and E, auto theft, crap like that. Last thing they was doing was boosting luxury vehicles on special order. Know those high-end SUVs? Greaseballs in LA and out east want them for their kids. Steady work. Only our boys get busted and Wade turns over on his cousin. DeReese gets sent up, Wade walks. He's a junkie, knows he can't make it inside. What's funny is, DeReese didn't carry a grudge. I hear they were close, like brothers.

Look like twins, Rule said.

Ditto, said Eastland, another thing that's interesting about this. I'm told they coulda been.

You're shittin me.

Naw, ol' boy in Lafayette says they were born the same day, same hospital. Only they was raised separate. Grew up as cousins down on some backwater bayou. Word is the grandpa might've been the real daddy. Big coonass family. Them swamp folks bad as hillbillies.

Sure throws a damn wrench in the works, Rule observed. He know where DeReese is?

No idea. Said both boys drifted over the state line after DeReese got paroled. They could be going by the same name. Or switched. They used to pass off as one another. Which raises a question.

What's that? Rule said.

How you know DeReese is the one you want?

Rule was silent, recollecting. No prints on the Abe Krishna shooting, or any other. Just video. And Moline's visual ID on DeReese. That was it. Jesus Christ.

I'll be damned, Rule said. Guess I don't.

Eastland chuckled. Nuthin like a good mystery, pardner. Why we pull down the big bucks. Listen, I gotta run. That headless corpse still in the morgue crying for a name. All I know is it ain't a Ledoux.

How's that?

He's Vietnamese. Eastland laughed. Stay in touch, hear? He hung up coughing.

Rule sat in the cab drumming the steering wheel. After a minute he dialed Moline at the lab. Moline said, You must be psychic, I was just about to call. His voice strutting a little. Got the ID on that body.

It ain't DeReese, Rule said.

Yeah, that's right. Moline in a nosedive, miffed.

That's only half of it, Rule said. He told Moline the rest, then the question Eastland raised. Moline sounded morose, observed video IDs can go wrong, Rule offered a mistake like that can happen. Maybe it was DeReese, maybe not. But what I want to know, hoss, is why Wade Ledoux jumped up and bit us on the ass. We didn't even know he existed. Why is that?

Well, shit, Moline retorted. He babbled about the computer system, NICI, Triple-I, network operations, official channels, informal contacts, appropriate requests for data and replies, how things worked. Defending himself.

What you're saying is that paperwork went out and paperwork

came in, Rule replied. You got answers to questions. Problem was, you didn't ask the right questions. That it?

Moline was silent.

What I figured, Rule said.

More silence, on both ends.

When Moline finally spoke, he did so quietly, his voice retrograde, distant, as if he'd fallen deep inside himself. You riding me pretty hard, Rule. So I'm gonna tell you straight out. Dana talked to a lawyer. I think she's gonna file. I'm already on the edge, don't push any more.

Rule eased off. All right, Moline. What you gonna do?

I got a gun. Comes a time I can't take it, I'll just end the misery.

Yours or hers? Rule speaking evenly.

Works either way, Moline said. I ain't decided yet.

All right. Rule paused. It's your life, pardner. It's what you make it. Long as you're undecided, though, just remember what I told you.

What's that?

Take the divorce. She ain't any good.

He heard Moline breathing. Then, How come you know so much about her, Rule?

I know her kind, he answered. That's enough to know.

And what kind is that?

A heartbreaker.

I don't care.

Rule said, Good to hear you admit it. Most truthful thing you said all day. That's it for me, hoss, I gotta run.

Okay, fine, Moline shot back, so you're tired of listening. Not your problem, fine. Now where you going?

Beaumont, then East Texas. Taking the roundabout way, down through Galveston and the Bolivar Peninsula.

Gonna check out that tip on DeReese.

Call it a hunch, Rule replied. You never know. I'll pass through, take a quick sniff.

What you want me to do? I ran the Matthews boy through vehicle registration. Big goose egg.

Then get what you can on Wade Ledoux. All the pictures you can find. Put them upside the pictures of DeReese. Then look at those videos again. See what you can see.

That all?

No, lay off the bottle or get rid of the gun. Or both.

Moline was silent. Then said, Don't think I will, Rule, think I'm gonna need 'em.

Maybe you need too much.

You finished?

Let her go, Moline.

But he'd hung up.

42

Nearing Woodville, the Tyler County seat, he backed off the speed. The slender pavement winding gently through upland terrain, green woods to either side now sparse, now dense. Logging trucks hurtled past, bulldog diesels grinding through the gears, huge pine logs stacked high on the trailers. In small dirt clearings along the roadside sat trailer homes surrounded by yard trash and chicken pens. More pickups than cars. Sandy ruts leading off toward unseen homesteads, handpainted offers nailed to trees: STUMP GRINDING, FRESH YARD EGGS, FIREWOOD, DIRT HAULING.

Grind my stump, baby, Ray Bob murmured, haul my dirt.

He drove on. Passed a one man sawmill, an open pasture fenced in post oak with grazing Herefords, a mule, then a small whitewashed church canting over brick piers. Full Gospel Tabernacle of Jesus Our Saviour. Shortly after, a propane gas distributor on a fenced lot with prefab aluminum buildings. The trees razed back from the lot. A feedstore with tack on discount, a tractor dealership. Low ranchstyle homes beneath the pines. Used bassboats on trailers set roadside with for sale signs.

Coming into Woodville, population four thousand, maybe five. Then another church, this with a mobile sign set out front: EARLY RISERS DON'T GO TO BED LATE, REMEMBER CHRIST JESUS DIED FOR YOUR SAKE. ARE YOU PREPARED? Followed by more churches. Nazarene, Assembly of God, Church of God, Apostolic, Pentecostal. Temples, fellowships, sanctuaries. And manifold Baptists: First, Shiloh, Zion, Ebenezer, Missionary and Pilgrim. Church every which way you turned. Goddamned religious place, Ray Bob thought, to be filled with so much meanness.

He passed the Woodville city limit sign, commercial outlets began in earnest. County seat, where everyone shopped. He braked into the Wal-Mart lot, stretched his legs. Late afternoon and a red sun hovered in the west. Still hot yet, but ready to cool down. Grackles policed the pavement, strutting scavengers foraging for tidbits. The thrumming of cicada and cricket from the treeline.

He went inside, bought a plastic twoliter bottle of Dr Pepper and a giant bag of Cheetos. In the exit area he picked up the latest issue of the *East Texas Peddler* and perused the bulletin board. Fresh catfish for sale, a Remington twelvegauge pump. Index cards listing acreage, used baby clothes, stud services. Handbill for a gospel music show at the high school starring Clouds of Glory and the True Light Gospel Trio. His eyes roved to the side, settled on a scrap of brown paper torn from a grocery sack: *Mayhaw jellie, Juss put Up, $2 a Cuart. Ethel Matthews, Jasper. Cawl me Now.*

Ray Bob smiled. No phone number. Aunt Ethel, his mother's sister. On her fourth husband, last he heard. Put the first under with food poisoning, the second with an ice pick. Third one disappeared. Kept the current one, Uncle Hardy, on his toes. If he was still around.

He cranked the Caddy and drove north, drew up to the redlight where the road intersected Highway 190. Center of town. Courthouse and bank on the left. Turn right and go on past the pawnshop, the road led east to Jasper. Place where Aunt Ethel lived. The whole clan, back down in the bottoms.

A hopped up Honda Civic eased up on the right, squeezed

between the Caddy and curb, trying to turn in that direction. Two young black men wearing gold chains and caps backward over cornrows, the car bouncing on its springs, stereo boosters booming out rap. Ray Bob glanced over, shot them the finger. They stared at him, then slowly turned. The light blinked green and he went straight through, past the Sonic Drive-In and Woodville Inn, then angled off onto Highway 287 headed west. Narrow twolane road through the nice part of town. Brick homes nestled in deep green magnolias, honeysuckled fencelines and gardens of azaleas beneath low blooming dogwoods. Several miles out he slowed, pulled into a lane up the hill into a small roadside park. Kirkland Springs, built by the WPA. He parked under an ancient beech above the springs and sat on a cement picnic table with the Wal-Mart bag.

It was cool in the hillside shade, and quiet but for bluejays and songbirds. No one else in the park. He drank the lukewarm Dr Pepper and munched Cheetos, reading the *East Texas Peddler*, free weekly publication for people selling personal property, nothing but ads. Anything from a fourwheeler to a genuine diamond engagement ring still in the box, guaranteed. Lots of used trucks and fiberglass bassboats. Plus tools, livestock, coon dogs, log chains, matching sofas and loveseats like new, you name it, whole world for sale. He carefully read the ads for bassboats. Wouldn't mind one of those. Neches River between here and Jasper, backed up with Dam B Lake, and the other big reservoirs nearby, Sam Rayburn and Toledo Bend, both famous for fishing tournaments. Spend an entire week there on the water if you had the right gear. He'd never been in a bassboat. Not one of those big twentyfoot fiberglass rigs with a fuel-injected V-6 Merc on the back, dual console with aerated baitwells, tilt steering, high performance Lowrance fishfinder, trolling motor up front. Cost thirty grand, setup like that. Maybe ten grand used, find it in the *Peddler*, someone just lost his job and can't make house payments.

He was so busy thinking about that he didn't hear the car drive up. Wasn't until the doors slammed he noticed the two guys in the Honda Civic. Parked right in front of him, black guys he'd flipped off. Hadn't been playing the music, he was pretty sure of that. They stood there staring at him, shooting spearchucker voodoo. Between him and the Caddy. Caddy where his gun was. He gazed back, framing the picture. Both wearing baggy pants and loose pullovers and flashed out Nikes. One tall and one short, the first one ebony skinned, the other high yellow with freckles, neither very large. Not muscular either, couple of skinny slumpshouldered dudes. Late teens, early twenties, hard to tell. Probably not that fast, weighted down by all the gold chains. Might be fun. Hadn't kicked a black boy's ass since prison, three four months now.

Then the tall one leaned backward and reached into the Honda, brought out an aluminum baseball bat. Laid it over his shoulder.

Ray Bob looked at the bat, looked at the guy. Said, Thought hoops was your ethnic group's game of choice.

Why you wanna fuck with us, man?

Let me ask sumthin, Ray Bob said, cause I'm curious. Has to do with social acoustics. What I wanna know is, why you think the whole world wants to hear Run XYZ and Snoopy Dogshit holler that jigaboo crap you call music.

The short one reached into his back pocket, brought out a stainless steel boxcutter. He slid the razor open. Uh-huh, he said, man think he a smart cracker, Lionel.

Ray Bob said, You need to get outa this onehorse town, bro, learn the latest lingo. Or watch the tube, one of them coon music channels. We ain't been crackers a long time. Honkies neither. He grinned. Be like me calling you a nigra.

Be callin me suh in a minute, the short one said.

Muthafucka be callin his momma, said the other.

What I be callin, said Ray Bob, is an ambulance, you two ass-holes don't get outa here. You got ten seconds.

But they didn't leave, and they were faster than he thought. He ripped the boxcutter away from the short one right away and kicked him in the balls hard, guy squealed and collapsed right there, but the second one called Lionel caught him upside the head with the bat. A short wicked cut. Made a metallic plunking thud and Ray Bob went down rolling in the dirt. Thunder in his head, and lightning. He came up on his feet reeling and plunged ahead, dodged the next swing so it caught a glancing blow off his left shoulder. Hurt like hell, though, worse than the first. He fell to his knees, left arm hanging numb, and ducked the third swing, sliced the guy's right thigh with the razor as he spun past. Heard the guy scream, but before he could rise or turn, the bat caught him flat across the back on the rebound, knocking his wind loose, and he fell forward on his face. Lay there in the dirt waiting, blow to finish him off.

Only it didn't come. Instead, the tall one called Lionel rolled Ray Bob onto his back and straddled his chest, stood over him breathing hard, clutching the baseball bat in one hand, the other pressed tightly against his right thigh. Not much blood, Ray Bob noticed, must've just nicked him. He closed his eyes, stretched them wide open. His vision was lousy, still seeing stars, but his breath was coming back. He lay there looking up, gripping his shoulder. Pains shooting through it. Then the black guy leaned down low, his ebony face close to Ray Bob's. He spoke quietly, almost a whisper.

Put down some respect next time, cracker, or you be dead.

Ray Bob grinned. Wasn't much of a grin, he could tell, but it was there. He lifted his right hand, shot Lionel the finger.

The guy snorted and stood up straight, shook his head, walked away. Ray Bob heard him help his buddy to the car, the motor started. The stereo came on full volume, all bass, like treble didn't even exist, nothing but distortion and mumbojumbo. He lay there gazing up into the high limbs of the beech tree until the thumping dropped down the hill and disappeared. Lay there watching the late navy blue sky through dark green leaves, listening to cicadas sing. Thinking his shoulder was gonna be sore for a while. Wondering why he'd walked away from the car without his gun.

Another fuckup.

Thinking, Shit what happens when you solo, when your runnin buddy pussies out.

Gonna teach that bitch a lesson.

43

You'd have thought she'd appreciate it, fact he had a job. Instead, she yelled.

Rufus? *Rufus?* What kind of dumb name is that?

Not Rufus, he replied, Rufus Slim.

Oh, great. What does that make me? Missus Slim?

He leaned back on the couch, rubbing an armpit. Cocked an eye, smiling. Saying, That mean you wanna get married, honeybunch?

She blew up her bangs in exasperation, marched into the kitchen area for a glass of water. He heard her over there running the tap, muttering, Rufus, Rufus.

It's Rufus Slim, he called out. One name, like Tampa Red or Big Bad Smitty.

She came back with a jellyglass of water and stood in front of the couch. Wearing cutoffs and bikini top, hipcocked. Big Bad Smitty?

Yeah, Eddie said, cool huh? It's a stage name. Like Gatemouth or Pine Top. Or Jelly Roll.

Jelly Roll? Her eyebrows arched, lips puckered, drawing out the syllables, making it sound silly.

He grinned. You know what a jelly roll is, don'tcha?

Well, I can imagine. Speaking *sotto voce*, wagging her head, eyes closed.

All this in the early evening, just after sunset. Just before he acquired the stage persona to go with the name.

I gotta get ready, he said, time's a wasting. He pulled off his T-shirt and borrowed her purse mirror, little round dinky thing, and disappeared behind the shower curtain. She heard him in there, moving around, chuckling. Half an hour later he threw open the curtain. Ta-daaa.

She sat in a kitchen chair, mouth open. Said one thing: My lord.

He winked and grinned, ran one hand over his head. Hair puffed up high in front, smoothed back along the top, feathered short on the side. All of it coming together in back, overlapping, squared off at the neck, no ponytail. Early Elvis. He slipped on a pair of dark shades, Roy Orbison. Took off the earring loop and put in a stud with a small gold star hanging from a chain. Who now?

A bad stray cat, Eddie said, straight from the Mississippi Delta. Big bad Rufus Slim. He raised his chin and howled.

She said it again: My lord, Eddie. Wade. Whatever your name is.

So, you dig it? He turned in a circle.

She waved one hand limplike, a moot question.

Yeah, me too, he said.

Then he stripped off his pants and shorts and stepped into the shower. Stood in there singing about chain gangs and sweet sugar mamas and backdoor hoochie coochie men until the water turned cold. Della sitting at the table listening, wondering how much money he was gonna make. A lot, she hoped.

Now, two hours later, he was perched on a stool in a corner upstairs at the Stingaree bar overlooking the Intracoastal Canal and East Galveston Bay. The bar a long room with screened windows on three sides, lit dimly. Warm night air smelling of fertile sea and swamp wafting through the screens, a salty tang. He sat on the stool cradling the Gibson acoustic, leaning into the mike. Sunglasses and the fifties haircut, cigarette stuck behind one ear. Banging the strings, bending the notes, growling cause he'd been re-buked and scorned. Song ended, without missing a beat he segued into another he called "Black Cat Bone"—

> *My baby got a black cat bone,*
> *She think everything I do is wrong . . .*

Della, sitting at a nearby table, stiffened. Good grief, what a thing to say. Like that was the only rhyme he could come up with. Besides, she wasn't anything like that. She raised a hand to her face, hid behind it. Just in case anyone had the notion she was Missus Slim.

Down to Dallas, Texas, down to Wichita Falls,
Got a thing about that greatlegged woman . . .

Della couldn't believe it. Calling her legs fat now, that was real nice. Next thing she knew he'd be on her eyes, for crying out loud, saying they were set too close. She kept one hand up, with the other lifted the wine cooler, strawberry flavored, and sipped. Thinking she'd better have a little talk later with Rufus. He needed some musical advice.

Someone sat down at the table, Della glanced over. Bubba Bear. He winked, reached over to pat her on the shoulder. She waved the fingers of one hand. Hello. Boy, he was big. She'd met him earlier, when he picked them up at the house, brought them to the Stingaree. Talked the whole way, telling about the time he lived in the Haight-Ashbury, back in the late sixties, before fascism made its comeback. People weren't afraid in those days, he'd said, everybody a friend. Love free, living easy, the summertime of life, like Janis said. Janis Joplin, from up the road in Port Arthur, same as him. Only he'd known her later, in San Francisco. Wild woman, liked to drink and talk nasty. Everything in excess, like Blake said. William Blake, eighteenth century poet, visionary mystic. The road of excess leads to the palace of wisdom? That guy. Also: I must create a system or be enslaved by another man's. Heavy dude. Probably used hallucinogenics, kept it quiet. The doors of perception? Blake. Then Huxley later. Aldous Huxley, famous writer. Brave new world, etcetera. Did LSD, wrote about it, quoted Blake. Nowadays they'd put him in prison. Huxley, that is. Blake, too, for that matter. Fascists hating any deviation as they do. Not so much the government. Not now. Corporate fascism, the new thing. Under the guise of free enterprise. Going global, too, just watch.

Bubba Bear telling all this between swigs on a big quart bottle of IBC root beer he kept between his thighs.

Wasn't until they reached the Stingaree that Eddie got a word in edgewise. Bubba Bear, he said, this is Della, my old lady. Sounding proud.

The huge bearded man had kissed her hand then, said he had

nothing but respect for any woman able and willing to put up with a bluesman. Smiling when he said it. Della smiling back, only thinking about what Eddie'd said. Calling her his old lady. Not sure she liked that, even if he was bragging. Seemed sort of trashy, like she was a biker chick.

Now she looked over the table at Bubba Bear, at his size. And the outfit. Old overalls, torn T-shirt. Not her picture of a successful restaurant owner. All that wild black hair, head and face and arms, probably all over his back, too. Like some caveman. Except the way he talked. And the boots.

He bent toward her, wagged his head, said, Rufus is damned good.

Oh yeah, she said. That Rufus Slim, he's full of surprises.

Bubba Bear said he figured as much. Life of a musician being so freeform, not bound by rules.

Della frowned, wondering what he meant by that. Hard to see how a musician could have fewer rules than a robber, for cripes sake.

What about yourself?

Me? Della reached up to fluff her bangs. Well, I'm a model. Only I ain't been working much lately, on account of . . . *things*, you know. My situation. She frowned again, wondering if she'd said that right.

Bubba Bear nodded like he understood, his gaze already turned back toward Rufus. Eddie up on the stool, doing another number. Della paid attention, thinking she recognized the tune.

> C. C. Rider, see what you have done,
> You made me love you, you made me love you . . .
> The blues ain't nuthin but a good woman on your mind.

Well, that was better. If he'd stick to songs like that.

Bubba Bear closed his eyes, listening. He wiggled his beefy shoulders in time with the beat. After a minute, he began snapping his fingers, bobbing his enormous head. Mister Wiggle. Della looked around. The bar was full of smoke, of people eating boiled shrimp and barbecued crabs, white ceramic platters overspilling with french fries and onion rings. Tables covered with ketchup bottles and Tabasco sauce and baskets of sliced bread, with empty Lone Star longnecks and Bud cans. Folks laughing and talking and smoking, listening to Rufus Slim. Someone near the back shouted, Get it on, Rufus!

Up on the stool, Eddie threw on the brake and finished with three slow notes down a minor progression. Everyone clapped. Eddie murmured thank you thank you thank you and took a break. He sat down with Della and Bubba Bear, took off the dark shades and asked the waitress to bring him a Coke.

You good, bud, Bubba Bear said, let's go to four nights.

Eddie nodded, wiped his face with a napkin. He was sweating. I gotta learn some more songs, though.

Della said she could suggest a few, some nice ones. Eddie said that was all right, he had a list. What he needed was a tape recorder. Plus some harps in different keys.

Got a whole set, Bubba Bear said, they're yours. One of them neck racks, too, hold the harps. I got everything but talent, friend. And you got that.

Eddie said thanks. Said it was mighty generous. Said, Man oh man, still can't believe this is happening. Thought you said they didn't like blues around here.

Bubba Bear grinned. I said they don't like *nigger* music. Least they think they don't. But put some on? Don't say what it is? Watch 'em shake, friend, they dig it. Got soul hid under all that redneck bullshit.

Always one asshole, though, Eddie said. He swallowed some Coke. We just ain't seen him yet.

Shows up here he gets bounced quick, said Bubba Bear. Don't come back either. Word gets around, you don't mess with the Bear. He smiled. I'll get you those harps in a minute. But what you really need is some wheels. So happens I got them, too.

Eddie stared at the guy. No shit?

No shit. Got an old Chevy truck, well, it ain't that old, just looks it. Runs fine, though. Sitting right out there in the parking lot. A Silverado. Better'n me playing cabdriver.

Outside the bar a tugboat passed down the Intracoastal pushing barges, pilot house even with the secondfloor bar. The diesel engines rumbled, the captain pulled his horn three times. The boat passed on, its wake churning foam by moonlight. Eddie leaned on his elbows and rubbed his face with both hands. Saying, Man, I ain't used to this. Everything too easy.

That right? You want me to make it hard? Bubba Bear sounding serious. Cause suffering, if that's what you want, what you need, we can arrange it. If suffering makes you feel better. He raised his shaggy eyebrows, saying it was possible.

Eddie glanced at Della. She stared past him, frowning, attention elsewhere. He looked back to Bubba Bear, saying, Naw, reckon I had enough to last a spell.

Who's that? Della asked.

They turned to see who she meant, saw a tall rangy man in a Stetson and bolo tie wearing boots and khaki slacks with a sidearm standing in the doorway between the restaurant and bar. His eyes scanned the room. Silver star on his chest. Texas Ranger, looked like.

Bubba Bear shrugged. Said, We get all kinds of folks in here, drug dealers to lawmen. Fresh seafood and cold beer, life's common denominators. You ain't wanted, are you?

Who, me?

Eddie and Della, both speaking at the same time.

They each looked at the other, surprised. Then Eddie picked up his shades and put them on. Della leaned over and fiddled with her shoe, head below the table. Feels like a heel's coming loose, she said from down there. Bubba Bear glanced at Eddie, at the top of Della's head, back to Eddie. Didn't say anything, just stood up and said he'd better show the Ranger to a table, the man looked lost. He ambled away.

After a minute, Eddie said, You can come up for air now. Della raised her head, studied the room. Where'd he go? she asked.

Why you hiding?

I'm not hiding, she retorted, I'm just protecting you . . . *Wade*.

Under the table?

She drew up straight in the chair and tossed her hair, indignant.

Her hands were shaking. Here I am thinking of you, she said, and that's the thanks I get. You . . . you . . . *Rufus*.

Eddie said, Gonna take more'n a broke heel if I get back on that stool. We need a diversion. Maybe you could get naked and dance.

She stared at him, trying to see if he was serious, decided not. She said, What I'm gonna do is, I'm gonna go downstairs to the pay phone and call my mother. Check on the kids.

Eddie lit a cigarette and grinned. What about me?

The big bearded guy offered to show Rule a table. Former Bandido, looked like, before he outgrew the bike. Dressed in those overalls, he reminded Rule of someone else, too. That big ol' boy on *Hee-Haw*, the moonfaced hillbilly. Junior.

Except for the Larry Mahan boots. Rule glancing down, surprised. Red pythons like that cost a bundle.

He followed the guy through the crowded room, through the smoke, weaving between tables to an empty one toward the rear. He sat down and put his hat on the chair to one side. The guy handed him a menu, said his name was Bubba Bear Guidroz, owner of the place. How'd you hear about us?

Saw the signs. Rule jerked a thumb toward the beach road. You got a passel of 'em, pardner. Everywhere you look. What you recommend?

You want it, my friend, we'll catch it, Bubba Bear replied. Bake it, grill it, or fry it. Anything but porpoise. They got bigger brains than we do, probably smarter. Folks like the barbecued crabs. Broiled snapper's good.

Rule ordered a seafood platter. Fish, shrimp, fried oysters, couple of crabs. Lettuce salad and french fries. A cold Bud.

A waitress brought the beer right away, the food shortly after. He was hungry. The fried shrimp were big and juicy, and he sprinkled them with Tabasco and ate slowly, relaxing, trying to get his feelers out. On his own again. No police on the peninsula, just a couple of county deputies, no help there. So he'd cruised the beach road in from the ferry landing, letting his mind rove, running on intuition. Knowing if DeReese was here, he wouldn't find him by looking. Too much space, not enough time. He'd have to follow his nose, maybe catch a scent.

He gazed out the screened window over the canal and across the bay, saw the refinery lights of Texas City twinkling on the far dark horizon. Back in 1947, a French freighter loaded with ammonium nitrate fertilizer exploded there. Set off a chain of fires and explosions, an inferno, worst industrial accident in U.S. history. Six hundred perished, including two of his father's brothers. They'd come down out of the piney woods to make a buck, just after the war. Bodies never found. Incinerated. Ghosts still out there, drifting over the bay. He finished the beer, wondered where the dead went. He heard a gull cry out over the water.

He felt lonely then, and knew he was tired. His mind working backward, conjuring the dead. In the cut between the canal and bay a single small boat rolled in the slop. Someone fishing by lantern light. How he'd fished for white perch in East Texas, when he was a kid. Shallow treestumped lakes filled with schooling perch. A good time, him and the old man. Hadn't fished much since then. Rivers and lakes around Austin, up in the hill country, didn't hold many fish.

Too clean, too deep.

Flash: call Katie. No, give her the space she's claiming. Can't give what you don't own. Conclusion: Let go.

Next premise: the past is beyond reconstruction, go forward. *Now.*

Man, it was hard. Accumulated regret, a fouled anchor holding fast.

The waitress brought him back. He ordered another beer and broke a crab, chewed the tender white meat and listened to the guy up front playing a guitar, singing. Sounded like that blues music. Lot of white folks went for it nowadays. The boy was going after it, had a steel frame around his neck with a harmonica. Rule watched, tilted his head. Something about the guy. Seemed vaguely familiar.

He drank his beer and ate, studying the guy on the stool with the Roy Orbison hairdo and shades. And the earring. Rule could barely make it out. Little gold thing hanging from his left ear. Lots of guys with earrings. No ponytail but a haircut's cheap. He wished he could see the boy's eyes. Had a wide mouth, big lips. Like DeReese.

Nothing in the files about a guitar.

Maybe another question Moline hadn't asked.

He'd finished the platter when the oversized Bandido in the custom made boots walked back to ask if everything was fine. Rule nodded. Said it was fine, real good, especially the shrimp. He wiped his mouth with a napkin, then motioned toward the front of the room. Who's that ol' boy singing?

Rufus Slim. You like the blues?

Rule shrugged. Listen to country mostly.

Bubba Bear laid one hand on the back of a chair, shoved the other into the bib of his overalls. Country's popular. You like the older stuff, though, that'd be my guess. The roots. Bluegrass, honkytonk drinking songs. No offense intended, the old stuff has integrity, like the blues. Matter of fact, you remind me of one of those fellas.

Porter Wagoner, Rule said.

Bubba Bear frowned, scratched his beard. Naw, I'm thinking more Randy Travis, sings "Digging Up Bones"?

Rule stared at the guy. Jesus Christ, he didn't look anything like Randy Travis. For one thing, most of Randy's face was forehead and brow. Or jaw. Middle part scrunched between like it'd been stuck in as an afterthought.

Rufus Slim, Rule said. Sounds like a stage name. Real one's not Ledoux, is it?

Bubba Bear shook his head. That's a coonass name. Rufus comes from Mississippi, down in the delta. South of Memphis, outside Clarksdale. Where Robert Johnson was from, and Muddy Waters, real name McKinley Morganfield. Reckon you never heard of him.

Rule shook his head. Can't say I have.

Well, you missing something, friend. Cat's a legend. Grew up sharecropping a plantation. Get enough black dirt and white cotton, you sing the blues. You good at it, you hit the road. Muddy went up to Chicago, knocked everybody on their ass. All those white boys copied him. Clapton, Stevie Ray, Johnny. Johnny Winter comes from up the road in Beaumont, him and his brother Edgar. Rolling Stones named after a Muddy song. Not that you could tell.

But Rule wasn't listening. He nodded toward Rufus Slim, said, How long he been around?

Him? Bubba Bear put both hands in his bib. He's just passing through, on his way from LA to Memphis. Likes the beach here, though. So do the wife and kids. I'll keep him busy if he stays. He's damn good.

He's married?

Bubba Bear shrugged. Don't know about that. But he's got an old lady and two kids. Can I get you anything else?

Another beer.

Coming up.

When the waitress brought the beer, Rule nursed it. Closed his eyes, let the feeling just be there. Wondering if he was making it up or not. He walked all around it, checking. No, it was real. Felt right, too, that was a fact. But all the rest made no sense. DeReese playing guitar, harmonica, singing. Wife and two kids. It didn't fit. The boy wasn't that complicated, a smalltime hood. Redhead was the one. Liable to do anything, too. Probably up there in East Texas right now planning another hit.

The thought got Rule moving. He called over the waitress, paid the tab. Picked up his hat, wandered up front and waited. When Rufus Slim finished his song, Rule stepped over and told him he liked the music.

Man, I appreciate it, Eddie said. He lit a cigarette, puffed on it. What I'm here for.

Camel straight, Rule noticed. Where you from?

Here and there, all over.

Mississippi?

Down at the crossroads.

Rule nodded, rotated the Stetson in his hands. Wishing he could get the guy to take off those shades. Couldn't see shit.

Ever been in Austin? A question he asked offhand. When what

ne wanted to ask was, You ever shoot a Hindu named Abe
Krishna between the eyes? Or maybe, When's the last time you
saw Johnny Ray Matthews?

Nossir, never been, Eddie replied, but I aim to. Got good blues
clubs, Austin. Antones, the Black Cat. Listen, it was good talking.
I better get back on it. Glad you stopped in.

He started plucking the guitar. Rule hesitated, then went on out
the door. Stood on the secondstory landing overlooking the parking lot and shadowed marina flanking the Stingaree. A small bait
camp with a gas pump down there, powerboats tied to mooring
posts. Overhead, a flotilla of low clouds moving inland off the
gulf, darkshaped mounds playing havoc with the stars. The wind
had picked up. Rain on the way.

He turned and put his hand back on the entrance door, paused,
then abruptly let it go and went on down the stairs beneath creosoted pilings, past the pay telephone on the wall beneath a bright
mercury lamp. A woman leaned against the wall, holding it up
with one foot, talking on the telephone. She turned her back when
he approached. Wearing tight bluejeans, a blouse, red high heels.
Nice ass on her. And big blonde hair to her shoulders. Kind of
woman he used to chase down for a horizontal rumble. Almost
always worth it, too. Might do it now if she was ten years older.
Or he was ten years younger. Or not so damned tired.

He walked on past. It was the fatigue that bothered him.
Wasn't sure where it came from, why it lingered. A bad sign. Nag-
ging worry buried in there: losing his edge.

In the parking lot he stood in the dark next to the truck, Lefty
inside curled up on the seat. He opened the door, called him out to
take a piss. Lefty opened one eye, shut it, refused to budge. Rule
stood holding the door, gazing back toward the Stingaree, up
toward the dim bar lights. He closed his eyes, took a deep breath.
There it was again. Couldn't hear the music, too far away. But
mixed in with the pungent sea and rank smell of swamp, he
caught the scent. Something there, all right. No telling what,
though. Could be off trail.

Focus.

Game right now was Redhead. He climbed into the truck and

cranked the motor, headed back to the beach road, going to Beaumont. Gonna run Redhead down.

All the same, first thing tomorrow, he'd call Moline, have him
check out Rufus Slim.

Della on the telephone with her mother—

You're so *mean*. How can you say that? I am not. I'm not running
around having a good time . . .

Well, it's not *that* bad . . .

I don't know when . . .

It is too the truth. If I had a phone I'd give it to you. No I'm
not. Why would I be hiding from my own kids?

Are you sure? I can't imagine Waylon doing that. Both ears? He
must've got that off the TV . . .

It's cause you stopped taking your iron again. How? Cause if
you're that tired, you stopped taking your iron, that's how . . .

About my car? The finance company? Well, you just tell 'em
they can have it back. That piece of junk ain't worth what I owe
on it . . .

I told you, I don't know when . . .

Well, call the post office then. Sometimes mailmen steal Social
Security checks. I don't know *how* they do it, they just do. I saw it
on some show . . .

Momma, listen, you sure it was the finance company?

That doesn't sound like Alzheimers. I forget things all the
time . . .

Of course they don't behave, they're little. You don't remember
when I was little? I had this habit of lying? When I was four,
maybe five, only I broke it. Well, you just don't remember . . .

I doubt it's a stroke, Momma. I just do. When you get older
you lose muscle tone. Plus your face *always* drooped some on that
side. Yes it did. Of course I'd tell you . . .

Is that Randy I hear coughing? Did you give him the medicine?
Then hold his mouth open and *make* him swallow. If he bites, just
slap him upside the head . . .

Momma, you *sure* it was the finance company?

I don't know when, I already said . . .

—when she looked up and saw the Ranger coming toward her. She turned her back and waited, not a doubt in her mind this was it. Her mother on the other end of the line talking about her face again, a funny droop on one side, how she was sure she'd had a stroke in her sleep. The footsteps of the Ranger drawing near. Della standing under the mercury lamp with her eyes closed, already feeling the cuffs. Thinking about those butch dykes. Remembering the pretty young woman sobbing in the cell, nice pink Laura Ashley dress ripped to shreds. Good lord.

Maybe if she told the truth.

Right.

Maybe if she begged.

When his footsteps passed on by. Then disappeared.

She swung her head after a minute, glanced over her shoulder down the way toward the parking lot, saw him standing by a pickup truck. Looking this direction. Oh boy. She kept her back turned, telephone receiver to her ear. Watching him discreetly. Waving off the mosquitos buzzing her face. After a bit he climbed into the truck and started the motor, pulled away. She slowly let out her breath.

So when are you coming for these kids? her mother asked.

For pete's sake, Della said, how many times do I have to tell you? I don't *know* when.

44

The rain he'd expected did not come though shortly after leaving the Stingaree he drove into fog and regretted not having put up the night in a beach motel. The narrow road threading the peninsula northeastward ran out ahead into a slatecolored veil, disappeared there, the headlamp beams scattered like birdshot. The fog hung suspended over the flat terrain, closing in to either side and front so that it seemed he was not moving, was suspended in it.

Dinner lay heavy on his stomach. He felt drowsy. The close gray mist played with his vision. He saw forms in the roadway—a rabbit, a horse, a hovering human figure—and touched on the brakes even as they dissipated into canescent night, into the nothing from which they'd come.

Crossing Rollover Pass he almost collided head-on with a car drifting over the line. It woke him up. He opened his side window for fresh air and ran the wipers to clear the windshield. He put on the Porter Wagoner tape for company and drove slowly, hugging the right edge of the pavement. After a minute he turned Porter off, his voice too lonely, too heartbroke.

The fog cleared at High Island where the peninsula joined the main coast. Straight ahead along the gulf the beach road lay closed to traffic, the asphalt collapsed and broken, the land beneath chewed away by high tide and hurricane. He turned at the barricade onto the road leading due north, a sinuous path through sawgrass and cane, treeless stretches of wetlands veined by bayous. The headlights swept over the dark verges of vast marshes and he thought he had never seen a land more lonely. Then he drove into more fog.

When he hit I-10, he stopped at an allnight station and bought gas and rancid coffee. He walked the gloamed periphery of the concrete drive stretching his back, the glaucous air sultry and warm. In the murksome beyond, a nightmantled chorus of moist frogs swelling, contracting. He finished the coffee and took the interstate eastward over the coastal plains toward Beaumont. Rice fields to either side, sometimes pasture, pitched flat in the humid darkness.

Near the Fannett cutoff he hit yet another patch of fog and slowed. Back off the highway appeared shrouded silhouettes, tall and bulky. Stands of loblolly pines and old oak. The southern edge of the East Texas woods. Lefty stirred and awakened. He was restless in the cab and Rule pulled into a roadside park. While the hound nosed the ground and set his marks, Rule leaned against the fender, phoned Eastland at home. He sounded drunk.

Watching the news, Eastland explained, and drinking whiskey. They still fighting in Kosovo. Mets player got busted for coke. Kid up in Milwaukee jumps off a bridge using nylon rope for a bungee cord. Tore off his foot. That's what they call the local news.

Turn it off.

I can take it, my loins is girded. Eastland laughed, began to cough, couldn't quit. Rule heard him put down the receiver. He waited. After a bit Eastland came back, saying, Think I'm getting a bug.

Might see a doctor, Rule said. Might get a complete workup.

Shit, thought you wanted that fifth of Old Crow.

Not that bad, pardner.

I already drank it anyhow. Why my balls're sagging.

Then put on some shorts, Rule said. Any more news on Ledoux?

Which one?

Dead one. Wade.

Yeah, my colleague Phelps filed a procedure complaint on me. Stuck it up the ol' yinyang. But I did learn how that guy ran down the wrong Ledoux. What's his name, death wish dude.

Lomax.

Yeah, religious fucker. That license Ledoux had was bogus, why it wasn't on the computer. Except Lomax has an old army buddy works in narcotics here at HPD. Guy named Myers, they're both gun nuts. Myers ran into Ledoux couple of times, knew he was dealing but couldn't get a collar. When he heard what happened up in Brookshire, he called Lomax, told him where to find the schmuck. Talk about correct fucking procedure.

Professional courtesy, Rule said. Figured the lord would do what the law couldn't.

We're results oriented here at HPD.

Only it was the wrong perp. Matthews is still loose.

Maybe so, but no one's crying. Lomax'll plead self-defense. No witnesses, Ledoux was carrying. Plus he's a junkie. Hell, the grand jury won't even indict. Your boy already walked without bail.

Reckon I'll see him again. If he knows where I'm headed.

Wouldn't know about that, Eastland said. But tomorrow morning's paper comes out, he's a hero, count on it. Upright citizen protecting the community.

Charles Bronson.

Yeah, only Bronson used a thirty-two dinker. This guy carries a three-fifty-seven Sig Sauer. He had a four-sixty Weatherby rifle with a Leupold scope in his truck. Elephant gun.

Rule grunted. Anything on the real DeReese?

I wouldn't know. Lieutenant put me on three day suspension. Maybe his running buddy took him out. Know how that goes. Where are you?

Close to Beaumont. Listen, Clint, I'm sorry.

Jesus, and you think Houston's a pisshole.

The line went dead. Rule whistled Lefty into the truck. As soon as he was back on the interstate he called the Beaumont police dispatcher, asked her to contact Kirkland, the homicide sergeant, have him call. The phone rang ten minutes later. They agreed to meet early next morning at the station downtown.

He was about to hang up when Kirkland said, You probably don't remember me from back in Woodville. James Kirkland. Went by Scooter.

Rule didn't say anything.

Didn't think so, the man said. No reason to, I was just a kid. Watched you play tight end for the Eagles. I came along eight years later, played the same position, same number.

How'd you do?

The detective chuckled. Your stats were better than mine. But I made all-district defense. Your dad was foreman up at the sawmill, if I remember right. Mine cut timber for Kirby.

I recollect your family, Rule said. Kirklands settled up there early. Got a Kirkland Springs out on the highway. Kirkland cemetery out past the airstrip.

That's us.

How much you know about the Matthews boy?

No worse than the rest until now, Kirkland said, but they're all mean. White trash backwoods folks. Before I got on the department down here I was a deputy sheriff in Tyler County. Knew Johnny Ray's daddy and uncles, that age group. Lived back in the bottoms, bunch of 'em. They'd come over from Jasper and raise hell, run back across the county line like it was an international border. Like they thought we couldn't reach 'em over there. Spent their share of time in the calaboose. Not very smart, but like I said, they're bad. Everything from burglary to bootlegging. Assault's pretty common, they like to fight. Handy with a knife. Most the men carry guns. The women are rough, too, got hair on their chest. Don't turn your back on one.

From what I recall, Rule said, they keep to themselves. Clannish. Don't stray far from the woods.

That's right. Active in the Klan, too, case I didn't mention it. Couple of homicides open up there, black victims, Matthews are the prime suspects but nobody can prove it. May be lowlifes, but they white.

So what happened with this one?

Johnny Ray? From what I'm told he killed his mother. Wasn't no arrest. Family circled the wagons on it. Par for the course. They handle that stuff themselves. Only this time it caused a real rift, I hear. They wanted to take Johnny Ray down. Some of the women, mainly his aunt Ethel. She was his mother's sister. Tough old woman. She's got three boys and they went after Johnny Ray. He lit out for parts unknown. This is the first I heard of him since. Saw from his sheet he served time in Huntsville on sexual assault.

It fits, Rule said. We might have a repeat. Him and a buddy up in Austin, couple of weeks back. Two gals from the university.

Kirkland paused. That'd be different. Other time it was a male.

Rule was silent, waiting for more. When none came, he said, You got any details on that?

Just what I saw on the report, Kirkland replied. He assaulted a fella over in Houston off Westheimer, where queers hang out. Sodomy, with anal penetration. Then he pistolwhipped the guy. Right on the street. Patrol team on bicycles happened to hear the guy screaming. Busted Johnny Ray cold.

Did he know the victim?

You mean, were they kissin buddies?

Something like that.

Don't recall anything about that in the report, Kirkland said, but you can take a gander first thing tomorrow. Heck of a way to treat a friend, if they were. Don't get much of that here in Beaumont. Queers're real careful in East Texas. Matter of survival, I suppose. Remember Gerald up in Woodville?

Gerald? Rule thought about it. Gerald who?

The old guy that drove a big Buick around town, lime green with whitewalls. Postal carrier, a bachelor. Real friendly, waved at everyone? All us kids knew to stay away. My momma told me, she said, Scooter, don't never get in that car with Gerald, never ever. Didn't ask why, either, tone of her voice was enough.

Guess I never noticed, Rule said. What happened to him?

Kirkland said Gerald was still there, far as he knew. Unless he'd died of AIDS. Lot of that going around. Only no one had ever hassled him, they let him be. Small town's like that, you know. Room for a town drunk, room for a town queer, long as he don't flaunt it. Get two of 'em and problems start. Just how it is.

Reckon so, Rule said. Listen, I'm coming up on Beaumont now, Kirkland, better run.

You'll see a whole slew of motels. Try the Hilton.

Appreciate it.

Rule hung up. Then remembered he'd forgot to ask why Redhead killed his mother. Ask tomorrow morning. Find out more on that assault in Houston, too, it said something about Redhead he hadn't thought about. Not that East Texas was unknown for homosexual activity. Gerald, for instance. Right there in Woodville, piddly little place. He'd missed that one altogether.

Then without preface or warning the fields and woods along the highway dropped away and he was in Beaumont. Car dealerships new and used lined the upbanked highway, hip to thigh with fastfood joints and discount stores, threestory brick office buildings, a Sam's Warehouse, strip malls, service stations. An army of fluoresced signs. The gaunt luminescence of lights hazing the damp night. And the smell. An acrid odor of sulphur and methane

bit at his nostrils, teared his eyes. Bad as Houston. The dense
cloudcover forming some sort of inversion layer, he supposed,
holding down the discharge from refinery smokestacks and petrochemical plants. Lefty rose on his haunches, nosed the side window. He whimpered.

Welcome to Cancerville Junior, good buddy, Rule said. Only
you won't be here long.

He took an exit spanning railroad tracks and pulled off the
access into a La Quinta Inn, rented a room. Once inside, he gave
Lefty a bowl of water and stripped and showered, lay down. His
back ached. Lefty curled up on the carpet between the bed and
window and went to sleep.

Rule turned on the TV and surfed channels with the remote.
Nothing new. He flipped it off, rolled over and reached into his
carryall. Brought out one of the paperbacks he'd bought in Houston and Katie's book of quotes. He opened the paperback first,
one by James Lee Burke. Guy sure could write. Rule liked the
main character in his stories, Cajun cop named Robicheaux, carried a government issue Colt .45 like his own. Unusual. Occurred
to Rule then that Robicheaux was always having flashback
dreams of a Nam firefight. Only he'd been there.

He read the first chapter in the novel. Robicheaux picked up a
guy on a DWI, a movie actor. The guy was talking about ghosts,
done seen a body in the swamp, dead black man. Good opening
scene, it set up the action, but Rule closed the paperback, feeling
weary. Then picked up Katie's quote book. Couldn't remember
the date so he referred to his watch, then turned to the correct
page. Quote from Shakespeare. Bard of Avon, the book said.

> *What win I if I gain the thing I seek?*
> *A dream, a breath, a froth of fleeting joy.*
> *Who buys a minute's mirth to wail a week,*
> *Or sells eternity to get a toy?*

He read it several times, the book resting on his chest, trying to
decipher the meaning. Damned hard. Good rhyme but the word
order was backasswards. Not a single one in the bunch he didn't

recognize. But put together this way they seemed cryptic. He finally decided it meant someone getting something he wished he hadn't.

Regret maybe.

Rule lowered his chin and read the editor's note at the bottom of the page. Quote was from some long poem called *Lucrece*, character called Tarquin, a king's son. Like Solomon, he betrayed a friend to usurp the man's wife. What did that mean? Sex, Rule supposed.

He lowered the book and rubbed his eyes. They were tired from the drive, the fog, and the strain. Whole body fatigued. He fondled his balls and pecker with one hand, briefly recollected the blonde standing at the telephone outside the Stingaree earlier. One in the red heels and jeans with a nice ass. Put her right here right now, though, buck naked, and he wouldn't even think twice. Go right to sleep. Not even sure Dana could keep him up. A sad situation.

He closed the book and climbed under the sheet, shut off the lamp. He lay in the dark room knowing he would soon pass into sleep. He pulled the sheet to his chin, shuddered, closed his eyes. An image of Redhead buttfucking a guy on a moonlit street blipped over the shadowy screen. Then the dim echo of Kirkland's voice: kissin buddies. Followed by the slightest transitory impression of an idea he knew was important but could not recall even as he let it go and passed into darkness.

A hunch why Redhead had hooked up with DeReese.

45

He believed it was raining when beads of water fell against his face and awakened him at dawn, but it was only dewdrops coalesced in the high canopy of beech, bending the ribbed leaves, tumbling earthward. He'd gone to sleep during the night with the

Caddy ragtop down. He climbed from the backseat and stretched his legs, looked about. The woods asleep yet. Towering beeches, black walnut, and hawthorn. A ghostly mist drifted among the trees, lay thick over the backwater slough.

He went down the leafcovered trail to the water's edge among cypress knees and palmetto, bent down to splash his face. A dull ache in his head and a bruise behind one ear where the baseball bat had caught him. His left shoulder felt stiff. He worked the muscles and joint with his right hand, probing deeply. Then he went along the low bank and skirted a baygall, the shallow water standing black and still over a tannin-leached bottom. Swamp tupelo rose from its soggy reaches, vinetangled among cypress and titi. At its edges, lapping dampdrenched air, pale lavender orchids. Soon thereafter he came to a planked footbridge, took it over a slough to a small treeless island blanketed in shrub willow and briar. A narrow path fringed its canebraked bank in either direction. He turned left. The weeds wet his boots and jeans to the thighs. When he came to the point he stood overlooking open water, leadgray and still.

Dam B.

What he'd always called it anyway. Steinhagen Reservoir, according to signs and maps, name the hotshots up in Austin had given it to honor one of their own. Local folks called it after the corps name, though. Dam B Lake. An old manmade impoundment at the confluence of the Neches and Angelina rivers, treestumped, backed up into hardwood bottomlands between sandy ridges overtowered by loblollies, its silty shallows clogged with hydrilla and water hyacinth beneath which pansized bluegill and goggle-eye fanned their slippery fins. Maybe twentyfive square miles of lake, counting sloughs and baygalled swamps, and fifty miles of ragged shoreline, a big lake until they built Sam Rayburn to the north, ten times larger. Then came Lake Livingston on the Trinity River to the west and Toledo Bend on the Sabine to the east, even bigger. Burying the rich bottomlands beneath stacked up water. Bottomlands where wildlife once lived. Turning East Texas into a publicly subsidized corporate tree farm interspersed with reservoirs called recreation areas for weekend

tourists. Calling it resource management. U. S. Army Corps of
Engineers on a rampage, following orders, any undammed river
an insult. Politicians scrabbling over which parks got named
after who.

He stood there on the point until the sun broke the treeline
behind and a warm breeze sprang over the rippling lake surface,
then he turned back up the trail to the car. When he reached it a
park ranger was standing alongside looking in.

This your vehicle?

Ray Bob nodded.

The ranger glanced at a clipboard in his left hand. A slim man
in his thirties with a sharp nose and sideburns. Behind him sat a
pickup with a Texas Parks & Wildlife decal on the door.

You realize this is a state park.

A statement, not a question. The ranger stood on the driver's
side of the Caddy and Ray Bob drifted up to the right rear fender,
leaned against it. He nodded again. Thinking the guy had a mid-
west accent, Michigan maybe, or Illinois.

This isn't a camping area, either.

I didn't camp here.

The ranger stepped forward and laid his hand on the Caddy
hood, checking its warmth. Letting Ray Bob know.

Sir, there's a park entrance fee of two dollars and an overnight
fee of nine dollars. He held up the clipboard. I don't see you registered for either one.

Ray Bob said, I come in late last night. Nobody in the booth up
there to pay.

There's a sign telling you how to register after hours. Put your
fee in the envelope, envelope in the box. Plenty of envelopes, sir.

The guy was all business, wasn't going to back off an inch. Like
some high school teacher talking to a kid. Ray Bob looked at him,
felt the Walther inside his right boot, muzzle rubbing his ankle.

I didn't have any change, all I had was a twenty.

The ranger shook his head and kicked the dirt with a bootheel,
gazing down. Making it clear the explanation didn't hold water,
he'd heard it a hundred times. The silence intended to give the
rulebreaker a chance to think about consequences. Park ranger in

uniform, state power invested. Basically, a cop. Let the anxiety build, easy way to teach a lesson.

Ray Bob leaned on the fender with his left elbow, waiting, right thumb hooked in his back pocket. The position put a strain on his shoulder and it throbbed but he ignored it. From there he could bend down to scratch his leg, a natural motion, come up with the gun before the guy knew what'd happened. Easy, just like that. Only if anyone heard the shots he was cornered in the park, just the one road out. Unless he swam out with a bad shoulder. Or mucked through the swamp, dodging alligators and water moccasins. Then he'd be afoot. Reckoned he'd chance the road. Woods might swallow up the noise anyhow. Though it was mighty quiet, with neither of them speaking. Nothing but the soft soughing forest, breeze swaying the treetops.

The ranger finally lifted his gaze and locked eyes with Ray Bob, face set rigid, as if he'd pondered the dilemma long enough and come to a decision. Ray Bob reached down and idly scratched his knee. Then the ranger abruptly slapped his thigh with the clipboard and said all right, this one time anyway, just pay on the way out. Don't forget. He casually strolled to the pickup swinging the clipboard and got in, backed up and turned around, pulled away up the treeshaded lane.

Ray Bob watched, hand beneath his shirt rubbing his belly. He should've taken the guy down. He had it coming, cocky sonofabitch. Stupid, too. Not even carrying. He listened to the low hum of the pickup engine fade into the woods. A bluejay queedled in the thicket, a fish slapped the surface of the slough. His stomach growled beneath his hand. He was hungry.

When the motor disappeared altogether he opened the Caddy trunk and took out a cloth rag and a small can of oil. He sat on a gnarled magnolia root and removed the clip from the Walther, unchambered the round, oiled and cleaned the gun. All the while thinking about the breakfast his mother used to serve back home. Cane syrup on buttered biscuits, grits and gravy, fried yard eggs, homecured pork bacon and smoked sausage. Wash it down with a steaming cup of chicory coffee.

A yellowbellied sapsucker swept through the clearing, lit on a honey locust, began its rat-tat-tat forage in the bark. The sharp insistent thumping echoed through the thicket. Otherwise, quiet. Ray Bob closed his eyes, inhaled the sweet aroma of the damp woods, the sweet honeysuckled air. He never felt so at ease as here, cloistered with the heaving earth, the deep green whispering forest, near surging waters collected in the fertile embrace, far beyond others of his species.

Safety here.

Among men, none.

He drove out of the park a half hour later beneath soaring loblollies and upland sycamore, the pineneedled floor of the forest opening auburn between the roughbarked trunks. The sweet smell of pine resin afloat in the warming air. Squirrels in the treetops, along the creepers, songbirds in the brush. A crow calling off in the deep woods. A paved turnoff to the campgrounds, another to the boat ramp. A park sign warning against feeding alligators. He took his time, driving slowly through the sundappled morning, and when he passed the park building and pay booth he didn't look or stop.

At the intersection of the park road and Highway 190, he put the transmission in neutral and lit a cigarette. He looked west up the road, to the right. Back across the raised causeway over the lake and fifteen miles farther on was Woodville, place he'd come from last night. He'd left Tyler County when he crossed the old iron-girdered bridge spanning the river channel midlake, sometime near midnight. He'd been in Jasper County since.

He sat at the intersection a while longer, smoking. He studied the twolane highway leading the other way, eastward. Sign there said eleven miles to Jasper. When he finished the cigarette he dropped it over the side and put the Caddy in drive, let off the brake. He turned left.

Going home.

46

Rule finished up early in Beaumont. He met with Kirkland in homicide and went through the paperwork on Johnny Ray Matthews, more than he'd expected. By midmorning he was on the way north toward Jasper, thinking about what he'd read.

Some surprises there. Turned out Redhead had known his assault victim in Houston. Fifty-year-old biochemist named Gary Arnold, unmarried, former scientist for Louisiana-Pacific, left the timber industry to work for the Sierra Club. Had run into Redhead in a Westheimer disco and put him up in his West University apartment. Planning to help him get on his feet because he was bright. Purely altruistic interest, according to Arnold. A humanitarian. Until the night Redhead turned on him. Unprovoked, the man claimed. "Sodomy with anal penetration" didn't quite cover it. Eightyfour stitches total, more than thirty in the anus, caused by repeated insertion of a pistol barrel. Arnold first refused to file charges, then flipped, said he was scared of Matthews.

Another surprise: fact that Redhead had graduated high school, had taken junior college classes during his stint in Huntsville. Couple of ecology courses, psychology, and something called mass communications. Decent grades, too. The boy could read.

News to me, Kirkland had said. He isn't your usual Matthews, tell you that. Smart kid, sounds like. Only problem, he's a sociopath, or whatever they call them nowadays. Full of the devil and wound up tight. He's a Matthews that way.

Maybe his family couldn't handle him, either, Rule'd said, sliding the paperwork back into its folder. Wondering what Redhead was driving. Could be stolen, could be borrowed. Freaky the way no one had seen the vehicle, all those chances. Damned frustrating.

Another black hole: nothing in the file on the boy's mother, how she died or why.

Before leaving he phoned Austin to have Moline check out Rufus Slim. He wasn't in. The lab tech said he hadn't called in sick, she expected him soon. She didn't know what progress, if any, he'd made on the security videos, DeReese versus Wade. Rule said he'd get back later.

At the Silsbee-Kountze Y above Beaumont he considered going the long way, through Woodville. No more reason than interest in the hometown, hadn't seen it in a while. Maybe drive past the old home on Dogwood, drop by the cemetery, see his folks. Only he couldn't afford the time. No telling what Redhead was up to, boy was on the prowl, bound to hit again soon. He took the fork toward Jasper.

The other side of Silsbee he pulled off the road beneath the Neches River bridge and let Lefty out. He stood on the high bank of the river watching its brown current surge, washing back into the hardwood bottoms downstream. The woods were thick in there, full of downed trees and brush, unlike the slash pine plantations along the road. Woods in their natural state, with deadfalls and rotting stumps, mulch ankledeep overgrown with muscadine and pawpaw, dark and humid. So thick in there a snake couldn't turn around, had to back out. He recollected a story his daddy used to tell. Hunter outlawing deer got lost in the thicket, came crawling out two days later on his hands and knees. Don't know how I got out, he told his wife. She said, The Lord was with you. Well, that might be, he replied, only I don't know how *He* got out. His daddy'd tell the story and laugh quietly, then lean to one side and spit tobacco juice. Big brown glob.

When Lefty was satisfied they continued upland through young pines, fields of seedlings and striplings lazing in sunlight, past the Temple-Inland pulp mill at Evadale with its nosestopping stink and up through old sawmill ghost towns and whistle stop junctions, fallen into decrepitude. He studied trailer homes squatting off the roadside, modern day tenant shacks, and stripped fields in which brindled cattle mouthed the ground. He passed an eighteen-wheeler and DPS patrol car on the shoulder, trucker shaking his head while the trooper talked. A mile on he flushed three turkey buzzards feeding on armadillo roadkill. The great birds lifted and flared out at the truck's approach, set their wings, returned in the rearview mirror.

Red Man chewing tobacco. That's what his daddy'd chewed. What finally killed him, the mouth cancer.

He picked up the cellular and dialed Katie's number in Austin. On the third ring the answering machine clicked and he punched off, laid the phone in the seat. Message to self: *Don't crowd.* Hard to do. Christ, all he wanted to do was say hello, hear her voice. *So?* So she's not a little girl anymore. Let go. She's got her own life now.

He took a deep breath, blew out. Might learn it after all.

A minute later he picked the phone up and dialed again. Different number. Dana answered.

Well, I can't believe it, she said, you never call. You missing your little pumpkin?

Thought I'd call you before you called me, Rule said. He hesitated, not sure what to say. Not sure why he'd called. Impulse overriding judgment.

Where's Moline?

At work, she said, where you think?

He drinking?

You kidding? Moline?

He's volatile right now, maybe dangerous. Rule paused. You oughta consider moving out.

No, no way I'm giving up this house, she said. Serious, her voice rock hard. It's mine as much as his.

Not if you're dead.

She laughed. Get a grip, darlin. Moline's all bluff. Where are you?

East Texas, where I grew up.

You were a kid once? Her voice light now, teasing. Hard to imagine that.

I know it.

Bet you were a handful. Bet you weren't nuthin but trouble.

I was a pretty good kid, he said, my daddy saw to that.

Whipped me regular up to the time I was baptized. Rule shifted the receiver and frowned. Couldn't decide what he was doing, talking to her this way. Revealing himself. Telling things he hadn't thought about in years.

You was baptized? She giggled. Well, it sure didn't take.

In a creek, he said. Turkey Creek, off this sandbar. Hardshell Baptist preacher almost drowned me.

Rule, you're plumb crazy. I miss you, honey. Why don't I come over there with you? Show me that place. I bet that's why you want me to leave Moline.

When he didn't answer she said, I been thinking about you ever since the other day. Know what I'm doing right now? Taking off my clothes. That's right. Down to my panties now. Whoopsie daisy, there they go. Okay, darlin, here I am. Ready and waiting. Look at my little pink nipples, they all excited. Talk to me.

Rule held the receiver to his ear, not saying anything.

Well, c'mon, sugar, I'm waiting.

That's not what I wanted.

What?

Watch your step with Moline.

He held the receiver out and disconnected, drove on holding it in his hand. When it rang after a moment he turned it off and laid it in the seat. He glanced over at Lefty, curled beneath the passenger window, watching. Said, Pardner, you looking at a sad sack of shit. Better get my head on straight. End up like Jedidiah down on the Rio. What you reckon?

Lefty cocked an eye, closed it, went to sleep.

What I figgered, Rule said.

He put the Porter Wagoner tape in the tape deck and listened but he still didn't like it, too damned depressing. The cornpone voice had a whine to it he'd never noticed until yesterday. As if Porter was overcome with self-pity because life had proved too much and love an inevitable sorrow. That last part maybe true, but the self-pity a weak man's response. Rule thinking about Moline. About himself. He turned off the tape and rode in silence.

Shortly before noon he hit Jasper and drove up through the commercial center into old town and parked in front of the county courthouse, a Victorian cathedral awash in sunlight. The sky spread baby blue and cloudless beyond the clocktower. He was at the door before he remembered the sheriff's office had moved. Some time back, like fifteen years. Something he knew. He backtracked and drove over to the new building near the Jasper Creosote works, across from the old chicken processing plant. Inside he learned that Stace Collins, the sheriff, had gone to Austin on business.

But don't you worry about that, the clerk said, cause he told Booker Wright, the chief deputy, to look after you. Just one second.

She went out a side door and returned followed by a tall black deputy wearing a highcrowned cowboy straw of golden jute with a Canadian crease. He was slimhipped and wideshouldered in his tan uniform and moved easily through the swinging half door to put out a hand the size of a catcher's mitt.

Ranger Hooks, he said, my pleasure. I'm Deputy Wright. Buckshot said he's sorry not to be here. He told me to treat you like one of our own, but I expect he meant well, all the same. He smiled.

I appreciate the help, Rule said. He had to look up. Guy was six-six, maybe. Not bigboned but rangy and well muscled. And young. He felt the man's hand wrapping around his, enclosing it. Said, I reckon you was a basketball player.

That's right. Played over at Baylor long enough to earn my degree, then came home. Five years now. Thought law work made more sense than hoops, least in the long run.

He smiled again. A slender face with a wide forehead and dark almond skin with a tinge of bronze. Friendly eyes. Kind of man women went for, Rule figured. An easy deep voice. If he'd made chief deputy in five years under Stace Collins, he was smart, too.

Buckshot tell you what I'm working?

Wright nodded. Johnny Ray Matthews, one of my favorite people. Went to high school with him. Hear he's on a spree.

You might say. Bringing it this way, what I figure.

The deputy wrapped a hand behind his neck, rested it there. We haven't seen him. But we put the word out yesterday, like you asked. Local police and deputies are keeping an eye open. We contacted the media, it's on the radio. Newspaper's a weekly, no help there just yet.

What can you tell me about the boy?

He don't like black folks, I know that much. But then, he is a Matthews. Wright pushed his hat back and glanced at his watch. What say we talk it out over lunch, Mister Hooks? My treat.

All right, long as we go in my truck. I got my dog. And long as I buy. Reckon the state oughta pay its help.

Wright held out both arms. Just being a good host, he said, trying to keep Buckshot happy. How about a little cafe I know serves fried chicken livers and chitlings, pickled pigs feet for dessert?

Rule hesitated, looked at the tall black man. Trying to decide how to say no without offense, disturbed by his own reluctance to just say it. He wasn't himself. Worried about Katie, the inept call with Dana. Forgetting where the sheriff's office was. Too preoccupied with the wrong things. Too many little mistakes. Needed to get his mind right.

Sir, I'm just kidding with you, the deputy said. His face broke into a wide grin and he extended a long arm outward, palm up, showing Rule toward the door. Saying, Why don't we go over to the Golden Corral? Buffet with a salad bar and steamed veggies, fried chicken if you want it. He patted his belly. It lay smooth as a flatiron. Saying, I watch my diet. We've got deputies here haven't seen their feet in ten years. He laughed.

Half an hour later Rule was partway through a heaping plate of fried catfish with mashed potatoes and gravy, turnip greens and blackeyed peas. Basket of cornbread and hush puppies, a big glass of ice tea. Chowing down. Watching the chief deputy eat a Caesar salad and a small side of cantaloupe. Drinking orange juice.

How's the grub? Wright asked.

Rule nodded. Reckon Lefty'd go for these hush puppies.

Glad you like it. Buckshot said you'd appreciate some down-home cooking. The deputy forked a tomato wedge. You think Johnny Ray's come back to Jasper?

Rule nodded again, wiped his hands on a napkin. I got a hunch he's running scared. Working alone, not comfortable with it. A bad boy's like any other boy, he heads home when he's worried.

Johnny Ray doesn't have much of a home, Wright said without hesitation. You know the family. Riverbottom folks, live off the land, more or less. Poach deer and hogs, cattle if they can. Womenfolk raise gardens, men make a little whiskey. Steal what they can't buy, feud for fun. Stay to themselves mostly, except when they're thieving. If it wasn't for the Klan they wouldn't belong to anything. Nobody'd let 'em. Wasn't for black folks they'd know what they really are.

Not that everyone who's Klan is ignorant and poor, Rule said.

Wright shrugged. At least not poor, you're right about that part. There's middleclass folks involved, some upperclass professionals who help bankroll it. They keep a low profile, play it safe, let the rabble do the dirty work.

Some things never change, Rule said. But I recollect the Matthews. They're ignorant and poor both. Common white trash.

Wright lifted his glass of juice chest high, leaned on an elbow and gazed at Rule. Only Johnny Ray is different.

Rule dipped a catfish filet in ketchup, chewed slowly. Waiting.

Problem for Johnny Ray is he knows what his family is, the deputy continued, and he knows what he is.

Rule said, What's that?

The angriest smart man I ever met.

What's he angry about?

How do I hate thee? Wright cocked an eyebrow. Let me count the ways. I'm not sure even he knows. He was always fighting, back in school. He'd take on anyone, any number. And not quit. He's relentless. I don't believe he's afraid of anything. Not even dying.

Rule drank some ice tea, studied the deputy. Almost sounds like you admire the boy. Or feel sorry for him.

I suppose you're right, about the last part anyhow. I always felt bad for Johnny Ray.

The deputy paused, made a wry face. As if suddenly aware there'd been a time in Jasper, and not so long ago, when being black, he wouldn't have said that, not even about riverbottom trash like the Matthews. Maybe especially about them. Even now it was a place where three young white men could pick up a black man walking along a country road and bind his legs and drag him by a chain behind a pickup until he was torn to pieces, limbless, decapitated, a ragged hunk of bleeding meat abandoned in a ditch. That was Jasper, a main street city, friendly on the outside but unwilling to dig deep, or to exorcise the demons it incubated.

Like any other place in America.

Rule broke into his thoughts. Me, I feel sorry for the folks he killed, and their families.

I hear you, the deputy replied. Speaking quietly. Seems like there's always enough grief to go around. It's not like Johnny Ray and I were ever close. He was damaged goods even then, a loner mostly. We talked a few times in high school. I believe we thought alike on some things, peculiar as that sounds. Outsider's view, you might say. But I'm black and Johnny Ray's a Matthews. He backed off quick. Then he watched me from a distance. It was a strange thing to see. Like his mind was going one way but the rest wouldn't follow. He's an intelligent man, Mister Hooks. Maybe even what you'd call sensitive. And he'd kill you in a New York second.

Like he did his momma?

We never proved that, Wright said, but we know he did. Everybody knew. Ella Mae Matthews was the meanest old woman ever lived. Hateful woman. She was born a Wiggins, they all related on both sides. Her husband was scared of her. Must run in the family, her sister Ethel Matthews puts the fear of god in men, too. Her husbands have a funny way of dying or disappearing. But Ella Mae was worse, what they say. Like that Greek goddess Medusa, with snakes in her hair, turn you to stone if you get too close. Even her own kids couldn't stand her, except for Johnny Ray.

Why's that?

Don't know. Maybe she had something he needed. She was his momma. This is grapevine stuff, you understand. How we know he did her. Not that many really cared. Being from these parts, you know how it is. Someone gets killed, first thing asked is if they deserved it. You'd be surprised at the number of folks didn't blame Johnny Ray.

I heard some folks did.

Part of his family, that's right. Ethel's bunch.

I hear that's why he left Jasper. They run him off.

The deputy fiddled with his fork, frowning. You know, I used to think that, too. But I don't believe Johnny Ray ever did anything he didn't want to do.

Ever have a girlfriend?

Not that I know of, but like I said, he was a loner. Girls were scared of him, same as the boys.

Is he queer?

Wright dropped the fork and leaned back in his seat, smiling. He looked surprised, then thoughtful.

I never heard that.

Rule shrugged. Any reason to think he was?

Like I said, it never occurred to me. That's a new one. You got something?

Nothing that makes a difference. It's all the same to me. I'm gonna get the boy, then I'm gonna put him away. If the system works, he'll go up on death row. Don't die of old age first, he'll be put to sleep. You ever hear of a boy named DeReese Ledoux?

Doesn't ring a bell. Friend of Johnny Ray?

Depends on what you mean by friend. From what you're telling me, he might be dead. Why'd the Matthews boy kill his momma?

Wright shook his head. I suppose you'd have to ask Johnny Ray.

Rule said, Maybe I will.

47

Moving east on Highway 190 through the piney woods toward Jasper, Ray Bob chainsmoked cigarettes and observed familiar landmarks etched into the landscape—country churches, trailer homes in disrepair, abandoned tenant shacks. The day promised to overheat by afternoon but for now lay easy over the forested

terrain, clear and mild, the sunlight bathing a rippling green
bucolic sea.

He passed rolling pastures carved from the woods, Santa
Gertrudis snoozing beneath spreading oaks and quarter horses
grazing the fenceline. Passed the farm to market road cutting
north toward the Angelina National Forest, another dropping
south to Beech Grove. Along the roadside volunteer bluebonnets
and Indian paintbrushes and an enormous sycamore that he'd
watched all his life, no telling what age it was, the things it'd wit-
nessed, storms endured.

He observed these things and in them recognized himself. He
was moving back in time and felt in it a deep abiding nostalgia
bordering on grief and the reassurance that the world had not
changed.

Closing in on town he scoped brick ranchstyle houses cloistered
beneath oak groves and pecan. Immaculate, well kept homes.
New pickup trucks parked in the drives. Hedges of oleander
blooming in the yards near bassboats on trailers and truck gardens fenced against rabbits and deer. A man in one yard raked
leaves onto a smoldering pile, the dense white smoke curling
upward. Ray Bob smelled the burning leaves and it seemed he was
ten years old again, a time before he knew what there was to
know that'd made life the thing it had become for him and any
other person who dared think about it. A neverending struggle to
hold back some things and to make other things happen, an
ordeal solitary neither by choice nor inclination but by natural
fiat, the whole world in forsaken opposition.

He came up on the city limits sign, population seven thousand
plus, then saw the Jasper Equipment Company with tractors and
cultivators lined in sparkling rows out front and the county livestock pavilion with its pungent smell of dung, and before long the
pavement spread into four lanes and he passed into the commercial district flanking the road. A sign reading WELCOME TO JASPER,
A MAIN STREET CITY. The main street being the highway. A Wal-
Mart Supercenter, Michelin Tire, a funeral home, the hospital.
Stores for drugs, furniture, appliances. Gasoline stations, fastfood
outlets, motels and churches. A video rental shop. Progress in con-

sumption, civilization on the move. Dollar bills making the loop. What everyone lived for.

He was cruising slow, trying to read the mobile sign in front of East Texas Chiropractic—something about workmans comp— and almost missed them. Right there across the road, two men climbing into a red Dodge pickup in front of the Golden Corral, one man he knew, Booker Wright. The other a Texas Ranger who would've seemed tall had it not been for the deputy. Ray Bob quickly raised a hand alongside his cheek, rubbing his forehead, concealing his profile. He drove on through an intersection on a green light, checking the rearview, and pulled into the parking lot of Kentucky Fried Chicken, parked on the far side so he could see back down the road. The Dodge pickup approached but stopped at the intersection and turned north, Booker in the passenger seat. It disappeared past the Dairy Queen.

Ray Bob waited a minute, then got out and raised the convertible top, locked it in place. Feeling chagrined he hadn't already done that, a stupid mistake. Then he drove on east to the Sonic Drive-In and parked under the awning, ordered two number-one burgers with jalapenos, onion rings and fries, a chocolate malt. The carhop was a chubby blonde girl with a ponytail and dark purple eyeshadow. When she smiled and said she liked the Caddy, flirting, he said he was just passing through, on his way to Leesville in Louisiana. She said she'd always wanted to go to Leesville, so he said he was going farther on, to Alexandria, and when she said she'd never been there, either, he told her to bring some ketchup. Her heavy shoulders slumped but she hurried off and returned with several packets, telling him to have a good day as if she was used to it.

Afterward he drove to the H.E.B. supermarket and bought groceries. Bread and peanut butter, cans of ranchstyle beans and sweet corn, crackers, canned Vienna sausage, a big jar of dill pickles. Enough to last a while. He added a large bag of oatmeal cookies and a case of Budweiser. Going up the housewares aisle he stuffed a can opener down the front of his jeans. He bought a carton of Marlboros at the register.

He was in the parking lot loading the sacks in the Caddy trunk when someone called his name. He ignored it. He felt the Walther in his boot pressing against his ankle and the person didn't call again. But when he closed the trunk lid and turned around cousin Donnie Ray was standing ten feet off watching.

Thought it was you.

Always was hard to fool, said Ray Bob, mind like a steel trap.

Don't take you long to get started.

I never quit.

They stood on the hot asphalt lot waiting to see what would happen. Cousin Donnie Ray, Aunt Ethel's youngest boy, nineteen or twenty, wearing a pair of oilstained coveralls and worndown rubber flipflops, a Red Man gimmee cap. Chaw working in his left jaw. He tilted his head to one side and spit, gaze never leaving Ray Bob. Slender guy with a turkey gobbler neck and no chin, light blue eyes fading to gray. Hands in his back pockets, where he carried a razor.

Surprised you come back, he said. Didn't figger you had the kay-honies.

Ray Bob said, Still fuckin your sister Wanda?

Donnie Ray said, You know we gonna come atcha.

Bring along some of Aunt Ethel's mayhaw jelly when you do.

It ain't gonna be that social.

Ray Bob grinned. How's the old man doing?

Which one.

Mine.

Donnie Ray spit again, wiped a dribble of tobacco juice off his lip with the back of one hand. The left hand, keeping the other down his back right pocket. Where the razor was.

Reckon he ain't no different, he said, done got hitched to some gal over to Holly Springs. Gotta bun in the oven already. Can't keep that horny old bastard down. Ain't interested in seeing you, tell you that much.

Might not have a choice.

Well then, go round, see for yourself. I'm telling it straight, you ain't wanted nowheres. Law's hunting you, what we hear. Just soon not draw them flies.

Ray Bob said, That ain't it.

Naw, it ain't.

Ray Bob grinned again, put a cigarette in his mouth, reached in his jeans pocket. Donnie Ray leaned forward, right arm tensed. Ray Bob said, Easy there, hoss, now ain't the time. He drew out his lighter.

Where you staying?

You'll know when I'm ready.

Never mind then. We'll find out noways. Billy Ray dreamed about you. Momma said you was dead.

Don't forget her mayhaw.

Told her you weren't. Told her you wait, we get our chance yet. Billy Ray and Ronnie Ray and me, we gonna be cummin.

I'll be there.

Ray Bob took a draw on the cigarette, blew out the smoke. Saying, Unless that is I come at you first. You ever seen a movie called *Deliverance*, numbnuts?

Donnie Ray stared for a moment, a brief flicker of disturbance passing through the flat, washed out eyes. Said then he wasn't much of a moviegoer.

Missed a chance to see yourself then, Ray Bob said, hear what you sound like. Some ol' hillbilly boys from Appalachia, they right cosmopolitan.

Don't see where that would interest me none. Donnie Ray bobbed his head toward the Caddy. This your car?

What you think?

Reckon you stole it. Mighty purty, too. Always wanted me a convertible. Figure I'll have to fight Billy Ray and Ronnie Ray for it, comes that time. I'm going in the store now. Momma sent me for sugar.

He sidled away up the parking aisle crabwise, keeping his eyes on Ray Bob. About thirty feet up the way, still watching, he said, Told momma you wasn't dead. We'll be cummin. Then he turned and slouched toward the store entrance, flipflops smacking on the cement.

Ray Bob waited until he was inside, then pulled out of the lot going the wrong way and made a turn several streets up, circling back a few blocks before hitting Highway 190 again well below the supermarket. Just in case Donnie Ray was watching. He drove up toward the hospital and stopped at the Wal-Mart. Inside he bought a propane lamp and a gallon can of fuel, a sleeping bag, cheapest they had. When he paid out he was left with a single ten dollar bill. He put his purchase in the trunk and continued on.

Just below Wal-Mart he angled off onto Highway 63, a narrow twolane road veering northwest toward the Angelina National Forest. A state sign said thirty-two miles to Zavalla. He punched the accelerator and passed the Kingdom Hall of Jehovah's Witnesses, was still picking up speed when he saw the cardboard placard nailed to a hickory tree beside a driveway leading back through mimosas to a twostory brick home. Printed in magic marker: FREE PUPPIES. He hit the brakes and backed up, turned into the drive. Fifteen minutes later he was moving again, a short-haired mixed breed pup in his lap. Big feet, black and white coat with floppy ears, nuzzling down in his crotch. He flipped the pup over in one hand and held it wiggling to his chest. Soft pink belly speckled with gray spots, a male. Flea powder on it smelled like pepper. The pup whimpered and Ray Bob set it down in the far seat. It scrambled back, trying to crawl up Ray Bob's thigh, so he held it against his belly and drove on. After a minute the pup settled down and went to sleep.

He drove out of the city limits and crossed Sandy Creek. The road shot straight ahead over gentle hills through loamed pine trees and pastureland, the grassy inclined shoulders dotted with winehued buttercups, purple thistle. Not far past the Tennessee Gas Pipeline station the roadway spanned the Angelina River. The main channel maybe a hundred feet wide, small fishcamp cabins along high cutbanks either way and trees leaning over the tobacco-colored water. Running medium to high, the stobs in the current nodding lazily. Another mile on, after a clapboard Baptist church, he cut back onto a spur road leading west. He took another left shortly thereafter into a sandy doublerutted lane and followed its shaded course down a ridge through the thick woods, headed directly for the river. In an overgrown field to one side perched a stilted deer stand tilting on bent legs toward a log cabin long collapsed in forlorn decrease, its mosscovered walls given to honeysuckle and creeper. A nearby shed storing remnants of tack stood hipdeep among briar. A spawn of yellow wildflowers circumvented the patch of briar, overfluttered by swallowtails and dragonflies. He passed by the abandoned homestead, breathed deeply the perfumed air.

Then the woods closed over the narrow course above and to either side and the land further declined. All about stood hardwoods, sweet gum and oak and their companion dwellers holly and ash layering the dark green tunnel down into the bottomland. The eclipsed earth between shadowed trunks vertical and twisting lay muffled in dead leaves, veined over with wrist thick vines. The air lay close and muggy, insects hummed a sonorous midday mantra. A chickadee whistled in the bush, echoed by titmouse. The doubleruts now carpeted with forest mulch curved sharply about a pillared beech, momentarily lost their way within the tight constraints of pressing brush, fingertips of buckthorn scraping the Caddy fenders as Ray Bob slowed it to a crawl. The narrow way reappeared, an illusion, ruts mere innuendo through the woods, insinuated beneath a cascade of vine and limb. Like moving through a dark brooding dream. He crept downward through it, skirting a flooded oxbow fringed with willow. A spike buck flushed from cover and leaped the trail, vanished into thicket with a flash of white tail. The wheels almost stuck in a shallow bog but found purchase and scooted the car forward around yet another tight turn and he stopped. There it was, before him. Another log cabin as the first but this still standing. The watermarked walls moldy and warped from floodplain rise and fall, the tin roof peeled away at the eaves but intact. Place he intended to stay.

Place nobody else came.

The river lay beyond a tangled thicket behind the cabin and a baygall beyond the thicket. West bank of the Angelina here, upstream and crossbank from the bottomlands where Aunt Ethel and her bunch lived. Far enough downstream to their shacks they wouldn't see him, close enough they'd never suspect. His daddy's side of the family farther on up, closer to the tailwaters below the Sam Rayburn Dam.

He put the Caddy in park and turned off the motor, studying

the cabin. In bad shape but it'd do. An old fishing camp his grand-father had shown him when he was a boy, as young then in man years as the pup was in dog years, the pup now stirring in his lap, whimpering. He picked it up and propped its belly on the steering wheel looking outward through the windshield. The warm mass of flesh squirmed in his hands.

Easy there, boy, easy.

He turned it around and studied the wet brown eyes. Said, What's your name, hoss?

The pup gazed back, curled a tongue out its muzzle and licked.

Gonna call you Eddie.

Ray Bob wiggled the pup and called the name again.

Said, We're safe here, good buddy.

48

Della put her head out the truck window and asked Eddie what the problem was. He didn't hear her, twice. So she peered through the lower windshield, trying to see through the long horizontal crack between it and the raised hood. She saw Eddie in there, part of his head and back. He was bent over the engine, practically upside down with one arm thrust into the machinery. His arm shot up and a wrench went flying.

Della heard him yell.

He climbed down off the bumper and disappeared below the truck front, reappeared holding the wrench kissing a knuckle, T-shirt stained with grease and sweat, his hair a mess. He dove back in.

She leaned against the Naugahyde seat and her blouse stuck to it. She puffed her cheeks, blew out. Boy, it was hot. Hundred degrees maybe, almost that much humidity, a real booger. Hot-ter'n a short order grill, and here they were stranded on Highway

6 in the middle of nowhere, between Hitchcock and Alvin was all Della knew, marsh grass to the horizon in every direction.

Thank *youuuu*, Mister Bubba Bear. The Chevy Silverado was a hunk of junk, just like her Hyundai. Third time it had broke down since Bolivar. Plus the air conditioner was shot.

She climbed out and went around front, high heels wobbling in the crabgrass, asked Eddie if she could help. Sure, he said, why don't you just scoot underneath with a ratchet and loosen the lower nut on this generator. Then pull it down hard and tighten the belt.

No thanks.

She went back to sit in the cab. Determined to stay in a good mood no matter what. When she'd suggested they go to Missouri City and get Randy and Waylon, Eddie had agreed right away. Surprised the heck out of her. No way now, knock on wood, she was gonna ruin it.

The idea had come to her in the middle of the night, after they'd both awakened horny at the same time and she'd rolled onto her belly and spread her legs, Eddie taking her from behind. That had been nice, way he held on with both hands while his balls slapped her ass, she'd noticed that as much as his cock going in and out. Made her realize it's the little things. She'd come twice.

Afterward she couldn't sleep so she got up and sat at the kitchen table with a pen and paper. What caused it was remembering that article in *Working Mother* at the beauty shop, one that told you How to Organize Your Life. Something everyone needed to do, if they had the presence of mind. Her own life for instance, being presently in a very disorganized state. So she'd sat at the table and followed the article's instructions best she remembered.

First she wrote down a list of the major problems: Mister Dreamboat, her job, the car, the apartment, her kids. Five was the maximum you were supposed to list, which fit with what she had, a good sign.

Then she considered each problem and rated it on a scale of one to ten in importance, meaning, she supposed, how soon it was about to jump up and bite you on the ass. Set your priorities that way. When she finished and looked at the points it so happened she'd listed the problems in the correct order to start with, another good sign. Not that the kids were *really* number five in importance, naturally, but her mother was taking the pressure off there.

After that she'd sat at the table analyzing the list, starting at the top and working her way down, considering solutions. What the magazine called brainstorming the options. Boy that stumped her. Mister Dreamboat in the way no matter what she brainstormed. It was a bleak situation, and depressed her so much she'd knelt over the La-Z-Boy holding the Bible to her chest to pray about it, first making sure Eddie was asleep.

Only thing that came out of that was the idea to get the kids. Which they were trying to do. Except she was beginning to think she'd misunderstood the message. Either that or Somebody Important had overlooked the condition of the truck.

She was fanning herself with the folded up *Houston Chronicle*— yet *another* day with no news—when Eddie slammed the hood and climbed in. He grinned and lit a cigarette.

Good thing I like to work on engines.

Uh-huh, Della said, and a good thing this contraption was free.

Can't beat the price, Eddie agreed. He cranked the motor and started down the shoulder, the truck trembling and quaking as they picked up speed. Around fortyfive it stopped shaking, which meant the front end needed alignment, he said, nothing serious. Generator might need a little work, no big deal. And the air conditioner, all it needed, most likely, was some Freon.

You're the mechanic, Della said, briefly wondering how much a good mechanic made. Not like Ralph who couldn't even fix a Hyundai but charged her all the same, the jerk. A good mechanic. She bet they made a better living than most folks realized, way cars broke down every chance they got.

I ever tell you I grew up in a Pentecostal church? Eddie said.

Said it just like that, out of the blue. Della frowned.

That's right, he went on, my momma switched over from being Catholic even though we was French coonass because she waked up one night speaking in tongues. Didn't know what it was until ld lady Grimes who lived down the street explained she'd got the Holy Ghost. It's in the Bible somewhere, what that means. Something about an upper room, all these people praying, they start talking in languages they never heard before. Meant they got the Holy Ghost, like my momma. I was about five or six then. What'd ou grow up?

Baptist, Della said. Sort of, at Christmas and Easter.

Well, old lady Grimes was Pentecostal, that's why she knew, only she was Sister Grimes after my momma joined the church. he had long hair, wore it piled on top, they don't believe in cutting hair, the women. That's in the Bible, too. They hold services bout six times a week, no joke. That's cause they don't watch TV or have fun.

He paused to flip the cigarette butt out the window and listen o the truck motor, leaning forward, and Della said, Why not?

Cause it's a sin, he said. Don't ask me why, I'm just telling you what the rules are. No TV, no smoking, no drinking, no dancing, you name it they against it.

He cocked his head, listening again. You hear something unny?

Lord, I hope not, she said, we're never gonna get there.

Eddie shrugged. Probably just the U-joint. It's a little loose, hat's minor. Anyway, my momma said getting the Holy Ghost hanged her life. She could quote that Bible, I kid you not. My old nan never attended, which was normal, Pentecostals being mostly women. Ones that ain't widow women are usually married to drunks and ne'er-do-wells, which they testify about in church, aking turns. It's a sad thing to hear, all them stories. You wouldn't believe it.

Della said, You never been in a beauty shop.

He agreed he hadn't, allowed it might be the same, except that rue Pentecostals didn't go to beauty shops or wear makeup, those being other sins.

Why'd you go?

Cause my momma made me, Eddie said, as if the answer was obvious. Least until I was a teenager and she couldn't handle me. But it wasn't that bad, they got great music. That full gospel holiness stuff is some righteous rock 'n' roll, honeybunch, they really get down. Elvis grew up in one, you know that?

She shook her head.

That's right, and so did Jerry Lee Lewis, Little Richard, all them cats.

Well, you sure wouldn't know it, she said.

That's cause they're backslid and living in sin. Happens a lot with musicians, artist types.

He tried to light another cigarette, elbows on the steering wheel. It shimmied so much he couldn't, so he drove with his knees. Thinking about Leadbelly, served thirty years in Huntsville for killing a man. Son House, the same, spent his time in Parchman. Plus some others. Man oh man. Thinking about that dead A-rab in Austin, that girl in the park, thinking about all the rest before, how time couldn't fix it, no matter where you spent it, in prison or elsewhere, nor regret nor grief, his own or any other's. Thinking about that shit all the time now, even when he wasn't. Couldn't run from it, couldn't shake it loose.

Take me now, he said, I'm the worst sinner ever was. Things I done, don't believe nuthin could save me, not even Jesus Christ hisself. And I tried talking to the man, believe you me, he didn't say a word. Not that I blame him. Probably got fed up, just turned off the tap. They say that happens.

Well, robbery's a bad habit, Della said tactfully, and pointing guns at people don't help, but at least you never killed no one.

He didn't say anything.

Anyhow, what I heard is you're already forgiven, she added, even if you ain't apologized. You're saved ahead of time whether you know it or not. Cause of Christ.

Yeah? Eddie made a wry face. Well, it sure don't feel like it. Maybe I need to use that little black box of yours. Here's Alvin, you want a burger?

He pulled into a Sonic Drive-In and parked in the shade under the awning, asked Della what she wanted. He placed the order, reminding the speaker not to put any mayonnaise on his burger, just mustard. Saying, I hate mayonnaise.

Della looked at him funny. She'd never noticed Eddie hated

mayonnaise, and it occurred to her then that there were lots of things about him she didn't know. Least not yet. It made her feel kind of strange, but warm, and hopeful, too. It was nice the way it took time to know someone.

Only then he said, I been thinking about Ray Bob. I miss that guy.

Della snorted.

He ain't as bad as he acts, Eddie said, and that's the truth, sugar-pie. He's got some good points.

He's a whacko, she retorted, an accident looking for a place to happen. Only with Mister Hothead it ain't no accident. Person like him's a lost cause, makes me doubt we're pre-saved.

He shrugged, thinking it was a subject he might as well forget. The carhop brought the order then and they spread out the food and ate watching the traffic on the highway. Heat waves rose off the asphalt pavement, causing the vehicles to appear like reflections in a funhouse mirror. He tried the truck radio again but it still wouldn't work, nothing but static. Loose wire to the antenna probably, easy to fix.

Reason I was thinking about him, he said momentarily—meaning Ray Bob, only not saying his name—is that I had this other best friend, and I been thinking about him, too. He's my cousin really but we was close as brothers. Then he got hooked on drugs and that fucked up the deal. He felt bad about it and drifted off, it's a long story.

He took a bite of his burger and gazed out the open window a minute, pulling on his earring. Della thought he looked wistful.

Thing is, he said, he lives in Houston now and I was thinking about looking him up, maybe see if I can't get him to kick before it kills him. Crank, junk, speedballs, that'll put your lights out fast. Only with the truck breaking down, I don't reckon there's time enough, not today.

What's his name?

Wade.

That's your name, she said. Sounding surprised.

Damn. He took another big bite and waved his hand, indicating he'd explain later, when his mouth wasn't full. Man oh man, he'd stepped in it now. He'd forgot all about that. He chewed for a while, a long while, like he might never finish.

Della waited.

Well, the thing is, he finally said, still chewing, the thing is we're both named Wade, after my mother's brother Uncle Wade.

How'd you tell each other apart? she asked.

That one surprised Eddie. Well, he said, now that you mention it, we did look a lot alike.

I mean names.

He dipped a french fry in ketchup, nonchalantly. Then said, Well, he usually went by his first name. DeReese.

I see.

Della returned to her hamburger, picking out the onion. She'd forgot to mention she didn't like onions.

Eddie watched. After a bit, he finished the burger and wadded up the wrapping, tossed it on the red plastic tray clipped to the windowglass. Thinking, Man, he was gonna have to start keeping better track if they stayed together, she didn't miss a *thing*.

49

The break came the following day.

After lunch with the deputy, Rule'd spent the first afternoon running the back roads off Highway 63 from the Jasper County side of Dam B north to the state fish hatchery. Twolane farm to market roads crisscrossed the area, though most ran roughly parallel to ridges fringing the eastern side of the lake and Angelina River bottom. Unpaved county spurs led off paved roads into piney woods, and narrow dirt lanes and logging roads off those. The timber companies clearcut and seeded the sandy upland terrain, acreage arranged in straight corporate rows of slash pine syncopated by denuded fields graded to the soil line.

The sun rode up high and white like a pearl wrapped in

alabaster. He didn't see much wildlife, a few birds. Wrong time of day, but early morning and dusk wouldn't make much difference. Squirrels couldn't thrive on pineburrs, deer and turkey preferred hardwoods, too.

Farther down the corduroyed watershed past the timber farms the logging roads petered out. Rutted dirt trails proceeding onward and downward into the bottomlands were so washed out and overgrown that it seemed to Rule he spent as much time in reverse as forward. The day was hot and sultry, the languid air beneath the canopied forest an overheated sauna. He rode with the windows down, sweating in the cab. He stopped now and then to let Lefty rove the woods.

He still didn't know what Redhead was driving and wasn't sure what he was looking for but he was looking. Never could tell, might stumble over something. Better than waiting. It seemed close, though, he could feel it coming.

Toward evening he gave up and drove back into Jasper. The sun was setting bloodred in the west. Cicadas sang back in the magnolias and sycamores. Porchlights flicked on at houses set in shadowed clearings along the road. From the windows came the warm yellow glow of inside lamps and the blue flicker of TV sets as folks settled in for the evening.

He realized then he and Moline hadn't spoken all day. Avoiding each other. It was no good in terms of work—he wondered whether it was DeReese or Wade on the videotapes, and Rufus down on Bolivar needed a closer look—but for the time being he didn't much mind. Moline too edgy, on a bender making threats, better to stay away. Plus Redhead the first order of business. Take care of the DeReese versus Wade problem later, or get the answer from Redhead, easiest way.

He checked into the Best Western on the main thoroughfare by the Cotton Patch, a country cafe, and called Deputy Wright. No word yet on Matthews but the patrols had their noses to the ground. The department had called in a couple of auxiliaries for backup. Rule told the deputy where he was staying and walked next door for supper.

The mention of auxiliaries jogged it loose: hadn't seen Lomax

since Houston. Cuffed in a patrol car, lanky bones rigid with triumph and restrained rage. Though he'd walked on bail hours
later. On the loose again, location unknown. Rule thinking maybe
one death satisfied an avenging angel's bloodlust. An eye for an
eye, not two. Or maybe he'd shaken Lomax in all the commotion.
He recollected the Old Testament fire in the man's grizzled face,
the set of his jaw. Decided then the guy was coming, just a matter
of time. Like a bad case of hives.

He ate light, a chicken-fried steak sandwich and fries, then
went to the H.E.B. supermarket and bought a bag of dogfood for
Lefty. He spent the evening in his room reading the Burke novel.
Or trying to. His attention wandered. He thought about calling
Eastland in Houston, asking for a status check on Lomax,
dropped it. He wondered what, if anything, to do about Katie.
Other than let go, but that part was about himself, not her. So he
let it go.

For a while he pictured Dana spreadlegged naked in bed,
smooth legs, pubic hair a thin blonde patch, playing with herself,
squirming. He got a half erection, fooled with it, then it too
passed away. Couldn't concentrate. His mind kept reaching out,
trying to make contact with Redhead, trying to crawl into the
boy's head. He fell asleep still trying but did not dream the dream
and he awakened early.

He showered and returned to the Cotton Patch for breakfast.
An armada of pewter clouds promising rain had drifted up from
the coast overnight. Backlit by morning, they glowed with a low-
grade neon haze, hovered low, held down the muggy air.

The cafe was busy with men wearing polyester slacks and half-
sleeved shirts with clip-on ties, smalltown businessman's uniform.
Kiwanis and Lions Club types. For the most part they were boisterous, vocal, and gutbellied. The waitresses joked, trading flirts
with men in passing as they carried plates stacked up their arms,
called out orders. From the kitchen came the sizzle of meat hitting
the grill, fried aroma and smoke, the low urgent voices of black
fry cooks in motion. Rule sat near the door and placed his order,
sipped his coffee.

He was eating a stack of buckwheat pancakes and sausage

when Jude Bevil walked in. Well, I'll be a monkey's uncle, Jude barked, lookit what the cat drug in.

Rule rose to shake hands, Jude sat down across the table. Slender and pinkskinned, white tufts above his ears, he was nearing ninety and stooped but he walked without a cane and his dark blue eyes sparked like a short in an electric plug. Publisher, editor and sole reporter of the weekly paper before he sold out to a chain from Atlanta. He'd been shot at through the newspaper office window for his politics and beaten up on the loading dock for his views on race and sued countless times for his barbed editorial comments. None of it worked. When they try to muzzle you, he'd boasted, howl louder. A born iconoclast, keeping the local compost turned. Motto of the paper back then was "First There Was God, Then Shakespeare, Then FDR." Nowadays, Jude said, it was "Patronize Our Advertisers." He ordered a bowl of oatmeal with whole wheat toast and coffee.

You looking fit, Rule said. How's retirement?

Better'n the alternative. The boneyard, I mean. The soapbox, I miss that. Get mad enough, I write a letter, they don't print it. You been following those peckerheads in Washington?

Jude's eyes flashed fiercely and he talked on, not waiting for an answer.

Democrats all turned Republican and the Republicans don't know which way to go. Political miscegenation. Only got one party now and it's schizophrenic. Democrats play with little girls, Republicans get caught with boys in the Greyhound toilet, only difference I see. Business Roundtable's running the show. Nothing left for those strutting peabrains in D.C. to do but dip their tallywhackers and run for reelection, keep one hand out for the honeymoney. They all got acting coaches. See a TV camera they get a hard-on. You chasing the Matthews boy?

Rule nodded and ate his pancakes.

Well, his family won't help you any, Jude said, spooning sugar in his coffee, but they won't help him neither. Sterling bunch of gooberheads. Halfwits and thieves. They're about the only natural predators we got left in the woods now that the woods ain't natural. All the longleaf's gone, the sandylands and prairie been planted over. The big timber boys are after the riverbottom now. Robber barons in our grand American tradition. Steal us blind, get glowing profiles in *Fortune* and *Newsweek*. Only difference between them and the Matthews clan is they dress better. Before they're finished won't be a pignut hickory or walnut left in East Texas. The music's almost done. And the voice of harpers and musicians shall be heard no more, for thy merchants were the great men of the earth, by their sorceries were all nations deceived. Book of Revelation. I suppose you looked in the bottoms already.

Rule nodded again, chewed a piece of sausage. One thing about talking with Jude, you didn't miss a bite if you were eating.

The old man poured sugar over his oatmeal and stirred it in. Said, I suppose you been on this side mostly, where the family lives, if you can call it a family. Never have advocated selective genocide, but that inbred cesspool makes a man ponder. Ethel Matthews' three boys stole a roadgrader last month. Planned to knock down nigger shacks with it, what they told Buckshot, proud of it, like they were performing a public service. Ever see what *they* live in? Johnny Ray's the only one with half a brain, and see what good it did him. But this side of the river won't be where he is. You looked in the westbank bottoms?

Rule said he hadn't.

Well then, Jude said, now that we got that cleared up, what we gonna do about those boneheads in Washington?

Rule reflected on what Jude had said, and when he dropped by the sheriff's office after breakfast and everything came up zeros, he drove out Highway 63 past the Tennessee Pipeline station. He crossed the Angelina River bridge, gave a cursory glance to the small Baptist church just beyond, and continued on toward Zavalla through the Angelina National Forest. The cloudcover overlaid the sky and enveloped the land in a soft bluegray patina of satin. The air lay unstirred and clung like hot mist from a steam iron. The lanky flourishing pines enfolded the heat, exhaled their resinous myrrh.

He rode with the window down, the wind rushing in. It smelled like warm pine sap and honeysuckle and the skin just beneath a woman's ear. Lefty sat alongside the far window, head up scanning the landscape for movement.

Ten miles this side of Zavalla, at Boykin Springs, he turned into the park road and followed it south through the trees over a cattle guard, past weedy heifers ranging in the sparse woods and a sign claiming the section for a hunting club. The road deadended at the springs and a twentyacre lake. He parked and stood on the lake levee watching a heron stalk minnows in the shallows, its long Egyptian neck a graceful undulating S curve until it swiftly uncoiled and flashed, a vicious downward strike. The tall white bird raised its beak skyward and swallowed.

Rule's gaze drifted over to the far bank where a ropeswing of thick hemp hung over the lake from the upper reaches of an ancient beech. His mind reached backward. He'd leaped from that rope as it swung over the water, dropping him fifteen feet or more, forever it seemed, arms and legs flailing air, downward falling into the cold springwater, breathless, rising to the surface with a gasping whoop. More than once, he'd done that, way back when. Time and again on hot days like this one. Right there, same tree, same rope maybe. It all appeared unchanged, yet not. A vague taunting difference. The past but a nostalgic sensation bound to a blurred image. Then gone. After a while he turned back and drove out of the park, returning eastward on the highway in the direction of Jasper.

Just shy of the Angelina bridge he yawed off right onto a spur road that cut back toward the Neches River, spanning the bottomlands tucked between the two rivers just above their confluence at Dam B Lake. The rivers running almost parallel here, several miles apart. A lot of country packed between, maybe one Redhead in it. He drove along the spur for a couple of miles, counted half a dozen sandy lanes leading off toward the Angelina's westbank bottoms. Could be down any one of them, or none. He U-turned on the narrow shoulder and cruised slowly back toward the highway, listening. A rustle in the verdant treetops, the plaintive caws of a crow, a distant answer, and quiet. Overhead the bluestreaked underbellies of the clouds swelled and parted, joined anew and coalesced in a shimmering ozoned dance.

It smelled like rain.

He stopped in the road and got out, stood next to the idling truck with a hand on the fender. The woods whispered, he cocked a closer ear. Then Lefty whined in the cab, wanting out, and he let the hound range the edge of the thicket while he listened some more, chin up, eyes closed, nostrils flaring. After a minute he walked to the border of the woods and heeled Lefty up. He squatted beside him, rubbing his head.

You hear what I hear, boy? Smell it?

He spoke quietly, barely a murmur. The Walker, head held high, rolled his eyes askance to look at Rule, who ran his hand over the smooth tricolored back, down the trembling flank, patted it softly.

Right in there, boy. All we got to do is flush him.

He gave Lefty a final caress, tugged one drooping velvet ear and stood up. He unholstered the .45 and checked the clip, chambered a round.

Or go in, hunt him down.

50

Ray Bob traversed the cypress shaded baygall, drew along a boggy trail from the riverbank to come up through the dense thicket halfbent with upraised arms, one hand holding an ax, the other his pants, his freckled forearms and naked legs lacerated with ugly welts, bleeding cuts, his torso drenched with sweat as if he'd been laboring crossties under a midday August sun. He was gaiting over the weedy nettled yard of wildflowers between thicket and cabin when he stopped midstride.

Froze in place, head cocked.

He didn't know then if it'd been something he'd heard or some sound he should've heard but hadn't. He glanced skyward at the shifting plumbago clouds which had been building since sunrise, lowhanging pregnant masses heavy with grumbling thunder and soon to term, bilious, threatening to part folds and break water in a coming deluge.

After a minute he went around to the front of the cabin and listened some more, gazing intently up the sandy ruts coming through the woods behind the Caddy. The moist breeze ruffling the treetops above, stridulous hum of insects below, warbling birds. Nothing else. Whatever it'd been wasn't there now.

He turned and went into the cabin where the pup was sleeping and put down the ax. He stripped off the wet T-shirt and removed his boots, dried off with a towel from his duffel. The cuts along his arms and legs smarted but they weren't deep. He pulled on a dry T-shirt and the damp jeans. Barefooted, he awakened the pup and carried it onto the porch, stood there cradling it, absentmindedly rubbing its rosy hairless belly.

Listening again.

First sound he'd heard was last night. He was sitting on the split-timbered floor feeding the pup Vienna sausages and peanut butter, eating a can of cold ranchstyle beans with crackers himself, chasing it with warm beer. The wavering halo of the propane lamp casting shadows into the dirtdobbered corners and along the cobwebbed pine rafters overhead. Slapping mosquitos to a black paste on his arms, smelling the close dusty mold and dampwood must which reminded him of an attic thrown ajar after years of disuse. When the distant baying of hounds passed through the open cabin door.

The sound was muffled by the woods, but they were running open in full cry. He listened. The hounds fell silent, then one struck again and they came on running a steady chop, drawing nearer. Trailing coon, no doubt, heading this way. He got up and blew down the lantern glass chimney, sat in the moldy charcoaled dark holding the pup for an hour as the hounds circled west and north from downriver, freetonguing on the scent, bawling, one with a sweet voice, redbone maybe, hard to tell. He heard the changeover when they treed the quarry. The urgent deepthroated keening raised the hair on his neck, the pup trembled and puled in the blackness. Then the bugling bays abruptly stopped, he heard the crack of a gun, one shot, then silence. He waited another hour before he lit the lamp again.

Afterward he went outside and stood on the porch watching fireflies lighting the near woods. Crickets chirred in the grass, an owl signaled close by once, twice, a third time. A chorus of treefrogs and bullfrogs from the baygall in concord swelled and fell in the moonlit night. The yammer did not seem as loud as what he recalled in years past, and he considered that there were less of them than before. Insecticides, he'd heard, and herbicides, killing off the supply line, abandoning them unlinked in the chain, mutating those that remained. That simple, that simple. For a while he listened to an armadillo snuffling in the brush, rooting for grubs and insects. He tracked its forage, swatting mosquitos until they drove him indoors.

He slept fitfully in the cheap nylon sleeping bag lined with cotton flannel. He'd forgotten to buy repellent and when he lay on the open bag the mosquitos swarmed, the sharp stings painful as needle pricks. He zippered it and crawled inside, could not sleep for the stifling heat, the flannel liner an oven, his body bathed in sweat. He finally rested near morning when the temperature settled on the dew. He awakened with the pup curled at his head.

In the false dawn he made his way through the thicket and baygall to stand on the riverbank watching the graygauzed current between the banks unveil at sunrise. Swallows flitted over tan-colored swirls between bobbing stobs, dodged the overhanging trees in their furtive dashing flight. Feeding fish broke surface beneath willows. He closed his eyes, felt the tingling vibrations in his arms and legs merge with the coming day's rhythm, seeking synchrony with the murbling riverflow and sighing trees, the slow cycling of his breath a bellows exchanging life for life as through the permeable membrane of a preternatural being.

When the dull red uprising sphere broached the slit between a flotilla of swollen clouds and the foliage in the upper trees and burned off the last shards of mist, he turned back to the baygall, removing first his boots and then his jeans before wading into its tannined reaches in undershorts and T-shirt. It was dark there yet, deeply shadowed beneath the dense hardwood canopy. He stepped carefully, an eye out for water moccasins, made his way under sweetbay and gallberry toward the swamp tupelo and cypress farther in. A silver haze filtered down as the cloud-occluded sun arced upward and a powderblue mark on a tupelo trunk caught his eye. Then another on a middling cypress draped in Spanish moss. Then another. He stood calfdeep in water as dark as brewed tea, puzzling the powderblue marks. Then understood.

Timbermen marking trees for cutting.

He pushed on then, more quickly, splashing through the shallows and bogs until he reached the solitary tree that had drawn him in. As it had before, many times, since that childhood time when his grandfather had first brought him to it. He finally stood before it breathing hard. A towering bald cypress reaching two hundred feet skyward, its lower trunk almost thirty feet in circumference, surrounded by cypress knees as tall as a man. A colossal spire that was not a mere tree but a massive being, a leviathan standing in inviolate testimony to passing centuries, to countless hurricanes and tornados and ice storms. To biblical flood, to fire apocalyptic, and drought. To a dozen generations of lesser trees and a hundred generations of lesser beasts. To leather-shod Indians passing in their silent communal stealth and imperial Spaniards who could not hold the land and the arrogant French who would quit it and to the somber streaming Anglo settlers who did not, who held it and finally would make it theirs in claim and title if not in spirit, would hold and conquer it or kill it trying.

Which now they were doing.

He stood before the tree and saw the powderblue mark on the great gray trunk that seemed as tender, muscular flesh.

Without pause he turned back through the baygall, emerged from it dripping to return to the cabin bootless and pantless, where he scavenged a junkstrewn corner until he found the onebladed ax and a fourfoot length of heavy iron rebar. He traipsed back through the bottoms to the cypress and drove the rebarred spear into its fleshy trunk with the blunt backside of the ax, pounding it in inch by inch, oblivious to the jolting pain in his shoulder, sweating and panting in the sultry shade of the very thing he was killing.

It took him most of the day. When he was finished the iron rod lay embedded in its entirety, piercing the cypress to its heart. He stepped back and wiped his brow with a wet forearm, gazed upward into the farthest reaches of the great tree. He felt like saying something but there was only the tree to hear and it was dying. He spoke anyway.

Whoever said evil will good on out was wrong. Goddamn them all.

Then he strode out of the baygall with the ax laid over one wide bunyaned shoulder and went up through the thicket pantless in his boots to the cabin, where he thought he heard something. Then changed into dry clothes and took the pup to stand on the porch listening some more. He didn't hear it now. Only the grumbling blueblack clouds bringing rain. But there was something else.

Something out there.

51

He decided to go in, hunt him down.

It would have been prudent to telephone the sheriff's office, request Deputy Wright bring out a dozen men with rifles and Kevlar vests and a brace of bloodhounds. And rainslickers. Or drive back to Jasper and meet with the deputy and work out a detailed plan. Prudent, by the book, certainly safer. But he worked alone, as he'd always done, because that's what the best Rangers did and he was a Ranger because that's how he liked it.

One riot, one Ranger. One bad boy, less than a riot.

What nailed it was the old man who walked out of the woods a quarter mile back up the spur road just as Rule drove past, trying to decide by which dirt lane to enter the bottoms. One moment the shoulder of the road was empty, the woods verging it a long scrabbled wall of leaf and dark trunks and brown fingered limbs beneath the heaving gray overcast. Then, an apparition instantly crystallized in flesh, the man was standing there. A wizened walnutcolored face, gnarled hands hanging loosely to his thighs, apelike, bentkneed, wearing a faded felt bush hat and faded blue overalls and a faded longsleeved denim shirt and brogans.

Rule braked, did a doubletake. The man stood just outside the treeline, motionless, not looking at Rule but regarding him nonetheless from beneath the downturned brim of the hat, his dark leathered face impassive. Shortly two hounds, a black and tan and a bluetick, slipped from the woods and heeled up on either side. They, too, seemed to watch without looking, as though their entire bodies sensed more than mere sight could comprehend, abstruse posture and demeanor as inscrutably sphinxlike as the man's.

Rule put the truck in park and got out, told Lefty to stay. Low rumbling thunder rolled in from the south, forked lightning veined the platinum horizon and a cool damp breeze sprang up when he walked around the tailgate and stood where pavement met road shoulder, touched one hand to his Stetson.

Howdy.

The old man nodded once, a barely perceptible motion, then spat a wad of brown juice sideways to the right. It skimmed the bluetick's mottled crown in its downward trajectory, landed in the pineneedled grass near the hound.

Live bouts here? Rule asked.

The man nodded again, or seemed to.

Rule couldn't see the man's eyes for the hatbrim but below it his face was etched deeply with lines and the chamfered corrugations of age and time spent more outdoors than in. His wrists below the buttoned shirtsleeves and both hands were dark brown and weathered as sunhardened parchment. Rule studied the hounds a minute. Both deepchested, plenty of lung, wellboned and muscular. Brown dots over the bluetick's eyes same color as the deep tan trim on the other dog, the black and tan with too much dewlap but strong, highknuckled cat's feet. Rule turned his gaze up the road.

Fine looking dogs, he said. Coon, I reckon.

The old man glanced down then, to one side and the other, as if surprised to find what he saw there. Then raised his head to look directly at Rule. His nose was a thin beak between small wideset eyes of a pale yellow flecked with light green. Panther's eyes. Though the cast of them did not change, Rule sensed the man's focus shift elsewhere.

Wonder how old that Walker might be, he said.

His voice flowed like soft water over stone, held the singsong southern accents of deep East Texas riverbottom. Language like what folks spoke when they first arrived by oxcart and mule-hauled wagons from Georgia and Alabama and the Carolinas almost two centuries back, from the Scots-Irish borderlands before that, the yeoman vernacular of freeholders seeking land by which to further traduce the traditions of easy subsistence and limitless hunting and free pasturage, rich unencumbered soil and forests without end, because they had worn out what they already had and wanted more, finding it here in East Texas, until it too would give out, then no more.

Rule swung his head about, saw Lefty in the truck cab with his head out the window, scrutinizing the other hounds. He's going on three, Rule said.

Once more the man seemed to nod, as if Rule had confirmed what was already known. Good Walker got grit, he said after a while, runs a track hard.

He does fine, never been trashy.

Hunts close, I reckon.

Naw, he's a wide hunter, Rule said. But he checks in, and he strikes with a clean, short mouth. Sired out of a line down in Brazoria County.

The man didn't say anything at that. His expression still indecipherable as alien code. He might've known where Brazoria County lay and every capillaried bayou and oaked knoll in it, or he might've never heard of the place. He spat again, this time shaving the broad skull of the black and tan. His gaze seemed to settle back on Rule, who momentarily realized the dog talk was finished, commerce completed.

He hung both thumbs in his back pants pockets, noted the

wind had come up stronger. The oncoming rain in it tasted as flat and metallic as gunmetal.

Name's Hooks, he said. Come from Tyler County, Austin now. I'm looking for a man, a bad man. Done killed five people I know of, maybe more. If he's around here he showed within the past couple of days.

Rule watched the old man, tried to glean any indication that he'd seen someone or heard. A futile effort. He'd known men like this growing up, backwoodsmen who moved through time leaving hardly a disturbance they did not will, yet where they willed they took anything they wanted, not caring what they left. Only they did not want much often, and then took it in places few others cared to go. In the bottoms, usually alone. Either the man knew something or didn't, would say it or not, beyond the circumference of Rule's need.

Several minutes passed. Rule touched his hat again, said, All right then. He turned to leave.

The old man spoke, his voice barely detectable on the gusting breeze.

Five men.

Rule pulled up. He said, Four men, and a woman. An old man and a young boy, a police officer and a black college boy.

Three men, the man said, a woman and a nigger.

Reckon I can't say how he's counting them, Rule replied, speaking evenly, I just know they're dead. They won't be the last. He's rogue.

Gonna kill him.

Only if I have to.

The old man looked away then, back down the spur road to where it folded into dark woods well before the twolane highway. After a minute he spoke, his soft voice textured as doeskin. Rule leaned forward to hear it.

Treed a bobtail cat yestiddy night. Down to the river, by the Grover place. Hided it this morning. Only one I seen since cain't member when. Last one, I reckon. Done give out. Used to be bear, they give out. Wolves done gone. Seen a light on down there. Seen a car.

The man stopped, the silence in the wake of his speech like a lingering inflection of the fatigue it had caused him, all those words at once, a rushing current of regretful noise, too much.

Which way's the Grover place? Rule asked.

Last road fore the highway.

At that the man turned and melted into the woods as if he'd stepped through a slitted veil, disappeared there before Rule realized he was gone. A phantasm fading on an instant. The two hounds vanished with him, the near edge of the thicket once more a scrabbled wall of green and ochered foliage and limb unfettered along its fringe. Rule listened for a twigsnap, a rustle of dead leaves stirred underfoot, heard nothing.

Gone.

He got in the cab and drove on down to the last sandy lane leading off into the bottoms before the highway. He paused there, considered calling the sheriff's office, rousting Wright and the deputies. He decided against it. When ghosts walk and give guidance, omens prevail. The waiting was done. He was going in alone.

Gonna hunt Redhead down.

52

He was in the cabin pulling on his boots when he heard the sound. Wouldn't have heard it then for the rumbling thunder coming from the south but the wheels must've bogged in a mudhole down near the oxbow slough and the engine whined momentarily, then subsided. He went out on the porch wearing one boot and listened, heard the low whirring of the motor in the woods. A car, or a truck. Couldn't tell what direction it was moving but there was only the solitary rutted lane so it was coming in.

He wiggled his jaw, popped his ears. The barometric pressure had fallen and he glanced upward at the swaying treetops and the dark blueblack sky, knowing the bottom would drop out soon, an early summer monsoon. He ducked back inside the cabin and pulled on the other boot, sitting on the floor. When the pup waddled over whining to lick his hand, he pushed it away and reached for the jar of peanut butter, unscrewed the top and plunged his fingers in. He scooped out a handful and wiped the oily mass on the floorboards. The pup went after it, tail wagging furiously.

He cleaned his hand on the damp towel and stood in the musty room among the floating dustmotes and checked the Walther automatic, making sure a round was chambered, then snugged it against the small of his back. He returned to the porch and listened again, the motor still coming through the woods.

Stepping off midst the high grass and nettles, he slipped around the side of the cabin to the back and waited, hidden there, surveying the front from a corner of notched pine logs. The shapeshifting underbellies of the stormclouds shuddered darkly overhead and the upper masts of the trees fluttered and quaked in anticipation, but the wind could not penetrate below and at ground level the air lay dense, still and muggy. His T-shirt was wet, dark splotches of sweat under his arms and along his belly. Beads collected on his face and he wiped his eyes in the crook of an elbow.

He wondered who it was. Could be his cousins coming like Donnie Ray promised only that wasn't likely. They wouldn't come in a vehicle, or if they did they'd leave it at the road and come afoot, in silence and stealth. More likely they'd come by river and up through the baygall and thicket, and then only by early morning or dusk when it was cooler. Wouldn't come during a thunderstorm either, stay inside high and dry. In any case, they wouldn't announce it, not with the kind of noise he was hearing. So it was someone else. Might be someone knew about the old camp, who used it, but he doubted that, he'd never seen anyone here in all the times he'd come. But it was someone coming for a reason because no one would otherwise come, not this far into the bottoms down a road that was barely ruts, not in this weather.

He waited, listening. Lightning streaked to the south in white-hot jagged splinters, ruptured the bruised sky. Thunder followed shortly, the clapping percussive din rolled over the landscape and dropped, shook the earth, entered his body through his legs and trembled in his bones. But still the rain did not fall, and the rumbling soon abated, then ceased.

The sound of the motor grew nearer. He glimpsed a flash of red through underbrush and foliage. A moment later another, and again, then he saw it was a truck and he knew it was the red Dodge pickup from town, one with the Ranger and Booker Wright. Backing slowly through weeds and wildflowers toward the thicket edge, he kept the corner of the cabin between him and the pickup, which now emerged fully from the woods and drew up behind the Caddy and stopped. He saw then the Ranger was alone. Unless there were others behind him. But the pickup motor switched off presently and it was quiet, there wasn't another sound in the woods besides the usual ones, and then it thundered again and the rain began to fall, tentative yet, a scattered descent of large warm droplets.

The Ranger stepped from the cab and pushed his Stetson back, stood by the open truckdoor looking at the Caddy, then the cabin. He was either careless or he knew what he was doing, one clear shot from inside would take him out. Tall lean man with a long face and a narrow chin, cowboy in a bolo tie. Reminded Ray Bob of that country singer, tall skinny one used to be on TV, wore sequined coats with rhinestones. Except he stood there watching the cabin like he knew it was empty, like he'd expected it. Cowboy knew what he was doing.

Ray Bob slipped along the edge of the thicket to the barely perceptible trailhead of the path leading down toward the baygall and river. He stood there in the open for a moment, turning to make sure the Ranger saw him, then ducked in beneath the elderberry and disappeared.

Rule was studying the cabin, an ancient construction of peeled longleaf timbers, straightgrained for sawing and rot resistant with pitch, kind that lasted, when the movement caught his eye, a bright white motion against green behind the cabin, and he saw Redhead stop and turn, then slip into the thicket. Boy playing cat and mouse, drawing him in like it was a game.

He paid no mind to the raindrops falling randomly, though he heard back in the woods upwind a persistent beating of leaves and knew it was about to come a downpour. Closing the truck door, he walked around to the passenger side, let Lefty out and told him to stay. He leaned in and got the Kevlar vest, put it on. It was going to be damned hot in those woods, the vest making it worse, especially if he wore the Gore-Tex rain jacket. He put it on anyway. Rather be hot than wet.

Removing his hat, he laid it in the seat, patted the holstered .45 Colt, reached in for his rifle, a .223 Ruger with a folding stock. He moved quickly but didn't waste motion. He'd done it before, no need to rush. He opened the stock, paused, refolded it, returned the rifle to behind the seat and unracked the twelvegauge Remington pump. A sturdy shotgun, stripped down, good for close-in work, better than a rifle in thick woods. He checked the magazine, pumped a shell into the chamber. Three-inch shells loaded with doubleought buckshot.

He glanced over the cab taking inventory, pulled the keys from the ignition, thought about bringing the cellular, decided against. Just another thing to rattle around, make noise, no good under dense treecover anyhow. Keys noisemakers, too. He took them and the loose coins from his pants pocket and put them in the floorboard, then shut the door.

He knelt then beside Lefty and talked to him, stroking his withers. Speaking quietly, calmly, saying, Listen up, boy, you need to work close, now ain't no time to drift or go wide. This ain't no coon. We got something here that's bad, that runs but won't tree. I need you to straddle the track and run a tight mouth.

Lefty held his broad head up, listening. Rule patted him, knowing it wasn't any good, the hound would range wide anyway once he struck, wasn't no changing it. Lefty would work to character, the only way he knew.

Rule strode off through the weeds past the cabin, Lefty heeled to one side. When they reached the border of the denser woods he kneeled at the elderberry where Redhead had gone in and put Lefty on the track. He was reminding the hound to work close when the sky exploded overhead with a ragged thunderbolt and groan and the moaning clouds let go their burden. The rain falling so torrentially that when he glanced back toward the cabin and Cadillac and truck he saw but a waterfalled curtain of silver lanyards roping downward into the steaming earth.

He bent forward and shouldered aside the leafy shrub and entered the thicket, Lefty in the lead. By the time he'd gone six feet and stood up straight with the shotgun cradled over his left elbow, the hound was gone. He wondered if he should've left him in the truck. Thinking a man who'd shoot a woman in the head or a young boy in the eye would as likely shoot a dog. A chance he hated to take, but he needed him. Only edge he had in these bottoms, following an armed man. Otherwise Redhead could wait behind any tree and drop him when he wanted. What a good dog was for when it came down to it.

The rain pummeled the treetops above, most of it collecting there in the canopy, falling only lightly below. He walked on down the slight trail beneath the trees through creeper vine and bush in the direction of the hound's voice, listening to it off yonder in the thicket on Redhead's scent, the familiar mouthing bark rising clean and short, a persistent, easy, deepthroated chop. It gave him goose pimples.

A beautiful sound.

He'd planned to follow the path around the baygall then veer off beneath a stand of pignut hickories, the trees flanking a shallow sandy branch where it mouthed the river. Other side of the branch was a cutbank six feet high, tree roots of an old overcup oak growing out the bank where the stream in flood washed it under. Haul himself up by the roots and lay there behind the trunk, wait for the cowboy to come along. A close safe shot, no way he could miss. If he did, he'd fade back into the woods upriver before the man could follow. Plan made sense.

Then there was a sharp crack of nearby lightning and thunder shattered the bottom and he heard the rain pelting the treetops overhead. Then he heard the dog.

Motherfuck.

Just one, sounded like, but that was enough. A hound, running his track. Hadn't seen it when the Ranger drove up, must've been in back.

Ray Bob turned in a small circle casting for another plan. The rain clammered in the umbrella of interlocking treetops overhead, gathered there and dripped below, a soft patter on the ground. Enough to turn the bottom into a vast bog before long, muddy up the soil beneath the mulch of dead leaves. Make it a hard slippery trek through the woods. Couldn't outrun a dog anyways. Only thing that made sense now was the baygall. Slowgoing, but a hound couldn't scent through water.

He took off his boots and held them in one hand, entered the shallow standing water same spot he had that morning. The brooding swamplike place stretched away through treetrunks and hanging muscadine, disappeared in shadows and Spanish moss and murky darkness. The baygall covered maybe twenty acres altogether along the river, longer than it was wide. He could carry its length, or go partway and cut back toward the thicket. Shorter that way. Then circumvent the gall, head downriver hugging the bank, swim it and knock on Aunt Ethel's door, say howdy to her and the boys, big surprise, do what he had to do and then take their boat. Figure it out from there later.

He sloshed through the calfdeep water beneath the sweetbay and gallberry, trying to make time, hearing the hound coming down through the woods, a clear sweet mouth on it. But the faster he tried to go the more his feet bogged in the bottom, a thick layer of gelatinous mush collected over eons, of decayed leaves and riversilt that when stirred smelled of sour mud, rotting cantaloupes and the rancid flesh of putrefied fish. He slowed, settled into a regular rhythm, taking short low steps, raising each foot just to skim the surface, bearing less weight.

He was moving better now, expending less energy, covering more distance. He debated the hound back and forth, decided it was a redbone, then changed his mind. Had the tongue but not deep lunged enough, he decided. A black and tan maybe, or a Walker. He plunged to one knee as his foot hit a soft spot, regained his balance. The teacolored water was warm, the surface peppered with precise circular ripples where rainwater dripped from the heavy hardwood mast. It was raining hard up there, he could hear it, but down below in the dark cloistered gall it was quiet, the cloying atmosphere hot and lethargic. His T-shirt clung to his body as if he had showered in it.

He'd gone less than a hundred feet when the hound fell silent, then soon began a steady bark back at the edge of the baygall. He couldn't see it for the trees and falling vines and he slogged on, urging himself forward, breathing heavily. Then the dog hushed and he heard the man call. He stopped moving, held quiet behind the broad trunk of a swamp tupelo.

Ain't going anywhere, the voice said, might as well come on out, Redhead.

The man wasn't speaking loudly. He spoke slowly, almost casually, as if he knew Ray Bob could hear and he knew where he was. Ray Bob didn't answer.

You ain't the first queer come out these woods, son, but that's no cause to kill folks. Come on out.

Ray Bob peered around the tupelo, couldn't see. He pulled the Walther from his pants and stepped away through the shallow water, boots in one hand and gun in the other, barely picking his feet up so as not to make noise.

The voice went on, still easy, almost conversational. But asking questions now.

What'd you do with DeReese? Or was it Wade? You fellas go the rump route?

Ray Bob moved on quietly past the tupelo and bald cypress, drawing away. He wiped the sweat from his eyes, thinking. Guy wasn't making any sense. Only DeReese he knew of was the coonass what snitched on Eddie. Other name didn't ring a bell. Who the fuck was Wade? Wade who? Sounded familiar, though, and recent. He grunted. Eddie's uncle, one the old man at that station up near Austin reminded him of. Old man he'd shot because Eddie was a pussy, except he hadn't known that yet.

We already got Wade, if it was him, the voice went on. Still relaxed, like he was making small talk.

He's dead. Was it him you was queer for? Maybe it was DeReese.

Ray Bob paused to brush a swarm of mosquitos from his face. Wondering what the hell the guy was talking about. He pushed on, the dark tainted water deeper now, up to his knees. He angled under a curtain of Spanish moss past a cypress to the right, away from the river. The baygall ended up there somewhere in the thicket.

The cowboy was talking again now, his voice farther away, less distinct. Only not making sense again. Maybe not coming from the same place, either, hard to tell, way a voice carried over water, through the woods.

—one or the other, it was saying, we know that much. We got video. Just not sure which one.

Then he didn't speak for a while and Ray Bob stopped wading. Stood next to a cypress knee, listening, maybe he could tell if the guy was changing position on him. Probably was.

He didn't hear anything. Ray Bob took another step, the water deeper, to his crotch, when a water moccasin thick as his arm slithered around the cypress knee riding the surface toward him, the triangular pitted head upraised, the white mouth wide open. He caught its musky odor almost before he saw it, a foul smell of black mud and rotting meat, the outreached fangs and angry slitted eyes snaking toward him, a vicious seething beast. Ray Bob fell back, sinking to his chest, slung his boots around as the viper struck. The sharp fangs caught the upper leathers of a boot and hung there and the broad gristled body swung over, laid across his arm, cold and wet. The heavy length of it twisted, the hard reptilian skin squirming against his own. The writhing mass was muscled and powerful and the overwhelming stench of it startled him more than its size or weight. He flung his arm up and backward and the thick uncoiled mass flew on past, the fangs unhinged from the boot. The moccasin landed against a nearby cypress knee. Ray Bob turned over in the water and shot to his feet, the Walther extended. He saw the long mud-colored serpent slide away, slow and sinuous, strangely graceful, head up in pendulous motion above the submerged body.

His head swam dizzily, he thought his legs would give way and he'd fall again. Felt like the unsprung shocks on a wornout jeep.

He teetered, found his footing, stood hauling in his breath as the shudders passed away. Then he went on.

When the voice next came it seemed nearer.

Can't figure why a queer'd rape a gal up in Austin though. Or maybe you flip both ways. Maybe you get off on rough trade, too. That why you pistolwhipped that old boy in Houston? Pistol-fucked him. It turn you on?

Ray Bob listened closely, decided the cowboy was still down on the other side of the baygall, back in the direction from which he'd come. He'd moved some but not much. Afraid to get his feet wet, maybe. Probably scared of snakes, or gators. Few of those in here, too. Or maybe he expected the dog to flush him, do the hard work.

He pressed on. The gall was shallower now and he moved more quickly, drawing little water so as not to make noise. After a minute he was stepping in bog, the thick black mire sucking his feet down, then directly ahead he saw a stand of water hickory and a big magnolia trailing a tangled veil of muscadine and he knew he was nearly out. He pushed forward, his toes gripping the muck, until he finally gained solid ground and leaned panting against the broad olivegreen trunk of the magnolia. He sat down on a buckled root and pulled on his boots. They slid easily over his mudslaked feet.

He noticed then it was still raining, heard it. He craned his neck upward toward the overhanging arbor of branches and saw glimpses of the swirling blueblack underbelly of the storm, the steady downpour rushing earthward.

He was still sitting there a moment later when he heard a sudden rustling in the near brush and the dog exploded through it growling and lunged. He raised the Walther and shot it in the chest. The dog rolled sideways and flipped with the impact and landed on its side on the wet ground a foot away, a dull thud. He looked at it. Broad head, long squared muzzle, oval tipped ears, a close smooth tricolored coat of white, black and tan. Mostly white.

A Treeing Walker. What he'd thought.

They were good dogs. Recollected his daddy used to run a

back, had five, sometimes six, called them after namebrand
liquors, said they had more speed and drive than blueticks or red-
bones.

Rule was bent double pushing through the underbrush and vines
rimming the outside edge of the baygall when he heard the shot
close by.

Lefty.

He stopped. For a moment, paralyzed. A black shape lifted in
his belly, twisted upward wobbling like the shuttle he'd once seen
on TV veering off into space uncontrolled and the premonition
constrained within that motion, knowing something terrible had
gone wrong and nothing could reverse a trajectory bound to cul-
minate in a bright red-orange ball of flame and smoke, a terrible
explosion like that which now erupted behind his eyes and
cleaved his head.

But not soundless. Crunching noise like a bone joint tearing,
cartilage and tendon ripped apart.

He'd known it might come to pass but was unprepared, and he
rushed forward through the wet thicket stumbling, rain streaming
down his head and face, thrusting aside the rough limbs and briar
with the shotgun barrel, almost blind, propelled by the bitter
indignity of that single gunshot, comprehending now what he'd
fathomed all along but had not admitted.

He wouldn't take Redhead alive, had never planned to.

He'd tracked the boy for ten days now since Austin counting
the waiting days, since the evening he'd shoved the pistol to
Bernie's face and pulled the trigger. Had waited endlessly. And had
tracked him relentlessly, down from the rolling hill country over
the green coastal plains, along the saltmarshed fringe of the gulf
through the poisonous discharge of refineries and chemical plants
up into the East Texas piney woods and bottomlands. Through
blastfurnace heat and jungle humidity and now thunderstorm and
deluge, through loneliness and boredom and the anguished inter-
ludes of his own diminishing potency, he'd tracked the trail of
Redhead's wanton rage, women and men old or young and a
young boy dead, for naught but one man's inexplicable violence.

He didn't know what had happened to cause it, but that was the world the boy'd made, the one Rule would finish. Life come full circle. A justice executed in proportion to the deed. As the deputy'd said, in the end it isn't a matter of right or wrong but whether one deserved it. He didn't know what Redhead might claim due and payable in the sums and calculations of a wider periphery, but within the configuration of his accomplishments and the circumscribed coordinates of this place he'd come to, he didn't deserve to live.

He was going to take the boy down, carry him out of the bottomlands in the back of the truck, a corpse.

Rule quickly caught himself, reined in. No use in getting shot. Redhead was up there, close, unless he'd taken off. He hadn't heard him in the brush but he hadn't been listening, too busy letting his head run, a mistake. He moved forward carefully, stalking step by step, the rain falling more heavily now, cushioning his boots in the wet mulch, the dense titi and thatches of briar as high as his head beneath the brooding canopy of hickory and magnolia. He pushed aside a wax myrtle limb and saw ahead among the drenched leaves on the ground a small form white and brown. He blinked.

Lefty. Oh Jesus.

The Walker lay prone on his side near the uptwisted root of an old broadbeamed magnolia. At first he believed the hound might rise up and walk if he called, then he saw the crimson stain over the broad white chest, blood matted in the smooth hair and pooled on the dead wet leaves. He stared, then scanned the deeply shadowed thicket beyond.

There was nothing to see and no sound but the unceasing rain in the treetops and his own ragged breathing when he stepped forward and raised his head, the grotesque black shape rising once more from his belly, a sickening sensation, wobbling upward, rising to his throat so that he reared back and howled into the monsooned darkness.

Sonofabitch! Where are you!

The hoarse reverberations of his outlandish scream had not yet subsided when there came a sharp explosive crack to his left and

omething heavy struck his left thigh, knocking him sideways. A
bright searing light flashed behind his eyes. His leg crumpled and
collapsed beneath him. A whitehot stabbing pain shot up his thigh
into his pelvis. The fleeting thought that all this seemed familiar
passed through him as he staggered and fell to the right bringing
the Remington twelvegauge up and around, but the gunbutt
snagged on the pocket of his Gore-Tex rain jacket and when he
fired the buckshot shattered a distant treelimb.

He landed on his right side with his face buried in the wet
leaves. The impact dislodged his breath, and when he regained it
the warm fecund aroma of the leaves and the moist black earth
below carried him back to days long ago, as in a dream, when he
wandered the deep woods alone after a summer rain and the lush
dripping land heaved and sighed with the possibilities of all that
waited him, youthful fertile promises of a profound and prolific
life. Which he knew now he had not had.

Which had come to this.

The Ranger lay on his side, cheek pressed to the muddy ground.

He picked up the shotgun and straddled him, rolled him to his
back, removed the holstered .45 Colt. He stepped away, gazing at
the tall prostrate man. The long narrow face set rigid against the
pain, wet hair plastered to his skull, dead leaves clinging in it.

Know who you look like? Ray Bob said. Porter Wagoner on a
bad day.

He grinned.

Like Porter just after he took a nine millimeter in the leg.

Fuck you, Rule said.

Maybe what you had in mind, but I don't think that's the sce-
nario now. What you reckon?

Rule was silent.

Ray Bob regarded the Kevlar vest under the parka, said, You
know I was aiming at your chest? Good thing I'm a bad shot. Left
dominant eye.

He took a step back and squatted, a woodsman's stance, flat-
footed with his ass dragging the ground, elbows crooked over
both knees, wrists hanging loose, the shotgun inside leaning

against his shoulder. He held the Walther in one hand, the Colt in the other. He studied Rule for a moment.

Shouldn't have brought the Walker in, though. That was stupid, Porter. Wasted a good dog.

Rule carefully pushed up with both hands, wincing, until he was seated upright on the ground. His left thigh throbbed like someone was pounding it with a ballpeen hammer. The bullet had struck bone, felt like, a wicked hit. His face was covered with rain and sweat but he felt cold. Shock coming on.

Coming after me alone, that was stupid, too. You the Lone Ranger?

Rule didn't answer. He examined his thigh, pressed his left hand against it, stanching the bloodflow. He was surprised at how light it was. He supposed most of the bleeding was internal. The leg was swelling.

Ray Bob said, Cat got your tongue now, but you sure was running your mouth while ago. What's all this shit about DeReese and Wade?

Rule looked at the boy. Stocky, thick shoulders, well muscled. Closecropped red hair, a wide fairskinned face with freckles, and cold eyes, gray or green. Gold earring in each ear. Just like the pictures.

Which one was it? he asked.

Ray Bob shrugged. You ain't making any sense. Which one was what?

Was with you, up in Austin, on the road.

You mean my runnin buddy? Dude is Eddie.

Rule shook his head. Name is Ledoux, either DeReese or Wade.

Ray Bob frowned, trying to put it together. All the names familiar, but not in any constellation he recognized. He wiped his face with the back of one hand. The rain was coming down hard up on top still, dripping through the trees with a steady patter. He heard it thundering down south again.

You all fucked up, Porter. His name's Eddie.

Rule took a deep breath, blew it out. Leg was pounding, using a sledge now instead of a ballpeen. He slowly leaned back to the side on one elbow. His head was going round, dizzy. Couldn' think clearly, the pain. He closed his eyes, opened them, feeling faint. Raped that gal in Austin, he said, thought you was queer.

Ray Bob snorted. You got it all wrong, numbnuts. Only fucked one woman in my life, and it wasn't her. Think I'd stick my dick in that strange shit?

He held up the Walther automatic, waggled the barrel.

Fucked her with this. Guess she didn't mention that part. Thought I was gonna blow her pussy off.

He grinned.

Should've seen her eyes roll, right before she passed out.

Rule said, You a sick man, pardner.

That's what they tell me. Reckon that's how I fit in this old world. Match made in heaven, you might say. Or hell, don't matter to me, take your pick, they the same.

Rule laid back then, closed his eyes. He felt cold, was trembling all over. The other watched, then stood and laid the shotgun aside and walked over to where the man lay on his back on the wet earth. Setting a foot on either side of his hips, he said, I gotta git before the rain washes the road out. Guess you know I killed my momma.

Rule nodded. What I heard, he murmured.

Redhead leaned down close holding both pistols, his face a foot away. A peculiar expression came over his features, twisting the pale freckled mouth, drawing the flat gaze of his graygreen eyes inward with a deranged glow.

Believe it or not, Porter, I loved that old woman. Reckon she was the only person I ever did love. But what happened, I didn't have no choice. What she called me, what she did—

His voice broke, words swallowed.

Eyes shut, Rule listened to him breathing, the low snuffling pants, heard the soft patter of the rain in the leaves beside his head, felt the warm drops falling against his face. He thought he felt Dana's tongue on his cheek, then remembered Katie's mom, how good she'd kissed. He'd forgotten that. A good woman. Then saw them together in the livingroom at Christmas, a family. Katie three years old, on the floor by the tree opening a gift, clasping a Barbie doll to her chest and rocking, singing it a lullaby. Prettiest

little girl he'd ever seen. He wondered what was bothering her
lately, hoped it wasn't boy trouble. Now she'd never know. Never
know he'd let go, was trying. That he understood why he didn't
know her, and couldn't. She wasn't *him*, and that was fine. Her
world to do what with. Only regret: no chance now to tell her he
admired her, that she'd made him proud. His little girl . . . a
woman. On her own. Still his sweet little girl, though. Always. *His*
secret. When he heard Redhead speaking again.

—nailed her while she watched, with this gun right here. And
then I fucked her while she was still warm. Showed her, I reckon.

He looked up into Redhead's face. There were tears in his eyes.

Tell you something else. It was the only time that old woman
ever held me close. Ain't that the shits?

Rule closed his eyes. It's a sad story, hoss.

Redhead laughed, lifted both pistols.

It sure is. I've seen grown nut doctors sit there and cry. How
you want it?

You don't shoot a man with his own gun.

Them's fine last words, said Ray Bob, think I'll write 'em down.
He raised up straight, pointed the Colt between the Ranger's eyes.
Said, Only this ain't your scene, Porter, and pulled the trigger.

53

They were sitting at the kitchen table drinking beer, late afternoon, TV on in the background. Randy and Waylon in there
sprawled out watching the Flintstones, Fred hollering at Wilma.
Eddie wanted to go watch but Della was sharing thoughts about
her modeling career.

To tell you the truth, she was saying, I've been getting tired of it
anyway, all that pressure.

He nodded and said, I can imagine. Sounding interested but
looking out the screen windows at the weather. It had poured

buckets all night and most the day, was letting up now, a light drizzle. Above the cabins down the beach the sky clearing off. Scorched orange, streaked with wide swathes of marine blue, a few scruffy clouds straggling up the rear.

Are you listening to me at *all*? Della asked.

Eddie turned back. You bet, honeybunch. You were saying the pressure.

Cause giving up your modeling career is pretty serious, even temporary. It's not like quitting Taco Bell. You know how long it takes to build contacts?

Well, I know it's a big decision, sugarpie, Eddie said, I surely do.

That's right. And then they just forget you overnight. Fashion people have a memory as long as my little toe.

He nodded, listening to Fred in there hollering at Barney, telling him what a goofus he was. Barney saying, Well uh, well uh. Poor Barney so confused he didn't know what a dumbass Fred was. The way they acted killed Eddie. He took a swig of beer, wondered what Ray Bob was up to, where he was.

Della saying, It's a big risk, but spending today with the kids made me think serious.

She sighed.

He looked at her. Wearing bluejeans and the red and blue checked cotton blouse, knotted at the waist, her blonde hair falling in long waves but tangled a little on purpose, the bangs fluffed over her forehead. She took care of herself, no doubt about it. Couldn't believe she was still pushing the notion she was a model, though. Except once you got going on something like that, it's hard to turn loose. He knew that for a fact.

Well now, look who's here, she said.

Waylon came shuffling around the stairwell opening and went up to his mother and leaned against her sucking his thumb. He pulled it out of his mouth and examined it. All puckered up and red like he'd stuck it in a deep fryer.

Eddie looked at Waylon's ears. They were red, too, with peeling scabs. He couldn't figure out where the kid'd got the idea to coat them with Preparation H, but it sure looked painful. The kid was a mess.

Della put her arm around the three year old, patted him on the shoulder. He laid his head in her lap.

I could be a better mother if I spent more time with Waylon and Randy, she said. Kids need lots of attention. She screwed up one eye. Would you just look at this ear?

She grabbed a scabbed red lobe and twisted it up for Eddie to see. Waylon yowled and jerked away. He stood off and stuck his thumb in his mouth, frowning, then returned to the TV.

That'll rot his teeth, Eddie said. You oughta get some of that hot stuff they sell for nailbiters.

Won't that burn his thumb?

I don't think it can get any worse.

I suppose. Her eyebrows knitted with vexation. Well, I'll get some. Maybe it'll cure their nervousness. Anyway, I should spend more time with them, just back off the modeling for now.

Eddie lit a cigarette and leaned his chair back on two legs scratching an armpit. It's your career, he said, your decision.

That's just what I was thinking. And here's—

She stopped midsentence, listening. You hear Randy in there?

Eddie nodded. The kid was coughing like a coalminer, had been ever since they'd picked him up in Missouri City. A deepchested rattling sound, like his lungs were equipped with exhaust baffles off a hopped-up hemi.

Need to give him his medicine, Della said, don't let me forget. Anyway, here's something else. You know this cabin, Eddie? Well, Ruby said LD don't care for it anymore, cause the doctor said he can't drink. I bet we could rent it cheap, almost nuthin. Cause they're such good friends.

She paused, waiting.

He stuck out his lower lip and bobbed his head, staring at the tabletop. Pondering the idea, listening to Fred in there hollering yabba-dabba-doo. Thing was, the beach still wasn't his idea of a great place to live, all the sand and heat, too much humidity and no trees. Especially the sand, man, it got everywhere, you didn't watch out it climbed right up your butthole. Except for the gig at the Stingaree, now that was cool. Just what he needed to get his chops back. Not like Bubba Bear was handing out hard-duty pay, but what the hell, it was a gig. Plus the guy was generous in other ways. Fact the gig meant staying at the beach couldn't be helped, a musician went where the work was, like a pipefitter.

The kids started yelling, shrill highpitched screams. Della jumped up and ran into the TV area. He heard her order Randy to leave Waylon alone, then several hard smacks on the bottom and Randy was crying, Waylon laughing. Then another smack and Waylon bawling, too. Boy, she was wading right in. Wasn't sure who he felt more sorry for, her or them, both boys being nervous thumbsuckers with health problems. Damn tough being a kid, he remembered that much.

Della came back smoothing her blouse and rolling her eyes. Saying, You see what I mean? They need more attention.

Eddie said, Wouldn't let 'em vote on it.

She sat down, flipped back her hair with both hands and asked what he meant by that. Cause if he meant what she thought he meant, he had a thing or two to learn about childhood discipline. He conceded that was probably the case, though he'd never much enjoyed getting whacked as a kid, and between his daddy and his momma he'd spent a fair amount of time feinting and dodging, mostly without success. They both had pretty good aim, he said.

Well, if you know a better way, she retorted, you can join right in anytime.

No need to get defensive.

He stubbed his cigarette out in the ashtray, watching the smoke curl upward. Surprised he'd said that, but feeling good about it.

I'm not defensive, she said quietly, I'm just explaining.

I know it, he replied, and I'm not passing judgment. It's hard being a single parent. I don't feel comfortable judging other folks anyhow. No matter what they do, I can always see myself doing worse.

That stopped her in her tracks. Then he glanced at the wall clock and observed he'd better head to the Stingaree. Going in early so he and Bubba Bear could talk business. He looked out the side screens, saw the sky blushing deep rosy orange with sunset. It had stopped raining. Out over the gulf the horizon had disappeared, lights from offshore rigs twinkling, just visible.

So what do you think about my idea, about renting this place? Della still speaking quietly, her hands now folded in her lap.

I think it might work, he said, for a while anyway, until I can get a better gig, a bigger town. That'll take some money, a move like that. I need to get us more scratch first. We got those boys to think about.

Della slowly traced her fingernail in the tabletop, watching it. Thinking she'd never seen this side of Eddie, him being so authoritative and all, like what a man ought to be. Responsible. It was nice, made her feel warm all over.

Well, she said, I was thinking I could help on that. She looked up at him. There's this beauty shop over on the beach road? The Curl Up and Dye Beauty Salon? Maybe I could use my fallback skills as a beautician, see if they might use someone. Just part time, I mean, so I still have time with the kids.

Eddie said he thought that was a good idea. Plus working nights, he'd be around during the day to help out. Help break that thumbsucking for starters.

That made her feel even warmer, him offering to do that. The kids needed a good male role model, she'd read enough in every magazine there was to know that much. Not that you needed a magazine. Common sense told you a daddy was as important as a momma. Well, almost.

She said then she was sure glad they'd talked, that's how grownups ought to handle problems, even if it isn't always easy. She planned to get the thumbnail stuff soon as possible, she added, then remembered she hadn't given Randy his cough medicine. She called to him and got the medicine off the shelf and a coffee spoon. He came around the stairwell opening to the table sucking his thumb, Waylon right behind, ditto.

Della sat down in the chair and pulled Randy close, jerked his thumb out, stared at Waylon with her eyebrows raised until he pulled his thumb out, too.

Eddie watched. He lit a cigarette and scratched his belly, saying, You never can tell, either, I might even turn out to be a decent daddy to these kids. Who the fuck knows?

Well, you might start by watching your mouth, Della said,

holding Randy's jaw as she put a spoon of cough medicine to his mouth. She gripped his jaw tighter, saying, Now, open your mouth, sweetheart. Cause you know, Eddie, how kids pick up things from grownups.

He said, I guess you're right.

Then Randy shook his jaw loose and bit Della between her thumb and forefinger, chomped down on the tender web of skin and drew blood, hard, holding on like a pit bull.

She yelled and swung an open hand around and smacked the kid upside the head twice before he let go. He dropped to the floor and sat there silently, as if satisfied, and began sucking his thumb again.

Della contemplated him a moment, bewildered, then said, Goddammit, Randy, you ever pull that shit again, I'll slap you halfway to Houston and back.

54

When Ray Bob came up out of the thicket holding the shotgun and pistols he saw a green truck parked behind the ranger's pickup. He heeled up in the weeds and studied it. A wrecker.

Motherfuck. Place was turning into a parking lot.

The rain fell in warm silver sheets over the cabin and clearing and he backed up into the elderberry wiping water from his eyes, watching. No movement. The wrecker cab was empty.

Snugging the handguns down his pants, he slowly pulled the ribbed forend on the Remington rearward, ejecting the spent shell, pushed it forward to slide another in the chamber.

He approached the cabin from the rear, hugged the timbered wall around to the front carrying the twelvegauge at port arms. When he put his head out from the notched pine corner, he saw a man in coveralls standing ten feet away on the porch, looking in the opposite direction, holding a deer rifle in one hand and a small book in the other. A Bible, it appeared. Country preacher with a gun come a calling, a little door to door evangelizing in a dangerous part of town. Ray Bob couldn't believe it.

He leveled the twelveguage and stepped into the open just as the preacher turned, the man's grizzled face as wild and forlorn as an Old Testament prophet's and a look of immediate recognition therein, one Ray Bob did not comprehend, never seen the old fart before. Though he perceived the fire of Jehovah in the crazed eyes as the man lifted the Bible aloft in one hand and loudly intoned, Vengeance is mine sa—

Ray Bob pulled the trigger and the shotgun discharged, roaring, the voice stopped. The man staggered backward, his weathered face twisted with incredulous despair as he gazed downward at the splotch of red spreading over his coveralls. Ray Bob pumped another shell into the chamber. The man dropped to his knees and tried raising the rifle with one arm, an agonizing effort, his gaunt features concentrating fiercely on this final act of will. Ray Bob fired again, thinking it sure was lucky he'd come across the scattergun, though the pattern held damned tight. Must be buckshot. Recollecting then he'd always been better with a longbarreled gun, made it easier to aim.

The second impact knocked the man over backward, sprawled him on the porch. He lay there still. Ray Bob stepped over the outstretched legs and through the cabin door. The pup was hiding in a corner under a scrap of tin, trembling. Ray Bob picked it up and held it close, said, You ready to head out, hoss? We got to git.

After that he moved quickly. The doublerutted lane out of the riverbottom was likely flooded in low places, reduced to mudholes and mire, no way the Caddy could make it, not enough clearance or traction. The lowgeared wrecker with its doubleaxle a better bet but too conspicuous on the road. He decided to take the Dodge pickup, realized he hadn't checked the Ranger's pockets. Damn keys down in that baygall. Probably walked off from folding money, too, when he was already short, only a tenspot. But he was lucky, found the keys in the floorboard along with some loose change.

In the pouring rain he moved the wrecker out of the way and

removed its license plate with a screwdriver, exchanged it for the one on the pickup, same as he'd done with the Caddy when he nabbed it off a Wal-Mart lot in Dallas and twice since. He returned to the cabin and went through the preacher man's pockets and found almost two hundred dollars in cash. As an afterthought he checked the man's ID. He'd never heard of him, never seen him, had no idea where he'd come from or why. World was full of crazy people.

Inside the cabin he set aside his dry jeans and the only dry T-shirt he had left. He rolled up the sleeping bag and carried it and the propane lamp and the fuel can and groceries and what was left of the beer out to the pickup. He returned for the Remington and coming back out on the porch he picked up the preacher man's rifle and paused there, surprised, looking at it. A bigbore 460 Weatherby with a scope, an expensive gun. He put it and the shotgun in the truck and went to the wrecker, tossed the blanket in the floorboard and turned up a .357 Sig Sauer. He put that in the pickup, too. Then pulled the Ranger's government issue Colt from his pants and laid it on the seat.

He stood there in the warm driving rain for a minute staring into the truck cab. Looked like a fucking arsenal.

He shut the door and returned to the cabin, slogging through the mud in his boots. Inside he stripped away the rainsoaked clothing and changed. Then he sat on the floor and broke down the 9mm Walther, dried it and oiled it and released the slide. He wrapped it in a plastic bag to keep it dry and put it down his boot. Then gathered up the pup and left.

He almost didn't make it out. The pickup sank to its rims down by the oxbow. In near darkness beneath the trees he spun the tires throwing mud, the chassis bucking and sliding to the side until the wheels found purchase and the truck eased on forward slowly and out into the dripping undercarriage of the bottomland. After that he hit the low spots gunning the motor and skated over, roostertailing slop, the dense underbrush scrabbing the fenders in short rasping shrieks. The pup curled up on the seat beside him whimpering.

He came out climbing the ridge past the decrepit homestead

with its sagging mosscovered walls draped in honeysuckle and the stilted deer stand tilting sideways like a faintly falling shadow. At the spur road he turned west. The forest lay deep green and drenched to either side, then faded into twilight as the graybanked sky darkened and then the rain let up, a near drizzle. He drove with the headlights and the wipers on low. When he hit Highway 69 he shut the wipers down and moved through the moonless and unstarred clouded darkness southward through Woodville toward Beaumont, aiming to angle off traveling backwater farm to market roads from the piney woods onto coastal prairies past Interstate 10, then follow the twolaner on to High Island and the beach road downcoast cleaving the Bolivar Peninsula. To where Eddie and the bitch were. Where he'd come from three days before.

He drove down into the damp night chasing the headlamp beams over glistening pavement through silent cloistered woods. He tried the Ranger's Stetson but it was too big so he handed it over for the pup to chew. The truck was rigged out well and he checked the gear by the overhead lamp listening to a country FM station out of Houston. Binoculars, a Nikon, what looked like a laptop computer. Sixtyfour channel radio, a cellular phone. He thought about using it but didn't have anyone to call. He was examining the Nikon when the telephone began to ring. He didn't answer. It stopped after a dozen rings, then started again. He picked it up, saying to the pup, Never know, it might be Momma.

Speaking low, he said, Yeah, a short grunt that might have been anyone's.

For pete's sake, Rule, I been trying you all afternoon, where are you?

A woman's voice. He held the receiver, listening.

Rule, answer me dammit. Don't you play games with me now and don't you hang up. I'm at the end of my rope with you, honey.

He didn't say anything. Had learned the Ranger's name, though.

Rule?

Silence.

Rule, I know you're there, say something.

Ray Bob spoke then, saying, He can't come to the phone right now.

This ain't Rule. Her voice surprised. Who is this?

This is Booker Wright, a negro. Is this the little woman?

You never mind who I am, where's Rule? Sounding confused now.

He's not feeling real perky. Out of commission, you might say. Will he know who's calling?

What's wrong with him? Her voice urgent now, frightened.

Migraine, said Ray Bob. Right between the eyes. But you hang tight, he's shacked up with some gash and says he'll feel better soon. You know he looks like Porter Wagoner?

He pushed the off button and returned the receiver to its carriage, turned down the cab light. He reached over and picked up the pup, cradled it against his chest.

What you say, hoss? Was that the cowboy's cooze?

The pup whimpered and he held it close, drove on thinking about what the Ranger had said down in the baygall. About DeReese Ledoux. And someone named Wade, dead, said he was a Ledoux too. He went over the ranger's words, reconstructing. Either DeReese or Wade in the videos, meaning he supposed the videos from the places they'd hit. Meaning Eddie, either one or the other. Doublecrossing dickhead. Had to be Wade then, cause Eddie'd said the other was the snitch turned him in.

Unless he was lying about that too. But to what end? Didn't make no sense.

Maybe Eddie was Wade, in which case he was already dead.

Unless the ranger was lying, about that part or all of it. Or all fucked up.

Shit, whole thing was a goddamn riddle.

He sped on into the darkness beneath clouds blowing inland, them parting and clearing until the sky was strewn with stars and he saw then he'd come down out of the woods and entered the wide coastal prairie, the land stretching away flat and lonely. He punched the accelerator and opened up the big V-8, the engine humming smoothly over the road transecting rice fields and pasture, the radio on low, sentimental country boy singing that a dream is like a river flowing, always changing, and the dreamer like some vessel on the current, following along. As if life was bound by fate and there was nothing to do about it but submit and sing some romantic bullshit.

He reached over and turned it off. Never could stand Garth Brooks, guy was shameless. He was nearing I-10 when the cellular rang again. He picked it up.

Yeah.

Rule, this is Moline. Can't tell whether it's DeReese or his cousin Wade on those tapes only I don't give a hairy rat's ass anymore. I done found out—

Ray Bob said, Wrong number, pardner, and disconnected. Voice had sounded drunk, slurring words. Thinking the Ranger hadn't lied, after all. Either DeReese or Wade, cousins named Ledoux. Fucking Eddie. Twist had lied to him. It still didn't make sense and he didn't know why, but he was gonna find out in the next hour or so.

If the pussy and his yellowhaired cunt were there.

Assuming they were, first thing he'd do is get some facts. Then he'd take care of both, biding his time. Start with her, let Eddie watch. Then deal with him. Show him what happens when a dude fucks his runnin buddy.

But first the bitch.

He reached over and stroked the pup's head, smiling. He was gonna enjoy that.

55

It felt so *good*, that spot there. Funny she'd never noticed it before. Or maybe it was something new, having to do with feeling all feminine warm and taken care of, what with Eddie's new attitude. Like a woman ought to feel, no kidding, and would if men were men. Which they usually weren't. Little boys or big bullies, mostly, either too nice or indifferent, and freeloaders, one way or the other, like they didn't have a clue.

There it was again. Right there. *Nice* spot. Mmmmmm.

When Randy rolled over on the bed and distracted her.

She pushed him back to his side, next to Waylon, who was asleep sucking his thumb. All three in one bed because the boys couldn't get to sleep, nervous in a new place. So she'd lain down with them and told them a story about a little boy who went to bed early and dreamed about a bicycle, when he woke up next morning there was one beside his bed. Randy complained he'd rather have a pony, or at least a puppy, so she'd told it again with the puppy.

Boy, she sure hoped he didn't wake up in the morning expecting one. Be crabby all day.

Worked though. They did go to sleep after that. She hadn't noticed just when, her lying on the bed waiting in the dark, hearing the crickets and frogs outside in the marsh, the waves breaking on the beach. But mostly busy thinking about Eddie, his new take charge attitude.

And then she'd got sidetracked exploring around down there, found that sweet spot. She reached back down into her panties, looking for it.

Thinking the thing about Eddie was, he had a good nature. So easygoing it'd thrown her at first, thinking he was aimless. Not that he was a Type A or anything, judging from the articles she'd read. Type A's hogged attention and made impossible demands. Whereas someone like Eddie just went along as if he lacked purpose or goals and suddenly you find out he does.

You could make a lot of money as a musician if you played your cards right and got discovered.

Mister Dreamboat, now, he'd been a Type A. You had to be if you wanted to run a corporation. Dress up like in *GQ*, get to work early downtown, a skyscraper office with a view, read the *Wall Street Journal*, sit behind a big desk talking on the telephone, making decisons, telling secretaries to bring you coffee all day because you're too busy to get it yourself. Someone like that gets spoiled.

Or weird.

Like Mister Dreamboat with his belt and cuffs. At least the boys' daddy had used his fists, hadn't gone running for a belt. Or handcuffs, which was definitely kinky. Eddie might not be perfect—might as well be honest about that, he was never gonna buy life insurance or invest in his future retirement—but at least he didn't beat up on women. Anyhow, Mister Dreamboat wasn't really Mister Dreamboat, either, as it turned out, he was a creep. So there you are.

She paused when she hit the spot just right with her finger and her legs began to quiver. Wow, couldn't believe she'd never found *that* place before.

Another thing about Eddie: He was good in the sack.

Plus he was interested in the boys. Not every day you meet someone interested in someone else's kids. A friend's husband or boyfriend might act interested, showing tricks and teasing, saying what great kids they were, only he's gonna walk out the door when the visit's over. Like an uncle or something. But available men? Maybe act interested long enough to get a piece of ass, but after that it was, Honey, I like you a lot but I'm not much with kids, *adios* and *sayonara*.

Whereas Eddie wanted to be a daddy. Kinda weird.

She wondered about that a minute.

Anyway, he was good in the sack. Plus he respected her, another important thing in any healthy relationship. Every magazine she'd ever read on that put respect right at the top, along with ability to communicate and expressing your feelings. And one other thing she was forgetting. Oh yeah, trust. Of course that depended on everything else. Only Eddie trusted her and she trusted him, well, mostly anyhow, and that was a good sign about the rest. Consider all that together and it seemed like a situation with a future.

If she didn't get caught and thrown in jail.

On account of Mister Dreamboat.

Boy, that would put a damper on things.

She almost lost it then. Her legs went slack and the feeling went out, not excited one bit anymore. So she closed her eyes and

opened the little black box and stuffed that idea right in there
tight, clamped down the lid. And started thinking about Eddie
again. Way he held her, way his bohunkus rolled around.

Pretty soon she found the spot again and her legs began to
tremble and shake, the warmth spreading down her thighs and
tingling up her belly. Her finger moving faster, working up speed,
pushing it up closer, closer, almost there, and she knew it was
gonna be a good one . . .

Thinking she needed to show Eddie that spot.

56

When he topped the rise at High Island he passed a seedy motel
with an unlit sign and a shutdown gas station and a solitary stand
of live oaks sleeping on the shoulder. Then the road dropped down
into the black night over salt-encrusted marshes and grassflats to
the beach a mile away. The gulf beyond. The only means of dis-
cerning horizon from heaving sea being the manner of stars
appearing in distant formation along the twinkling demarcation of
their ascent. Floating among them the worklights of offshore rigs.

Where the road hit the beach highway leading down onto the
Bolivar Peninsula a stormwrecked pier beyond the dunes extended
outward into the waves. A wooden ramp off the beach inclined
upward to a decrepit shack set on creosoted pilings. Subsequent to
the shack the pier struggled onward into surf and rollers until it
disappeared, nothing but gaptoothed pilings marching like hap-
less vagabonds in two straight lines toward Mexico.

He crossed the beach road, drove through a cut between the
dunes and parked on the sand at the foot of the ramp. Carrying
four loose beers lined along his forearm he strode up the incline
through the creaking screendoor into the shack. A lanky young
man standing between a plywood counter with candy bars and
peanuts and a rainstained wall hung with fishing gear nodded. His

long sunbleached hair was greasy, his skin the color of a polished mahogany box. He wore a muscle shirt saying SALTY SID'S FISHING PIER and cutoff jeans riding low on his hips and white rubber boots.

Ray Bob walked over the puckered plywood floor and set the four cans of Bud on the counter. The humid air in the shack smelled like seaweed, dead fish and marijuana. A clock radio on a shelf was playing "In-A-Gadda-Da-Vida". Headbanger music for dopers.

You got any canned dogfood?

The guy looked at him like he was crazy. Why'd we have any dogfood, man?

Thought that's what you used for shark bait.

Might use a dog for bait, only we wouldn't feed him first. The guy laughed with his teeth but his head jerked back and he stared with glassy bloodshot eyes.

Guess I heard wrong, Ray Bob said. I need to trade these warm beers for some cold ones.

The guy glanced at the cans on the counter and said, I don't need any beers been hot.

Ain't been hot. They just ain't cold anymore.

Don't know where those beers have been. No telling.

Ray Bob took two small bags of salted peanuts and laid a dollar on the counter. Tell you exactly where they been, he said, and where I can put 'em you keep jerkin my chain.

The guy frowned, blinking, like he wasn't sure he'd heard that right. Well, just a second here, man, you can't just come in a place of business . . .

He scratched one arm nervously. Against the law anyhow, trading cigarettes and beer.

Are you Salty Sid?

Naw.

Then why you give a shit?

He looked confused. Well, you can't just come in a place of business.

We got an echo in here, said Ray Bob. Tell you what, I'll pretend I don't smell the weed and you pretend you didn't see me exchange the beer.

Well, hell, man. Digging a finger in his ear.

Ray Bob took the four cans to the rusty upright cooler and set them inside and took out the cold ones. On the way out he glanced back and the guy was still standing there scratching his arm with a stunned expression, Iron Butterfly pounding a drum solo through the radio. He was halfway down the ramp when he heard the guy open the screendoor and say, You probably ought not come back no more, man. This is a place of business.

Ray Bob waved one hand.

He took the pup from the truck cab and lowered the tailgate, sat on it and opened a can of Vienna sausage. He handed them over one by one while he drank one beer fast and another slow. The pup gobbled the soft wieners wagging its tail until it gagged.

Easy there, pardner, act like you afraid they'll get away.

He sat swinging his legs off the tailgate drinking beer eating the peanuts, feeling the breeze rise up off the gulf, brackish and warm, the faint aroma of crude oil on it. He took the Walther pistol from his boot and removed the plastic bag wrapping, put it back. Overhead the ascending stars pinned and wheeled, and when the pup was finished he loaded it in the cab and turned back out onto the beach highway. He kicked the motor and flew over the narrow pavement between the saltgrass and reeds.

Less than ten minutes later he shot past Moody's weatherbeaten bait camp. The lights were out. Old onelegged Moody, blind in one eye. Cause of a hammerhead. With a parrot named Jim. Hunting buried treasure left by John the Feet, a pirate. Finding instead a dead man in a casket. Ray Bob grinned. Crusty old motherfucker.

Then he spanned the low concrete bridge over Rollover Pass and he knew he would be there in a few minutes.

Reunion time. He'd even saved a can of cold beer for Eddie while he watched.

57

Della was sitting on her and Eddie's bed painting her toenails by lamplight when she heard the truck drive up and park beneath the house. Painting them moonglow rose to match her panties and the pink I Luv Mom T-shirt. She glanced at the clock. He was home early.

The Bible lay open on the bed beside her—she'd been reading on and off about the prodigal son, how the other brother got jealous cause the irresponsible one had so much fun and didn't even have to suffer for it. She blew on her toenails, heard the truck door slam shut.

Thinking business at the Stingaree must have been slow.

She started on the other foot, pulling it up close, hunched over, squinting in the low light. Listening to his footsteps coming up the stairwell. Clomp, clomp, clomp. Louder than usual.

She paused, frowning, having a funny feeling.

Then he reached the top and turned the corner out of the shadows and she saw it wasn't Eddie. Mister Hothead. Oh dear lord.

He walked over toward the bed holding a beer and stopped near the end with a thumb hung in one pocket, smiling.

Love the shirt, he said. Where's Eddie?

He's not here.

I can see that.

Boy, she wished he was though.

Where is he?

He's got this job, she said. Only he'll be back any second. Adding that part quickly, wanting him to know.

He still going by Eddie?

She stared at him. How'd he know that?

Or is it Wade now?

That really threw her. Kind of pissed her off, too. That was a

ecret, Eddie'd said, just between him and her. Goes to show what
happens when you trust someone. Give that pissant a piece of her
mind, first chance she got.

Then Mister Hothead plopped down on the end of the bed and
stretched out and it stopped her. She screwed the top on the
moonglow polish and set it on the sidetable, pushed the T-shirt
down between her thighs with both hands. Suddenly feeling
naked.

She said, What are you doing back?

Ray Bob leaned on one elbow, looked at her hands gripping the
T-shirt and grinned. I was in the neighborhood, thought I'd drop
by and see how Ozzie and Harriet are doing. Bring Ozzie a cold
one. He lifted the beer can. How is Ozzie? Or is it DeReese now?

She stared at him, beginning to feel a little scared. Knew he was
a lunatic but he wasn't making any sense at all now. Smelled like
he'd been drinking. She didn't say anything. Then she glanced at
the clock and said, He'll be back any second and you can ask him
yourself.

Reckon I will.

Him staring back, mouth smiling with amusement but both
graygreen eyes as flat and mean as the very first time in the
rearview mirror that night. Gave her the creeps. The eyes briefly
moved to the open Bible, then back.

You ain't no model, he said. What you running from?

She picked up the book and closed it and held it in her lap.
Hoping the Stingaree was slow for real and Eddie'd get home
soon, like right now. Cause Mister Hothead was scaring her bigtime.

He said, What'd you do wrong?

I killed someone, she replied, a man who attacked me.

Blurted it right out, a surprise, but realizing why, knowing it
might be good information for him to have, just in case. She
pulled the Bible against her stomach, studying his face. He was
gazing off in another direction.

Them your kids?

She followed his eyes, saw he was looking at Randy and Way-
on in the other bed. They were curled up together beneath the

sheet, asleep, both sucking their thumbs. She thought to say, No,
borrowed them, but decided not to start anything. Watching the
thin sheet gently rise and fall as the two boys breathed at the same
time, goose pimples up and down her arms.

He abruptly rose up and swung his boots to the floor, walked
over to their bed and leaned down close, observing, her saying
Don't wake them up. After a minute he said, Yep, looks like
they're still nervous, and came back and sat on the end of the bed.

So you killed a guy.

She nodded.

What'd he want, some pussy?

She didn't answer.

You got a tight pussy? he said.

When she still didn't answer he said, Or is it all loosed up
from having those kids, and she said, Ask Eddie, he'll be here any
second.

He grinned again. You sound like this guy down at the pier, he
knew maybe one complete sentence, kept repeating it over and
over. I think he was nervous. You nervous?

No. She squeezed the Bible. Her hands were sweating. I got the
Lord protecting me.

He laughed shortly and shook his head, tickled. That might be,
he agreed, but the bad news is if he's protecting you he's protecting me, too. He's an equal opportunity man. Ain't that the shits?

I don't think he protects someone like you, she replied curtly.
You got to want his protection.

Maybe I do.

You got to deserve it.

Suppose you're the judge of that.

She didn't say anything.

Woman who killed a man, he said.

She said, He attacked me. And I asked for forgiveness.

Right convenient. He's still dead but you feel better about it.
What I always liked about Jesus.

I'm not gonna argue religion with you, she said, someone who
don't try.

He bent his head down and scratched behind one ear, saying

There you go, judging again. See it all over, people using that religious shit halfway. Want forgiveness but don't wanna give it. Sure
wish dickhead would get here. Can't start the party til he does. No
use letting this beer get warm, though.

He popped the tab and took a swallow. What kind of job he got?

Playing music.

That right?

She nodded, feeling a bit more hopeful, thinking about that.
Saying, He's changed. He don't want your kind of life no more.
Why don't you just go on and leave us alone?

Ray Bob said, You ever watch westerns? That sounds just like a
line out of a western. Outlaw shows up to see his old runnin
buddy, and the little woman says, He's changed. He don't want
your kind of life no more. Why don't you just go on, leave us
alone? And if he's a good outlaw, he understands and rides off and
you feel sorry for him, being all alone again. But if he's a bad outlaw, he hangs around waiting, playing with his gun, making her
all nervous. Ever notice that?

She didn't bother to answer.

Only nowadays, he said, people think that kind of scene is
corny, a tired cliche. Not enough action in it. They want to see the
outlaw—only now he's a drug dealer, or a psychopath—they want
to see him fuck the little woman and then kill his buddy when he
shows up. Or even better, wait and fuck the little woman while the
buddy has to watch, then kill him. Maybe take the kids out, too,
if there are any. Lots of blood spurting and writhing bodies, some
radical torture, cranked up screams and heavy panting, all spliced
with close-ups of rage and fear. Cause people get bored otherwise,
know what I mean?

For a minute neither spoke and she listened to the surf crashing
on the beach and the frogs in the marsh, and then Randy snorted
in his sleep and rolled over. Ray Bob stood up, said, That reminds
me, I got something downstairs I better bring up before it pees all
over my truck. He walked away, went clomping down the stairwell.

As soon as she heard the footsteps disappear she scooted off the
bed and began digging in Eddie's duffel, breathing hard, thrusting

her hand around inside until she found it. She pulled it out and looked at it, hoped she knew how it worked. Then she went over to the TV area and turned on the overhead light. Stood several feet back by the La-Z-Boy waiting, both arms extended holding the gun pointed at the top of the stairwell.

When he came back up he was holding a puppy and for a moment that seemed so spooky, her remembering what Randy wanted and her telling him the story, worrying he would wake up in a bad mood because of it—knowing a coincidence like this meant something but she wasn't sure what—that she dropped her arms halfway before she got a grip. Then she raised them level and pointed, her finger on the trigger.

He stopped there cradling the puppy looking at her. Said, Look what I got. Like he didn't even notice the gun.

She said, You just have a seat over there on the couch, buster and we'll wait for Eddie. Waving her outstretched arms with the pistol in that direction as she said it.

He went past and sat down holding the puppy, leaned back against the cushions and crossed his legs, grinning.

What'd I tell you? he said. I knew you'd seen that movie.

58

The bar at the Stingaree was smoky and loud and Rufus was feeling good. The Gibson in fine mettle, perfect tone, his left hand dancing the frets, right fingers popping the strings. Plus that special groaning break in his voice. Only happened on certain nights. Like tonight. Rufus getting it *on*.

He finished Robert Johnson's "Hellhound on My Trail" and wiped his face on a bar towel, adjusted the Roy Orbison shades. Then acknowledged the applause, the shouted comments, offering an appreciative nod and streetwise weary grunts, holding character, especially toward the table up front by the windows.

Three women there dressed casual neat on a girls' night out, nursing cold Buds and trying to act hip. Short shiny hair, manicured nails, smooth skin. Good posture, too, like they had steel rebar up their ass. Divorced, he figured, and not gonna make the same mistake twice, least not until they hit thirtyfive and got scared. Trying out life in the meantime. Been giving him the eye all night. Junior League groupies.

He swallowed some beer and lit a cigarette, leaned into the mike looking their way. Said, Yeah, baby, just heard from my buddy Ray down in Nuevo Laredo, he opened a bar and cathouse down there.

Speaking low, laid back, intimate. He paused, looking directly at the women, who smiled and nodded, then he went on.

Yeah, ol' Ray said the whorehouse upstairs was making good money, five grand a month, but he had to close the bar downstairs. Too much fucking overhead.

He strummed the guitar hard once, a burlesque hall hi-hat bump, checked out the three women. Eyes glazed over, reaching for their beers, a little strained around the mouth, but still smiling. Digging life on the wild side. He gave them the jaded Rufus grin.

Next thing Rufus knew Bubba Bear was standing next to him saying, Ease off, friend, this is a family joint, Jesus Christ.

No problem, Eddie said, time for a break anyhow. He propped the Gibson in the corner and went over to the bar, inspected his hair in the mirror, grooved on the new look, smoothed the sides. Then he turned and leaned back against the bar on his elbows, standing next to Bubba Bear, who was eating a platter of barbecue crabs and drinking a quart of IBC. The big guy poured some into a glass and handed it to Eddie, who stared at it, said thanks.

De nada.

How'm I sounding?

Bubba Bear shook his head, stroked his mountain man beard. Damn good, Rufus, outside that last joke, damn good. Takes me back to cats like the Wolf and Lightnin', Sonny Terry, the roots. You got this *je ne sais quoi*. Got a rough raw edge on it. White boy blues with a rockabilly twist, sort of a psychobilly blues *noir*, know what I'm saying?

You bet, Eddie said. What's *noir* mean?

Black. It's French.

He took a sip of root beer. I forgot you was a coonass.

Bubba Bear sucked on a crab claw, wiped his hands on a napkin and grinned. Said, Registered pedigree. Grandpa from Vermilion Parish, a pirogue pilot. My old man worked at the Gulf refinery up in Port Arthur. Place is a toilet now. Funky demographics, white flight. Oil companies stripped it and split. Full of crackheads and gangsta rappers don't know blues from Liberace. No roots, no future. Here, grab you some of these crabs.

Naw, thanks. Eddie lit a cigarette, heard a tugboat pushing barges up the Intracoastal outside. Through the side window he could see lights across the bay. The last remnants of rain had blown inland.

Listen, he said, you know what Ledoux means? In coonass?

Bubba Bear paused holding a crab between his hands, the light blue oval shell crusted with sauce. He shrugged. Far as I know, it's a name. Could mean two, maybe, or sweet. But I'm not a linguist. All I know is you get born, they hand you a name, say, Get going boy, the rest is up to you, good luck, don't poop in your pants, watch out crossing the street. And don't do drugs.

The big man took a long swallow of root beer and burped, adjusted a strap on his overalls and said, Now, I can tell you what Bubba Bear means, it's a name I chose myself. Tell you the story sometime. Goes back to the Haight-Ashbury and a windowpane of acid in Golden Gate Park during a Santana concert. Got a story behind it. Like Rufus Slim. Bet there's some meaning behind that name, am I right?

Eddie said absolutely, nodding vaguely. He fiddled with his ear ring. Man, he didn't have a clue, name'd just popped into his head.

Well, that's what I'm saying. Name means something if you know the particulars. But what's Ledoux mean? Or Guidroz? don't mean jack, been Americanized. Boxer played by Bruce Willis talked about that to a female cab driver in *Pulp Fiction*. Good flick, you see it?

Eddie shook his head no, said he didn't catch many movies

Thinking a discussion with Bubba Bear was like listening to Cousin Wade on speed, only stranger. His brain all over the place, making weird connections, circles and arcs, a stoned jazz riff.

Cause you a roots man, Bubba Bear was saying, cause you're not modern, postmodern, avant pop, all that wonka-wonka jive. World's gone theoretical, friend, vicarious and abstract. Image over substance. Folks bored of the real thing, not that they see it much. Disconnected from nature. But not you. Am I right or wrong?

Eddie said he reckoned so, one way or the other.

Bubba Bear laughed. You're sharp, Rufus, you got that inborn native intelligence. Comes from having your feet on the ground. All that black Mississippi mud between your toes, the wisdom of the gut. You're not a spectator, man, you're a creator. I built my soul a lordly pleasure-house, wherein at ease forever to dwell. That's Tennyson. I celebrate myself and sing myself. Whitman, another roots man. What I'm saying, friend, is you're too busy creating the universe to pay attention to ancillary bullshit. You're rooted. Otherwise you'd be living secondhand sucking off TV and pop music, reading *People* magazine, have a soul as big as my left nut. Know what you'd be?

Eddie allowed he wasn't sure but had a notion.

That's right, Bubba Bear rolled on, a consumer. A corporate subject. Someone whose sole allegiance is to money. Someone who lives within the borders of his debt in permanent political exile. Make it, spend it, finance the difference, living on the installment plan. Eats what they throw at him, says yum-yum. Garbage, his only creation.

Bubba Bear threw up a hand saying, But don't get me started, Rufus, the point is, that person could be you. But it isn't. You rejected that. Instead, you're a bluesman. You're an artist.

Eddie stroking his chin, surprised, half smiling. Most of it'd gone by him, but not that last part, the artist part. Man oh man. Never been called an artist before, not by somebody else, somebody who knew. Gave him chill bumps.

Myself, I'm no artist, said Bubba Bear, I know my limitations. What I do here at the Stingaree? Nourish the body a little, provide beer and ambience to relax the mind, offer up some music for the soul. I don't have the answers, Rufus. I'm just a friend helping folks along. Guess you'd call me a middleman, know what I mean?

Eddie nodded, sipped the root beer. Said, Being an artist is like being a criminal. He studied the bottom of the glass. Thinking, Whoa, where'd that come from?

Bubba Bear laughed heartily and broke off another crab claw and said it was so. Said to truly live for art was like living a life of crime or a monk seeking visions of god. Said they all put you on the outside, put you face to face with your own inherent frailty and corruption. Said they all forced an encounter with the need for redemption.

Eddie listening, smiling now, knowing he wasn't getting it all but the gist was right there, the truth in the overall construction of words singly beyond him but as real as the scent of jasmine on a moonless night where you can't see the blooms. Thinking it was weird how things connected up, ways you'd never considered, like crime and salvation and art. Thinking all the same he might not run the idea past Della, least not the artist as criminal part. Though it occurred to him Ray Bob might understand. Wasn't sure why, but he had a feeling about that.

You check out Jean Genet sometime, Bubba Bear was saying, he was this French cat, a professional thief who wrote some fine books, only he was gay so he didn't get far in the good old U S of A, homophobia being as *de rigueur* here as fruitcakes at Christmas.

Eddie didn't say anything, wasn't even listening, tell the truth. He felt a little dazed, as though something remarkable had just transpired, an internal shift of balances that had been in progress for some time without his realizing it but had come now to a full blown rearrangement of who he was. Something he hadn't seen coming and could not in retrospect even pinpoint in conception and couldn't describe in words. But there it was. Like he was another person. Man oh man oh man. Put that together with Della and the kids, him becoming a daddy, and the whole world was a different place, and his place in it. A real asskicker.

He smiled to himself again, barely noticed as the three women from up front passed by with their purses and told him they'd enjoyed the music, didn't even watch their rumps when they went out the door. Too dazzled.

Thinking maybe his skinny ass been forgiven after all. Thinking maybe he'd got the Holy Ghost and hadn't even known it, just like his momma.

Then heard Bubba Bear's voice saying, You might want to strap on your guitar, Rufus, folks getting a little restless. So what do you think of the Stingaree so far? We get a good crowd in here, they dig what you do. You gonna stick around a while?

Eddie nodded. Said, I reckon I will.

I'm glad to hear that, friend. We'll go fishing in my boat.

Long as it's calm, Eddie said. I get seasick in a bathtub.

59

He was still feeling good an hour later when he wrapped the final set and wiped down the Gibson and packed it in its case— one he'd picked up in Missouri City for a song, cheap cardboard but it worked—and headed for the house. Said good night to Bubba Bear, collected his pay, went downstairs to the truck. Stood for a minute in the parking lot soaking up the stars and distant calls of nightbirds in the marsh.

Then he started the pickup and eased along the road toward the beach highway. He rolled the window down and hung out his elbow, lit a cigarette. The night warm, a soft breeze sidling off the gulf. He drove slowly. No hurry to get anywhere because he'd already arrived. Wherever he went, he was there.

An artist.

Imagine that. The words echoed in his brain, lit up his thoughts like heat lightning, spread like summer smoke. He smiled.

Just wait til Della heard.

He turned off the highway, and nearing the sandy lane end

where the house sat against the dunes he saw a vehicle parked on the slab underneath. Wondered who it was. Could be the owners, most likely, the guy with initials for a name, LD, and the other, Della's friend Ruby. Maybe decided on impulse to drive down, stay a couple of days. Plenty of room, all those beds. He pulled into the crabgrass yard and parked, the Silverado headlamps illuminating the vehicle, a late model red Dodge pickup. Occurred to him then it might be Ray Bob, done boosted another ride. Man oh man, that'd be a charge, seeing his old running buddy again. Kick back, drink a few beers and catch up on things, tell about his new gig.

And damn if it wasn't.

He got upstairs and there he was sitting on the couch petting a puppy, Della in the La-Z-Boy holding the boys in her lap, they were up late. Della looking sort of peculiar, worn out maybe. He set the guitar case down excited and gave a thumbs up.

Ray Bob.

What you say, hoss.

Della said, He's got a gun, Eddie.

Course he does, honeybunch, Ray Bob always got a gun.

He went over grinning and shook Ray Bob's hand. Said, Where the fuck you been, man? Noticed then the Walther on the couch at his right thigh and the little Police Positive .22 beside the left. Pistol from his duffel. He stared at it, puzzled.

She drew down on me, Ray Bob said, you believe it? I walk in here with a puppy for the kids and she's got this little peashooter pointed at me.

He's gonna kill us, Eddie. Della talking, her voice shaky.

Ray Bob winced. She's a TV movie buff, pardner, you know that? Watching all that late night stuff'll put bad shit in your head, make you paranoid.

Eddie looked at Della. Her face was pale and drawn. Randy curled up on one side, Waylon on the other, both sucking their thumbs, staring at him. He went over and pecked her on the cheek and tousled the boys' hair. Saying, It's okay, sugar, you was just scared's all, being here alone and Ray Bob surprised you. You really pull the gun on him?

She didn't answer.

Ray Bob said, Thought she was gonna shoot me, no joke. Almost shit a brick. Had to take it away.

Well, y'all never did get along, said Eddie. You want a beer, man? He went around the stairwell opening to the kitchen area and brought back two beers and a straightbacked chair. He handed a beer to Ray Bob and sat down facing the couch, jerked at his earring. See you found some new wheels. Where'd you get the puppy?

Same place I got the truck. Up in the piney woods.

Thought you was going to Houston.

Got sidetracked. He pulled on the pup's ears. Guess what I named him.

What?

Wade.

Eddie said, No shit? He glanced at Della and shrugged. Then said, After my Uncle Wade, right?

After your cousin, hoss.

Eddie shrugged. Don't have a cousin named Wade.

Not what I heard.

Where'd you hear that?

Fella I run across. Says you're either Wade or DeReese.

Eddie said, Guy the other night told me he'd been kidnapped by aliens. Took him up in a spaceship. Asked him what it was like, told me he didn't know, they'd wiped his memory clean.

Della said, He's gonna kill us, Eddie.

Ray Bob made a face. Just listen to her.

Eddie studied her a moment, her staring at him wide-eyed, and shook his head, smiling. C'mon, honeybunch, take it easy, Ray Bob's my runnin buddy. Man, you must've really scared her, he said, turning back. What'd you do?

Walked through the door. Ray Bob lifted both hands palms up like that was it. Told me she already killed one guy, though. You know about that? Why she's on the run. Sounds to me like you paired off with a black widow.

She said, Don't listen to him, Eddie, he's lying.

Ray Bob finished his beer and played with the pup's ear. Said,

Don't get me in the middle of it, that's your business. Got another cold one?

You bet. Eddie brought another beer from the kitchen saying, Sure wish you two would stop it, gets on my nerves. Then Ray Bob popped the tab and said, So I hear you're playing music.

He bobbed his head. It's righteous, man. Got a gig four nights a week and I'm getting my chops back. I'm digging it, Ray Bob, no shit. Guy hired me, he told me tonight I'm an artist. Says I got a unique sound.

That right?

Yeah, then he went into this rap on how music is like religion, then how they're both like crime, man, I can't explain it. But I knew you'd understand if you heard. It was some heavy shit.

Ray Bob nodded. Everybody getting religion, one way or another.

Eddie said, See? What'd I tell you?

Well, for one thing, you told me you were my runnin buddy, Ray Bob said after a moment, and then you pussied out. Now you something else. You don't understand loyalty, that's your problem.

Man, don't start. I thought you'd be happy for me.

You're right. Jesus, what am I thinking? So what name you going by these days, hoss?

Eddie smiled, took out his Zippo lighter. Said, My stage name's Rufus Slim. He sat there flipping the top of the Zippo open and shut in one hand. Something I just thought up.

What's your real name?

He lit a cigarette and leaned back in the chair. It's Wade, he said, still smiling. Tried to tell you that once before, you weren't listening.

Ray Bob shook his head no. Saying, Got it straight from the horse's mouth.

Who was that?

A Ranger.

Texas Ranger?

That's right. One looked like Porter Wagoner.

No kidding, said Eddie, surprised. I met him.

Well, he's dead.

Jesus, you gonna kill everybody?

Ray Bob grinned. Told you I might.

They didn't speak for a minute. Drinking beer, Eddie smoking, Ray Bob gently caressing the sleeping pup's ears. Over in the La-Z-Boy the kids had fallen asleep. Della had her eyes closed, too.

Eddie said, Why you wanna do that?

Ray Bob said, Gimmee a reason not.

Cause it's wrong.

So when'd that ever stop anybody?

For a while they were silent again, and then Eddie asked where he was going from here. Ray Bob raised one hand and slithered it up and away, saying, Wherever the road takes me, just like always. You wanna come?

Naw, I got this gig. Plus them. He pointed his head toward Della and the kids.

Whatever bakes your biscuit, Ray Bob said, you wanna play family man that's your problem. Who's DeReese?

Guy who snitched on me, like I said.

Your cousin.

Ranger tell you that, too?

Said you're either DeReese or Wade Ledoux. Only Wade's dead.

Bullshit.

What he said.

How?

Never said, didn't ask.

Eddie frowned. After a minute he spoke, quietly, saying, Man oh man, I told him not to use my name.

Ray Bob's eyebrows knitted now. You're Wade?

It's a long story. Eddie leaned over with both elbows on his knees and rubbed his face with both hands. Outside the wind had picked up and he heard it blowing under the house eaves, moaning, the waves breaking on the beach and the nightmarsh sounds. Thinking about his cousin, missing him again, wondering if it was the drugs got him after all.

Just what is your name, Eddie?

Della talking.

He looked at her. The boys were awake again and all three
were watching him. He flipped the Zippo open and shut with one
hand. Snap, snap. He said, Why don't you put those kids to bed,
honeybunch? It's late. Take the pup, too, they'll cuddle up. That
all right, Ray Bob?

Might as well. He rubbed the side of his nose with a thumb,
regarded Eddie with flat graygreen eyes. Get this party started
right.

Della got up slowly without speaking and took the boys to the
far corner bed and tucked them in, returned for the puppy. She
stood away and reached out to take it from Ray Bob, not meeting
his gaze. When she was done she returned to the recliner and sat
down, leaning forward, watching Eddie.

He gave her a wink, said, How about a song, hon? I'll play
quiet, won't wake the kids. Do one for my old runnin buddy here,
let him see how I'm coming along.

She didn't say anything.

Put it on me, Ray Bob said, and make it a sad one. About losing your old lady, seeing her with another man, something like
that. Lots of heartbreak and grief. He grinned at Della.

Eddie smiled, said, Reckon I can handle that.

He got up and laid the guitar case across the chair, opened it.
He picked the old Gibson up gently and turned it around, holding
it by both hands high on the neck. Then stepped back and lifted it
chesthigh and swung it like a baseball bat hard, the wide body of
it slicing through the air sideways. The leading edge caught Ray
Bob right in the forehead, made a ruptured splintering sound, the
strings twanging loudly. Ray Bob's head flew back and hit the wall
behind the couch with a clunk, then shot forward, eyes blinking
wildly as he grabbed for the Walther beside his thigh.

Della dove for the .22 revolver, fumbling, down on both knees,
finally got her hand around the butt and a finger in the trigger
guard just as Ray Bob lifted the 9mm pointing at Eddie, who
stood holding the shattered guitar dangling by its neck. She pulled
the trigger without aiming and the gun bucked. Ray Bob jerked,
his right arm dropped. He looked down at the small hole bored
into his chest, his freckled face pinched with a bewildered expres-

sion, then abject rage. Fucked up the goddamn script, he said softly, shoulda done the bitch first. Then he raised his chin and lifted the Walther once more toward Eddie and she fired again. His left eyeball exploded and he slumped on the couch.

They both stared.

After a bit she said, Well, now I done it twice.

He said, There went my guitar.

She started to say, I told him, I asked him to leave us alone, but then they heard a child's urgent voice across the way, and they looked over to see both boys sitting up on the bed, Randy rubbing a fist in his eye holding the puppy, saying, Momma, what was that noise? Lookit what I got.

60

We can't just leave him there.

I realize that, honeybunch.

We got to think positive.

That would be a help.

Cause you know what the police'll do.

Ask a lot of questions.

Put me in jail.

We don't want that.

Eddie and Della sitting at the table in the kitchen area drinking instant coffee, chainsmoking cigarettes. Della smoking Camel straights cause she was out, had been for several days and thought she'd quit, not even telling anyone. Eddie hadn't realized until she lit up one of his.

You ain't been smoking, he'd said.

Listen to you, she'd replied, just now noticing.

Well, I knew there was something.

Good thing I didn't dye my hair.

I'd've noticed that.

Or cut it.

Wish you wouldn't. I like it long.

Both of them making small talk until they got around to the subject at hand: what to do.

Not like I killed someone nice, she'd said.

To which he'd replied, You never saw his good points.

I'm not gonna start looking now, either, so don't ask.

Well, he'd observed, suppose it's too late anyhow.

Still not ready to broach the subject, lighting one cigarette off the other, drinking lukewarm Sanka, talking around it.

Until Eddie finally said, Okay, here's what we need to do. We got to get rid of the body.

Man oh man, it sure sounded funny, calling Ray Bob a body. All he was now, though. Ray Bob here one minute, gone the next. There, then not. Dead, man. *Gone.* Just like that.

Della saying, I already got *that* far, Eddie. The question is how.

He made a face.

What?

Man, it sounds awful.

What?

Gators. Or sharks, only we don't have a boat.

Della made a face, too. Good lord, she hadn't been thinking along *those* lines. I thought we'd just take him somewhere and leave him, she said.

Well, there's that.

They drank more of the tepid coffee and smoked, thinking. Both the boys asleep in the bed, snuggled up with the puppy. That'd surprised Della, way they went right back to sleep. Boy, she wasn't gonna sleep for a week, so much adrenaline. Eddie looking pretty relaxed, though. Or dazed.

She said, Sorry about your guitar.

He didn't hear, already saying, Okay, I got it, just remembered. Up past High Island there's this state park, off the beach road below Sabine Pass, almost to Port Arthur. They got boardwalks out in the marsh so you can watch gators and nutrias, only mostly it's birdwatchers. Place called Sea Rim State Park. Guy told me about it, he poached some otters there.

Della nodded, waiting.

Thing is, see, the beach road above High Island's closed due to hurricanes and shit, it's all tore up. But this guy said you can go around the barricade, if you got a truck. We can take him up there, out that boardwalk in the marsh, find a gator hole.

She shivered. Why don't we just leave him in the parking lot of some bar? The Shipwreck or something. That'd be simpler.

Simpler for the cops. He shook his head. Then they'd be knocking on doors, hanging around asking questions. Plus up there's another county, case they find him. They'll start in Port Arthur, place run over with crime, Bubba Bear said.

Well, if you really think that's best.

I do.

Okey dokey, you're the one with the experience.

Thing is, though, we're gonna have to take both trucks.

She thought about that. Jesus, she sure hoped Bubba Bear's heap didn't break down.

Eddie rolled the body in the frayed piece of outdoor carpet LD and Ruby'd used for a livingroom rug, almost tripped and fell carrying it down the stairs breathing hard. He put it in the bed of the red Dodge pickup, came back up and wrapped the two handguns in a towel after wiping down the .22. He carried them down to the cab, took a moment staring at all the guns in there. Man, Ray Bob'd been loaded for bear. Plus a computer, a radio, other different things. Looked like a cop vehicle, the Ranger's maybe. No telling what Ray Bob'd been up to. Pretty sure he didn't want to know.

Della upstairs put a sheet around each boy and he helped carry them to the Chevy Silverado, laid them on pillows in the floorboard. What about the puppy? she said.

That stopped Eddie. I just don't think I could do that, Della.

What?

Give him to the gators.

For pete's sake, I mean you want to leave him here or take him?

Oh.

He went upstairs and brought the puppy back, put it between

the boys. It hardly stirred. When he handed Della the Silverado keys she hesitated, rolling her eyes.

What if it breaks down?

Then I'll fix it. You want to drive Ray Bob around?

She took the keys and got right in. He saw then she'd brought the Bible. She set it on the seat beside her. He told her to follow close, said he'd go slow and keep her in the rearview. She said she certainly hoped so and he told her not to worry.

Why'd I worry? Just cause I'm driving a brokedown jalopy following someone carrying a dead body in the middle of the night?

Eddie said, That's my girl.

It was fifteen miles north to the barricades on the beach highway at High Island, another twenty to the state park. The second part took better than an hour.

Except for an occasional stretch where the asphalt pavement was merely potholed and mauled, the road at best was a broken mishmash of scattered asphalt chunks strewn among drifting sand, oyster shells, washed up seaweed, and plastic bottles and trash and waterlogged lengths of scarred wooden floorplanks drifted up from offshore rigs and workboats. At its worst, the road disappeared completely, along with the beach, consumed by the surging gulf. There the headlamps dimly lit a speculative curving path between lapping waves and wetlands, a thin strip of loose sawgrassed sand in which the truck slipped and spun.

He steered carefully through the darkness, the twin lights of the other truck just behind. A stiff wind came off the gulf through the passenger window, warm and muggy, smelling of saltwater and dead fish and diesel. The worklights of distant rigs blinked starboard beneath lower stars. He wondered then how he'd escaped them. Almost everyone he'd grown up with worked the oilfields, offshore or inland. Roughnecks, drillers, roustabouts. He'd watched them: missing hands, twisted broken backs, limping on misshapen legs, slowly cannibalized. A hard life. Different from the refineries and plants. Not as likely to get cancer but the rigs ate you a piece at a time.

Halfway there the headlights behind disappeared and he

stopped, walked back with a flashlight he'd found behind the cab seat to where the Silverado had died. Took him fifteen minutes to discover a wire'd shaken loose. He fought off the swarming mosquitos and reconnected it and they drove on, passing junked washing machines and refrigerators dumped along the way, a pile of discarded car tires, a dumptruck load of old roofing shingles.

He counted three live possums and fourteen cottontails, another dozen sets of red eyes in the beams that faded back into the dark marsh before he could identify them.

Then the pavement slowly began to reappear, and then it rolled out smoothly ahead in the damp starlit night and they were there.

The park was divided into two zones. On the gulf side, beyond the visitors center and headquarters complex, it stretched along several miles of low windswept beach. Inland it reached clawlike up into salt tidal marshlands filled with silt from longshore currents, nursery grounds for marine life and migratory waterfowl. Where most the wildlife was. The gators.

They parked in the empty visitors lot and he got out, went back to the Chevy.

You wait here, he said.

Don't worry.

No need to get out.

Who's getting out?

All right.

He walked halfway back to the Dodge pickup and stopped and returned. He said, I'll be right back.

Well, you better.

I will.

Where'd I go?

He took a deep breath and stared off across the road into the vast blackness of wetlands where the boardwalk would be and said, This ain't easy.

You said it was best.

Yeah, I did.

Okay.

I'll be back.

He opened the pickup tailgate and pulled out the rolled-up carpet with the body and balanced it over one shoulder and holding the flashlight in the other hand set out across the road. The small yellow beam scanned the far side back and forth, then settled in one place and moved ahead. After a minute it disappeared.

The mosquitos were terrible so she rolled up the windows and sweated. Sat holding the Bible between her hands, wondering how someone who tried so hard to do what was right could end up killing two people without even planning it. Thinking life was full of surprises and some weren't so nice. Not that it was news, but you just kept learning it, over and over.

Then she saw the flashlight again and he came across the road carrying the piece of carpet and took some things out of the red truck and went back. She waited. Thinking it sure was different seeing something like this on TV and being right in the middle of it.

When he returned the second time she saw him wiping off the steering wheel of the red truck with a towel, then he brought the piece of carpet and towel and put them in the bed of the Silverado. She scooted over when he got in and they turned around and headed back down the broken road.

They didn't talk much. He stopped at one point beside a heap of black plastic garbage bags full of who knew what and a collapsed sofa with rusty springs without cushions, tossed the piece of carpet and towel into the tall grass behind them. They went on.

She said, Did we think of everything?

He said, I hope so.

Can't think of anything else.

I can't either.

Well, then, it's over.

He looked at her funny.

When they rounded the barricades at High Island and returned to the open road along the peninsula she said, Do you think they'll find him?

I'd be surprised.

Hope not.

It ain't likely.

They rode in silence again for a while, the empty highway unfurling ahead between grassy dunes beachside and the marshy wetlands extending in darkness toward the Intracoastal Canal and East Galveston Bay. She glanced down at the Bible she was holding and said, I suppose we should've said a few words or something, that would've been right.

He said he had.

What?

He lit a cigarette, gazed through the windshield at the road. I didn't know the right verses, so I just quoted a song I know.

Want to tell me?

If you want to know.

I wouldn't mind.

He smoked the cigarette, flicked the ash out the side window, and said, not turning to look at her, It's from the blues. The words go—

> *The old folks told me long time ago*
> *Don't trust nobody that I don't know*
> *I don't trust nobody*
> *Not even myself*
> *Now I don't trust you*
> *Don't trust nobody else*

After a minute she put her arm on the seat behind him, rested her hand on his far shoulder. Saying, You don't really believe that, do you?

No, he said, but he did.

They drove on not talking, over Rollover Pass, through Gilchrist, on to Crystal Beach, the kids sleeping in the floorboard with the puppy snuggled between them. When they turned off the highway into the lane to the house, she said, Is there anything else we need to talk about?

You have something in mind.

I was wondering, she said, what your real name is.

He turned and looked at her. Said, My name is DeReese
Ledoux.

They pulled into the parking space beneath the house and he shut
down the truck. It was quiet but for the surf on the beach and
wind whispering in the sawgrass. She said, Okay, I have something to tell you, too.

What's that.

Well, I'm not really a model.

Reckon I knew that, he said.

Boy, that surprised her.

Epilogue

Golden beams of morning. They flushed an eastern gulf sky stacked with backlit lavender clouds, suffused the back bay, illumined the platinum surface of whitecapped chop. Off metal boat trim flashed small sparkling stars. The boat bucking a head wind due north toward Smith Point.

Bubba Bear backed off the throttle.

North wind's gonna push water from the marsh, he shouted. Water starts falling out, so will the bait. Specks and reds'll hang around to forage.

Eddie sat on the low bench in front of the console wearing a gimmee hat turned backwards and lifted one hand. Waving to indicate he'd heard. Hadn't understood, but he'd heard. Man, his stomach was flipping. Boat going up and down, up and down.

Randy and Waylon enjoying it, though. Sitting there wide-eyed, taking it in, the vast heaving surface of water, the sky dropped over horizoned marshes, the wind . . . the motion of the boat. Man oh man. Bubba Bear hit the throttle again and the hull thrust forward, front end lifting until it planed out and fell, skimming the chop. Randy and Waylon grinning.

They passed the point and skirted the marshy edge, then slowed, almost stopped, the boat lifting in its own surging wake. Bubba Bear steered into the mouth of a shallow cut, saying, Tide's turning, too. Here come the mullet and baitfish, chasing those shrimp. Speckled trout chasing them. We'll just extend the ol' food chain another link, get us some lunch. You ever fish specks?

Eddie shook his head.

Don't know what you're missing. Put up a good fight. Smell that.

Eddie lifted his head and sniffed. Smelled like rotting vegetation and sour mud. Smelled like a swamp.

That's the aroma of fertility, said Bubba Bear. How it is in a
tidal marsh. The living feeding on the dead. One neverending
cycle.

The boat drew up into the mouth of the slough, the water
calmer there. Eddie's stomach settled. The big man cut the motor,
dropped anchor. Saying, You ever tasted a woman when she's
ovulating, Rufus?

Said he reckoned he had, tasted a little sour.

Well, that's what I mean. Fertility, friend.

Bubba Bear handed him a rod and reel, then rigged out smaller
rods for Randy and Waylon and they fished as the sun rose blood
red over the clouds, the two men pulling in gasping threepound
specks with shimmering silver sides and the boys small croaker
and hardheads caught on frozen shrimpbait. The boat exploded
and rocked with shouts, the big man's rumbling laughter. After an
hour Eddie laid his rod aside and leaned back against the console
in the sun, feeling sleepy. Bubba Bear put his gear down, opened
two beers, handed one over.

Too bad about your old Gibson, he said.

Eddie shook his head, eyes closed. You know kids.

Well, if you ask me, the new one sounds better. Pretty to look
at, too.

Eddie pictured the guitar. Cherry sunburst finish on a Sitka
spruce top, mahogany back and sides, engraved pickguard. Gibson Hummingbird, a real piece of work. Picked it up used at a
Galveston music shop a week ago. Bubba Bear co-signing the
note.

Hear about that Ranger's truck up at Sea Rim?

Eddie nodded, eyes still shut. Been all over the news for days
now. Found the body up in an East Texas riverbottom, along with
another fella, the truck all the way down by Port Arthur. Everybody speculating. Saying it looked like the handiwork of Johnny
Ray Matthews, now lit out for parts unknown, target of a man-
hunt.

Ray Bob.

Gone.

TV news saying he'd been part of a twoman crime spree leaving

a trail of murder and mayhem across half of Texas, the other partner believed dead.

Meaning Cousin Wade.

Gone.

Man oh man oh man.

Well, its a big ol' bad ol' world, Bubba Bear said, but it's the
one we made. He crushed the empty beer can in one hand. What
say we haul anchor and head in?

Sounds good, Eddie murmured.

You got some fine boys here, Rufus.

He opened his eyes to see Randy and Waylon in their orange
lifevests standing in the boat holding rods over the side, squinting into bright sunlight reflecting off water, watching the fiberglass rodtips for a wiggle. Neither one sucking a thumb, too
busy.

Yeah, he said, they are. They surely are.

A pair of pelicans winged overhead against the tealblue sky and
the boys pointed upward and turned to him, both of them,
mouths open.

Them's my buddies.

What I heard, you order the bean burrito and use all the picante
sauce you want.

Just avoid the sour cream.

Right. At McDonald's, you get the junior burger, not a Big Mac.

Okay.

Save like five hundred calories.

Della and Melinda Crane at the beauty shop, midafternoon,
discussing how to eat fast food while not getting fat, Della saying
it was the size of portions that got you, and milk products.
Melinda in the chair, getting a perm, said, Where'd you get your
information?

Della frowned. *Cosmo.* Believe we're ready to wash now.

They went over to the sink. Susie Green, the shop owner, working at the other chair on Mrs. McFaddin, said she'd heard eat anything broiled or boiled but avoid fried.

Fried foods are just terrible, Mrs. McFaddin said, gripping the chair arms, cause of the lard. But how else you gonna eat seafood? She made a helpless face and shook her jowls.

The Stingaree uses vegetable oil, Melinda said. She waited tables at the restaurant weekends. We certainly do *not* use lard.

Well, for heaven's sake, I didn't say you did, the older woman replied.

Della changed the subject, asked Melinda how her love life was. She said her boyfriend Larry Lee was working a construction job up in Fort Worth. Said they never got along as well as when he was out of town. Know why?

Why? asked Mrs. McFaddin.

Because then he isn't around to remind me he's a butthole.

They laughed, and Della said she and Rufus hadn't reached that point in their relationship yet. Saying Rufus as *Roo-fus* because she still wasn't sure how to say the name, sounded silly no matter how it came out.

Those aren't his boys? asked Susie.

No ma'am, they're by my first husband. Only Rufus is twice the daddy he ever was. You know he took 'em fishing? Can't imagine their real daddy doing that. Have to get away from his Jack Daniels and TV.

Men, said Mrs. McFaddin.

Never met one I couldn't learn to hate, Della quipped, adding, That's just a saying from a friend of mine. I don't necessarily agree.

Mrs. McFaddin said, Well, you're young.

Why, thank you. And Rufus said the boys didn't even suck their thumbs out in that boat. They have this problem with that? So we got some hot stuff for nailbiters, which works, but he forgot to put it on. Only it didn't matter. His theory is, long as they're occupied they don't have time to get nervous. That's when they do it.

Do what? asked Mrs. McFaddin.

Well, I'll say one thing, said Melinda, I sure do like his music. Bubba Bear swears he's the genuine article.

He certainly is, Della said. Real dedicated. We've been talking about moving back out to LA, you know, after he writes some more songs. More opportunities there, as far as being discovered and all. That's his dream.

Mrs. McFaddin observed that dreams were just fine but living in a place like California was a high price to pay, and Della admitted it was probably true, only fame didn't come cheap. When Mrs. McFaddin asked just how much they were willing to pay, Susie pointed a comb in the mirror and told her, I think we're done here, now don't you look cute?

Peering at herself in the mirror the fat woman frowned, saying, I don't know if that's the word I'd use.

When she left Susie whooshed her breath out saying, She's always a trial, bless her heart. Then Melinda was gone, too, and Susie and Della began cleaning up. The owner said she was glad to have Della's help. It's hard to get skilled beauticians down here, she said, it's not exactly life in the fast lane.

It's not so bad, Della replied. It's a good place to relax, charge your batteries. She smiled, excited. Plus guess what?

What?

Susie smiling, too, at the way Della was.

Can you keep a secret?

Get outa here, girl, you know I can.

I think maybe I'm pregnant.

Early evening and the beach lay quiet beneath the approach of first stars. Frogs in the vespertine marsh warming canonical throats, Eddie getting ready for work. Della said she needed to run to the store first, get some milk for the boys.

She took the truck down to the Gulf Coast Market, bought a half gallon, got five dollars in quarters. Outside at the telephone she called Houston information for the Holiday Inn on I-10 near the Highway 6 loop, dialed the number, asked for the desk clerk. A young man answered.

Good evening, Della said, this is Mrs. Green calling from Kalamazoo.

Lies, lies, lies. She hated it, but how else could she learn the truth?

Yes, ma'am?

Well, I'm calling because my husband and me were staying at your hotel recently—we were visiting his family in Houston—and there was this unusual incident. And being curious, I'm calling to see what happened.

The clerk waited, cleared his throat. Yes, ma'am?

It was about, oh, three weeks ago, she said, and you had a guest that was stabbed in his room. I think he was killed? Then we came home the next day. So I never heard what it was over. That's why I'm calling, cause I'm a curious person.

The clerk was silent.

Anyway, I'm just wondering who did it, and why? Were you on duty that night?

The clerk hesitated, then said, Yes, ma'am, only I'm not sure I should be talking about it. He wasn't dead, though, I can say that.

Good lord. Della almost dropped the telephone.

He wasn't?

No, ma'am, but he was critical.

Who was he? When the clerk didn't answer, she said, I'm calling from Kalamazoo, you know, who would I tell?

Well . . . this is just what I heard, cause it was all pretty hush hush, the clerk finally said. He was Mister Delahoussaye, from New Orleans. A couple of his . . . I guess you'd say *associates*, they found him. What I heard is they're like with the Mafia or something.

My lord, Della said.

Yes, ma'am, and they called an ambulance and took him to the hospital. They said he fell on his letter opener, and not to call the police. My boss wasn't too excited about that, what with insurance and all. Lawsuits, I mean.

Well, I'm not surprised. Did you?

What?

Call the police.

Yes, ma'am, and our bartender told 'em there was a woman with him. But it didn't go anywhere. Like I said, his associates claimed it was an accident. And my boss said we didn't need the

ublicity anyways. So it just got kinda swept under the rug, I
robably shouldn't be telling you this.

It's safe with me, Della reassured him, I never mess with organ-
ed crime. So Mister Delahoussaye's alive?

No, ma'am. I mean, I don't know. What I heard, they trans-
rred him to some hospital in New Orleans, he died there. Only
aybe he didn't, cause it's all rumors. People in that line of busi-
ess, you never know for sure. Don't quote me on that.

Of course not, Della said.

Whole thing was bizarre though. Like something you see on TV.

Amazing what can happen right under your nose, Della said.
isten, I better not run up a bill, my husband'll kill me. Thanks
or the explanation.

Yes, ma'am, only I didn't say anything.

Mum's the word.

She hung up the receiver. Stood there holding the sack with the
ilk and truck keys thinking she couldn't believe it. Mister
reamboat alive, maybe. Or dead. Anyhow, way over in New
rleans. Boy oh boy, that was gonna free up some space in her lit-
e black box.

And him a gangster, for cripes sake. After all that Big Executive
lk. Wouldn't you know it? Mister Dreamboat a liar. He'd
emed so nice, too. Except for there at the end.

Della thinking when it comes to people, you just can never tell.
hey're real characters, worse than some made-up book. Which
e oughta write someday. Maybe she would, too. Only no one
ould believe it.

So there. Wasn't that the truth?

nother late night in the Stingaree bar. Outside, the churning
ake of a passing tug, lights in the bay among reeling stars, a
lty breeze off the surging sea. Inside, a rising swirl of smoke
d noise, of clinking beer bottles, the juicy tang of barbecued
abs, people elbow to elbow and knee to knee, the loud commu-
al fest.

Midst this scene, Bubba Bear standing at the bar in his happy devotion, Rufus on the corner stool sweating over his Gibson bending notes, blowing the harp, singing his guts out.

Singing about lost love, love gone bad, love unrequited or stolen in secret or revealed in all its wayward desire. Love and pleasure, love and pain. Hope against loss, trust and betrayal. Yet love, more love, and more love yet.

What it's about. What we do.

And redemption there in his anguished face, the breaking voice, the bent blue notes and wails.

Singing—

He'd been a bad man, a bad man, a thief and a liar, shot a man between the eyes and got away. He'd run with bad men, worse men, had seen them pay with the very thing they did not value.

Not a good man, no. Not good. Only bad.

Listen—

A bluesman, a bluesman, an artist robber stealing a moment in time, the eternal poet paying for everyone's crimes. Looking in the face of the face and what dwells therein, not blinking but singing, singing of salvation and sin. His own, and every other man's.

And smiling about it.

He smiles in anguished joy and sweats, closes his eyes and sings. Verse upon verse, the longing refrain, the final lines, the lingering notes. Then a moment's quiet, echoes among innuendo.

The giant bearded man at the bar drinks his root beer, eyes closed, listening. Hearing in it the story of his life and yours. Knowing the singer knows what we all know only the singer says and dares. This solitary singer and all the others, the poets of time timeless.

No meaning therein—none at all—but what we give it.

The big man listens, taking note, hears the song come to an end, knowing there will come yet another, mere pauses of rest between the restless everchanging stories, each scene connected to any other, endless.

Yet there is silence between.

So he smiles into his bardlike beard, and lifts his glass to Rufus knowing this one, too, in this late midnight hour, has reached a moment of repose, must make a swanlike end . . . tender, graceful, and low . . . fading in music.

Gone.